The Midas Factor

To order additional copies, please contact us.
BookSurge, LLC
www.booksurge.com
1-866-308-6235
orders@booksurge.com

The Midas Factor

A NOVEL

Donald Reed

2005

The Midas Factor

AUTHOR'S NOTE

The tapestry of Gold Rush times in California would be incomplete without inclusion of some historical figures. To some, notably John Sutter, Dr. Robert Semple and Sam Brannan, I have attributed speeches and actions. Others, like General Mariano Vallejo, appear simply to illuminate this intense historical period. Historical events and conditions, too, such as the Christmas Eve fire in San Francisco and the flotilla of deserted ships in San Francisco Bay, impact the lives of my fictional characters.

For Erica, Kelsey, Lucas, Danielle, Deanna and Drew.

CHAPTER I

Pine smoke drifted through fog shrouding his camp. Adam Stuart stirred and groaned. Down river an ax rang on wood. On a gravel bar nearby, iron clashed with stones as shovels sliced through the gravel bar. Adam stretched and groaned again. Other miners had begun their day, but he lay in his blankets flexing his wrists and fingers. They ached, as did his feet and legs. No doubt about it. Panning for gold through the winter had sapped his strength. His gold had grown by thirty to forty dollars per day. But now he wished he had wintered in San Francisco or New Helvetia. The miners who did returned with renewed energy and drive.

Drops of water fell from the great live oak overhead. They spattered on the mildewed tarpaulin – part of a sail from a vessel anchored in San Francisco Bay – stretched over his bed.

He struggled up onto one elbow, peered out and froze. Not three feet away stood a pair of new leather boots. Above them a pistol waved, mostly at his head. The boots' owner bent down, black moustache and beard thrust toward him. A slouch hat concealed the man's face. Adam brushed hair out of his eyes the better to see.

"Get your hands out where I can see 'em. Quick, or you're a dead man!"

There was something familiar about the man. Was it his voice or the glimpse Adam caught of his eyes beneath black brows? Where had he seen the fellow before? Sailor Diggins maybe, or Mormon Bar?

"What do you want?" Adam demanded.

"Your gold."

Beneath the blankets Adam tensed. For nearly a year he had worked undisturbed. Now miners poured into the country. Some spoke languages he never heard before. Others passed by, giving him a wide berth. Adam had not built his camp beside the trail. Rather, the trail grew beside his camp as miners penetrated deeper into the canyon. He had had no trouble, but stories grew about robberies, beatings and even murder. He thought about obtaining a gun. But the lure of gold, hope for a big strike, made him put it off.

"What makes you think I have gold?"

The stranger shifted his feet and thrust the pistol in Adam's face. "Oh, I know, all right. You left Oregon with six hundred in gold."

Adam's mouth fell open. He peered into glittering eyes beneath the hat. "Mal? Mal Wilson? Is that you?"

"None other."

"Mal, put the gun away. What are you doing here?"

"Well now, that's easy. I come for the gold you stole off the Squire. The boys. . . ."

"I didn't steal your father's gold. He put it in my hand. You saw him do it. But how did you find me?"

"Boys down the river says to look for the loner camped under an old sail. And by God here you are. I've got you dead to rights. You come here with the Squire's gold, all right, but you didn't come back with the cattle."

"But how did you come here, to Brown's Bar?" The pistol waved again but never far from his head. "For God's sake, Mal, put down the gun. My sister is your wife. We're family."

"Not no more we ain't. Your own sister disowned you. She don't know why you didn't come right back."

"I wrote to the Squire saying why. I couldn't send the gold, or come myself. No ships sailed out of San Francisco, and the Rogue Indians were killing travelers. Least that was the story here. For a while I couldn't even send a letter." A mosquito buzzed around Adam. He slapped at his forehead. At once the drifting gun swerved back to him.

"You been writin' letters to Mary Jane Carr, ain't you?"

"Ah!" breathed Adam. "She told you where to find me. She must have kept close touch with your family."

Mal Wilson hunkered down on his heels. "You might say that."

Adam moved to roll out of his bed.

"None o' that!" barked Mal. "Keep your hands out. Likely you got a gun hid in them blankets."

"I don't have a gun, Mal."

"Expect me to believe that?" Mal's head flicked to the dressed carcass of a deer hanging from the live oak. "How'd you shoot the critter hangin' yonder?"

"When I need fresh meat," Adam said, "I borrow a long gun from Danny Fisher down there on the gravel bar. Ask him, he'll tell you."

"I will, don't you fret. But I ain't putting this weapon down until you hand over the Squire's gold."

Adam glanced at the smoldering fire he kept the night before when he wrote his weekly letter to Miss Mary Jane Carr.

"I can't show you right now, but I've got it all except forty dollars I used to outfit myself."

"It figures. Usin' money that ain't yours."

"Mal, green as I was, I made it back and more the first week."

"The hell you say! Out of that river down there?"

"From gravel bars down by Auburn. And bedrock here

3

when the water went down. I picked nuggets out of holes worn in the rock. I want to get up, Mal, and fix breakfast. Then I'll show you how to find gold. You hungry?"

Sudden wariness tightened Mal's face. His gun, which had sagged, came up. "No tricks, Adam. I got the drop on you. I already ate down at Brown's Bar."

"Slapjacks and molasses," said Adam. "That's all they eat. How about bacon and biscuits and coffee?" Mal's eyes lighted up at the mention of bacon."

"Bacon, maybe," he allowed, "after you give me the gold."

Moving carefully, Adam crawled out, grabbed his pants and shirt and stood up. He bent beneath the canvas, careful not to touch the underside and start water dripping through. He hopped about pulling on his pants one leg at a time. Next he sat on a rock and dragged damp socks over his feet. Finally came the hardest part:, stamping tender feet into soggy broken knee-high leather boots.

He glanced toward the river. Had the water come up again? Yesterday he shoveled sand and gravel aside to expose more bedrock. Today he intended to pick nuggets out of water-worn pockets in the rock. But with Mal's arrival all his plans went awry.

How did miners know his name at Brown's Bar? He had little to do with them. Especially he avoided newcomers. Many of them spent a few hours searching for gold and the rest of the day carousing at the whiskey tents.

"You never got my letters? Mal, put that gun down. You might hurt somebody."

"Not until you hand over the Squire's gold. We never got a letter from you."

"I wrote to the Squire. I said I would bring his gold. There are cattle to buy in California but nobody to help drive them north. The men I wanted were digging for gold. Don't worry, I have the Squire's gold and a lot more."

Mal's eyes darted to the gear under the sail. "Got the gold in there?"

"Not so loud!" Adam looked around. He shifted his weight to ease his aching legs. Once more the gun wavered forward. "If you'll get that gun out of my face. . . ."

Mal stepped back and lowered his pistol. "No funny stuff Adam. I'd as soon blow your head off as look at you."

Adam sighed. Mal had fixed treachery in his mind. It seemed nothing would dislodge his notions. "Did you come through San Francisco?"

"I did."

"Then you saw the ships anchored there. I couldn't return to Portland. Captain Howlett's crew deserted, every last man. I couldn't wait around for a ship, and I was cautioned not to go overland. Now I'll start a fire and fix breakfast."

He pulled dry kindling and small wood out from under the tarpaulin. Soon he had a fire going and water boiling. He dropped a handful of coffee grounds into the pot. When the aroma of bacon and coffee drifted his way, Mal sniffed the air like a hound dog. "Maybe I'll have some coffee too."

Adam poured coffee into tin cups and forked bacon onto tin pie plates. From his grub sack he fished yesterday's cold biscuits, which he split and warmed face down in bacon grease.

"Sorry I don't have eggs," said Adam. "They cost dear when I can find them. Cost a dollar apiece last time."

Silently they ate. Mal rested the pistol in his lap. Adam watched the other miners on the gravel bar. The trio upstream had settled into their daily routine. One man shoveled sand and gravel into their cradle while one hauled water to wash away the useless slickens. The third man sat on a log rocking the cradle back and forth. As he watched, they rotated. The man sitting now shoveled.

If Mal wanted to dig, cradling would be the way to go. One could shovel sand and gravel and haul water while the other rocked the cradle. Spell each other off. A third man would help, but Adam knew no one he trusted. Most successful miners had left the diggins. Those still here would not hire out on shares.

Many newcomers arrived with strange glints in their eyes. They asked questions, prying into his affairs. But not all were bad men. Most simply tried to learn where to find gold. Some tried to learn how much gold he had and where he kept it.

"Tell me," said Adam, snapping a slice of bacon with his teeth, "did you know about the gold before you came?"

Mal nodded as he chewed his last biscuit. "Heard about it last fall. Didn't put much stock in it. Then we figured you ran off to the mines. Figured right, didn't we?"

Adam hadn't run off, as Mal put it. He started to say so but said, "What's the news from home? Have you seen Mary — Miss Carr?"

"Folks is fine." Mal's rough features turned hard once more. "About the gold, Adam. . . ."

Adam waved a strip of bacon in the air. "Don't worry. I have most of the gold coin." At the further tightening of Mal's mouth he went on. "You'll get it and then some."

"You said so before, but I ain't seen it. If you got so much gold, how come you look like a scarecrow? And why ain't you got any eggs?"

Adam grinned. "Dress up to shovel rocks? If I did, every man here would know I've got gold. Some would roust me for it. And on your way in, see anybody raising chickens? When I can buy eggs, they cost a dollar apiece, as I said, sometimes more."

Mal studied the river swirling past the gravel bar from

which heat waves now rose. "You really find gold here? Looks like poor country to me."

Adam stared at him. What made him such an expert on placer mining? "Would I live like this for nothing, Mal? Not much better'n a critter, camped under this tarp? Cold, wet, hungry half the time? Later on the bar heats up something fierce. Come on, I'll show some pay dirt down on the bar."

But Mal persisted with his fool notions. "Why do you go hungry? If you have so much gold, you can buy all the grub you want."

"It takes three days to go out for food. Sometimes you plain run out of grub. When a peddler comes through, he can't pack much. I buy what I can. Then I don't waste time on the trail."

Mal pointed to the trio upriver. "How are they doing?"

"Mal, I don't ask. They run through more dirt than I can, so I guess they're doing fine."

"Where do you get a — what's that machine down there?"

"A cradle. Works just like rocking a baby. They sell them down at New Helvetia — Sutter's Fort."

As they watched, one of the trio looked at something in his hand, yelled and danced around. "Looka here!" he yelled. The others stared at his hand and they too hopped about.

"Found a big nugget, I'd guess," said Adam. "Go down and talk to them while I clean up. Then we'll pick gold off the bedrock under the river. Maybe pan a little dirt too."

Mal studied the miners, who were still jumping about, whooping and laughing. "I'm powerful curious," he said. "But maybe they don't want me there."

"Danny Fisher and Zeb Brackett are all right. They picked up a new partner a while ago. I don't know him. Keeps mostly to himself. He's gotta pee or something whenever I go over. Wanders off into the brush. But the other two won't mind. Tell them I sent you."

"Well, if you say so."

As he cleaned breakfast dishes Adam glanced down at the miners. When Mal approached, the man rocking the cradle reached for a rifle leaning against a boulder. Mal pointed up toward Adam and said something, and the miner returned his rifle to its rest.

Mal leaned over, pointing now and then. Soon he came running back. "Gold!" he said. "I seen 'em wash it out myself. We gotta go down to Sutter's Fort and get one of them machines."

Hands on hips, Adam grinned "Want to try mining?"

"Hell, yes! The nugget they was fussin' over is near as big as your fist! How soon can we get one of them contraptions?"

Adam stared. "You really mean it, don't you?"

"Damn right I do."

Adam sighed. "I just came from New Helvetia. It's a long way. Take us two, three days, even with a shortcut or two I know about."

"New Helvetia? You mean Sutter's Fort?"

"Same thing. Didn't you come through there?"

"Sure did. Some fella standing outside the fort dressed up like a tin soldier yelled and shook his fist at me. Said I stole his cattle." Mal frowned. "When are we getting started?"

"Tomorrow at daylight," said Adam. "We'll need all day and then some. Right now I'll show you some gold. Want to see dust or nuggets?"

"Nuggets! Big ones."

Adam couldn't help smiling. Just a few minutes ago Mal waved a gun in his face. Now he jumped about like a little boy, anxious to pull a fortune out of the river.

On the bar Adam studied the river. During the night the river had come up. Water swirled over the bedrock he exposed, but it remained clear of gravel. Adam could see the glitter of gold in the pockets.

"Keep downstream of the place you're working," said Adam. "Don't muddy the water. Look for bright color. With your knife, pry the pebbles out of the pockets in the bedrock. If there's a nugget in the pocket, it'll show."

Mal looked at the water. "What'll I do with my boots? Take 'em off?"

Adam shook his head. "Too many sharp rocks. You'll have to work in wet boots."

When Mal stepped into the water, he went rigid and his eyes widened. He stepped back. "My God, but that water's cold! How do you stand it?"

"It's the hardest part, getting into the water." He watched Mal step into the water again, bend over and with his knife blade scrape out a pocket. A flash of color gleamed against the dark bedrock. Mal reached down and picked out a nugget the size of a pea. Adam would have grinned happily at such a find, but Mal scowled.

"I thought they'd be bigger," he grumbled, "like the chunk they found yonder."

Adam shook his head. "You don't see many like that. Find three, four nuggets like yours, add some dust and you've made wages for the day."

Mal hefted the nugget in his hand. "What do you call wages?"

"Fifteen, twenty dollars a day. Maybe more."

Mal gazed at the gravel beneath him. The river swirled by, cold and swift. His brows knit in thought. Finally a long, low whistle escaped him.

"You been here maybe two hundred days. At fifteen a day, that's near three thousand dollars!"

Adam grinned. "Sometimes I do better."

Mal's eyebrows shot up, and a gleam leaped into his ryes. "The hell you say!"

"And sometimes I do worse."

"That six hundred in gold. That was Pa's lifetime savings. Not counting our place in Lafayette, of course." Mal's eyes narrowed. "You still haven't showed me Pa's gold, Adam."

"I have it," said Adam. "Most of it anyhow."

"Well, where it?"

"Buried up on the hillside, where it's safe. Don't worry, I'll pay back the gold I borrowed, with interest."

Mal turned to watch the three miners upstream. "How about those fellers? What do you suppose they're making?"

Adam thought a moment. "This bar shows color no matter where you dig. I'd guess twenty-five a day. Probably more."

"That's all?"

"Apiece, that is."

"You reckon they're digging seventy-five dollars every day?"

"It wouldn't surprise me."

"Adam, let's get one of them cradles!"

A wide grin split Adam's face. "Mal, you're getting the fever."

"Getting it? I got it! Let's get going."

Adam choked back the refusal on his lips. What a revelation this must be to Mal! He had come to retrieve his family's gold, unaware Adam earned more than the Squire Harley Wilson had acquired in a lifetime.

Now before Mal's fevered eyes gleamed a vision of wealth. Since Adam had known the Wilsons, the Squire held a tight rein on his son. He forever reminded Mal of his duty to help increase the family fortunes. Which meant Squire Wilson's fortunes.

Despite the pain when he stepped into the water, Adam could not refuse his brother-in-law. Hadn't he dreamed of gold himself? "We'll go at first light, Mal. Now let's pan for dust, and nuggets if you're lucky."

That night at the campfire Mal gazed at the nuggets and dust he had washed out. "Can't wait to get that cradle and dig some real gold."

"Then we'd better get some sleep. It's a long, hard walk to New Helvetia."

Later, when they lay in their bedrolls beneath the tarpaulin, Mal said, "I forgot to tell you. The other feller on the gravel bar. You said you didn't know his name. It's Johann Leinenweber."

"A Dutchman? Foreigners usually keep to their own kind."

"He's no more a foreigner than you or me. He's New York. Speaks English as well as we do. He came to California with the army. You know, during the war with Mexico. Said he stayed when his enlistment was up. Came to the mines."

Adam did not reply. What could he say? The man had made no effort to be friendly. Rather, it seemed he went out of his way to avoid Adam. Well, that was all right. Johann Leinenweber had no place in his life.

But sleep would not come. Thought of Squire Wilson and his gold also invoked images of Miss Mary Jane Carr. He recalled lying in his bedroll reviewing his weekly letter to her, addressed to Twality Plains, Oregon. Finally he drifted off, only to jar awake and start all over again.

Unable to form a clear picture of Miss Mary Jane, he drifted to another subject that always amazed him: how he came here. When he boarded the brig *Western Star* in Portland, Oregon, he had no intention of remaining in California. He had no notion of living under a tarpaulin. He had no thought of gold. He had come to buy cattle for Squire Wilson and push them north to the Willamette Valley as Ewing Young had done some ten years earlier.

After a rough voyage down the coast the ship swept between towering cliffs half hidden by fog. Her captain brought her into San Francisco Bay, finally dropping anchor off a miserable village huddled among sand dunes on Yerba Buena Cove. The vessel's stern swung south or east, whichever way the cold wind blew. Wisps of fog trailed past the ship, dissipating in warmer air inland. Halyards, whipped by the wind, drummed against the masts.

Adam stood at the railing with Captain Howlett, trying to see the town through drifting fog. When the mist receded, the captain shaded his eyes against the sun's glare on the water. He tugged at his chin whiskers.

"Something is amiss, lad. Maybe an outbreak of smallpox, or cholera. When a ship makes port, folks turn out. But I don't see a soul. It's not right. We'd best remain aboard."

But Adam would not be denied. "I'm going ashore, sir. My business is there, and it won't wait. I want to start back to Oregon before the rains set in."

"We'll both go then, lad," said the captain, "but carefully."

The crew lowered the gig. Two sailors stood by as Adam Stuart followed the captain over the side and down the rope ladder. While Adam took his seat in the stern, Captain Howlett stood in the bow, squinting into the sun's glare. "Nary a soul on shore, lad. Something's afoot. I don't like it. I'll not wade into a plague."

At the word the sailors missed a stroke on the oars. Adam

sat in the stern peering around the oarsmen. Fifty feet from shore the ship's boat nosed into mud.

Without leaving the boat the captain and Adam peered about. The town appeared deserted. As they watched, dust whirled up from sand hills behind town and blotted out the village. When the cloud dissipated, a man in a black suit strode toward the beach.

Ready to order the sailors to back oars, Captain Howlett waited. "What's the news?" he shouted. "Where is everybody? Quick, man, is it the fever?"

The man laughed. "Yes, sir," he said, "it's the fever all right!"

"Thunderation!" shouted the captain. "Back oars, lads!"

"But not what you think."

"What's that you say? Belay, lads. Well, man, out with it!"

"I'm talking of gold fever, sir! The whole town has got it."

The captain glanced at the sailors standing at the oars. They stared at each other, mouths agape.

The captain stepped out into water up to his knees and made his way ashore with great sucking sounds. "When will you build a wharf? To arrive during low tide is an abomination, like the sand and dust whirling about our heads."

Reluctantly, seeing the captain's discomfort, Adam stepped over the side. He thought he would leave his boots in the mud, but he dragged them loose and wallowed ashore after the captain.

"Gold, did you say?" asked Captain Howlett.

"More than enough for everybody. Almost everyone has left for the mines. See for yourself." The man thrust out his hand. In it he held a quinine bottle for them to see. Its contents gleamed in the sunlight. "Gathered it from the American Fork myself, at Coloma."

Adam stared. "You dug it yourself?"

"Yes, sir," said the man. "From the gravel bars in that river. It was easy as pie."

Demanded the captain, "If it was so easy, sir, why haven't you gone to mine gold yourself?"

The man stuck out his hand. "Brannan is the name, sir. Sam Brannan."

"Captain Phineas Howlett of the brig *Western Star*, just arrived from Portland. This is my passenger, Adam Stuart. But you haven't answered my question. Why haven't you gone to the mines?"

"My business keeps me here, sir, and at Sutter's Fort on the Sacramento River." Brannan studied Adam. "Have you come, Mr. Stuart, to seek your fortune in the mines?"

"No, sir. Until now I never heard of gold in California."

"Then why did you come, if I may ask?"

"I came from Lafayette, in the Willamette Valley of Oregon, on business. Maybe you can direct me to the proper person or persons."

Brannan inclined his head. "I would, sir, if I knew. . . ."

Adam studied the man standing before him. They were of the same height. Brannan's face was slender but with a wide brow. His dark hair receded somewhat at the temples. Mutton-chop whiskers curved down from his sideburns, and a tiny patch of whiskers dotted his lower lip. The man said business kept him in the city. With his open features, clear gaze and fine voice, Adam would have pegged him as a preacher.

"My business is simple enough," Adam said. "I came to buy cattle and hire drovers to help me drive them north."

"An ambitious undertaking," observed Brannan.

"But it can be done, sir. A man from our district, Ewing Young, did it some ten years ago."

Brannan smiled. " I came here two years ago," he said. "I haven't heard of him." "Brannan shook his head. "Thousands of cattle abound on almost every rancho. Obtaining what you want would be easy, I dare say. Hiring men to herd them north may be another matter. A few *Californios* have gone to the mines. But most of them stayed home, having nothing to do with mad Yankees who scratch for gold. I doubt you could hire a man. They avoid Americans when they can and scorn them when they can't."

"What do you think I should do?"

Brannan gazed past Adam toward the interior. "Seek your wealth in the mines. You came at a most fortuitous time. If you do so, stop by my store for supplies."

"Thank you, sir," said Adam, shaking his head, "but I am resolved to return at once to Oregon."

Accordingly he rented a room in a mud hut for two days. Then he looked up Captain Howlett. He found the captain slumped over the railing of his vessel. The *Western Star* appeared deserted, with several sails hanging loosely, flapping in the wind.

"When are you sailing for Portland, sir?"

Growled the captain, "When they learned of the gold, my crew jumped ship and headed for the mines, every one of them. I cannot hire even one man to sail with me."

Thus Adam Stuart's decision was made for him. Looking up Sam Brannan, he informed the merchant he intended to seek his fortune in the mines. Brannan smiled and rubbed his hands briskly. "Why, then, you'll need equipment and supplies. That's my business. Come along and I'll outfit you with the best."

Buying a pick, shovel and tin pie plates along with other gear, he headed for the Middle American River. There he was surprised to learn there were no mines. There were only sand

and gravel bars along the streams. He stood in icy water from sun-up to dark each day panning for gold. Or he knelt at the river's edge swirling water around in his pie plate, washing the slickens out until heavy sand and gold remained. He worked until it seemed his knees would never straighten out again.

At night he wrote to Miss Mary Jane Carr, teacher, of West Tualatin Plains, Oregon Territory. Adam rummaged into a canvas bag for paper, a steel pen in a wooden holder, and a bottle of black ink. Setting his ink carefully on the ground, using a piece of warped pine board for a desk, he scowled at the blank paper.

Mary Jane's cool blonde vision floated before him. The girl had ridden beside him on the wagon crossing the plains to Oregon. When the wind swept over them, threatening to lift her skirts, she clasped her hands firmly about her knees. Her poke bonnet largely hid her face from him. Was that why her vision remained so shadowy? One memory pleased him. When Indians drew alongside their train, she moved closer to him on the wagon seat.

What could he write? He already described panning and picking for gold. He described the country, including the canyon of the Middle Fork. What could he say to keep him in her thoughts? His scowl deepened, and he began to write.

Dear Mary Jane:

He stopped. That would never do. Since they had no understanding, she would think him forward using her name so familiarly. He crumpled the sheet of paper and drew another — his last — from his bag.

Dear Miss Carr:
    Again I take my pen in hand. I have not received

a letter from you since October although I wrote every week. I do not say this against you, for mail here is uncertain. Unless someone goes out to New Helvetia for grub, there is no one to bring the mail in.

Mining is a hard life, but things go well. The past winter was difficult but spring has come to the diggins.

He set his pen down and stared at the paper. What more could he say? That he lived under a tarpaulin with brush piled against one end to break the wind? She would think him no better than an animal in a burrow.

He could say he was too busy digging gold from the river to provide better shelter. Or that he would move on when the color gave out. Would she think him greedy, grasping for gold?

Or would she think him shiftless, quick to move from one failure to another? He wished he knew how she would take what he wrote. In short, he wished he knew her better.

His tongue protruding from his lips, he wrote on.

Food has been hard to come by. What we can find costs us dear. Coffee, flour, beans, sugar at a dollar per pound. After lacking bacon for two months I bought some off a trader passing through. When I can't work the gravel bar I borrow a rifle and hunt for game. But more miners arrive every day, driving the deer higher in the mountains.

A change has come about that we — most of my fellow miners and I — do not like. Arrivals include men — and a few females, I hear — new to the diggins. Just down the river a rum-mill and a gaming hall have appeared, both in tents far grander than mine. We see more drunken men and gamblers and less regard for the persons and property of others.

Some fellows have given up hopes of finding a rich strike. They spend much time frequenting these places. They think us odd for sticking to our tasks so diligently.

Cramps gripped his legs, shooting pain through the muscles. He pointed his toes straight out and grasped his calves. Slowly he massaged the knots out of the sinews.

That would be news. Increasing frequency of the cramps, sometimes requiring him to leave the gravel bar, worried him. But he did not want to pass his sorry state on to Mary Jane, so he dismissed mention of his growing infirmity.

The task is hard, but I am nearing my goal. I shall work until autumn but I will not spend another winter here. The means to begin a new venture is already at hand. Will it be opening a store or operating a first-rate farm? I have not decided yet.

Thoughts of you remain a shining beacon to spur me on. I hope you will allow me to call upon you when I return to Oregon.

The rain has stopped, so I must get on with my work. As ever, I remain

Your obedient servant,

Adam Stuart

Stretching to find an envelope, he addressed it and stuffed the letter inside. A miner might come down the trail at any time. He would take letters or messages to New Helvetia for posting.

With Mal's arrival the letter seemed spurious, somehow.

Yet his arrival didn't really change anything except to make Adam yearn for home. Now with Mal's arrival and their plans to obtain a cradle, his vision of home faded farther into the distance. He sighed, rolled over and listened to Mal snoring the night away.

CHAPTER 2

"What's the matter, Adam? Got a rock in your boot?"

Over his shoulder Adam glanced at his brother-in-law. Two hours on the trail, they were sweating heavily. "What makes you ask?"

Mal pointed toward Adam's feet. "You're walking gimpy."

He hoped he could hide his pain. But Mal, never big on guns, had shown the sharpest eyes in their train over the trail to Oregon. No movement of buffalo or hostiles escaped his attention. What he saw and what he thought did not always come together, but he had sharp eyes.

"It's these boots. Stones come up through the cracks in the soles." Which was true enough. He didn't tell Mal of his pain or of his doubt about lasting through the summer.

"Next to a cradle and another pick and shovel," said Mal, "you need new boots. Your toes are leaking out of them boots you got on."

They lapsed into silence. From the Middle Fork they climbed to a saddle between grassy hills dotted with pines and oaks. From there they dropped down to another river bottom.

Dust rose from the treetops ahead. Adam had seen it for an hour, but Mal kept his nose to the ground. Finally he looked up and pointed. "What do you make of that?"

Adam shook his head. "Don't know."

S'pose it's Sutter's Fort?"

"We're nowhere near there yet. Too far up in the hills to be Sutter's cows."

They soon had their answer. They met men, singly and in groups, headed toward the Middle Fork. Some sized up the trail before them. Others' eyes glittered as brightly as their red or blue calico shirts. Butternut pants were tucked into black knee-high boots. Floppy-brimmed hats and neckerchiefs completed their costumes. Gold crossed the counter of Sam Brannan's New Helvetia store as he outfitted these men. Adam knew what caused the feverish looks in their eyes.

A dozen men blocked the trail. Newcomers looked over Adam's rags with poorly-concealed disgust before turning to Mal.

"Hey, mister," said a man, "can you point us to the gold?"

"You're asking me? Talk to this fellow. He's been here awhile."

A sour-looking man, whiskey bottle in hand, had been staring up and down Adam's long frame. He stepped forward, his lip curling. "What's a scarecrow like him know?"

"Brother," said Mal, "He's been panning gold nearly a year now."

The sour one spat in the dust at Adam's feet. He pulled at the bottle. "Obviously he ain't found it yet. Me, I'd o' been out o' here with treasure months ago."

"Now let me tell you. . . ."

"Let's move on, Mal."

A good-natured fellow stepped ahead of the grouch. "Don't mind Jud here. He wakes up mad and stays that way. Grumbled all the way around the Horn."

Adam, who seldom let anger show, retorted, "Mighty strange somebody hasn't drowned him by now."

The sour one stepped forward, bristling. "Now see here! Ain't nobody goin' to talk thataway."

But the other man held him back. "Don't pay him no mind. What do you say, feller? Can you point the way or not?"

Adam shrugged. "Gold is where you find it."

They stared at him. The grouch said, "That don't tell us nothing." He turned to the rest of his party, tipping the bottle up, shaking it, tossing it beside the trail. "He ain't sayin' even if he does know."

Again Adam shrugged. "Hard to point you anywhere from here."

When the miners pressed on, Mal said, "Maybe you should have given them some pointers."

Adam stopped and faced Mal. "What would I say? If they dig and stick to it, they'll find gold."

Mal said, "I see. I got a lot to learn. "

Yes, you surely do. First thing is to keep your mouth shut, especially about gold.

Earlier they greeted men civilly and wished them luck. Now Adam, eyeing the dusty file of men, nodded and eased past them. Mal turned to watch them hurry toward the notch they passed through earlier.

"Seeing them fellers starts me thinking, Adam. Maybe we'd best head back. I don't want to lose our camp. Likely we'll find somebody squatting on your gold."

"Big country," said Adam. "It'll swallow them up. Besides, Danny said he'd hold down camp for us."

"Are you sure? You mean, he'll take time off from digging?"

"Nothing like that. He'll work the gravel I was working."

Mal stared at him. "That all right with you?"

"Why not? He can't work it all out, and we can move on if paydirt gives out. Might even improve our luck."

Mal shook his head. "I dunno. When you got a good thing going, you don't give it up, seems to me."

"Count on Danny," said Adam. "He owes me. I saved his bacon a while back."

"What happened?"

Adam laughed. "Fished him out of the river. He saw color in the water and went after it. The hole was deeper than he thought and the current stronger. He can't swim."

"So you saved his life?"

"You might say that."

They came to another river. Unlike the Middle Fork, this one flowed quietly from pool to pool. In between the pools water slid silently over gravel.

Gazing at the river, Adam said, "Folks talk of damming the rivers to get at gravel bars under water. Might happen someday."

"Sounds too much like work to me," said Mal.

The trail stopped abruptly at the water's edge. Mal looked upriver and down. "Now what? Which way do we go?"

Before Adam could reply, a voice crackled from the far bank. "Fixin' to cross, gents?" A shaggy gray-haired fellow sat in the shade near a boat drawn up on the bank.

"Sure thing, Ben!" called Adam. "Fare still four bits?"

Nodding, the grizzled fellow got up from a log and stood with the aid of a home-made crutch. A dirty bandage covered the stump of his right leg. Gingerly he shoved the boat into the water and clambered aboard. With powerful strokes he propelled it across the river.

Adam pointed upriver from the stern. "Coloma is up that way, Mal. Where Marshall first found the gold. This is the South Fork of the American River."

"Pullin' out, Adam?" asked the ferryman.

"Going in to buy a cradle," said Adam. "We're settled on a bar that shows good color and nuggets now and then."

Ben spat over the side. "Hell, the way you stuck to it, I'd o' thought you cleared out rich by now."

Adam grinned. "I'm greedy."

On the western bank they paid the ferryman, climbed out of the boat and hit the trail.

"Poor fella," said Mal, "stuck here, unable to dig for gold."

"Brought it on himself," said Adam. "He found good gravel in the high Sierras. Stayed too long last winter and froze his legs. Lost the one. Ben Merwin is a good fella. He just didn't show good judgment."

They continued on. Adam could say the same about himself, going to New Helvetia for a cradle. He should pull out for good. But he wouldn't leave Mal in the lurch.

Evening found them nearing a river once more. Here it was wide, with gravel bars that had been worked over. Yet men in strange hats and baggy trousers carried gravel in buckets hung from their shoulders on a double yoke. Others washed gravel in long sluice boxes Adam called long toms. One thing struck him as strange. The men swarmed over the old diggins, silent as ghosts as they toiled.

"Mormon Island. Some of the first big strikes came here. Sam Brannan brought a shipload of Mormons to San Francisco in '46. Some of them were already on the ground when Marshall found gold. They worked for Captain Sutter, building a sawmill."

"Who are these scarecrows?"

"Chinamen. They pick up gold others left behind."

"I never seen Chinamen before. What're they like?"

"Same as anyone else. You'll find good Chinamen and bad."

"Why ain't they up on the Middle Fork diggin' in good dirt?"

"White miners ran them out. Beat 'em, hung 'em upside

down, mean tricks like that. By grab, Mal, I'm plumb tuckered out. Let's find some grub and bed down. We still have nearly eighteen miles to go."

After they ate, they lay under the stars in their bedrolls. Adam, slapping constantly at mosquitoes, tried to think of Miss Mary Jane Carr. But around them sounds of music and shouts and drunken laughter wafted through the night. "One thing for sure," said Adam, "the gents making all the racket didn't shovel much gravel today."

He just about drifted off to sleep when Mal's voice drew him awake. "Adam, you never did show me your gold. How much you got buried back in camp?"

"Five, six thousand, maybe more not counting your pa's money."

"Hope none of them fellers find it."

Adam fretted about more than gold. His legs were cramping. He worried about getting rest, about toting a cradle back to the Middle Fork and working after that. He lay watching stars whirl in the sky until sleep overtook him.

At first light they found a breakfast of Johnny cakes and bacon washed down with bitter coffee. The sun appeared over the hills when they hit the trail to New Helvetia.

The country leveled out into gentle rises, hardly enough to call hills, dotted with oaks. Willows lined watercourses. The hills were green following the winter rains, but already patches of dried grass heralded the arrival of summer's stifling heat — and mosquitoes.

Cattle dotted the hillsides, some standing, others lying beneath the oaks. They watched Adam and Mal and the men who streamed in the opposite direction.

"Captain Sutter's cattle," said Adam.

"Way out here? He must own a huge farm."

"Way I heard it he obtained a land grant of forty thousand acres from the Mexican government in Monterey. But he lost his rancho when the U. S. took over California. The gold stampede makes some men rich, but it's ruining Sutter."

When they crested a rise, a group of men clustered around something on the ground. "Sutter's hide tanners, I'd guess," said Adam. "They say he does a big business in leather."

But as they approached, they saw men butchering a cow beside the trail.

"Stealing Sutter's beef," muttered Adam.

Men cut chunks of meat from the hind quarters and crammed them, still dripping blood, into packs. Black flies swarmed over carcass and butchers. Adam shook his head. Most of what they took would soon spoil.

Mal stopped. "That animal belong to you?" he demanded of the butchers.

One man stepped out from among the cutters and looked down his nose at Mal. Two pistols stuck in his belt and a rifle nestled in the crook of his arm. "This your critter, Sonny?"

"No, but. . . ."

"Then butt out." The rifle swung toward Mal.

"Come on," said Adam, "this is no business of ours." Beyond hearing of the butchers he continued, "You see the kind of men coming in. Last year I never heard of anybody taking anything, except maybe a cow or two. But times are changing. We won't take another partner. We don't know who to trust."

"Maybe we better stock up on guns too," said Mal.

"Guns lead to trouble. You already have one weapon. That's enough."

The sun was midway down the western sky when they reached New Helvetia. Fine dust in the air clung to them, sweaty as they were. It coated their eyelids and coursed down their faces as muddy rivers of sweat.

On a small rise before them an eighteen-foot adobe wall jutted up from the bare earth. Behind the wall a rooftop rose. As they neared, Mal said, curling his lip "Isn't this just the grandest sight? Except maybe what's inside the wall, it looks like a pigsty."

Outside the walls, hastily-erected buildings lined a dusty road. Already their yellow pine boards warped and bleached to a uniform gray beneath the blazing sun.

"Ho, lads! The show is beginning for fair."

A figure slouched against a shed whittling on a stick. Shoulder-length hair fell from his floppy hat down to his shoulders, where a red kerchief covered a dusty shirt.

"What do you mean by that?" demanded Mal.

The fellow spat into the dust. "Stick around. Ye'll see." With the stick he pointed to the main gate in the adobe wall. Adam leaned against the shed also. As long as he kept moving he put the pain out of mind. When he stopped, his legs ached beyond ability to stand.

A single drum began to beat inside the wall. Out marched a detachment of men clad more or less uniformly in costumes of green and blue. They marched more or less in a column and somewhat in step. The column turned left and halted outside the wall beside the gate. The drum fell silent.

"It's his nibs' army ye're privileged to see. He bought them uniforms from the Russians when he bought Fort Ross over on the coast. Maybe ye'll even see the cap'n himself."

Adam had never heard of Russians in California. Scanning the detachment with renewed interest, he was astounded to see that they were all Indians.

"Now the real treat!" said the wood carver.

Through the gate marched a stocky man resplendent in a dark blue uniform topped by a gold-plumed helmet. Golden epaulets fell from his shoulders, and about his middle he wore a golden belt with golden sash hanging from it. In his gauntleted hand he carried a sword. He stood, rigidly at attention, and rested the point of his sword on the ground.

The native troops sagged beneath the sun as if they were melting. The great man, however, remained erect. But eventually he too succumbed to the heat. He removed his headpiece and cradled it in one arm. Even from across the road Adam saw sweat roll down from his high bald dome of a head. Fierce concentration made his mustaches bristle.

"Ain't he the toff!" But the idler kept his voice low.

"What's his name?" demanded Mal. "He's the feller ragged me when I was comin' in to the Middle Fork."

"Captain Sutter himself," said Adam.

Sounds of a horse's hoofs drummed on the hard ground as a young rider dashed up and pulled his horse to a stop. "They're coming, sir!"

Adam and Mal peered down the road. Distant riders were approaching. A sudden explosion shook them and rattled the buildings outside the fort. A giant smoke ring rolled out from a small cannon placed in the wall.

"Big man coming," offered the bystander. "Mighty important man. Sutter don't fire his cannon for a pipsqueak."

The cannon fire brought people spilling out of buildings along the road, shading their eyes to see the spectacle.

Riders approached the fort ahead of a dust cloud. A man rode at the head of a double column of twenty soldiers.

Sutter settled his headpiece on his head. When the column halted before him, he raised his sword in salute.

"Welcome to New Helvetia, General Riley!"

Before the general could respond, another cannon blew another smoke ring out from the walled enclosure. The horsemen struggled to keep their panicked mounts under control. The general returned the salute, dismounted and turned to a man at the head of the column.

"Dismount the men, sergeant, and stand them at ease."

"Who's this new feller?" asked Mal.

"Don't worry about him, mate," said the lounging stranger, looking over Adam's rags. "Ye got nothing to do with the likes of him. Down from the mines?"

Adam nodded.

"Made out pretty good, did ye?"

"Found some color."

"Come in to town, did ye? Ye come to the right place. Jimmy Devlin's is right down the road toward the river. Best whiskey saloon in Sacramento City. Tell 'em Chalky sent ye."

Mal eyed Captain Sutter. "Somebody should tell him he's losing cattle to the miners."

"I expect he already knows," said Adam.

"Was it me, I'd drive the animals away from the trail. No use putting temptation in the miners' way. Hold up, Adam. I'm going over and tell him."

Before Adam could stop him Mal bounded across the street, where Captain Sutter was speaking. "We seldom see units of the army or officers of the government here, Governor."

"I shouldn't be surprised," said the general. "California is a huge territory."

"And a lawless one. Miners overrun my land, trample my grain and steal my horses." Sutter's eye fell on Mal, who had edged near. "Yes," demanded Sutter, "what do you want?"

Mal swelled up. "We just came in from the American Fork. Men were butchering one of your cows right beside the trail, and we saw dozens of other carcasses. If I was you. . . ."

Captain Sutter turned to the general, arms outstretched,

palms upward. "You see? Even as we speak, the outlaws destroy me."

"You ought to drive the cattle away from the trail," said Mal.

Captain Sutter scowled at him. "I have no vaqueros. They have deserted to the mines or gone back to their ranchos. Will you work for me? Tend my cattle?"

Mal stiffened, as if he had been offered an indecent proposal. "No, sir. Soon as we find a cradle, we're back to the mines."

"You see how it is, General Riley. The Americans dig gold. Even my *Californios* desert me, and my Indians flee to the mountains to escape the miners' cruelty. But come. It is hot. Over good wine in the shade we will talk." Turning his back on Mal, Captain Sutter marched with his guest through the wall.

The troop dismounted, each man sweating in the heat stood by his horse. The army sergeant paced back and forth in front of Sutter's troop. Nervously Sutter's soldiers stared at him. Then one by one they slipped away, around the corner of the fort.

The lounger beside Adam spat into the dust. "Yer mate sorta puts his oar in where it ain't wanted, don't he?"

"Takes after his pa," said Adam.

Mal rejoined them, a sour look on his face. "It's like they don't want to know. Makes you wonder if anyone is in charge."

Adam turned to the idler. "In the diggins they say Mr. Brannan has a store here."

"That he has, mate. Head west to the river, to the steamboat landing."

"Steamboat?" asked Adam. "Last summer I had to walk from Carquines Strait."

"Ye been in the tules, mate. They even talk of running railroad cars to Folsom. Save the lads a few steps an' separate 'em from their dust quicker."

Adam shook his head. The world had rushed in while he sifted through gravel on the Middle Fork.

He limped badly now, but they reached the Sacramento River and Sam Brannan's store. Inside, Adam's senses were assailed by the sight of merchandise piled everywhere. Smells of fresh-roasted coffee beans and clothing and manila rope and leather tickled his nostrils.

He was drinking in the sights of plenty when he found Brannan staring at him, a puzzled expression on his face. "Pardon me," said Brannan, "but you remind me of someone. Did you sail to San Francisco with me aboard the *Brooklyn*?"

Adam shook his head. "Last spring when I landed, San Francisco was almost deserted. I arrived aboard the *Western Star*. You urged me to come to the mines."

Brannan laughed. "I remember now. I still tell friends about the man who nearly turned his back on fortune for cattle. Do you know what some of them say? There's a man who kept his head in this time of madness. Have you enjoyed good fortune?"

"Tolerable," said Adam.

"So now you're going home?"

"No, sir, we came to buy a cradle. This is my brother-in-law, Mal Wilson of Lafayette, Oregon Territory."

Brannan offered his hand to Mal. "You came to dig gold with Mr. Stuart?"

Mal colored and mumbled, "Something like that." He wandered off to examine several cradles.

Adam wondered how much he should tell Brannan. The man seemed honest enough, but it also seemed that he turned every scrap of information to his own profit.

"You will find whatever supplies you need here. Will you stay in California when you have dug enough gold?"

"There's a young lady in Oregon."

"I understand. Should you decide to stay," said Brannan, "look me up. I'll sell you a fine lot in San Francisco, or maybe here in Sacramento City. I'll give you a good price.

"Thank you, sir. I doubt I'll stay. Until Mal arrived I hadn't seen family for a year."

Brannan smiled. "A common complaint in the mines, isn't it?" Brannan beckoned to the counter and called, "Mr. Sinclair, would you please help Mr. Stuart here? Mr. Donovan and I will serve the other customers."

When Brannan left, Mal, who had returned, looked after him. "Got his fingers in a lot of pies, ain't he? Wouldn't surprise me to see that feller governor someday, even president of the U. S. of A. If California ever becomes a state."

Mr. Sinclair approached them. He was a small bald-headed man with a fringe of gray hair curling about his ears. His open coat revealed a vest of green tartan. But his eyes glinted and a smile played about his bloodless lips. He looked Adam up and down, his eyes resting longest on the wreckage of Adam's boots.

"Ye look pretty duddie, Mr. Stuart," he said. "Shall we start with new pants and a shirt or two?"

"I'd like to see a mining cradle first," said Mal, but Adam waved him off. "First things first, Mal." To the clerk he said, "I feel a wee bit duddie. I haven't heard that word since Grandfather said it back in Indiana."

For the next hour Adam and Mal selected their purchases: clothing, new boots, a couple of sacks of beans and bacon, and of course fresh-ground coffee.

Now I need a bath," said Adam, "before I climb into these new clothes. And a laundry to wash the old."

Mal's mouth fell open. "Surely you're not keeping those rags."

"They're good for work," said Adam. "I'll save the new for traveling home. Besides, it doesn't pay to look too prosperous."

Mr. Sinclair, smiling broadly, tapped his head. "Ye've not lost the touch, laddie. Look for the third tent down the road. The Chinaman will fix ye up good as new."

Adam smiled wistfully. He wanted to believe Mr. Sinclair. But his exhausted, aching body told him otherwise.

After a bath and their need for food met, Mal said, "Now to get one of them cradles."

"Back to Brannan's," said Adam.

An hour later Adam pronounced himself ready to start back. But the weight on his back brought misery. He was afraid he couldn't follow through. They couldn't go far in the daylight remaining, but they could make camp on the road to Mormon Bar.

CHAPTER 3

"Can't go a step farther, Mal," groaned Adam. He let his pack drop. Staggering to a down tree, he sank onto the log and rubbed his legs. Across the South Fork, Ben's ferry deposited two miners and their packs on the bank.

Mal looked from Adam to the ferry, now crossing toward them. "We can't stop here, Adam. It's only a little way to camp."

"If you call six, eight miles a little way," said Adam. "I shouldn't have come back. I should have kept on going."

"And leave all your gold? What's wrong with you anyhow?"

"Rheumatism," said Adam.

"That's an old man's disease," protested Mal.

"I stood in cold water too long. Made an old man out of me."

Ben nosed his skiff in to the bank. When neither of them got up, he stood up and leaned on his crutch, waiting. Finally he asked, "What's yer pleasure, gents? Fixin' to cross or not? Oh, hello, Adam. Couldn't see it was you, new duds an' all." Ben peered closely at him. "You ailin', Adam?"

Adam nodded, mopping his brow with a bandanna. "It's the cold water sick, Ben. Stayed at it too long."

Ben shook his head and clucked. "Beats hell, don't it, bein' stove up?"

"Tell you what, Adam," said Mal. "Tote what you can. I'll come back for the rest."

Mal was talking sense. Adam sighed and struggled up. He

stowed the beans, flour and the bucket aboard the skiff and climbed in. "All right to leave our gear until Mal comes back?"

"You bet," said Ben, letting his crutch clatter into the boat, scrambling in. "Hell to be gimped up. Now an old man like me, it don't matter, but you're a young feller."

"I'll get by," said Adam. He wished he believed it.

He endured the climb over the low ridges lying between the forks of the American River. Finally they spotted the sail that had been Adam's home for half a year. His shoulders sagged, crying for relief, and he sighed. As they drew near the canvas, his relief turned sour.

A staggering amount of baggage was stacked beneath his tent. There was nobody in sight. Four men were panning for gold on the bar. Danny and his boys still worked the upper end.

"Damn!" said Mal. "I knew this would happen. Now what?"

"Somebody moved in on us. Probably those men down there."

"Well, we'll just throw all that truck out."

Adam held up a hand. "When we explain we went in for supplies and were coming right back, they'll move on."

"Don't be too sure of that, sonny. Don't lay a hand on our gear."

A bearded man stepped from behind the huge oak, his rifle pointed toward them. He looked as though he knew how to use it. Adam recognized him as the man who stood guard while his party butchered Captain Sutter's cow along the trail.

"This is our camp and our diggins," said Adam.

"Not no more it ain't. This here is Kaintuck Bar."

Adam pointed to the men working the cradle at the upper end of the bar. "Wasn't Danny, the fellow rocking the cradle down there, wasn't he camped here?"

"No, siree, wasn't nobody here when we come. It was plumb deserted."

Something was wrong. In the five months Adam had known him, Danny Fisher never went back on his word.

"No matter," said Adam. "We'll help you fellows find another dig."

The rifle swung to bear directly on him. The bearded fellow let loose a piercing whistle. Almost before he could count them, four men lined up behind Adam and Mal, their hands on the butts of pistols stuck in their belts.

"You see how it is, feller," said the bearded one. "If this was your camp, which I'm doubtin', it ain't no more."

Adam pointed to several tools leaning up against a stump. "We left our pick and shovel to show we'd come back. That's what everybody does here."

"Well, if you ain't the most argufyin' feller," said the bearded one. "But it ain't good enough. You didn't stake your claim."

"Stake our claim?"

"Drive stakes in the corners like we done. Them's the boundaries of our diggings. Miner's law. An' accordin' to law, you ain't drove no stakes, so you ain't got no claim."

"We've never had miner's law," said Adam, "whatever that means."

"We do now. Boys down to Brown's Bar voted it in yestiddy."

"But we were in Sacramento City yesterday."

"Tough luck, sonny. This here claim is staked out by the Kaintuck Company, meanin' us. Right, boys?"

Adam pointed to shallow holes around camp, with piles of dirt beside them. "These your prospect holes?"

The bearded one shook his head. "They was here when we come."

Adam gazed at the trio working the cradle upstream. Now only two men were working. He thought of having it out with Danny and his pards. Danny had promised to work their digs until they returned. But why argue? Whatever happened, there was no use crying about it. He smiled easily at the rifleman. "How wide is a miner's claim?" he asked.

"Hunnert feet, like the boys decided."

"Well, then, we'll pitch camp down there on the flat and work the bar next to you folks if you don't mind."

"But Adam," protested Mal, "the gold!"

The bearded man whirled on Mal. "What gold?"

"Why," said Adam, "the gold we'll take out as soon as we set up our cradle. You keep the old sail. It lets the rain in some, but it'll keep the sun off your grub. We'll camp down there under the oaks. Dry weather coming on."

"You cain't do that," said the rifleman. "This bar is claimed by our party."

Adam looked over the gravel bar and the hillside above it. He turned back to the bearded one. "I see one set of stakes. Don't see any more."

"But. . . ."

"Miner's law." Adam grinned.

The man's mouth fell open, and his jaw snapped shut without speaking.

"Where's the rest of your company?" asked Adam. "There were more of you when we met on the trail."

The man's glance slid downriver and back at him. "I reckon that ain't your concern."

"You're right," said Adam. "Mal, we'll set up camp down below."

They moved away. Out of earshot Mal said, "You're giving up on the gold you got buried? Or did somebody find it?"

Adam frowned. "Mal, you're so all-fired concerned about that gold you almost gave my secret way. Don't say anything, all right? The gold is safe for now. We'll worry about it later."

"With that crowd here? Shouldn't I at least know where it is?"

Adam wondered how much he should tell Mal. When it came down to it, he knew his brother in-law only slightly. He had not met Mal back in Indiana. On the Oregon Trail, Squire Wilson demanded each man keep to himself and tend to business. Idle chatter never got a man rich, he said. In the settlement of Lafayette on the Yamhill River, Mal and Adam's sister had settled on their own farm. Lacking capital, Adam had gone to work for the Squire.

Mal stared at him, waiting for an answer.

"The gold is safe," said Adam. Mal talked without thinking. Too, as the loafer at Sutter's Fort said, he stuck his oar into other people's affairs. It could cost them the gold, even their lives. There were things Mal didn't need to know.

"Most miners don't work on Sunday. Unless I miss my guess, these fellows will go down to Brown's Bar."

"What for?"

"The whiskey tent, and maybe the gaming tables. I reckon that's where the rest of them are now. Did you see the empty bottles tossed around?"

Mal's eyebrows shot up. "You don't miss much, do you?"

Adam wished Mal's alertness on the trail showed now. Probably he saw nothing but gold. "In your camp alone with a poke of gold, you get a mite watchful. Down at the whiskey tents they might hear of some big strike and go running off. Happens all the time."

"You know what?" said Mal. "You got a head on your shoulders."

"What do you want to do?" said Adam. "Go back for the rest of the cradle tonight or wait until tomorrow?"

With a sigh Mal gazed toward the trail on the hill above them. "I'm tuckered, but I sure want to see gold color. Got plenty of daylight yet. I'll make it back tonight."

When Mal vanished down the trail, Adam looked for a new campsite. Finding a fairly level spot beneath several live oaks, he placed their gear there. With a shovel he dug a fire pit and lined it with round stones. From the hill he dragged several dead trees for firewood. Then he paced out roughly a hundred feet of gravel bar and with a rock drove pegs into the ground.

His legs, still aching, cried out for relief. He did the only thing he had found to help besides laudanum. Near camp lay sand washed up against the hillside by high water. He dug two trenches. Sitting on the sand, he placed a leg in each trench and pushed hot sand over them, burying them. At once the heat gave him relief.

Sitting on the pile, he contemplated their plight. Except for his bedroll he left his gear in camp. Without the frying pan and coffee pot, how would they cook? Without an ax, he would have to break limbs into sticks by hand for their fire.

But most of all he missed his canvas possibles bag. He had brought paper from Sacramento City, but the bag contained his pen and ink. Without it he could write no letters. Four days had gone by without thought of Mary Jane Carr. He was too busy by day and too tired by night to even think of her.

The warm sand made him drowsy. He was nodding off when a noise behind him made him spin about, lifting his legs out of the sand. It was Danny, looking sheepish, carrying a cast iron frying pan and an ax. Danny stared as Adam rubbed his aching legs.

"Hurting again?" Danny asked.

"Still," said Adam. "The pain won't let up. What happened up there in camp? They run you out at gunpoint?"

Danny shook his grizzled head. "If they had, I'd feel better."

"With these new folks coming in," said Adam, "I thought you would stay until I got back."

Danny stared at his feet. "Yeah, well, our new man, Leinenweber, said he'd stay up there. But he wandered off to hunt camp meat. When he come back, them jaspers had moved in. I said you were coming right back, but they said the camp and claim was abandoned. They outnumbered us eight rifles to one. They wasn't going to move. I wanted your gear but they said no."

"I appreciate your trying," said Adam.

Danny held out the fry pan and ax. "We figured you could use these. We got extra. Haven't got a spare coffee pot, though."

"I've made coffee in a fry pan," said "Adam. "This new fellow of yours. . . "

"Leinenweber."

"This Leinenweber," said Adam. "I don't see him over there to your camp. Did he pull out?"

"He up and grabbed the rifle and went hunting for fresh meat. Maybe he didn't want to look you in the eye after what he done. Makes us short-handed working the cradle, but truth is, we're about out of grub."

Adam pointed to the bacon tied on a short rope and hung over an oak limb. "I'll cut off a slab for you. And some flour. If you go out, bring some back for us."

"Don't know as we deserve it, losing your camp to them jaspers. but bacon and slapjacks would go good." Danny pointed to the cradle box. "Where do you figure on setting up?"

"Right here between you and those fellows," said Adam. "If we aren't crowding you."

Danny waved an arm over the expanse of rocks. "Hell, we couldn't work all this bar this summer. We get good color here. You should too."

"That'll please Mal. He went to Ben's Crossing for the rest of the cradle. Be back tonight."

Later, after a dinner of bacon and coffee, Adam lay in his blankets watching shadows settle into the river bottom. Constant yells and curses rolled from his old camp. A fire blazed in the fire ring, lighting up his old sail, and flames leaped toward the lower limbs of the great oak. The way the Kaintuck Company were burning firewood, they would have little fuel within easy reach.

Only moments before, he stuck some sticks into his own fire to guide Mal should he return during the night.

Again voices raised, and a pistol shot shattered the calm. The bullet went splat against a rock on the gravel bar. Adam, still inside his blankets, rolled behind an oak tree.

"Damn it, Jethro, put that gun down!"

A drunken voice rose. "Now who's to tell me. . . ." A second shot rapped through the night.

Almost at Adam's shoulder a voice whispered, "You all right, Adam?"

Mal stepped into their firelight, keeping a tree between himself and the bonfire on the hill. With a sigh he eased the pack off his shoulders and looked about. "I thought you were frying bacon, but it's those fellers upriver. Damn it, Adam, after they gave up our camp, you shared our grub with them?"

"I've borrowed their rifle, and I expect I will again. And they brought us a fry pan and an ax. Did you bring the rest of the cradle?"

"Sure did. I want to see some gold tomorrow. But now I'm hitting the hay. I ate down to Brown's Bar." Mal laid out his bedroll, squirmed around in it for awhile and said, "Sure wish I had some hay."

The next morning, as Adam and Mal set up the cradle, they heard constant bickering among the Kentucky men. A piping voice complained, "Damn! I ain't seen a nugget yet. No wonder the scarecrow lit out. These diggings are as bum as them hard-scrabble ridges back home."

"Could be the reason he left," said a second voice, "but there must be gold here. Else, why would he come back?"

"Well, if you think so, you try diggin' tomorrow instead of runnin' down to the whiskey tent."

"Probably wants his tent and other truck. They're hangin' around waitin' for somethin'."

Adam and Mal stared at one another. "What's he mean by that?"

"If ye fellers are so powerful curious," said another, "whyn't ye go ast 'em?"

When he had arisen, Adam stowed away his new clothes and boots. He donned his tattered garb and the broken boots. He grinned at Mal and muttered, "This here scarecrow won't say a word, but they're working the ground I spent months picking clean. They're not very smart."

"Did you find gold?" asked Mal.

"Lots of it. We're walking around on it. They would be too if they moved over a few feet."

"If we tell them," said Mall, "they'll push us right off the bar. But I don't see any gold."

Adam started to poke gentle fun at Mal. But he recalled that his brother-in-law was as green as the crowd next door. "It's down two to four feet. This gravel sits on bedrock. When the water comes up and disturbs it, the gold works its way down."

Mal looked up from the nail he was about to drive into the cradle. "You mean the water comes clear up here?"

"It will in a couple of weeks. Sooner if it turns off hot and dry."

"How so?"

Adam jerked a thumb over his shoulder. "Snow melt up in the high Sierras. There could still be eight or ten feet of snow up there."

Mal's face went slack-jawed. "I thought we'd work here all summer. How long will the high water last?"

"Through June, maybe July. Then we can work until November, maybe even December. We'll work gravel nearest the water. When it rises, we'll back off. Maybe we can work the edges clear through high water."

His jaw set, Mal drove the last nail home. "We better get a move on. Folks expect me back home for harvest."

Adam watched Mal level up the cradle and start shoveling gravel furiously into the hopper. The point of the shovel scraped through the gravel, jarring him as it butted up against a boulder. He grunted, found another purchase, and crashed through the gravel once more.

It was just like him, thought Adam. Bang and shovel. Go like hell. No sense of pace, no backing off to study the task. More than once on the trail Mal had nearly drowned his team and family. Adam figured it was that way long before Mal and his sister Abby met. Mal had come along, sweeping Abby off her feet. By the time she came down to earth, they were married and on the trail to Oregon.

Mal was staring at him. "Aren't you going to tote some water?"

Adam grinned and picked up the pail. But his grin faded when he stepped into the river. Pain shot through his feet and ankles and coursed up his legs. He said nothing, nor would he ask Mal to fetch water while he shoveled and rocked the cradle.

Once, when he turned from scooping up water, he saw Mal slip something into his shirt pocket.

As Adam dumped water and Mal rocked the cradle, large gravel slid down the hopper and spilled onto the gravel bar, while fine sand and gravel fell though the screen to the cleated bottom. Here too the dross jiggled out the open end, leaving flakes and dust piled up behind the cleats. Mal's mouth opened in a soundless laugh. His eyes gleamed avidly, expectantly, as the day wore on.

Finally Adam asked, "What have we got?"

"Color, but no nuggets."

"We'll find them," said Adam, "when we get down to bed-rock."

For three days they worked their way down. Several times Adam thought he detected Mal hiding something away. Suspicion grew, along with it a sick sense of disappointment. His brother-in-law was picking out the nuggets. Adam didn't want to believe it, but he knew the presence of gold worked strange behaviors in men.

They drew gold flakes and dust from the cleats and very small nuggets. Adam shook his head. "I don't get it. Two of us working together are coming up with less than I earned by myself without a cradle."

For a moment a funny look — was it guilt — crossed Mal's face. "Maybe you hit a streak of paydirt earlier," he said.

"I reckon, but I don't understand it. They're taking out nuggets. There should be nuggets everywhere."

Three more days passed. Adam kept a close eye on Mal. At times he thought his partner was hiding nuggets, but he couldn't prove it. He wanted to trust his own kin until he couldn't.

During his watchfulness, as Adam was shoveling gravel into the cradle, an irregular piece of rock caught his eye. He picked it up, and was struck by its weight. He set his shovel aside and scraped with a knife. His heart leaped. The rock shone dull yellow.

"Hey, Mal," he said to his brother-in-law, who was cleaning up the morning dishes, "What do you make of this?" He tossed the nugget to Mal, who stared at it, turned it over, scraped the surface with his thumbnail. Suddenly he snatched his floppy hat off his head and threw it up.

"Not a word!" urged Adam. "You want to be robbed?"

Mal clamped a hand over his mouth as he turned it over and over, and hefted it in his hand. Finally he whispered, "What do you think it's worth?"

"I'd guess three hundred, maybe four."

Mal held the rock gingerly. "A year's wages."

"Toss it back," said Adam. "I'll put it in a safe place. Don't say a word. You know what the Kaintuck bunch is like."

Mal gazed admiringly at Adam. "You have all the luck, Adam. Just the right touch."

Adam grinned. "We made good wages, and the day hasn't even started yet."

Shovel in hand, one of the Kentucky company came down from the sail tent, which they had hoisted higher into the trees. The Kentuckian peered into the cradle. "Always wondered if these contraptions was any good. We ain't doin' squat down there." He pointed with his shovel to Adam's old digs. "That machine o' your'n, is it doin' any good?"

Adam wondered if he had seen them find the big nugget, which weighed one side of his pants down. "Not so you'd notice. We're making about four dollars a day apiece. I could hire out for more than that."

The visitor leaned on his shovel. "Ain't enough gold on this here bar to keep a man in whiskey and tobacco. Speakin' o' whiskey, I come down to invite you up to our whiskey tent. Goin' to have the finest drinkin' establishment on the Middle Fork soon's we get a bigger tent."

"Why, thank you," said Adam. "We'll be along directly."

When the miner left Mel frowned. "First I seen or heard you talk about drink, Adam. You ain't going to start now, are you?"

Adam smiled. "We need to know our neighbors better. Maybe plant some rumors to move them on. Our time here is growing shorter. The river came up five inches since yesterday morning."

"The hell you say!" Mal shrugged. "If we're making only four dollars a day, best we move on."

"Oh, we're doing lots better than that, Mal, but don't tell those fellows. But I wish we found nuggets. They add up in a hurry."

Mal looked away, out over the water. "When we get down to bedrock, maybe we will."

Something in Mal's voice made Adam look sharply at him. But again Mal shrugged and said, "Well, might as well get at it."

For two more days they worked as the river came up another half a foot. Now Adam knew Mal was holding out on him. But still he hadn't caught his partner in the act. Adam decided to solve the problem: dig up his buried gold and pull out. He would leave the cradle to Mal.

CHAPTER 4

Two weeks passed. During the day the sun beat down on the bar. Crinkles of heat caused trees across the river to dance before Adam's eyes. Flies buzzed about his head. When he brushed them away, they settled on his hands and arms and bit viciously. All too painfully Adam recalled summer a year ago, when flies multiplied wherever miners gathered. With the stink drifting from the Kentucky camp, the flies would soon drive them wild.

By now he knew Mal was pocketing nuggets. When they talked, Mal's eyes met his briefly but slid away. Too, whenever they started or returned to work, Mal grabbed the shovel and filled the cradle hopper, leaving Adam to haul water. Constant wading in the icy water took its toll. He had to move on.

One morning Adam threw down the bucket, glanced at the bickering Kentucky men on the bar and said to Mal, "Time for a drink."

His brother-in-law stopped rocking the cradle and stared at him, open-mouthed. "*You?* A drink?"

"We're not taking enough gold out to make it pay."

Mal looked stricken for a moment but recovered. "If it's all the same to you, Adam, I'll stay here and wash out pay dirt."

"Suit yourself." Clamping his slouch hat upon his head, streaming with sweat, Adam forced his aching legs up the slope to the whiskey tent. A man stood behind a raw plank set on whiskey barrels and poured drinks for half a dozen miners. They were all resplendent in red calico shirts, canvas pants and blue neckerchiefs, none of which showed a speck of dirt. The brims of their hats were pinned back the better to see.

"Yo!" said the bartender. "Wondered if you'd ever show. What'll it be?"

"What've you got?" asked Adam.

"Whiskey." The bartender poured him a drink.

The spanking new miners looked over Adam's tattered rags. One of them said, "You been here a spell, friend. Know a good place to dig?"

Adam, aware that the bartender had paused in pouring himself a drink and stared at him, looked the new men over carefully. He looked around as if afraid of being overheard. "You look like men who can keep a secret."

The newcomers drew toward him. "We sure can, friend."

Adam stepped closer and lowered his voice. "Friend of mine came by. Said he made a big strike up at Poverty Bar."

The men inched closer. "Just where is this Poverty Bar?"

"Why, just a few miles up this branch," said Adam. "No more than twelve, fifteen miles. Rough country in there and not much room for miners. Don't say a word. He doesn't want it to get out. I'm heading up there myself, soon as I pack."

The newcomers glanced at each other. "We'll keep it under our hats." They downed their drinks, shouldered their packs, lifted picks and shovels and started up the trail.

"Good luck!" Adam called after them.

The bartender gazed after the departing newcomers and looked at his fellows on the gravel bar. Adam poured his whiskey into the dust and covered the wet spot with his boot.

"Mind watchin' the bar for me?" asked the Kentuckian. "Got to have a word with my pards. Pour yourself another drink." He shoved the bottle forward.

"Don't mind if I do," said Adam, reaching for the bottle, pouring a generous drink.

The fellow slid down the bank in a cloud of dust and talked earnestly to his fellows. They gathered up their tools and followed him back to the tent.

"We been talkin' about movin' some'eres else," explained the bartender. To his companions he said, "I'm going down to Brown's Bar to get the rest of the boys. We'll catch up."

For the first time since the Kentucky company arrived, their camp was deserted. Adam found his old shovel, which the departing miners had left behind. Furiously he shoveled the hot coals and ashes away from the campfire. Then he dug in the soft, dry dirt.

Down a couple of feet he unearthed a leather bag with a drawstring fastening it tight. It was dried out and cracked from the heat.

"Lucky for me those big fires didn't burn my poke up," he grumbled.

Looking around, he saw no one. He lifted the boot out, brushed off dust and ashes, and hefted it. Whoever had dug the holes looking for his cache had skipped the fire ring. Adam filled the hole and scraped ashes and bits of smoking wood back together. With a branch from the oak tree he brushed the area, scattering dirt to cover signs of digging.

Mal watched him approach their camp. "What's going on, Adam? What have you got there?"

'Mal," he said, "I can't take the heat and the cold water. I'm going to Oregon. This is my cache of gold."

"But we just started! We'll get rich working the rocker."

"We're make three, four dollars a day. Hardly worth the hell I'm going through."

Mal frowned. Apparently he had never expected his pilfering to discourage Adam. "How am I going to work the cradle?"

"You can do it," said Adam. "It'll just go slower. Or take on a partner, if you find someone you can trust. Maybe the Dutchman over there will team up with you."

Mal pointed to the leather boot. "The gold you stashed away. How much you got there?"

Adam regarded Mal carefully. He saw nothing more than curiosity in his brother-in-law's question. Still, the less said the better. "My diggins and the Squire's gold. You want the six hundred in coin now?"

Mal stared at his feet. "You're going home for sure."

"Any longer in that water, I'll be plumb crippled," said Adam. "Sometimes I want to take opium to get through the night. I bought some, but I never used it."

"Why didn't you tell me about your legs?" demanded Mal.

"Would it have made a difference?"

"Sure would. I would have fetched the water."

Adam's eyes bored into his. "The way you grabbed onto that cradle, I figured you'd never give it up."

Mal paled and stared upstream. With the toe of his boot he kicked some rocks around. "Look, Adam, I got to tell you."

"No need to.

White-faced, Mal stared at him. "You knew?"

"From the start. Forget it. Gold does funny things to a man." Blood rushed to Mal's face. "But I was holding out on you. Cheating family."

Adam shrugged. "I figured you needed it more than I did. Besides, I've got my stake. Lift up the boot. Get a heft of it."

When Mal picked up the leather pouch, he whistled. "My God, Adam, it must be worth thousands!"

Adam held up his hand. "Not so loud!"

Again blood rushed to Mal's face. "Seems I do something stupid every time. I'm sorry. I truly am. Pulling out for sure?"

"When somebody comes down the trail heading out," said Adam. "It's no good traveling alone. Used to be folks left other folks alone. But this spring it changed. Like the Kentucky bunch. If they knew my gold was buried under their fire, they'd kill me for it."

"Under the fire?" marveled his brother-in-law. "My God! Think of those whopping fires they built."

"It fretted me some. It singed the leather. Wouldn't have hurt the gold even if the leather burned. Well, I'll pack my gear up to the trail and wait for somebody to travel with. But we need to agree on what we dug. Tell you what. I figure we have about the same in dust and nuggets as I have in the big nugget. I'll keep that, you take the rest."

Wrapping his boot of gold inside his bedroll, rolling his new clothes inside as well, he picked up his possibles sack. All the while Mal fidgeted, looking miserable.

"You're going off and leaving our cradle," he said, "because I got greedy. Can't I pay you for it?"

Adam waved his offer off. "I'm not complaining. Do you have any messages for the Squire? When you plan to go home, anything like that?"

"Tell 'em I'll be there for harvest. Adam, do me a favor, will you? Don't say anything about my holding out on you?"

Adam held out his hand. "I've forgotten it already. See you in Oregon. I doubt I'll settle in Lafayette, but I'll look the family up, and give the Squire his money, of course."

Beside the trail Adam leaned against a live oak tree, spread his legs on the warm earth and sighed. For the first time in nearly a year he had nothing to do. No rocks to turn and move, no icy water to endure, no gravel bar throwing heat into his face until he staggered to the shade. He was going home.

From his possibles sack he removed a cloth money belt. He dropped into it a double handful of small nuggets and forced the big one into it as well. He tied it about his middle. The large, flat nugget made him sit up straight.

For the first time in days his thoughts turned to Miss Mary Jane Carr of West Tualatin, Oregon Territory. Since Mal's arrival he had scarcely thought of her. Racket from the whiskey tent distracted him all day; almost every night somebody whooped and fired a gun. Each time he rolled to the shelter of a tree trunk. Soon after the hullabaloo stopped, Mal's deep snores punctured the night calm. But Adam had lain wide awake. After a year of solitude he came to think of night and early morning hours as his own, when he pondered the future and his good fortune.

From the bag he drew writing materials and spread them out. Everything was there, even the small board he used as a writing table. The Kentucky Company had disregarded his writing implements. Otherwise they would have turned his writing table into kindling.

He put paper on the board balanced across his knees, dipped pen in ink and began to write. First he described his astonishment at seeing Mal and their brief partnership but nothing of Mal's cheating. Next he speculated on his future. Perhaps he would start a business. Oregon men said Portland, no longer a struggling stump town, had become a trading center. Or perhaps he would search out the best land he could buy and settle down to farming.

Here he paused, pen in hand, and wondered. Could his legs carry him through plowing and support him to scythe grain with a cradle? More likely he would open a store and hire a clerk or two to attend to custom. He doubted whether he could stand behind a counter ten or twelve hours each day.

Looking at the page he had written, he puzzled over what else he might say. Suddenly he slapped his forehead with his open hand. Why was he writing this letter? He would reach Oregon and see Miss Mary Jane when the letter arrived, perhaps on the same ship.

He crumpled the letter and tossed it aside. Writing had provided a pleasant diversion while he waited beside the trail. He was going home. He would call upon Miss Carr — even now he could not bring himself to call her Mary Jane — and tell her what was in his mind.

He settled back against the tree. Miners passed both ways on the trail, eyeing him curiously as they passed. He knew men who had gone up the Middle Fork. Some of them would be pulling out. He need only wait.

Under the sun's heat, the buzzing insects, scrapes of shovels on rock and voices from the gravel bar, he nodded off to sleep.

"Stuart!"

He jerked awake to stare at worn boots and shredded pants cuffs. Above them a bearded man grinned from beneath a greasy slouch hat.

"Terence!" Adam grinned back. "Terry Small."

The miner stuck out his hand. "How the hell are ya? First time I ever seen you taking it easy. Down at Sailor Bar and Mormon Island all you done was work, work, work."

Adam got to his feet. "I'm pulling out, Terry. Going home."

"Me too. Which way you going, Indiana or Oregon?"

"I'm heading north. Nothing in Indiana for me. Mind if I string along with you to New Helvetia?"

"They still call Sutter's place that? Fellers coming in call it Sacramento City now."

With a grunt Adam lifted his bedroll onto his back.

Small's eyes narrowed as he studied Adam's gear. "Hey! By the heft of your pack you got a big stake."

"Not bad," said Adam, regretting the grunt. "Could be better. My bedroll isn't all that heavy. Sitting here, I stiffened up some." He had known Small since he started panning gold, even worked beside him at times. Even so, he didn't know Terry very well.

Shadows deepened as they headed out. Small constantly looked over his shoulder as if expecting someone to overtake them.

"Trouble?" asked Adam.

"I wanted to reach Mormon Bar before nightfall," said Terence Small, "but we won't make it much past the South Fork. Can you hurry it along, Adam?"

He tried, but his legs would carry him only so fast. Already he was beginning to limp, although he tried to hide his weakness. They crossed the low divide at Pilot Hill and started down to the South Fork.

"How are we going to cross the river, Adam? I don't hanker to swim."

"Remember Ben Martin, the fellow who froze his legs last winter? He's got a boat at the crossing. He'll ferry us across."

"Somebody said he was dead," said Small. "Somebody else said he left the country."

"I crossed the South Fork with him a few weeks ago."

"Shows how much you can believe anybody, don't it?"

When they reached the South Fork crossing below Sutter's sawmill, where gold was first discovered, Ben had just discharged two miners. He grinned at Adam and nodded coolly to Small, whose eye ran from Ben's crutch to the stump of his leg. Ben's eyes narrowed, and a snarl curved his lips. Hurriedly Adam said, "You remember Terence, Ben. At Mormon Island?"

Ben's grim manner relaxed a little. "That's where I seen ye. I recollect now. Step aboard, gents."

Ben stared when Adam's pack thudded into the boat. Ben said, "Kinda late for the trail. Be dark soon. Ye might stop here. Ye'll not reach the Island tonight."

"We'll keep moving," said Small.

Ben's eyes slid over Terence Small, bringing Adam alert. Did Ben Martin know something about Terence? For a moment he resolved to keep Ben company tonight, but that meant the trail alone tomorrow. He vowed he'd go on, keeping his wits about him.

Across the river they paid the ferryman.

"Sure you won't stay the night?" asked Ben.

Adam shook his head. They struck out for Mormon Island, on the main stem of the American River. Before long Adam was sweating heavily. His legs had become wooden channels through which intense pain coursed. He tried shifting his pack, walking straighter, swinging his arms. Nothing helped. With a bandanna he mopped greasy sweat off his face.

Miners were still going in. Others had stopped and pitched camp for the night. They fried meat in dusty camps by the trail. *More of Sutter's beef going to feed the crowd.*

He settled into a pronounced limp. Meanwhile the sun had gone down, a red ball in the dusty sky before it dipped behind low hills. Twilight settled into dusk with night looming out of the east. Terence Small's eyes shifted often to him.

"Say, what's wrong with you?" he finally demanded in his high-pitched voice. "Can't you go no faster?"

Adam stopped and leaned against a tree. "It's the cold sick. My legs hurt so I can hardly walk," he gasped. Sweat poured down his forehead into his eyes. Salt nearly blinded him.

"We can't stop here," grumbled. Small. "We got to reach Mormon Island. If you can't go faster, I'll have to go on."

"Might be best," said "Adam. He had noticed the bulge in Small's pants pocket. Terence had always sported a short-barreled pistol and a hideout gun in his boot: a derringer he called a pepperbox.

"Got a gun I can borrow or buy?"

Terry's eyes slid away, down the trail. "No," he said, "I don't. Luck, Stuart."

Terence Small vanished in the night.

When the dust kicked up by Small's footsteps settled, Adam let go of the oak sapling to which he had clung. He had to make camp off the trail. Here were low, hilly grasslands dotted with oaks. They provided little shelter and less screening. He had to protect his back. He leaned against a large live oak. There the grass was thick, if covered with dust. He settled under the tree, his pack beside him.

Adam nodded off when the smell of dust brought him alert. A snuffling sound shook him. Over him loomed a dim shadow. He raised his hands, fists doubled, when a breath of wind washed the sharp tang of cow over him. Adam thrashed his arms. The animal snorted and lumbered off into the darkness. His heart pounding, Adam settled back against the tree. Why didn't Sutter keep his damned cows closer to home?

He wanted to rest, but not to sleep. His trembling legs cried for relief. Hands shaking, Adam dug into his possibles sack and brought out a small bottle. Twice in the last year he needed laudanum. If ever he had need, it was now. He pulled the cork and lifted the bottle to his lips, letting the bitter liquid trickle down his throat. Putting the bottle back in his sack, he leaned against the tree.

Slowly the pain in his legs eased, and a sense of calm settled over him. With luck he would reach Mormon Island by morning, where he would find safety among friends. There he could rent a horse or board a coach which ran between the Island and New Helvetia. It was simply a wagon fitted with wooden seats, but he would welcome any sort of conveyance.

Without warning a blinding light flashed before him and great pain surged through him. He toppled onto his bedroll. Hands sought to pull it free. Desperately he grabbed and held on.

"What's going. . . ."

"Sing out and you're a dead man." His assailant's voice whispered, harsh and grating and dry as dust. Foul breath and odor of sweat washed over him as a man leaned over him.

Adam struggled to see his assailant, but the man's knee in his back pinned him down. "Turn around and I'll shoot," he hissed.

Half stunned, Adam lay as the assailant pulled the bedroll out from under him. The robber tore loose the rope bindings and spilled everything onto the dusty earth. With a grunt he lifted the leather boot and eased his body off Adam. Adam raised up on one elbow, straining in the darkness to see his attacker.

Again blinding spirals of light pinwheeled before his eyes. Pain and nausea swept over him again. Into the dust he collapsed. Silence. The robber was gone. Before his eyes eerie patterns of red swirled in gray fog. He could not form words; he could not think. Slowly fear wormed its way through the gray swirls. Was this how he would die?

No! Showers of sparks burst through the gray curtain. He would not die! When he lifted himself to a sitting position, nausea overwhelmed him again. Gut-wrenching heaves racked him until he had nothing left. When they subsided he lay in his own vomit.

In a great flash, clarity broke through the fog in his brain. He would not die. He would find his assailant and reclaim his gold. He would. He had to.

CHAPTER 5

For a long time Adam lay in the dust. His head pounded; sickness washed over him in waves of pain. He put his hand to the back of his head. It came away sticky. Two huge lumps had raised behind his ear. He wondered if the blows had cracked his skull.

He heard voices. Raucous laughter broke out nearby. Opening his eyes, he saw the orange glow of a campfire. Had miners set up camp there? Or were they there all along? He wanted to call for help, but what could they do? His new clothes lay strewn on the ground, and he still had gold in the money belt. They might take what he had left.

When his mind cleared, he lifted himself onto an elbow. Again nausea racked him. When it eased he sat up, clutching the oak against which he had rested. With shaking hands he pulled his clothes and blankets together. Anger flared into white heat as he hefted his bedroll. But it made him dizzy. He sat still until his head cleared.

Someone threw wood onto the fire nearby, sending up a shower of sparks. Flames leaped up to shed light on a knoll. The campers were farther away than he first thought. They had been too far away to help and had probably been asleep when the robber attacked him.

Slowly he put his pack together. Then he got to his knees. Using the tree to steady himself, he struggled up. Sweating, he closed his eyes, fearful his trembling legs would collapse beneath him.

Where did the trail lie? He faced the campfire and lifted his right arm to point the way. Soon he should reach the trail. If he didn't find it, he would reverse his direction. He had to keep the fire in sight. It alone told him which way he was going.

Still shaky, he lurched to the wide, dusty track. With a rising moon behind him, he struck off toward Mormon Island.

Through the night he staggered. Daylight found him nearing camp. When he panned for gold there a year ago, it was a tent town. Now frame buildings fronted the American River and several brick buildings were rising. On he trudged, meeting miners going toward the mountains. Some walked a wide circle around him; all of them stared. Dust hung in the air as the sun edged up over the hills.

On the river bank he found a familiar tent. A man, his back to Adam, was frying bacon over his campfire. A blackened coffee pot steamed amid the coals; the aroma of coffee pervaded the air.

"Hello, Will."

Will Adair turned, glanced up and turned back to his task. Then he stared and whistled through his teeth. "My God, Adam, what happened to you? You wrestle a grizzly bear?"

Adam leaned crazily, sucking air. "Worse," he croaked. "I was robbed. Had near eight thousand in gold."

Will's eyes blazed. "Damn this new bunch coming in. They're buying every weapon in sight. Pistols sell for a hundred dollars in Sacramento City, if you can find one."

"I don't think it was a new fella."

"You saw him? Well, let's get up a gang and run him down."

Adam shook his head. "I never saw him. I don't know where he went. He got away in the dark. Could be right here in camp."

"I doubt it, Adam. If he's an old timer, he knows what we'd do if we catch him. Do you know who he is?"

Adam hung his head. "I did a stupid thing last night. I took laudanum to kill the pain in my legs. Will, did Terence Small come through camp last night? You remember Terence, don't you?"

"He came about midnight, got something to eat and kept on going. He looked like the devil was on his tail. Do you think he did it?"

"I doubt it. We came out together. When my legs went bad, he left me and pushed on. He kept looking over his shoulder. Maybe someone he knew was following us."

"That's funny," said Will. "He done the same here. If I'd been bent on mischief, I'd have pegged him as a mark and laid for him outside camp."

"You look done in," said Will. "How about I clean the blood off your head? Flies are settling on you. Then I'll fry up some more bacon and Johnny cakes. We'll start with coffee."

Adam allowed himself to be repaired and fed. He didn't make the job easy, falling asleep and spilling coffee on himself. Will gently bathed the gashes in his scalp and bandaged them.

Finally, his wounds tended and food under his belt, Adam thanked Will Adair and said he'd move on.

"Adam, you ain't fit to travel."

"Got to find the man," he said, "and I want to see if Terence knows anything. Thanks, Will, for your help."

Adam visited the saloons and whiskey tents. He knew Terry Small's weakness for hard liquor. At one saloon a bartender crossed massive hairy arms and called, across the heads of men at his bar, "What'll it be?"

Adam shook his head. "I'm looking for a fella."

The bartender jerked a thumb toward the street. "Out. You're taking a drinking man's place. Out or I throw you out."

Mostly men ignored him. Many looked down and out, but few seemed as ragged as he did. Adam wandered among them, watching them drink and gamble.

Finally he decided the robber would move on. Once more he hit the trail, bucking the tide of miners flowing toward the mountains. Darkness caught him miles short of Sutter's Fort. Drawing away from the trail, he spread his blankets beneath a giant oak.

Mosquitoes plagued him even beneath his smelly blankets, and the tree held the day's heat captive. His face became greasy with sweat. With his coat sleeve he toweled himself dry. Exhausted, shielding himself against the insects, he finally slept through the last cool hours of the night.

The next day at Sutter's Fort he pondered where to search. Two towns had grown up, merging into one. The older town clustered around the fort; the other sprawled along the Sacramento River. Maybe Sam Brannan could tell him where to locate a sheriff or constable. At Brannan's store Mr. Sinclair, the clerk, greeted him.

"Mr. Brannan has gone to San Francisco on Captain Sutter's boat, the *Sacramento*. We don't expect him back for several days. Perhaps Captain Sutter can help you."

Adam retraced his steps to Sutter's Fort. There he asked to see the captain. A servant vanished up a stairway outside the central building in the compound. Adam, waited below. Just as he decided the captain wouldn't see him, Sutter descended the steps from his office. He looked Adam over and lifted his nose. "What do you want?"

"I need help, sir," said Adam. "Can you tell me. . . ."

"You I should help?" demanded Sutter. "You trespass on my property, trample my crops, eat my beef, drive my Indian workers away."

"Mr. Sutter, for a year I panned gold on the American River. I crossed your land twice, when I went in and again when I came out, except for two times I came in for supplies."

Apparently Sutter had not expected such a reply. His ramrod straight back bent a little. "Well, then, what do you want of me?"

"I have heard you uphold the law here. Where can I find a sheriff? Two nights ago near the South Fork I was robbed of my gold."

"You ask me for help? For half a year I have begged the law to protect my property. But there is no law. There is only the army. Many soldiers have deserted to the mines. I am sorry for you, young man, but I cannot help. How much did you lose?"

"Somewhere around eight thousand in nuggets and dust and almost six hundred in gold coin."

Sutter's eyebrows raised. "So much?" He studied Adam's long hair, his tattered clothing and seedy bedroll. "A year's work, hmmm?"

"Yes, sir. Gone in half a minute."

"Where are you going now?"

"To San Francisco, unless I can find the robber here."

"Ah," said Sutter. "You know your assailant then."

"Well, no."

With the palm of his hand Sutter struck his forehead. "Then how do you expect me to help you?"

"Somebody knew I had gold. He knew what he was looking for."

Captain Sutter sighed. "I would offer you passage to San Francisco aboard my boat, but it sailed this morning. I am sorry for you, but I can do nothing."

Adam thanked him and left. Up on the American River he had heard Captain Sutter called every name in the book. Today he felt the sting of the captain's scorn. Yet Sutter would have made room for him on his boat. He would have helped run the man down if he could. Adam couldn't trust others' opinions. He had to rely on his own hunches.

He made the rounds of the saloons in Sacramento. A number of men drinking there looked villainous enough to attack a crippled man. But none of them had the dusty look of a miner just come to town.

Probably the robber had gone to San Francisco. Almost everyone went through the tiny port town eventually. He should go there and search for his assailant.

Boats lay three abreast along the river bank. Some would surely leave for San Francisco soon. But Adam considered his dwindling gold. He still had his large nugget but little else. If he walked out, it would cost him some gold to cross the Sacramento River and the Carquines Straits and yet again San Francisco Bay.

Remembering the lack of drinking water on the road to the straits, he found an empty whiskey bottle and filled it with fresh water. Then he paid a man to row him across the river. There he chose two stout limbs to use as walking sticks — and as weapons.

Beneath towering cottonwood trees he paused. Blinking away salty sweat, he studied the flat plain ahead. The road ran west and south, clearly marked by a line of dust. Above the dust mountains appeared in the distance. At the southern tip of that range he would ferry across Carquines Strait. Perhaps there he could escape the stifling heat.

Shrugging, he set out across grasslands burned by the sun to the color of ripe wheat. He angled away from the road and trees marking the Sacramento. Beside the river he would encounter travelers' dust and swarms of mosquitoes.

But the river swollen by snowmelt had overflowed its banks. It filled dry watercourses, forming small sloughs and pools of stagnant water. They blocked his way, forcing him back to the road. Mosquitoes swarmed over him without mercy.

Through it all he thrust out his walking sticks and leaned forward, throwing himself off balance, forcing his legs to catch up to his body. His brain, numbed by the heat, sparked with hatred for the man who had reduced him to poverty. He would find the robber and reclaim his gold.

Throughout the day and into night he trudged toward the low mountains. When he could see no longer, he sank to the earth and slept. At daylight he went on, chewing on tough beef jerky he had bought in Sacramento City and sipping water from his whiskey bottle.

People going inland stared and put distance between them as they passed. A woman, the first he had seen in a year, looked down from her horse.

"Look at that man," she said as if he weren't there, "his clothes hang from him like rags. Just imagine how he smells. He's no better than an animal. Someone should put him in a pig sty."

Adam watched them go on toward Sacramento City. "Good luck, ma'am," he murmured. "I won't wish my bad fortune on you." But she didn't hear as she passed with her nose in the air.

He saw their future: crude housing, poor food or none and filthy living conditions. Her nose would soon tell her she landed in the pig sty she meant for him.

It seemed he would never reach the hills. On the third day they loomed abruptly before him, rounded grassy buttes dotted with oaks. The air turned cooler and a steady breeze blew in his face. Long shadows reached across the land toward him from the hills ahead.

At last he reached the hills. A large bay appeared. Low in the sky, the sun sparkled on its surface. He followed the shoreline, drawing the smell of water into his lungs, until it narrowed into the strait.

He could not see the ferry. Every muscle and joint ached now, but Adam forged ahead. The ferry dock appeared, spindly but serviceable, and a house loomed in the shadows. It was like many in Sacramento City: a frame of rough board sides and a canvas roof. A stovepipe stuck out a wall and curved upward. An open shed stood behind the house.

Now he saw a part of the larger bay west of the mile-wide strait. The giant ferryman who carried him across Carquines Strait a year ago called it Bahia San Pablo, part of San Francisco Bay.

Wearily Adam eased the rope straps of the bedroll from his shoulders. Letting his pack slip to the ground, he sank down beside it and rubbed the calves of his legs. They screamed with pain, even more when he took his weight off them. From his vial of laudanum he took a tiny sip.

He looked around. Two men waited to be ferried across. They sat apart from each other and from him. Did they put space between themselves out of mistrust, even fear, of each other? Most miners made it out with their stakes, even some who flaunted their gold.

What had he done wrong? He had looked the part of a miner, broke and discouraged. One thing he had done unwisely. He had remained in the diggins too long. Perhaps someone on the Middle Fork noted this and concluded he had gold. Most miners he knew wintered In San Francisco, but he stayed to pan and pick for gold. The icy conditions took their toll. Had his persistence marked him as one who accumulated gold?

Somehow he had revealed his wealth, but how? Had someone lain in the trees up the slope or across the river and watched him increase his hoard of pay dirt? The robber had known he was carrying it out. He put his bad fortune behind him. It did no good to puzzle over what went wrong or agonize over his loss. He could only try to recover his stake.

So far he had pursued the man who stole his future. Or had he? He had no idea whom to seek. He only believed the man had gone to San Francisco. It was the port through which virtually all traffic funneled. Would his man still be there? Had he even gone there?

When his aches eased, a new thought occurred to him. Could he go back and start over? Could he stand another year? Perhaps he could hire men to work the cradle he had left with Mal. Yet they could cheat him as Mal had done. It might take years to regain what he lost in moments.

Most men would have cursed their bad luck. They would have heaped vile epithets and empty threats upon the robber. Adam sighed. He was not a cursing man. But if it helped, he would have cursed. He rejected the idea of going back. He could only go on to San Francisco.

The two men stood up and shaded their eyes from the sun, now a red orb hovering above the horizon. Adam saw where one pointed. The ferry appeared and was approaching the dock. It was not the scow in which he had crossed. Now a sailboat approached, her sail billowing, white water curling from her bow. The ferryman, the tallest man Adam had ever seen, made an imposing figure as he steered from the stern.

When the boat docked, the passengers tumbled over the side, anxious to regain solid ground. It had been a cold, wet crossing and, Adam suspected, a little scary. They shouldered their packs and edged past him, staring at him openly.

"Good luck to ye in the mines, gents," the ferryman called after them.

Most of the passengers turned up their noses at Adam. "Disgusting fellow!" snorted a man decked out in brown suit and beaver hat. Adam clenched his fists on his hips and glared after them. He wanted to knock the beaver off the man's head, but he knew he couldn't.

"They do not ken what ye went through, lad."

The ferryman had come up behind Adam, mast, sail and rudder in his grasp.

Adam's hands relaxed and fell to his sides. "You're right, I suppose. I should feel sorry for them. They don't know what they're getting into."

"Some gents come out with a full poke; others have nothing to show for their work. Can't ever tell by looking at them."

"I started out with a full poke," Adam said bitterly. "A man robbed me on the American River. Eight thousand in gold. A year's work."

"The hell you say! What are you going to do now?"

Adam shrugged. "I was going back to Oregon, but I've got to find the robber first."

The ferryman gazed at him, his head cocked to one side. Finally he spoke. "Want a job here? Ferrying folks across? It'll give ye a chance to look folks over. Maybe your man hasn't come out yet."

Adam looked at the boat secured to the dock and then at the tall man. "I hadn't thought about stopping anywhere."

"I'll pay five dollars a day and found. Extra two dollars if ye take someone across at night."

"I never handled a boat before," said Adam. "I wouldn't know how."

"A bonfire at the landing would mark your course. Don't worry. Ye wouldn't do that right away."

"But I don't know anything about boats," said Adam. "I

grew up in Indiana. The Wabash isn't much more than a creek at Lafayette."

"Came from Kentucky myself. Learned how to sail and I haven't drowned anybody yet."

Adam looked out at the strait. The sun had vanished, leaving the surface the color of pewter beneath a faintly orange sky. The ferryman said nothing about crossing tonight. That meant the added cost of food. His gold was going fast. After he ferried twice to San Francisco, he would be nearly broke.

"Look, Mr. . . . ."

"Semple. Robert Semple." The giant extended a hand.

"I'm Adam Stuart," he said, taking the huge paw, thankful for the gentle pressure Semple exerted.

"Look, Mr. Semple, my legs gave out. I stood in the cold water too long. I don't have the strength for it."

"Ye don't need legs as much as ye need strong arms, Adam. And a good head on your shoulders."

Again Adam looked at the water. "I can learn, I guess," he said.

Semple clapped him on the shoulder. "First thing in the morning. Ye'll sail across with me. Learn about wind and tide."

The other men had approached and were listening. One of them asked, "We're not crossing tonight?"

Semple shook his head. "We sail at sun-up. Might as well bed down. Sorry I'm not running a hotel. Too busy carrying folks across to build one."

With a sour expression the passenger turned away.

"It's settled, then," said Semple. "Wash up first. Don't want passengers downwind of ye. I'll cut your hair, else folks will think they're sailing with a grizzly bear. Then we'll dish up some grub." The ferryman called to the other two men. "Join us for beef stew in about an hour? Won't cost ye."

One of the men looked up from making camp for the night. "We'd be pleasured, sir."

Semple pointed to a tin tub in a corner of the room. "Bring that rig out, Adam, and we'll fill her up."

They set the bathtub outside. The ferryman had warm water ready, probably for his own use. Adam thought to decline, but his itching, sweating body cried out for relief. Gratefully he peeled his clothes off and sank into the warm water. He soaped himself and lay there, trying to remember the last time he had a bath. Then he scrubbed off layers of dirt.

"Don't know what I have ye can wear," said the Kentuckian. "I can't rightly have a scarecrow running my ferry."

"I have a new outfit," grinned Adam. "The best for Sunday wear in the diggins."

Adam put off getting out, luxuriating in the bath. But the aroma of beef stew was too great to resist. The water turned cool by the time he stepped out and dried himself with an old flour sack.

Dressed in long johns and bare feet in his good boots, he sat on a chair while Semple combed the tangles out of his hair and studied it.

"Couldn't tell before you washed what critters might crawl out. Didn't see any."

"I washed an acre of Captain Sutter's land off," said Adam. "Strange he didn't say anything. He accused me of stealing everything else."

"Sutter's a crusty feller," offered Semple. "Sometimes he sails by grand as a lord on his boat. Other times he waves like a common feller. Well, let's get at it." He threw a muslin bed sheet over Adam's shoulders.

"You sure took a lick or two on the back of your head. You owe one, I reckon. I'll be careful." With that the ferryman turned to.

Adam, lulled by the snip-snip of the scissors, would have fallen asleep but for the aroma of beef stew simmering on the stove. His hair fell in a circle about him. Then Semple trimmed his beard, and held up a broken piece of mirror.

"I've done all the damage I can. Ye might want to shave the beard off all the way later. Now for some grub."

He ladled out bowls of beef stew thick with chunks of turnips and peas and corn. He cut slabs of crusty bread. Calling the two travelers from their camps, he set the meal before them. All was quiet, except for fervent sighs, for half an hour. Finally they sopped up the last of the gravy with bread and pushed the bowls away. Semple packed and fired a pipe and leaned back, puffing contentedly.

"Sure obliged," said one of the passengers. "Best meal I et in a year. Looks like we et you out of house and home."

The ferryman chuckled. "Don't worry. My good friend, General Vallejo, will send a *Californio* over soon with a beef or two and some garden truck."

"No miners on his property, apparently," said Adam. "They'd kill his beef the way they're slaughtering Sutter's cattle."

"No danger of that. Sonoma's off by itself."

Again the passengers thanked Robert Semple and retired to their bedrolls.

"Now," said Semple, "we'll bed ye down. Grab your gear and follow me." He picked up the lantern. Outside, shadows of his legs made giant strides across the land as he walked around the house. A board and canvas shed piled with oars, sails and rope opened toward the house.

Semple cleared rope and other gear off a lumpy mattress on a platform "Corn shucks, but it beats lying on hard ground. I slept here while I built the house. Got another house up town, but it's too far. We'll rig up some spare sails to keep out the wind. It's not fancy, but it'll do."

"After a year crawling under a sail stretched out for a roof," said Adam, "this is like a hotel."

Later, when the lantern was doused and the canvas house was dark, Adam lay on his bunk and stared out at the sky. Stars shone dimly in the velvet night. Moisture in the air, likely, from the Pacific Ocean, some twenty miles away. The heat of the day faded, too, bringing a dampness he hadn't felt for months.

He pondered his situation. Semple's offer of work blunted his search for the robber. Gone was his driving need to return to Oregon. The pale image of Mary Jane Carr floated before his eyes. He would have called on her in a few weeks after quick passage to Portland. Now he couldn't even buy his way. And he had lost Squire Wilson's six hundred in gold.

Suddenly he felt himself falling. He grabbed the bed and held on until he sensed his muscles relaxing. Funny how a bath and a square meal could relax a man. He had known neither for too long.

Now he let himself go. Just before he drifted into sleep, the face and form of Mary Jane came before his eyes once more. She was looking at him, and he started toward her. She came, a smile on her lips, her hands reaching out. But she drifted beyond him, her eyes looking into the distance.

"Mary Jane!"

He tried to reach for her, to catch her. But somebody gripped his shoulder. "No!" he shouted. "Keep away! The gold is mine!" He tried to sit up, to push his assailant away. Corn shucks rustled beneath him and the hand fell away.

"Ye all right, Adam?"

"Semple! What are you doing here?"

The ferryman held a lantern up, shining it into Adam's face.

"Why," he said mildly, "I live here. I came out to check. Ye were yelling at the top of your lungs. Sounded like a nightmare."

Adam came fully awake now. Sweat drenched his face and neck, and his hands shook.

"Ye all right? Who's Mary Jane?"

Suddenly self-conscious, he mumbled his reply. "A girl I rode across the plains with."

Semple straightened to his full height, a smile on is lips. "I'll get back to sleep. Long day ahead of us."

When Semple was gone, he toweled his face and neck with a sheet Semple had left for him. He rolled over and closed his eyes. Morning would come too soon.

CHAPTER 6

Hearing a persistent bang, bang, bang, Adam stirred. He lay in darkness. Where was he? Who or what was pounding? Clawing his way out of a sleep-drugged stupor, he settled back. He was at the Benicia ferry. The pounding came from the wall of the tent house.

"Awake out there, Adam?"

"Sure thing. Be right in."

But he allowed himself the luxury of a few more minutes. He had punished his body without mercy. He hadn't felt this good in days. But the boss was calling. The aroma of brewing coffee and bacon mingled with the smell of salt in the air.

Yawning, gingerly he stretched. He feared his stiff legs would cramp. Sitting up, he swung them to the ground. For a few minutes he massaged his calves. Then he slipped into pants and shirt and eased into his new boots. When he opened the door and stepped into the lamplight, Robert Semple looked him over. "Right down to the kerchief around your throat," he said, "ye look like a proper Argonaut."

Adam looked down at himself. "I look like what?"

"Ye don't know the story of Jason, then."

"Never heard of him. Did he work on the American River?"

Laughing, Semple turned slices of smoking bacon over in his pan. "In Greek mythology he was a gold seeker. He and his crew became known as Argonauts, after the name of his ship, the *Argo*."

Adam shook his head. "I haven't read much about the Greeks."

"No matter. Set down and I'll dish 'er up."

Adam would been thankful for bacon and coffee. But eggs fried sunny side up in bacon grease? And fluffy biscuits? Butter and a clay pot of jam?

Semple set a plate before him. "Dig in. Long day ahead."

They ate by lantern light. Before they finished, a knock came at the door. His eyes rolling upward, Semple opened it. A traveler, bedroll on his back, sniffed the air as he shifted his weight.

"Why aren't we leaving? It's almost daylight."

"Do ye see the sun coming up?"

"Well, no, but. . . ."

"Ye've seen the sign? We depart at sun-up." Semple shut the door. "Always someone trying to tell ye how to run your business. Did ye see the sails and tiller I brought up last night? When ye've eaten, Adam, tote them down to the ferry while I clean up."

While Adam carried the gear, Semple inspected a rowboat drawn up on shore. Adam joined him, and together they shoved the boat into the water. At once the craft filled with water and swamped.

"Ye'll row this boat across when need be." At Adam's dismayed look he chuckled. "She's been out of the water. In a day or two her seams will swell shut."

Semple tied the rowboat to the dock and turned to the ferry. Raising the sail, allowing it to flap in the breeze, he stepped the rudder into brackets on the transom. Then he turned and smiled at the eight men lined up on the dock. "We're ready to board, gents. Fare is five dollars. I'll value your dust at seventeen dollars to the ounce."

At once the passengers brightened. The first man aboard handed his poke to Semple, who weighed out the fare on his scales. "Them belly robbers in the camps give six, seven dollars if you buy their high-priced goods and whiskey."

"Bad food and worse whiskey," added another.

"We're not pirates here," said Semple. "Passengers back of the mast. Adam, ye go up front and cast off."

Adam stared at him. "Do what?"

"Untie that rope from the dock. Sun's coming up."

The sun glared, a red ball casting a bloody streak across the strait. Small waves, gray only minutes before, glittered as if on fire.

Semple pulled the sail around to catch the breeze. The boat left the dock. Waves lapped at the bow, sending spray over the weather rail to brush Adam's face and arms. He leaned back against the gunwale, sighed and drank in the salt air. This sure beat shoveling rocks and sand and wading in the river.

Streamers of fog rode the wind from San Pablo Bay to the west. Soon it lay dense and solid at the mouth of the strait.

"See that point?" Semple indicated a low headland etched against the fog. "Beyond it is Point Pinole. Maybe a dozen miles farther on is San Francisco. Adam, when the fog moves in fast, as it's doing now, we'll see a fresh wind out yonder. Crossing goes faster, but ye need to stay alert. I'll show ye how she handles when the wind kicks up."

Adam peered around the passengers. "Do you mean for me to steer this ferry across?"

"I don't see why not. Rough or smooth, I take her across a dozen times a day. We'll give ye a stab at it."

Adam's gaze traveled from the growing chop on the water ahead to the wide sweep of the far shore. Except for his voyage from Portland, he had never seen so much water. Why had he hired on? Yet he knew the answer. Five dollars a day looked good to a man who was broke. Now he realized it wasn't much for this work.

The far shore which seemed so distant now loomed close. When they left Benicia, they faced a high ridge following the curve of the strait. They rushed toward the shore until it seemed they must pile up on the beach. But Semple bore away toward an inlet slightly to the east.

Adam made out the dock ahead. People sitting on the ground stood and shaded their eyes. A string of men lined up on the dock, baggage in hand. Semple shook his head. "Can take only so many, but they line up forty deep anyway."

The ferryman pushed the tiller hard over. The bow came up into the wind, and the gaff-rigged sail cracked and flapped like a dog shaking a bone.

The craft bumped the dock. Adam grasped the dock and made the rope fast. Semple rose to his full height and scowled at the men on the dock.

"Gents, if ye'll back off and let the passengers by, ye'll reach the diggings sooner." He muttered to Adam. "Same thing every trip, on this side. Some fellers don't have a lick of sense."

Men backed slowly, stepping on others' feet, cursing, clinging to their places in the line. Some would knock others off the dock before they would yield. Adam tried to count the number in line but gave up. Enough travelers herded together to make half a dozen ferry loads. They would likely see an even bigger crowd the next time they crossed. The makeshift camps up the slope gave the place the smell of gold camps on the American River.

Finally the ferry passengers crowded ashore. Semple followed them and spoke in his deep but soft voice. "We can board ten men," he said. "Five dollars for the crossing."

Six men promptly stepped forward and paid. The seventh man hung back. "Five dollars?" he growled. "On top of what it cost for my outfit?. That's robbery. I'll not pay."

Semple gazed calmly down at him. "Your pleasure, sir. Kindly step aside for those bound for Eldorado."

The man stood his ground, blocking access to the boat. Semple took a step forward. "If ye don't want to pay," he said, "ye can swim across or walk near two hundred miles around the delta."

Men stirred restlessly behind him. Finally someone in line said, "Pay up or step aside, man. Don't keep the rest of us waiting."

The angry one scowled and dug into his purse and came up with several coins. Robert Semple accepted them with a gracious nod and stepped aside. Men filled the seats, peering at the waves rolling past. Totaling up their fares, Adam calculated the number of crossings the ferry made each day. Semple said he crossed a dozen times, often more. An inkling of what it meant worked into his brain.

Although the sun still cast long shadows across the hills, already Semple had taken in a hundred dollars. At this rate, ten crossings would net around a thousand per day. It beat Adam's best month on the American River. No wonder Semple could afford good food.

"Cast off, Adam!" called the ferryman. Adam unfastened the rope and pushed the bow away from the dock. Slowly the craft turned as the sail filled. She moved steadily away from shore. Spray leaped over the blunt bow, drenching him, and the craft heeled over. The wind chilled him through to the skin.

Passengers turned pale. Adam guessed why. Some of them, perhaps all of them, could not swim. They watched foam rush by under the lee rail low to the water. Instantly it brought them face to face with their own mortality. If the ferry capsized, they would drown in this cold water."

The canvas sail billowed taut. Semple's calm face studied it as he held against the tiller. When the wind gusted, the sloop lay over until water rushed past only inches from the gunwale.

"Ye see, Adam," Semple called above rush of wind and water, "when the valley heats up, the wind blows stronger. Ye're wondering when we'll tip over, aren't ye?"

To a man the passengers nodded vigorously, but no one said a word. Adam swallowed and nodded with the rest. He could swim across a small stream. But this?

Semple went on. "See how she lays over when I hold the sail in tight? When I let it out, some of the wind spills out." He slacked off the rope holding the sail. The boat righted herself and the water rushed by more slowly. "Got the idea?"

Adam nodded.

"Read the wind," said the ferryman. "More than the tides, pay attention to the wind."

Again Adam nodded. Maybe someday he could hurtle across the water like this. For now he would settle for slower, safer passage.

As the shore approached once more, Adam thought about the ferry operation. Semple was paying him only five dollars a day.

Suppose he handled the craft while Semple collected the fares. Suppose he even made crossings alone. Even further, suppose he pressed for speed, making an extra passage or two each day. It did not add up. Only a fool would stay for five dollars per day. He'd move on, after he earned enough, of course, to pay his passage.

Expertly the ferryman landed his craft despite the freshening breeze. Adam scrambled onto the dock and tied up. If the Kentuckian could learn to handle the boat, he could learn also. For the first time in weeks Adam's legs didn't ache constantly. Perhaps he should stay on, at least until he regained more strength.

At the end of the day, when the sun set behind the mountain west of San Pablo Bay, he carried the rudder and sail to the shed while Semple told men wanting to cross that the ferry was shut down until sun-up. He shucked his wet clothes, donning his rags. He spread his good clothes to dry by the stove while Semple fried bacon and heated an earthenware pot of beans.

Silently they ate. Semple tore huge chunks of bread off a loaf and dipped them into his bowl of beans before popping them into his mouth. Now and then he glanced at Adam, who ate quietly. Finally he stopped eating, rested his forearms on the table and spoke.

"Out with it, lad. What's bothering ye? Ye've been wearing a log face half the day."

Adam said, "I've come to a halt. I'm not looking for my man and the trail is getting cold."

"The trail? He came this way? Would ye know him if ye saw him?"

Adam didn't reply.

"Have ye followed the right trail? No, Adam, it's something else. Ye saw the proceeds from the ferry today. Ye think I'm paying a paltry wage. Is that it?"

Adam turned red to the roots of his hair. "In the diggins I earned twice five dollars every day, most days more."

"I don't doubt it, lad. Ye're heady enough to figure things out. But ye had nothing, and nothing coming in, when ye arrived last night. Isn't five dollars and this —" he indicated the food on the table — "better than nothing?"

"Don't think I'm greedy, sir. I appreciate the wage. But I had eight thousand dollars. I want to get it back."

"Good. A man who'll settle for whatever isn't much of a man. Look ye, Adam, do ye think me a grasping man?"

"No, sir. You found an honorable way to earn a living. And you want to make your pile like anybody else. But you're not grasping. If you were, you'd collect near an ounce of dust per man and you wouldn't give the miners full value for their gold."

"Thank ye, sir. Tell ye what I'll do. I'll double your wage starting tomorrow. Ye learn how to sail. Ye take the ferry across a time or two."

Alarmed, Adam half rose. "By myself? I couldn't do that, sir."

"Hear me out, lad. No, I'll go with ye. But I want ye able to do it alone."

"Won't you be here?"

The ferryman bit into a chunk of bread and shoveled a spoonful of beans into his mouth. He spoke through his chewing.

"There's something come up. I'll be gone for awhile. I need a good man to operate the ferry. Else by the time I return somebody else will have my place."

"But, sir, I could hire out for ten dollars a day with no responsibility except to do the work."

"I appreciate that. Here's what we'll do. When I'm gone, we'll split the profit if ye stay on."

Adam set his spoon down and stared at Semple. "Seventy-five to a hundred every single day?"

"That's what I said, lad."

"That's better than most days in the diggins!"

"There's more, lad. After I return, I have other business that'll need my attention. If ye stick, ye'll profit a tidy sum."

This was a whole new situation. In a week he could earn

enough to repay the Sqire's six hundred. In several more weeks he could return to Oregon with a small stake.

"How long will you be gone, sir?"

Semple leaned back, closed his eyes and sighed. "Ah, there's the rub, lad. I don't know. A week or two for sure. Maybe a month. Can ye bear it not knowing?"

He would give up pursuit of the robber. But the chase was chancy at best. Who knew which way he went, if he left Sacramento City at all? On the other hand, if Adam stayed, he saw clear his passage home with a tidy stake.

"Yes, sir," said "Adam, "I'll stay. May I ask where you will be going?"

"I can't say, but it's mighty important for California. Ye'll know before I leave. Now let's eat before these vittles get cold."

The next morning, while travelers fidgeted at the dock, Adam and the ferryman pulled the swamped rowboat ashore. Dumping the water out, they pushed her back in. Hands on hips, Semple shook his head. "Not tight enough. Seams are still open. Needs a day or two yet. Ye'll sail with me today, Adam."

All morning the wind blew steadily from the west. Before they reached the opposite shore, mist streamed overhead. The summit of Monte Diablo to the southeast vanished and the sun, a faint yellow ball, disappeared.

"Interior's heating up," observed Semple. "Pulls the fog clear into the delta sometimes." Adam's mind filled with memories of the heat. Waves shimmered above the gravel bar while icy water flowed over the gravel. Then miners' bodies suffered a double blow. Here on the ferry, spray curled over the bow and splashed into his face. It too was cold, but it lacked the punishing chill of the placers.

The fog thickened until only the lower shoulders of Diablo remained visible.

"How do we cross," Adam called, "when the fog settles over the water?"

"Mainly the fog stays high. Sometimes a tule fog sets in. Then we stay put and whittle. No wind. Happens mainly in the winter." Adam couldn't imagine Semple sitting on shore whittling.

He watched closely everything the ferryman did. One day he would operate the craft alone. There didn't seem much to it. He surprised himself to realize he was looking forward to sailing the ferry, until Semple's next words fell on his ears. They had made two crossings. Now, as the ferry approached the landing, Semple spoke.

"Ye'll take her back across, lad."

Sweat broke out over Adam, and the wind poked at him with icy fingers. "You mean now?"

Passengers eyed him curiously. Had he revealed the near-panic he felt?

"Why not?"

One passenger grumbled, "Glad I'm not crossing again."

Semple glared at the fellow. "Ye learn fast, Adam. Just do as ye've seen me do. Ye'll do fine."

Semple brought the boat up into the wind alongside the dock. As Adam made a line fast, he despaired. Could he match Semple's strength and skill?

The passengers scrambled ashore as if wanting to put distance between themselves and the ferry. Semple collected the fares and ten newcomers settled onto the hard benches.

"Now, Adam, if ye'll step back to the stern, we'll shove off."

They exchanged places. Semple untied the ferry and shoved the bow away. Slowly the sail filled and the boat moved away from shore. As they sailed out into the strait, the wind picked up. The boat headed up into the wind, and the sail flapped, useless. Dodging the snapping canvas, the passengers peered in alarm at Adam.

"Push your tiller over!" called Semple, gesturing into the wind. "The way ye saw me do."

Semple had said nothing about the tiller, and Adam had not seen what he had done. He pushed the tiller as Semple said. Slowly the ferryboat fell off the wind until the sail filled. Within minutes they were hurtling across the strait. Spray broke in sheets over the bow. Water began to slosh back and forth in the bottom of the boat.

Once Adam drove a runaway horse and buggy. The vehicle lurched over a road filled with holes, filling him with terror. He had pulled on the reins but to no effect. He felt the same lack of control now.

Terror mounted in him and fed upon the fear reflected in the passengers' eyes. He gripped both the tiller and the rope holding the sail in tightly. The agony he had felt coming here stabbed once more at his arms and legs. He didn't know how much longer he could hang on.

"Mr. Sample!" he shouted, "I can't keep this up!"

"Ye're doing fine, Adam." The ferryman had no idea of his pain.

A new threat appeared from San Pablo Bay. A schooner, her sails billowing, entered the strait bound toward the rivers. It seemed they must collide in mid-channel. Frantically he looked to Semple, but the ferryman was studying the vessel closing on them. Icy sweat broke out anew over Adam.

The schooner bore down on them. Semple gazed from the vessel to Adam. His voice roared over the heads of the passengers. "Ease up, Mr. Stuart! Let the sail out! The rope in your hand! Let it out a foot or two!"

Adam stared at the rope. At once he realized what drove them so hard. Bracing trembling knees against the tiller, holding it steady, with both hands he paid out line. At once the ferryboat righted itself and settled into the water. The sharp pain subsided to an ache that left him shaking.

The ship swept across their bow barely fifty yards ahead. Passengers lined her rails, cheering, their voices born away by the wind. Clearly they had no inkling of the disaster Adam had avoided

The rest of the crossing seemed calm, but the passengers remained tense. Finally one man, burly and broad-faced, tugged at a tarred pigtail on the back of his neck. glared at Robert Semple. "Ye're training this man on my watch? Wait'll we're across, man!"

Semple looked upon him calmly. "Would ye wait at the landing for two or three days while I broke him in? And while the ferry crossed without passengers? Ye might miss your bonanza on the American River or the Yuba."

The fellow scowled, and the other passengers, obviously frightened, huddled together and gripped their bedrolls and packs.

Even though he shivered as the wind searched out the sweat on his body, Adam suddenly discovered a peace he had not known before. He could cope with danger. After being robbed he had questioned himself. But it was more than that. The wind and water which threatened to upend and sink them only minutes before had somehow become allies, tools he could use. From them Adam gained confidence and a sense of power.

At the Benicia landing he brought the bow up into the wind and slammed the dock only moderately hard. The passengers tumbled over one another to escape.

For the rest of the day Semple commanded the ferryboat,

allowing Adam to rest and reflect on the experience. For this he was grateful. He never told Semple how close he came to collapse, nearly giving in to fear and weakness. Later, when he must depend upon himself, he would recall how he conquered that fear. He would never again fight the elements. He would make them work for him, as the tools they had become.

CHAPTER 7

For three days ferry passengers lined up, shuffled their feet, cursed under their breath and yearned for the opposite shore while Semple and Adam checked the rowboat. On the fourth morning the ferryman said, "She's right enough. Now ye'll get your lesson in rowing."

Semple approached the passengers. "Gentlemen, crossing will be delayed one hour. I must teach Adam how to handle the rowboat." A collective groan went up from the men waiting to cross.

Adam looked upon the surface of the water. Already cat-spaws ruffled the tide surging inland. Beyond the far shore, Monte Diablo, tipped with sunshine, reared its shadowy bulk on the horizon.

Commotion on the dock turned Adam's attention that way. The first passenger in line had slammed his pack down. "The hell you say!" He pulled a revolver from his waistband. "We'll cross now, damn you!"

Semple stood, arms akimbo, hands resting on his hips, his feet wide apart. A frosty smile touched his craggy features. "Crossing will be delayed one hour, gentlemen."

All was silent on the landing. Then one of the men said, "Put the gun away, George. The man has his work to do."

"Like hell I will!" The gun pointing loosely at Semple waved around.

"If ye were in such a sweat to go to San Francisco," said Semple, "why did you boys spend two days drinking in Sacramento City?"

The wielder of the gun stared at Semple. "How the hell did you know?"

"Ye told me yourself. Ye made enough noise last night to keep the dead awake. Put the gun away."

The man glared at him before shoving the pistol into his waistband. He snorted. "Hell, for two bits I'd take the ferry across myself."

"Would ye now?" Semple's gaze traveled along the line of passengers. "And would ye gentlemen cross with him?"

Shakes of heads and shuffles of feet gave the answer. Finally one man said, "Naw. I can't swim. George talks big, but he can't swim neither."

"Well, then, tell you what we'll do. We'll bring ye a pot of coffee and some cups. Sorry I have only three, but ye can share."

Adam, hearing Semple's offer, started for the house.

"Fetch the oars too, Adam! They're leaning against the house."

Oars over his shoulder, a bandanna wrapped around the hand carrying the coffee pot, three tin cups dangling from his fingers, Adam returned to the dock."

"Make yourselves comfortable, gentlemen," said Robert Semple. "We'll return within the hour. I promise ye."

Semple placed the oars between thole pins in the gunwale and let them float on the water. Manila rope tacked around each oar kept them from sliding out and drifting away. The thole pins, worn where the oars rubbed on them, were sturdy oak pegs. Adam had seen a sack of them in the shelter behind the home. Now he knew what Semple used them for.

"Now, Adam, step to the stern and watch what I do. It's all in the wrists and back."

Pushing one oar, pulling on the other, Semple turned the

craft upstream parallel to the shore. Above them rocks and chapparal dotted the slope, with grasses and tules waving along the shoreline. The ferryman pulled the oars with long, powerful strokes. The boat shot along beneath the village of Benicia.

"I didn't think we could travel so fast," said Adam."

"Wind and tide working for us. Fifteen minutes up and forty-five back."

They rowed in silence except for a gurgle in the stern each time Semple pulled the oars, and the rattle of oars rubbing on thole pins.

"Mr. Semple, would that man have shot you?"

Semple shook his head. "Ye learn to sort them out, lad, the four- flushers from the dangerous ones. No, he was a blowhard trying to bluff. Now ye take the oars."

Gingerly Adam slid around him. Semple's weight tilted the gunwale down to the water dangerously until they settled into their seats. Adam stared at the oars, their thin blades trailing alongside in the water.

"Go ahead," said the ferrymen. "Grab the oars and row."

Adam grasped the oars and held them straight out, but he couldn't extend his grip all the way around the handles. Stretching his fingers threatened to cramp them.

"Pull the oars back, set them in the water and pull."

On one oar he felt the resistance of the water. But the other oar turned, its blade flat, skidding across the surface. The boat turned slightly.

"It's in the wrist. Control the oar with your wrist."

On the next stroke both oars caught. The boat moved ahead smoothly.

"There ye've got it, just like that. If ye want to turn, pull on one oar. Let the other trail in the water, or push it away from you."

For the most part Adam pulled evenly. Now and then an oar rolled and the blade skipped across the water. Sometimes he didn't lift the oar high enough on the return sweep. Then the blade caught the surface abruptly, sending a sheet of spray out ahead of the boat.

Semple said rowing involved wrists and back. But Adam's legs ached as badly as they had on the gravel bars. He needed something to brace them against. but he could not reach the blocks Semple had set on the bottom for his own feet. All the old pains returned, rendering him weak and feeling useless.

The ferryman watched the shore slid past. From his pocket he drew a watch. "We'd better turn back," he said. "Our passengers might try to cross without us. They'd drown themselves and put us out of business."

Adam got the boat turned around but could make no headway against wind and tide. The wind turned the bow this way and then that. He spent most of his energy correcting their course. And when his oar caught on the return sweep, sending spray into the air, it flew back on the wind and struck him squarely in the back. So it went. They made slow progress while Adams hands cramped and his arms ached.

'Let's switch," said the ferryman. "I like my passengers fat and sassy. Of course, not many of them are fat. Some real scarecrows come down from the diggings."

"Like me?" asked Adam as they carefully traded places.

"Ye're fat alongside the ones I'm talking about. The gents who spent their time in the whiskey tents."

Adam shook his head. "I was in pretty bad shape."

"Ye tuckered yourself out, lad, chasing the feller who robbed ye. Ye look fat and sassy, not like them who drank instead of eating. Like the gent waiting up there at the landing."

With powerful strokes Semple propelled the boat downstream. Adam marveled at the strength in the man's huge frame. With each stroke of the oars he felt the boat surge forward. How could he hope to match, or even approach, Semple's skill and power?

Soon they reached the ferry dock. Semple looked at Adam. "What do ye think? Can ye learn how to row?"

Adam flexed his hands to work out cramps. "Maybe, if I could fit my hands around the oar handles."

Semple's craggy brow lifted in surprise. "Didn't even think about that, lad. Hold out your hands."

The ferryman matched his own bony hands and fingers to Adam's. He shook his head. "The oars were made for me. Tell ye what. I'll take the ferry across today. Ye stay here and cut them down to fit. Do ye know what a drawknife is?"

Adam nodded. "I've used one a time or two."

"Ye'll find one in the shed ye call home. Cut the oar handles down and smooth them. Ye can't have slivers in your hands. We'll row again tomorrow."

Semple turned to the waiting ferry passengers. "Now, gentlemen, I'll collect the coffeepot and cups." When a passenger handed them over, Semple frowned. "Only two cups here."

Silent men shuffled nervous feet. Adam sensed the suppressed anger building in the giant ferryman. Up to now Semple had never displayed a trace of temper.

"Well, gentlemen?"

One man looked at Semple briefly before looking away. "George here threw his cup into the river."

Semple advanced on the man called George. The other passengers backed off the deck. "Sir, I trust ye can walk on water. Ye'll not cross on my ferry."

The man grabbed at the pistol in his waistband. But Semple's hand shot out, closed upon the man's hand and forced the pistol down. Finally the man yelled, "You're breaking my hand!"

Slowly the ferryman increased the pressure. With his other hand he pried the weapon loose and handed it to Adam.

"Ye're lucky I'll not break your head. Step off the dock. Ye'll not cross here."

The fellow glared at him. "I know my rights!"

"Off the dock or into the water. Which'll it be?"

The man, standing rigid, suddenly sagged. He backpedaled onto dry land, whining, "I'll pay for the cup."

Semple gritted through clenched teeth, "Ye'll pay six fares, sir. One for the cost of the cup. One for the time and fuss of having it shipped here. One for the pleasure ye'll be denying me of my morning coffee. One for delaying our passage. And one for general damages. In addition to your fare, of course. That will make six fares in all. And ye'll not step aboard with a loaded gun to hold to my head. Do ye carry a knife?"

"In his boot," said one of the others. "We've been delayed long enough."

"Out with it, man," ordered Semple. "Adam, if he so much as scratches me, blow him into the water."

The fellow bent down, lifted the knife and handed it to the ferryman handle first. Semple passed it to Adam.

"Now, sir, what's your pleasure? I won't keep these other gents waiting any longer."

"I'll pay," growled the man, drawing a leather poke from his pocket.

"Now then," said Semple, all business. He drew his tiny scales out. "I'll weigh the fares and we'll cast off." He regarded the fellow's companions with a severe eye. "Keep an eye on your prickly friend while he's aboard. And Adam, I'll take the gent's weapons and return them on the other shore."

With relief Adam shoved them away from the dock. As the ferry pulled away, fully loaded, he carried the pot and cups up to the house. In the shed he located the drawknife. It had begun to rust, so he coated the blade with whale oil from the lamp.

On two sawhorses he tied the oars down. Careful not to dig into the grain and gouge the wood, he cut each handle down. Then with his belt knife he shaved each handle round and smooth.

As he worked, Adam wondered whether he was doing the right thing staying here. The robber's trail grew colder. Yet he didn't really have a trail to follow, hadn't had one to begin with. And he was slowly accumulating gold.

Semple returned, discharged passengers and loaded new ones and departed for Martinez. Adam took the oars down to the rowboat. Fitting them between the thole pins, he sat in the boat and held the oars poised above the water. Already the cut-down handles gave him more control. But a nagging fear tugged at him. Did he have the strength to handle the boat against wind and tide?

He got out and walked onto the dock. He peered at the water. Unable to detect flow either way, he tossed several wood chips into the stream. Slowly they drifted upstream. It was nearing slack tide. He had perhaps half an hour of the flood remaining. He could row upstream and return on the ebb.

Tacking wooden cleats onto the bottom of the boat, he untied it, stepped aboard and sat down. Bracing his legs against the cleats, he pulled on the oars. Relaxed, free from Semple's keen eye, he worked on form. He liked the rhythm of the stroke, the squeak of leather where oars rubbed against thole pins. He rolled his wrists to feather the oar blades. Now he didn't fear catching the water on the return stroke.

Past Benicia he rowed. Above town he saw a log on the

rocks a few feet above high water. It looked like yellow pine, the kind of wood Semple burned in his stove. The next time he came, he would roll it into the water and tow it to the landing to cut it into firewood. He had seen a crosscut saw hanging in the shed.

Adam returned to the landing as Robert Semple was tying up for the day. He carried the gear up for the ferryman, along with his own.

"What say ye, Adam? Did ye find the rowing easier?"

"Much easier! It will take time to work everything out." He held out his hands to show broken blisters, a couple of them bleeding.

"Um," was all Semple said.

Adam glanced sharply at him. Did the ferryman think he would make a good boatman? Did Semple regret hiring him?

"Mr. Semple, do you want me to move on?"

"No, lad, of course not. Why do ye ask?"

"You seem disappointed in my rowing."

Semple shook his head. "It's not that, Adam. The rum fellow this morning spoiled my whole day. After he got away from the bank, he took a shot at me. Would ye believe it? That he would be so stupid? Men waiting for the ferry chased him up the hill. If he'd shot me, they would have hung him. They didn't want their crossing hampered. They wait over there two days sometimes."

Later, over bacon and beans and coffee, Adam asked, "Mr. Semple, was he really trying to shoot you?"

The ferryman shrugged. "Who knows, lad? Lord knows, enough crazies come through every day. Put it out of your head."

"I can't," said Adam. "When you go away, I'll have to deal with folks on my own. I don't like guns. Crossing over the trail to Oregon I carried one every day. I never shot at a hostile or even for food. In the mines I shot a deer now and then. It was that or starve."

"Worrying wastes your time, lad, and tuckers you out."

"If you say so." Adam leaned his elbows on the table, coffee cup in is hand. "Sir, how did you start this ferry? It's a real money-maker, isn't it?"

"That it is. I ran the ferry before all this fuss about gold started. Brought folks across the strait to see my town."

"What town is that, sir?"

Semple set his fork and knife down. In his eyes showed surprise. "Why, Benicia, of course."

"You owned the town?"

"Still own most of it with a man named Larkin. Ever heard of him? No? He was the American consul to the Mexican government at Monterey. President Polk's secret agent too, I hear, but he won't say."

Adam went back to his dinner, chewing thoughtfully. "It helped to be here first. Like Mr. Brannan, who met me as I landed in San Francisco.

Sample cocked his head. "Ah, Sam Brannan. He's a sly one. He started the gold fever, you know."

"He discovered the gold? I thought a man named Marshall did."

Semple nodded. "Marshall found the gold, all right. Sam and a partner had a store up at Sacramento City. They called it New Helvetia then."

"I bought supplies at his store, like my good duds."

"Like just about everybody else. Sam heard they found gold in Sutter's millrace. So did other folks, but nobody took it seriously. Sam bought up all the picks and shovels and tin plates and all that truck. Put them in his store. Then he went up to the

American and got some gold. Maybe he dug it, maybe he bought it. Anyway, he put it in a bottle and flashed it around the plaza in San Francisco. Folks got excited then. Most of them up and left for the mines."

Adam nodded. "He showed it to me in San Francisco. Did you go to the mines, sir?"

"Humph! Only a damn fool will kill himself trying to dig gold." At the sudden rush of blood to Adam's face, Semple added, "Oh, some come out rich, but most lose their gold one way or another. Look here, Adam, men who engage in business usually do better. Most fellers in the mines come out ruined."

Adam got up, took the coffee pot from the stove and re-filled their cups. Sitting down, leaning back, he pondered Semple's words. The man was right enough. He himself was proof of that. Many escaped the crippling effects of heat and cold only to find ruin in the whiskey and gambling tents.

Semple had founded a city. The idea appealed immensely to Adam. Not only might he realize a fortune, but also he might make his mark in the world.

Robert Semple seemed withdrawn, dreamy. Was he falling asleep? If so, he would soon chase Adam out to his canvas shed. Candle light was no substitute for the warm light of the whale oil lamp.

"Mr. Semple?"

The ferryman started to his feet, sat back down, passing a hand over his eyes and drank from his cup. No doubt the coffee was barely warm by now.

"Yes, lad?"

Adam leaned forward, resting his arms on his knees. "I've never met anyone who started a city. How would I go about do-ing it?"

Semple looked at him as he were daft. "Ye want to start a city? What for?"

"I want to leave my mark on the land."

Semple stared at him until he felt foolish having proposed it. Yet some left their mark by the farms they tilled. Others left business establishments. Was it so strange to leave a city?

"Ye would need money, Adam, lots of it, to buy raw land in the right place. And ye need a sense of history. Understand why great cities grew where they did. New York, Boston, Charleston, New Orleans. What do ye know about them?"

"I've heard of them is all," admitted Adam. "How did you start Benicia?"

"Not much to tell," said Semple. "Larkin and I talked it over. We went to our good friend General Mariano Vallejo at Sonoma. He gave us this land along the strait."

"I've heard of him. But why did he do that? And why here?"

The big ferryman seemed lost in thought for a moment. Adam saw his eyes glow as if he were seeing a great vision. Finally he spoke. "San Francisco has a great harbor, that you know. One of the best in the world, they say. One day there will be a great city worthy of this harbor. We want Benicia to become that city. San Francisco is miserable most of the year. Wind, fog, blowing sand, not enough water, these are just some of its faults."

Adam nodded. "I came there a year ago. I saw all those things, even in the summer. And I had to wade ashore in deep muck."

"Especially in the summer, lad. Here we have fine weather and deep water. Ships can tie up next to shore. No crawling across mud flats here."

"But why did the general give you the land?"

"Simple, lad. He figured if our town grew, he could sell his land around it."

Adam saw Robert Semple with new eyes. This giant of a

man was more than a simple ferryman. Semple knew and mingled with important men. He knew Brannan and Sutter, and the man Larkin. What was he going to do several weeks or months from now? Business important for California, he said. Did it have to do with these other men? Thinking this over, he wasn't prepared for Semple's next statement.

The ferryman chuckled. "If we hadn't been too late, this place would be named San Francisco. As it is, we named our town after General Vallejo's wife. Benicia is her middle name. A little flattery here and there never hurt."

"You must know him very well."

Semple nodded. "We wanted to call the town by her first name but somebody beat us to it."

"Her name is Francisco?"

"Francesca. A couple of years ago they changed the name of Yerba Buena to San Francisco. That left us high and dry for a name, but we settled on Benicia."

"That's a pretty name. You came here, then, before gold was found."

Again Semple chuckled. "Ever hear of the Bear Flag Revolt, when we took California from Mexico?" Adam had thought Semple looked tired a moment ago, but his eyes danced. "I helped capture my good friend Vallejo. Some of us went to Sonoma, where he commanded the Mexican garrison. We had a glass of wine with Mariano and then we arrested him. Took him to Sutter's Fort. Promised Francesca we'd treat him gentle. But enough of that. Are ye sticking with me here, Adam?"

"Yes, sir. If I knew who robbed me. . . ."

"But ye don't. Ye won't regret staying, lad. Now let's turn in. That business of the pistol tuckered me out."

Later, lying in darkness, Adam thought about Semple's

advice. He earned as much here as he did in the mines. When he operated the ferry in Semple's absence, he would earn much more.

CHAPTER 8

Weeks went by. Inland the heat built up, sucking ocean air in from San Francisco Bay. Each night fog streamed overhead through the strait of Carquines. The sun melted it away, but not before it obscured most of Monte Diablo.

Adam recalled days on the American River when heat waves crinkled up from the gravel. Salt sweat poured into his eyes, often blinding him temporarily. With the heat, snowmelt from the Sierra Nevada Mountains rose. The river's cold flood rippled over most of the gravel bars.

Adam had stood, sometimes hip deep in the water, day after day. In the first summer of the gold, he did not know he could dig pay dirt out of dry ravines. No one knew. In the icy water his weakness had begun.

When Robert Semple released him from the ferry, he spent days in the rowboat. He rowed until his muscles screamed for relief. Then he sat, drenched in sweat, quivering until the pain eased. But he persisted. His senses told him his strength was returning.

Afraid of venturing toward San Pablo Bay, he rowed upstream into Suisun Bay and Grizzly Bay to the north. Sometimes he reached the mouth of the Sacramento River, using the flood tide to offset the snowmelt pouring seaward.

Adam brought down the pine log on the shore near Benicia. From it he cut and split firewood. Using Semple's cumbrous wheelbarrow with its wooden wheel, he toted and stacked the fuel behind the canvas house. After his day was done Semple stood, hands on hips, nodding approval.

"Ye might go up the Sacramento for oak and sycamore. They make a slow fire, not like the pine. But sure as hell ye'll wear yourself out chopping trees down only to see them sink in the river. Been up Montezuma Slough, behind Grizzly Island?"

"I've seen it."

"Ye might find dry, cured wood there. Floods bring pines down the Sacramento and the wind pushes them up there."

Adam set out at daybreak, saying he would be gone a day or two. An hour of hard rowing brought him to Montezuma Slough. As he pushed up the slough, great blue herons stood on stilted legs in the shallows. When he came too close, with a raucous *grak* they rose into the air. Skimming over the water, necks folded back on their shoulders, long bills thrust forward, with steady beat of great wings they sought refuge farther up the slough.

There he found all the pines he wanted, washed up in the grass and cottonwoods on the banks. On shore, wading through mud, battling swarms of mosquitoes, Adam chopped off limbs and sawed off roots. At times he staggered with fatigue. Clutching cottonwood saplings to stand up, he rested until the mosquitoes drove him back to work.

Finally he cut and trimmed four yellow pine logs. With a stout limb he pried them into the water. Pushing and pulling, he lined them up beside each other. With a rope he tied them into a raft. Hands bloody from smashing mosquitoes, he loaded his tools into the boat and shoved off, towing his raft.

The sun plummeted behind the hill. Twilight brought even greater swarms of insects. As he slapped at them, his notion of staying overnight vanished. Still in Montezuma Slough, he towed his raft out into midstream. There he slipped over the side and washed the mosquitoes and blood off. The water was brackish, neither salt nor fresh but tending to the latter as the rivers poured their snowmelt into Suisun Bay.

Pulling out into the bay, he saw lights downstream. Slowly, almost lazily, he rowed into the wind toward them. The tide would flood for some hours yet. To waste energy pushing against it would be stupid. Until it turned, he stayed offshore to avoid the insects.

After several hours of languid rowing he felt strength returning. Lights appeared, the largest cluster marking Benicia. When they loomed closer, he knew the tide had turned. He pulled hard to the northern shore, afraid he would lose the raft if he slipped past the ferry landing.

Dawn stained the eastern sky when he reached the landing. Travelers huddling around campfires boiling coffee stared curiously at him and his log raft. As he was tying up, Semple emerged from the house.

"Ye've done well, lad," Semple rumbled. "Far better than I expected. For this work ye have two extra days' pay. Woodcutters up the Sacramento are charging dear for fuel this summer. And ye've already put in a day. Stay here and relax."

"I'll begin cutting firewood," said Adam, "if I can roll a log or two out of the water. But I'll have some breakfast first."

Adam had started frying bacon when a knock came at the door. "Cap'n wants to see you," said a miner. Adam shoved the frying pan to the side, hoping his bacon wouldn't burn, and followed the messenger to the dock.

Semple was bending the sail onto the mast. "That you, Adam? There's a sick feller over in camp by the shore." Semple glanced at the sun, beginning to appear blood-red through the interior haze. "Would ye help bring him here?"

Adam strode to the camp, where two men struggled to lift a third man and his gear. Adam said, "If one of you will help me and the other bring along his gear, we'll walk him to the ferry."

Before he reached the man the overpowering odor of vomit

and sweat and dirt engulfed him. He almost recoiled from the familiar smell — the smell of himself not many weeks back. The fellow could not get up. Adam pulled him to his feet and wrapped an arm around him. At once the smell of stale whiskey sickened him. The man peered from under a slouch hat, sagging as his knees buckled.

"Throw your arm over my shoulder. Help me to help you."

With his right arm around the man's waist, his left hand grasped the arm flung across his shoulders. The other miner propped the limber fellow up on the other side. Together they half walked, half carried him to the dock, where they eased him into the ferry. He collapsed on the bench, eyes closed, mouth hanging open, shallow rasps of breath heaving his chest.

"I doubt he'll remember to think kindly of ye, Adam, but I will. We'll get under way."

Adam watched the ferry catch the freshening breeze. He swallowed a time or two; he almost vomited himself. The man had marked him with his odor.

Adam stripped off his shirt and went up to the house. He poured hot water from the teakettle into the tub in which he bathed. Throwing in a bar of rough soap and his shirt, he scrubbed the garment until he washed out the rank odor.

Now he scrubbed himself. Then he hung his shirt to dry.

As was his habit, he scanned the strait and its shoreline. Something arrested his attention. Was it a pile of rags left behind by the party? The more he gazed at it, the more it excited his curiosity.

The rags had once been blankets. The debris would not please his employer. In a fire ring nearby, coals still smoldered. He kicked the rags into the fire, but they did not move. Slowly, with his toe he pushed the cloth aside.

His heart leaped. Beneath the rags lay a leather boot like the one he had lost but smaller. He pulled it up and lifted it out at arm's length, his heart pounding. It was a miner's stake. Hefting the bag, he guessed there were four or five thousand inside.

Quickly he looked about. Men approached on the shore trail, but they were far away. Hugging the boot to his chest, he hurried back to the house, entered and closed the door, dropping the bar into place.

He lighted the whale oil lamp and set the boot on the table. Reaching into the leather, he lifted out several pokes of soft leather. All of them were crammed with gold dust and small nuggets.

He stashed the poke in the boot and set it under the table. Searching for a weapon, he grabbed a butcher knife and waited. He could hear voices outside.

"Ho, the house!" a voice called. "Anybody there?"

The door latch rattled.

Another voice said, "Semple's gone. Ferry's gone — there it is, out in the strait."

Still another voice said, "There's some gents coming. We'd best line up, be the next ones to cross."

The voices faded. Cautiously Adam withdrew the bar and cracked the door open. Five men settled on the ground, intent upon the ferry. Half a dozen more, apparently seeing the ferry, hurried to assure themselves of passage.

Adam slipped out with the boot and rounded the corner to the shed. He had to hide the gold. Setting it down, he laid the sack of oak thole pins over the leather.

Breakfast forgotten, he was rolling a pine log out of the water when Semple docked the ferry. Semple hurried to the camping area. Soon the ferryman returned.

"A few minutes, gents. Adam, I'd like a word with you."

Semple led him out of earshot.

"Lad, did ye find something where the last bunch camped?" The ferryman peered into Adam's face.

For an instant Adam hesitated. Then he said, "Yes, sir, a boot with several thousand in gold dust and nuggets."

Semple leaned forward. "Ye did! And where is it now?"

"Under a sack in the shed."

"Why didn't ye put it in the house?"

Adam faced him squarely. "Mr. Semple, that is your home. I don't intrude when you're away."

A smile broke over the ferryman's tense face. "Adam, my home is yonder in the town. This is my office, so to speak. The gold belongs to the lad ye assisted. Would you bring it down while I collect fares?"

The ferry passengers stared at the leather boot Adam brought to Semple. Their eyes remained on it as the ferryman lodged it firmly between his feet.

That night, over dinner of bacon and beans, the ferryman studied Adam. Finally he said, "Ye're a Midas, Adam, and then again ye're not."

"Midas," said Adam. "Another Greek, like that Jason fellow?"

"Right. Midas attracted gold. It got so bad everything he touched turned to gold. Even his grub until he couldn't eat."

"Well," said Adam, shoveling a spoonful of beans into his mouth, "my grub hasn't turned to gold yet."

"Ye're different, lad. The gold comes easily into your hand, but then it slips away. Tell me, did you intend to keep the boot and slip away some night?"

Adam turned startled eyes on him. "Why do you ask?"

Semple drank coffee before replying. "Well, uh, lad " – after a swift intake of breath he said, "ye hesitated. The thought crossed my mind."

"I see, sir. No, I never meant to keep the gold. It seemed I'd recovered my stake. Now I was giving it up again, and it pained me to do it. But I wouldn't do that to a man. He'll need his gold if he hopes to recover. He'll need good food and rest."

"In him I saw myself," Adam went on. "He used spirits to kill his pain; I used laudanum."

Robert Semple rose and went to the cupboard. There he drew out a leather poke of gold, which he put before Adam. "The gent realized what happened. He was so glad to get his gold he left this poke for you."

"I can't take it," protested Adam.

"Would ye have me chase him down to return it?"

Reluctantly Adam took it. It more than doubled his stake.

The incident behind him, their firewood needs resolved, Adam turned to the ferry once more. He became almost as skilled as his employer in handling the vessel. More relaxed, he spent less time watching the sail. He began to notice his passengers, especially those returning from the placers.

There were men like himself. Shaggy, tattered, faces pinched by poor food, bodies shattered by icy water and hardscrabble diggings, they shambled to the ferry. Aghast at what he saw, he asked himself, *did I look that bad when I came here?* Yet he knew he did.

A second class of men emerged, men he seldom saw on the gravel bars. Sour in body and face, they traveled with a bottle. They were the quitters. They came to simply pick gold off the ground. Finding themselves scrabbling with pick and shovel, they abandoned the placers for whiskey tents and gambling hells.

A third group of miners puzzled him. Some, quiet satisfaction written on their faces, were headed home. Others laughed boisterously and bragged openly. They left some of their gold with barkeepers and gamblers in Sacramento City.

Now they headed for San Francisco, talking of nonstop drinking and gambling there. He found the stories hard to believe. He recalled dust and squalor, sand blowing and fog rolling over the town. To think anyone *wanted* to go there, well, it was too much.

Why they left the diggins puzzled him. The best panning was at hand. Snowmelt provided water to wash sand and gravel, and potholes in river bedrock showed when the water went down. Soon the summer heat would subside. Yet they left when existence was becoming bearable.

As he thought about it, he came to understand. Loneliness and privation drove them out. They needed bright lights and the excitement produced by crowds. They needed to touch human beings again.

Passengers crossing to Benicia were hot-eyed, fretful, insolent. As the ferry approached, they crowded the dock. They had to back off to let those aboard go ashore. Grudgingly they did so. Adam strove to serve everyone, but each time he took on passengers, the line waiting to cross grew.

Only two men among these passengers took interest in the ferry. The first, a Chinese, held his place in line although men around him said they wouldn't cross "with no rat-eating heathen."

"If not," said Adam, "kindly step aside. Catch a later crossing." But no one did. The Chinese, dressed in black pantaloons and a padded black silk tunic, took his place aboard. He gazed with interest at the sail. Finally he spoke, his voice thin, high-pitched.

"You movee sail, work like China boat." When he stood and crouched beside the mast, the wind snatched his wide-brimmed, flat-crowned silk hat from his head. He caught it and jammed it down, but not before it revealed his shaved head. His long queue, wrapped around his head, flung out with the wind.

He stood again, touched the gaff and slid his hand back, indicating where the spar and mast should intersect. "Movee sail, boat go like hellee. Like China chop-boat."

He sat down and settled into himself, black eyes staring impassively at the approaching shore.

Adam wondered whether he could deal with hostile stares from everyone as the Orientals did.

That night Adam told Robert Semple what the Chinaman said. Semple shrugged. "Sail's always worked fine for me. No need to change."

Adam decided to forget the Chinaman's advice. He didn't have time to make changes. Nor did he want to handle new gear.

One day, as he loaded passengers at Martinez, a gimpy one-eyed man stepped aboard sidewise, crablike. He glanced at the sail. Adam studied him. He knew sailors deserted ships and flocked to the diggins, but he had never seen one up close. The man was small, bandy-legged, dressed in canvas pants and shirt. His flat straw hat with wide brim and red ribbon was coated liberally with tar. He squinted out of his one good eye and pointed to the patch covering the other.

"Ye noticed me badge, eh, mate?"

Adam flushed. He had not meant to stare.

The man put a hand to the leather patch. "A bucko mate done it. Flogging me, he was, an' he got careless. His knot took out me eye."

They were halfway across the strait when the sailor spoke again. "Hard to handle that sail, ain't it? Main sheet pulls hard, looks to me. Tuckers ye out some?"

He said nothing more until they reached Benicia.

"I got a idee," he said as he stepped ashore. "Might make yer work easier."

"I'm always ready to listen," said Adam.

"Ever sailed on a ship?"

"From Oregon to San Francisco."

"Then ye seen a jib. Three-cornered sail forward of the masts, on the bowsprit."

Adam nodded. Aboard the *Western Star* he had spent hours leaning over the fiddlehead watching the cutwater slice through the sea.

"Cut a sail, a big 'un, like a jib an' rig it fore an' aft behind the mast. Run yer halyard up the mast to raise and lower yer sail." With a stick he sketched in the dust a diagram of the sail. "Put a traveler rigged with a couple of blocks fer the main sheet. Reeve yer main sheet through the blocks like this." He drew another sketch.

"What's a main sheet?" asked Adam.

The sailor rolled his eyes to heaven. "Yer sailin' and ye don't know? The rope that holds the sail in, mate. The one ye got in yer hand." Again he sketched the main sheet running from the boom through the blocks to a hand. "It'll take a lot of pressure off yer arm."

Passengers bound for Martinez crowded onto the dock. One of them growled, "Come on. We want to reach San Francisco before nightfall."

Adam held up a hand. "In good time. You'll not make it anyway." To the sailor he said, "We have canvas here, but I don't have anything to sew it with."

The sailor dug into his bag and pulled out a canvas folded over and tied by a string. He opened it, revealing a package of stout needles and a spool of heavy linen thread. "This here's a sailor's palm. Put it on yer hand, push yer needle through the canvas with the heavy leather in yer palm." He held the package out to Adam. "Won't need it no more. Sailor Jack ain't never goin' aboard a hellship again. An' you ain't seen him neither."

Adam returned the sailor's crossing fare. "Never heard of him. Never charged him for crossing the strait."

While passengers loaded, Adam transferred the sailor's sketches in the dust onto a sheet of paper he found in the house.

When Semple returned from his business in Benicia, Adam explained Sailor Jack's idea. Semple chewed thoughtfully on his food, appearing to think it over.

"I never was a seafaring man, Adam, so I can't judge the worth of his plan." He chewed his lip, his eye running over the sketches Adam had made. "Tell ye what. I'll run the ferry. Ye make the sail. Ye'll find canvas in the shed. And there's a traveler and blocks if ye dig around. I took them off because drunkards tripped over 'em getting aboard."

"Yes, sir. Can you tell me yet when or where you're going?"

"To Monterey, lad. The new governor, General Riley, called together a convention to write a constitution for the state of California. There'll be men ye know and heard of at Monterey — Sutter and Vallejo — and some ye don't."

"I saw General Riley at Sutter's Fort." Adam looked at Robert Semple with new respect. Obviously his employer was more than just a ferryman. Known throughout the territory, he was respected. Semple had taken part in the Bear Flag Revolt and had founded a city.

The next morning Adam cut lengths from a bolt of canvas and sewed them together, but not without pain. With the leather palm he pushed the heavy needle through the canvas and drew the heavy thread to make stitches. But it didn't always go just right. Then he sucked blood from a punctured finger.

Finally he cut the sewn canvas into a triangle. Later he would make the remnant into a new sail for the rowboat. It had once been rigged for sailing, with a centerboard well built in. The board was still in the shed, and a tiller leaned against the wall.

For two days he sewed. At the corners he sewed extra canvas where the greatest stresses would occur. The days marched toward Robert Semple's departure date. Finally Adam finished his sail.

At daylight he bolted the traveler into place. Semple quieted the usual grumbling at the delay. "Gents," he said, "if we don't make these repairs, nobody will cross today."

After everything was in place, Semple said, "Want to try her out? Ye did all the work."

Adam sagged. "I'm too tired. I couldn't hang onto the sheets."

The ferryman's face went blank. "What?"

"The rope you hold in your hand."

Semple shrugged. "I called it the rope. Sails just the same."

They loaded the passengers aboard. With Adam in the bow watching, Semple pointed for Martinez. The spotless sail billowed, virginal, rosy in the morning sun. The old sail had been stained by mildew and dirt and hard use.

"She works fine," said the ferryman. "She's faster, I do believe, and certainly she handles easier. Your Sailor Jack had a good idea."

Adam ran the ferry while Semple prepared for his trip. Finally they reached the eve of Semple's departure. Darkness had fallen when they quit for the day. Already campfires dotted the shore. Robert Semple didn't allow his passengers to foul the landing, so he had built a privy for their use back a ways. The travelers tended to settle around it for the night.

"We'll fix supper, and then we'll talk about how ye handle money and such. But we'll eat first."

CHAPTER 9

They fried ham and eggs and sat down to eat when a knock came at the door. The ferryman rolled his eyes upward. "A simple 'no' is not enough. And some folks can't read the sign."

He rose and opened the door, and his eyebrows shot up. A man dressed unlike anyone Adam had ever seen stood in the lamplight, his weight mostly on one leg. Adam knew the pose well. The traveler was tired to the bone. His wide-brimmed black hat and flowing cape were coated with dust. He looked important, but in what way Adam had no idea. Semple did not seem to recognize him, suggesting he was a newcomer to California.

"No ferry before sun-up," said Semple firmly. "Plenty of room to make your camp back a ways." He pointed to campfires burning along the shore.

The man shifted his weight to the other foot. "Sir, it is imperative that we cross tonight."

The man's voice surprised Adam. He was not a large man, but urgency in his clear baritone sounded through his fatigue. He pronounced every word precisely.

Semple shook his head. "We work since sun-up. We must have our rest."

"A word with you, sir? In private?"

Semple shrugged, glanced at his supper growing cold and stepped outside. They walked toward the landing.

At first Adam did not see the other figure. His surprise turned to shock when she edged into the lamplight. A girl! Except for Indians at Sutter's fort he had not seen a female. Her eyes fell on the food and rested there longingly.

"Would you care to eat?" asked Adam.

"I'm starved! We've had nothing since breakfast."

Adam got up. "Here, eat mine. I haven't touched it."

With a smile she sat down and attacked his dinner. At the same time she inspected him frankly. "That man, is he your father?"

Adam shook his head. "His name is Robert Semple. Mine is Adam Stuart. I help him run the ferry."

"I didn't think so." She wolfed down his ham and eggs without showing poor manners, unless hunger would qualify. "I never saw anyone so tall. He looks mean, not at all like you."

Adam's face warmed. "His speech is blunt. He has to be. People expect him to do this or that, but there is nothing mean about him."

Pushing the hood from her head, she looked directly at him. He felt hot blood rising in his neck. He had never seen a female with such high coloring or direct manner. Her cheeks, the color of peaches touched by summer sun, were framed by dark hair tumbling about her shoulders. Her brown eyes danced, and her teeth gleamed in her travel-stained face. Vaguely Adam recalled the blonde pallor of Miss Mary Jane Carr, who came off a distant second by comparison.

"Do you live here?"

"I work here." Her directness put him off. He remembered his mother admonishing his sister Abigail — Abby – to listen often but speak seldom, especially if she wished to acquire a husband. Maybe this one had never entertained such a notion.

"Have you always worked here? I mean, since you came to California? Don't you want to get rich in the mines?"

"I spent a year," he said, "digging for gold."

"But you didn't find any, so now you work for him?"

"I was robbed on the way out," he ground out. He was angry with himself. It was none of her business, but he lacked words to blunt her speech.

"Oh. Papa tried mining, but he was too delicate. Now he gives readings and acts out parts of Shakespeare's plays. That's why we're going to San Francisco."

The men's voices came to them, too low for Adam to hear what they said. Then they appeared in the lamplight spilling out the door.

"I thank you, sir," said the man in the cape. "You are most understanding." He looked at the girl finishing Adam's ham. "Francine!"

"He offered his supper to me, Papa, and I was hungry, so I accepted."

The father threw his hands up. "What am I to do with you?"

Robert Semple stepped forward. "Adam, ye will row these folks across tonight. This is Professor Langford Wilmott and his daughter Francine. They must hurry on to San Francisco."

Adam stared at his employer. The ferryman knew he'd never taken the rowboat out into open water. And only once at night. He had seen scattered lights slightly upstream from the ferry dock along the far shore, but that was all. He understood the place to be Martinez.

"They need to cross now, Adam. I'll make sandwiches while ye break out the oars. The folks — uh, the professor — hasn't eaten since morning. They are hurrying to an engagement in San Francisco. And while ye're at it, bring a bullseye lantern. Ye shouldn't meet any traffic on the water, but if ye do, ye need to show a light."

Adam hoped Semple would reconsider. Why could they

possibly want to cross the strait tonight? Had they seen it before, with its swift currents and tides? Semple turned at once to prepare the food.

Adam carried the oars down to the rowboat and waited. Above Monte Diablo a half moon shone through wispy streamers of fog. Its silver reflection glittered on the water. The fog meant wind. Beyond Benicia Point he could expect rough water.

Semple carried a basket of food and the shuttered lantern which he had lighted. Adam shoved the boat into the water and moved it to the ferry dock. To Professor Wilmott he said, "Sir, I'll put you in the bow and the lady in the stern with your baggage."

The dim figure nodded and clambered into the boat. Adam took his place at the oars. Semple helped the girl into the boat and stowed their bags on the seat beside her. Then he gripped the transom and turned the boat, bow pointed to the far shore.

"Remember three things, Adam. Don't look into the lantern light. It'll blind ye. The tide is coming in. Mind it doesn't carry ye into Suisun Bay. And keep the wind on your left shoulder. Got that?"

"Yes, sir."

"One other thing. Best ye stay the night over there. I'd keep a fire to show the way back, but I travel tomorrow and I'll need rest. Ye can sail the ferry and tow the boat back."

"We'll make out, sir."

"Good." Semple gave a shove, propelling the boat away from shore.

They were scarcely out of earshot before the girl said, "Why do you work for him? He's bossy. Imagine telling you what to do. As if you haven't done this before."

What could he say? He'd never rowed across? Or he'd never

crossed at night? He hoped she wouldn't find out before the night was done.

He's a good man to work for," he said. "He wants to make sure everything goes right."

"Not only that," she said. "He thinks himself very important."

"Mr. Semple *is* important. He's going to Monterey to help write a constitution for California. He helped lead the Bear Flag Revolt, you know, freeing California from Mexico. He has important friends – General Vallejo, Captain Sutter. Mr. Larkin is his partner. He says Larkin is a special agent of the President of the United States. So you see, he is important."

"Oh."

With the weight of the two passengers and their baggage, the boat did not pull easily, but the load steadied it in the water. Adam needed to keep the lights of Benicia over Francine Wilmott's left shoulder. Now the lights were directly behind her. He pulled harder on an oar until he was on course again.

"Before you came to California," she asked, "where did you live?"

The girl was full of questions. He needed to save his breath for rowing. But she was persistent, asking him again.

"I grew up in Lafayette, Indiana."

"Why, we are practically neighbors. Papa taught literature and philosophy at Kenyon College. That's in Gambier, Ohio. Do you know where it is?"

"No," said Adam.

"Well, I'm not surprised. Gambier is a tiny place."

"You left a place like that to come here?"

Francine peered around him, frowning. Adam looked over his shoulder to follow her gaze. Her father, wrapped in his cape, slumped forward, asleep. His hat had fallen into the bilge. Adam put it on the seat beside him.

"Poor Papa," said the girl softly, "he's so tired. He's not very strong. And he worries about me. Why did we leave Ohio? Two reasons, actually. First Papa was passed over for a post in the college. It disappointed him terribly. Then his wife died."

Adam thought it strange to talk about her mother as if she were talking about a stranger.

"Was she your mother?"

"Why, of course! Mama took sick with the fever. She just wasted away. After she died we didn't want to stay."

Out past Benicia Point the wind picked up. Waves rolled by, now and then slopping water over the side. Several times on the back sweep Adam caught an oar on a wave, showering spray over Professor Wilmott. Finally the professor cried out.

"I'm sorry, sir. Sometimes I can't help catching a wave."

Wilmott grunted, jammed his hat on his head, pulled his cape more tightly about himself and slumped once more.

For the next half hour Adam rowed silently. In the moonlight filtering through the fog he saw the girl's eyes fixed on him. He had never looked into a girl's face so closely or for so long. Heat not related to his exertion flooded over him. He was glad of the dark.

Adam sensed they drifted with wind and tide. He angled farther into the wind. Waves broke over the bow, sending showers of water over them. He searched for landmarks on the shore ahead.

"You're not well, are you?" The girl's voice startled him as much as her words. "I can tell. You're not rowing as hard as before. Will we reach shore safely?"

"We will." Adam put more back into his effort, but he was tiring rapidly. He despaired of reaching Martinez before the tide swept them into Suisun Bay. The boat began to wallow in the choppy waves as more water settled into the bilge.

Abruptly the black outline of land rose before them. Only a hundred yards separated them from shore. It gave him new energy. Avoiding the girl's eyes, he pulled with his remaining strength. They neared a strip of white marking waves breaking on the shoreline. The bow nudged into soft sand.

Sweating, his body trembling, Adam hunched over the oars until his pounding heart eased and his breathing slowed to near normal. Francine made no move to help him or to get out of the boat. But he saw her look of deep concern in the moonlight.

"Thank you for helping us," she whispered. "I saw how much it hurt you. You never rowed across before, did you? That's why Mr. Semple gave you so much advice."

He stepped into knee-deep water and pulled the bow up the beach. Professor Wilmott sat up and peered around, bewildered. He stood and would have fallen had Adam not grabbed his arm.

"We thank you," said the professor. "I hadn't realized how hazardous the crossing might be. You're a brave young man."

"Just doing my job," said Adam. He still had to unload the boat, dump the water out, pull it higher and learn where they landed.

He offered his hand to Francine Wilmott and guided her over the seats. When she lifted her dress to step over the bow, he glimpsed slender high-button shoes and trim ankles. He piled their baggage on the beach, pulled the boat higher and opened the lantern shutters. Then he looked about.

"We'll continue on our way," said Wilmott. "Can we buy or rent horses here?"

"I don't know, sir. I've never stepped ashore here. But this is not the ferry landing. If you and Miss Wilmott will wait here, I'll climb to higher ground to see where we landed."

With a sigh Wilmott sank onto the sand and slouched forward. But Francine stood close to Adam. "I'm going with you. And call me Francie."

"Don't you want to rest?"

She faced him. "I'm not as tired as you are."

He nodded. "Sir, I'll leave the lantern here so we can find our way back."

As they started up the hill, Francie took his hand. Her warm touch startled him. He had never held a girl's hand before.

They climbed up through dry grass and scrub chaparral. Several lights twinkled downstream.

"Martinez," said Adam. "Our ferry landing is down there."

She squeezed his hand. "You did very well in the dark."

He was glad the darkness hid the warmth flooding his face.

"We'd better go back," he said, "and start a fire. Your father got wet coming across. He'll be cold soon."

Professor Wilmott turned a tired dusty face up to them as they trudged down the slope. In his eyes Adam read discouragement. Could the professor care properly for his daughter in San Francisco?

"We're in luck. Our ferry landing is just downstream. At first light we'll row down."

Wilmott struggled to his feet and staggered. "We must go now and get away before daylight."

"Oh, Papa," said Francie, "Adam is so tired. Can't we rest?"

At her use of his name so familiarly Adam started, but he wasn't prepared for the expression on Wilmott's face. Did he see fear there? Something was driving the professor. Did Francie know?

"Sir, we'll stay here until daylight. There are no lights at the landing, and the tide will be going out. We might miss the landing. Even if we found it, you couldn't find your way in the dark through camps there. I'll start a fire, and then we can eat our sandwiches."

"My goodness!" said Francie. "I ate your dinner last night."

Wilmott's shoulders sagged. "It's best, I suppose. I had hoped to be on our way. I'll help gather firewood."

"You and Miss Willmot rest. I'll do it."

With a fire burning brightly, the smoke drifting into the darkness, they ate. Adam sat on the sand, Francie beside him, again raising concern in her father's eyes.

After they ate, Adam gathered wood to last the night. He had been up since daylight yesterday. No doubt they had too. After putting fresh wood on the fire Adam nodded, lurched upright, nodded again.

Streaks of light stained the eastern sky when he stirred. He had fallen asleep, and Francie had moved closer until her head rested on his shoulder. Fearing her father might think the worst, he knew he should break away, but he couldn't give up the warmth of her. Finally she stirred and looked up at him wide-eyed, her lips parted. Their eyes met and held. Adam felt himself leaning toward her. With an effort he drew back, breathing deeply. Professor Wilmott was stirring.

Sand was softer than rock, yet it was unforgiving. Adam rose and stretched the ache out of his muscles.

"I'd better go up and make sure it was Martinez we saw last night. I'll be right back."

Up the slope, out of sight, he emptied his bladder. Of course it was Martinez downstream. Looking across the Strait of Carquines, he saw Benicia's cluster of houses near the water's edge, rounded hills beyond. Flaming orange and pink touched fleecy clouds in the east.

Professor Wilmott was fleeing from something back there. The haunted look in his eyes when he looked across the strait gave him away. Adam returned to the beach and shoved the boat into the water.

"We'll reach the ferry landing by the time Mr. Semple leaves Benicia. He always sails promptly at sunrise."

The professor whirled to stare at him. "Are you positive?"

"As sure as I am of anything."

"We want to leave before the ferry arrives."

As he rowed them to the ferry landing, Adam avoided Francie's steady gaze. Again he felt a strange stirring within himself.

They reached the landing as the sun broke over the horizon. Adam helped Francie out of the boat and put their bags on shore. Across the water the ferry's new white sail caught the sunlight as it moved away from shore.

"The ferry is coming," he said. "I'm to wait for it here."

The professor cast a nervous eye at the sail, then thrust out his hand. "We thank you, Adam. Come along, Francie."

She held out her hand. He took it and held it a couple of seconds. She murmured, "I wish you were coming too."

Adam shot a glance at her father, who seemed not to have heard. He was gazing, fearfully, Adam thought, as the sail grew larger.

He watched them thread their way up the slope through the camps until they vanished.

Several horsemen appeared from Martinez leading a riderless horse. No doubt they came to meet Robert Semple. They stopped a short distance from the landing, where passengers already lined up peering at the sail.

The ferry grew larger in his view. By the time it landed, the Wilmotts vanished from sight. Semple tied the ferry, letting the sail flap in the breeze. He glanced at the rowboat and then at Adam. As passengers disembarked, he said, "Ye made it, I see, and your passengers are on their way." The ferryman stepped ashore with a single leather bag.

"Hey, mister," said a man, "ain't you goin' back? We been waitin' since yestiddy noon."

"Well, then," said Semple, "ye won't mind a few minutes more." He pointed to Adam. "This man will take ye. But I have words for him first." Aside, Semple said, "Take care of the money. Don't show more'n ye must." He slipped a pistol into Adam's hand. "But mainly I'm warning ye against a man named Charles Dupre."

"Should I know him?"

"I doubt ye've seen him. He's the man Professor Wilmott is running from. Up at Bidwell's Bar the professor gave readings and the girl sang. Drew a crowd, she did. This gambler Dupre was mightily taken with her and paid her attention. I reckon she was flattered and returned his interest, not knowing his nature. Wilmott pulled out with the girl in the middle of the night."

"Francie is a very forward young lady," said Adam. "She's outspoken, but I'm sure she's proper." But he wondered. She seemed to warm to men. He understood why men would flock around her, especially with so few females in camp. She would find the attention flattering, and she had no mother to advise her. He doubted her father could do more than spirit her away.

"The professor said Dupre is tracking them."

"They wanted to go before you landed."

"Wilmott probably feared Dupre was on the ferry. If he shows up, don't admit ye've seen them. Dupre will find them anyway. Wilmott will be a public man, and the girl will draw crowds wherever she goes."

"Hey, old man!" yelled a skinny kid in brand new boots, pants, red calico shirt and floppy hat with the brim pinned back. "When is this here boat leaving?"

Semple shook his head and muttered, "Hurrying to seek his grave, unless I miss my guess. I'll leave him to ye, lad. My friends are waiting. Good luck!"

Adam turned toward the ferry. The youth who complained eyed the pistol in Adam's belt and sank down into his seat. But Adam paid no attention. Responsibility already weighed upon him. He wished for Robert Semple's return. Semple had not paid him for the night crossing. But he didn't dwell on it. Helping Francie was payment enough.

CHAPTER 10

Adam threw himself into his work. From sunrise to sundown he carried passengers back and forth. During the ferry's first days, in a scow Semple ferried two wagons at a time with their teams across the strait. He never knew where wind and tide would land the ungainly craft. But he knew one thing. No matter how many he carried from the south bank, more arrived. Sometimes men camped for days, not always patiently, waiting their turn.

Adam sensed the pressure Semple felt in those days. He felt the same now. Each morning he fisted sleep from his eyes, hurried breakfast, made sandwiches for lunch and carried the gear to the ferry. Did he imagine it, or did he find more surliness than had his employer? It didn't hurt, he guessed, to stand six feet eight inches tall. Many gold seekers took boats from San Francisco to Sacramento — those who could afford the steep tariff and who could find space on a vessel. Among those who walked were the poorer and the rougher elements.

Each night he sighed, putting off travelers who begged him to cross one more time. He was barely able to count and hide away his ferry tolls. As in the mines, his only satisfaction lay in the growing pile of gold. He worked hard enough for it.

Each time he returned to Benicia he scanned waiting passengers for the man Charles Dupre. He didn't know what Dupre looked like, but he had an idea, from what Robert Semple had said. At sundown on the fourth day after the Wilmotts crossed Adam saw him. He knew the instant he saw the man. Instead of coming along the shore trail, the man strode down from the town.

Adam saw no trace of hard, feverish pursuit. No dust or sweat stained his black frock coat or gray trousers; his knee-high boots had been freshly brushed and polished. Yet in the gambler's steps he sensed the man's relentless persistence. Adam knew before he spoke a word that Charles Dupre had come to the crossing. He appeared as different from the miners as had the professor and his daughter only days before. In the self-assured, casual way he carried a riding whip, Dupre seemed to be stalking rather than pursuing.

Arms full of canvas, Adam stopped. Deliberately the man set his leather valise down and tipped his hat. "Do I have the pleasure of addressing Mr. Semple?"

"No, sir. I am Adam Stuart."

Black eyebrows raised. "I understand Mr. Semple operates this ferry."

"He does, but I've taken his place for a while."

"Where has he gone?"

"I'm not at liberty to say, sir."

"No matter. I wish to cross at once."

"The ferry stops at sundown," said Adam. "Mr. Semple's orders."

"It is a matter of utmost urgency. I will speak directly to Mr. Semple." The man glanced toward the canvas house.

Didn't the man listen? Adam shook his head. "He is not here. He hasn't been here all day." But he didn't elaborate. The fewer people who knew Robert Semple had gone to Monterey the better.

Dupre tapped the butt of his whip against the palm of an open hand. "Can someone else take me across?"

"There's no other ferry, sir."

Lifting his chain, looking down his nose, Dupre fixed him with a long stare. "I am trying to catch up with dear friends. Professor Langford Wilmott and his lovely daughter Francine."

"They didn't cross on the ferry, sir."

"You've seen them then."

"I would know if a young lady boarded the ferry. Not a single woman has crossed on the ferry bound for San Francisco since I came here."

The man's dark brows knit together. "Strange. I have it on good authority they came this way."

"Maybe to the town, sir. I wouldn't know."

"I came from Benicia, sir. They didn't stay at the hotel, nor have they dined there. No one in Benicia has seen them."

"A road goes from Benicia on to Sonoma. Maybe they went there."

"Why in God's name would they go there? They were bound for San Francisco. No, sir, you are not telling me the straight of it."

Under the load of canvas in his arms, Adam was beginning to tire. He started around the man, but Dupre quickly blocked him. Adam said, in a wooden voice, "They did not cross on the ferry. I am aboard from sunup to sundown."

"Yesterday also?"

"Every day."

The thin-lipped man's mouth became a faint line across his face. As he looked across the strait toward Martinez, he tapped his whip. He spoke through gritted teeth.

"Enough! I will speak to Mr. Semple."

"Fine," said Adam, "if you can find him. Mr. Semple has many interests."

"Fellow," hissed Dupre, "I could compel you to ferry me across." He shook his arm. Into his hand dropped an over-and-under derringer.

Adam's stomach lurched. He hadn't expected this. But he looked from the weapon into the gambler's eyes. "Mister. . . ."

"Charles Dupre, sir!"

"Mr. Dupre, you can't make me cross. And you won't shoot me. Seven men camped by the river are watching us right now."

The gambler glanced where Adam pointed. Genuine surprise widened the gambler's eyes. Obviously he had not noticed them before.

"You came from the gold camps," said Adam. "You know they'd hang you on the spot."

A sneer settled on Depre's lips. "Nonsense! What are you to them?"

Adam shifted the load of canvas in his arms. "I am their way across the strait. They want to go to San Francisco too. They're miners. They settle trouble their own way. With a rope."

The gun remained steady in the gambler's hand. From careless arrogance Charles Dupre's presence changed to pure malice. Wide-brimmed black hat shadowing narrowed eyes, mustache curling around his cruel mouth, dead white hands, fingers curving over the triggers of the small weapon, his entire person from his stance to the glitter in his eyes spoke of murder. Adam talked fast.

"Mr. Dupre, I have nothing on the other shore to guide me in the darkness. You can shoot me and take the ferry across yourself. That is, if you escape the miners and if you can sail. Sometimes the wind blows hard out there, and the current is strong. Other times it fails at night, leaving you at the mercy of the tide. I have never crossed at night. I doubt I could find the dock in the darkness, and less idea where you might end up if you go on your own."

Dupre stared a long time before slipping the gun into his coat pocket. When he spoke, Adam had to strain to hear him, though no more than ten feet lay between them.

"If I find you have deceived me, sir, I will hunt you down and kill you."

"In the morning, then. At sun-up." He turned on his heel, picked up his valise and started toward Benicia.

His gut cramping, greasy sweat running down his face, his knees trembling, Adam watched him retreat. He started toward the house, where he dumped the canvas in the shed.

Inside, he mopped the sweat off his face. He had lost his appetite. Putting several slices of cold fried bacon between slabs of bread, he washed the sandwich down with lukewarm water. He didn't need a fire and decided against lighting the lamp. It would throw his shadow on the canvas in case Dupre returned. With darkness rapidly settling, there was no telling what the gambler might do. He would pursue any advantage that fell to him.

Sitting in the dark, windowless house, he felt trapped. Slipping out to the shed, he gathered his blankets and a remnant of canvas. Behind the house a ways a grassy dry wash provided cover. There he spread his blankets and stretched out. He felt the familiar hard lumps and smelled the dusty earth. How quickly the difficult days on the Middle Fork came back! How much better he had it here, sleeping on a bed with a roof over his head. But he would stay where he was until Dupre was gone.

Lying on his back, head cradled on his arms, he gazed up at the stars, thinking of Francie Wilmott. What a delightful girl! So forward, yet sweet. How could she cope with Dupre when he caught up with her? For catch up he would. Only by leaving San Francisco could the Wilmotts evade him. Where could they go? The professor depended for his living upon an audience of men yearning for diversion.

If Adam raced to San Francisco ahead of the gambler, he could warn father and daughter. But why? If they remained there, how could he protect Francie from Charles Dupre? The answer followed hard on the question. He could do nothing. Leaving here would risk everything with nothing to gain.

He closed his eyes. The vivid face of the girl from Ohio appeared before him, tender when she observed his physical distress on the crossing. Adam had never seen a hard woman; he wouldn't recognize one if he saw her. But he did know this. Francine did not have the toughness she would need to cope with Dupre. The gambler's manners would be immaculate if all went his way. Or he could be heartlessly cruel. Adam pictured him bending over Francie's hand. Though the night air was balmy, he shivered.

An hour before first light he rose. Long-familiar aches from sleeping on the ground tormented him. As he stretched his back and moved his arms, he listened. There were only sounds of water birds gabbling among the rushes along the shore. Pistol in hand, slowly he walked to the house, shaking the stiffness out of his legs. Half a dozen campfires already dotted the shoreline; wayward puffs of wind carried the aroma of coffee.

By the time he finished bacon and the last of the eggs and drank a last cup of coffee, the eastern horizon blazed with orange. He stepped outside and looked toward town. He expected to see Charles Dupre approaching in his deliberate stride. If he arrived at the last moment, would he demand that one of the men already waiting at the dock surrender his place? If Dupre forced the issue at gunpoint, would Adam dare intervene?

Looking over his shoulder for Dupre, he carried his gear down to the ferry. Something seemed wrong, out of place. He couldn't put his finger on it. He bent the sail onto the mast and booms and let it rattle in the light breeze as he hung the rudder on the transom.

Ready to take fares and load passengers aboard, he let his

eyes drift over the landing, searching for whatever bothered him. Then he saw it. The rope by which he tied the rowboat to a stake driven into the ground had been cut. The rowboat was gone.

"Sorry, gents, but I forgot something. I'll be right back." Ignoring their grumbles, he hurried up to the house. The oars he always stood against the shed were gone also.

When the ferry was halfway across the strait, Adam spied a small white boat against the shore above Martinez. Drawing closer, he recognized Semple's rowboat. A man was rowing it toward the ferry landing.

As Adam brought the ferry alongside the dock and tied up, a stranger rowed the boat alongside. He rested the oars on the water and called, "A word wid ye, mate."

Adam gestured toward shore. "Beach her. I'll be right with you."

The man touched a knuckle to his forehead and propelled the boat onto the sand. Adam stood aside to let his passengers disembark and held up a hand to stop the men crowding forward. "One minute, gents. Please hold your places in line."

He stepped to the beach where the man waited. A scar coursed angrily across his cheek just below the eye. No doubt punishment from a mate's fury aboard a ship halfway around the world.

"Who be ye?" demanded the fellow. "Where's Semple?"

"I'm Adam Stuart. I work for Mr. Semple. He's gone to Monterey on business."

The man appeared to think this over. Then he nodded. "Me name's Bestwick. Walkin' on the beach this mornin'" – he gestured upstream – "I sees this bloke pullin' Semple's boat up on shore. Dressed all in black, he was, an' sweatin' like a pig. He gives me a hard look an' walks off. So here I am wid the boat. Can ye tow her back across?"

"Can do," said Adam. "You're lucky you didn't challenge him. He dropped a pistol into his hand last night when I refused to cross in the dark." Adam put a gold coin in his hand. "Thank you. I'll mention you to Mr. Semple."

"A bad 'un, he was." Again Bestwick knuckled his forehead. "Thankee. I'll be on me way."

Two weeks passed. One night, as Adam tallied his day's receipts, he made a discovery. He made fewer crossings then just a week ago. Between sunrise and sunset the sunlight grew shorter. But that did not account for the fewer trips. The wind had eased in the straits. Fog rarely scudded overhead. He had no clock or calendar to consult, but he reckoned he must be nearing the end of September.

Each day, as he approached the dock at Martinez, he scanned the passengers waiting at the dock. But no figure stood head and shoulders above the rest. Adam's pile of gold grew, but he wanted to move on. He hoped to return to Oregon before the rainy season set in. He could easily repay Squire Wilson and still have a tidy stake, although far less than what he had. He sighed. Chances became slimmer each day of finding the man who robbed him.

When sailing grew easier, he reacted automatically to shifts in the wind. Often, since Charles Dupre took the rowboat Adam thought about the craft. According to Semple it had nested on board some ship as the captain's gig. It had once been rigged for sail. In the boat's hull were chain plates for fastening stays. The mast and other gear were probably stored in the shed.

That night he lighted the whale oil lamp and set it where its light flooded the shed. Working toward the back wall, he moved everything out about two feet. Eventually he uncovered a spar with rigging that he thought must be the mast. Digging further, he found a bundle of canvas. Although it was stained, smelling of mildew, it was still serviceable. Beneath it lay the boom and gaff. Finally, he found rudder and tiller like the one on the ferry but smaller.

He saw himself bounding across the strait in the small boat, spray flying in the sunlight. He wanted to rig and sail her, but there was no time. First he had to meet the unceasing demands of the passenger ferry.

During the last crossing to Benicia one day the wind died to little more than a whisper. In the lee of Benicia Point, still well offshore, the ferry slowed and drifted on the flood tide. The passengers looked toward the ferry landing and then at him. Their brows furrowed. Some gripped their bags as if they would leap into the water and swim for shore.

Adam felt pressure ease on both the sails and the tiller. Under the eyes of the passengers he felt a different kind of pressure. They wondered whether he could reach shore. To counter their drift upstream he pointed the craft higher into the wind. This slowed them even more although they gained against the tide.

In the hour it required to reach the dock, Adam learned how to point into the wind without losing headway. But that hour took them through sunset and twilight into the dusk. When they finally made land a subdued group of travelers stepped ashore and trudged silently along the shore toward Sacramento City.

As he started up from the dock carrying the sails, he heard noise coming from the house. Someone alternately rattled the padlock and hammered on metal with some object. He set his load down and slipped behind the house. In the shed from beneath the pillow on his bed he lifted Semple's pistol and stuck it in his waistband. He felt further for the shuttered lantern hanging on its nail. He took it down, struck a lucifer, lighted it and closed the shutters. Gun in one hand, lantern in the other, he edged around the house.

He pointed the pistol at the intruder. The man was pounding on the hasp with a rock and muttering to himself. Setting the lantern at his feet, Adam drew the pistol's hammer back with a loud click. The shadowy figure froze.

"Put your hands in the air!" ordered Adam.

"Don't shoot!" squeaked the intruder.

Adam opened the lantern to throw light on the man's back. It was a miner, his clothes faded and ragged from hard use.

"Turn around. Slowly!"

When the man did so, Adam gasped and stared at him. "Terry! Terry Small!"

Terence Small peered into the light trying to see beyond the lantern's glare. "I know your voice. Is that you, Adam?"

"It is. What are you doing here?"

Terence Small hesitated. His mouth worked as if to form a reply. Finally he said, "Looking for food. I haven't et in two days."

"There's a hotel up in town," Adam said. "They serve meals."

Terry's thin voice wavered. "I'm broke. Know what it's like to have gold and then lose it all?"

"Why don't you ask instead of trying to break in?"

"There wasn't nobody here. Besides, I'm not a beggar. Please, Adam, point that gun some'res else."

Adam held the pistol on him steadily. "I see. You're not a beggar, Terry. You're a burglar instead. Were you robbed?"

Terry Small hung his head. "I lost my poke in Sacramento City, bucking the monte and faro tables."

"You weren't as smart as you thought you were."

"I didn't say that."

Adam lowered the pistol and opened the lantern wider. Fishing the key from his pocket, he unlocked the padlock and slipped it off the bent hasp. Inside, he lighted the lamp. Terry remained outside.

"Come in," said Adam. "We'll fix supper. Then you can bed down and I'll take you across in the morning."

Terry nodded. Adam started a fire and made coffee. Terry sat at the table with a cup. He chattered about bad luck at the gaming tables. Several times he doubled his stake before seeing his last ounce of gold slip away. He concluded glumly, "Once lady luck turns on you, you're a goner. But how about you, Adam? What are you doing here?"

"Working the ferry," said Adam. He fried bacon and sliced some bread. "Terry, did you know someone followed us from the Middle Fork?"

"I swear I never knew. Why?"

"But you suspected. You kept looking back over your shoulder."

"I was scared we were being followed. I heard stories about robbers before we left the diggins."

"You didn't see anybody behind us?"

"Not a soul. But why all these questions?"

"Minutes after you left me I was robbed. I thought you might have done it."

Terry held out his hands, palms up. "Aw, now, Adam, you know I'd never do that."

Adam wasn't so sure. "I took laudanum for pain in my legs and wasn't thinking straight. But I figured you're not the one. Your voice is too high. The robber growled like a grizzly bear. But I wondered. Were you making it easy for someone, leaving me behind?"

Terry opened his mouth but Adam said, "The bacon is done. Let's eat."

They ate the bacon between slices of bread sopped in bacon

grease and washed down with coffee. Terry kept his eyes on his food, glancing now and then at Adam. "You had a pretty good stake, didn't you, Adam?"

"I figure eight thousand."

Terry whistled. "That much! You were toting a load, the way you bent over and leaned sideways. So lady luck did you in too."

Adam disagreed. He had lost all, but hard work was paying off again.

After dinner Terry's eyes swiveled about. He must have assumed Adam would sleep in Semple's bed, for he said, "I can throw my bedroll in any old corner."

Adam shook his head. "Sorry. Nobody stays near the house. You'll have to camp down where the other gents have built their fires. Come up for breakfast at daylight."

Watching to see that Terry joined the men at their campfire, Adam locked the house and doused the lantern. He lay in bed, listening for Terry's return. Throughout dinner Small's eyes had darted this way and that as if searching for gold. Finally Adam fell asleep with the pistol close by his hand. He was up and making coffee before dawn.

Adam was relieved when he deposited Terry Small on the opposite shore of the strait.

Another week passed. Since the encounter with Terry Small, Adam brooded over the hold Robert Semple had on him. Men continued to stream across the strait in both directions. Life flowed by him, but he was going nowhere. During the day he ferried passengers, but at night he tossed and turned. He worried about his passengers. Which among them were corrupted either by having gold or by the want of it?

Adam couldn't help but wonder about Terry Small, whether he had always been weak or whether desperate prospects turned him into a thief. He wondered too about Terry's truthfulness. Terry had said he was broke. Was he, or did he say that as a way of disarming Adam's suspicions? He denied complicity in the robbery that left Adam broke But suspicion lingered in Adam's mind.

He was scarred, he knew. Once a victim of robbery, he became more suspicious of others. He was piling up gold by honest effort again. Who among the men flowing past him was honest? If he could get inside their heads, maybe he could foresee another robbery attempt and forestall it.

As his gold accumulated, he grew more distrustful. Everyone saw him collect gold each day. Who among them wondered where he kept it? Who among them would disappear along the shore trail only to return at night? Every man bound for the mines seemed intent upon finding his own bonanza. But not everyone intended to become a miner. Some of them meant to mine the wealth of those who found gold.

When Robert Semple was here, he had not considered being robbed here. The ferryman's size alone would deter a robber. Yet a gun became an equalizer in any man's hand.

Adam became increasingly nervous about keeping his gold in one place. Each night he buried the day's receipts, wrapped in canvas, along the back wall of the house. With a broom he swept each site clear of any signs of digging. Each evening he inspected the area before he cooked dinner.

Adam was thinking about the day's events when a man slouched along the shore trail, his shoulders slumped with fatigue. Even in the gathering shadows the fellow looked familiar. Maybe it was how he carried himself; perhaps it was the set of his head on his shoulders. Adam had just made his supper and was about to sit and eat when he recognized Mal Wilson.

"Mal! Come on up here!"

His brother-in-law stopped and gasped.

"Adam, for God's sake! Why haven't you gone home? And damn me if that frying bacon doesn't smell good!"

They threw arms around each other's shoulders and grasped each other's hands. Always before, Mal Wilson had clasped the other in a vise-hard handshake. Now his brother-in-law's grip, weak and tentative, shocked Adam. He shook his head. Only a few months of heat and icy water had robbed Mal of his vitality.

"You still haven't answered my question, Adam. What are you doing here? Why haven't you gone home?"

"Let's eat, Mal, while the grub is hot. Then we'll talk."

At the table Mal leaned back in his chair and watched Adam pour batter for slapjacks into a frying pan. Mal stuck his feet out and stretched his legs as far as he could without falling off his chair. He sighed. "In the cold water I felt like I was cut in half. Even stretching out full on the ground didn't help."

"I know," said Adam. "Sometimes on the ferry I still feel that way."

Mal eyed him curiously but contained himself. They tied into the food. As they ate, Adam flicked a glance at Mal's boots. When Mal had showed up at Brown's Bar, they were almost new. Now they ran down at the heels, and the soles were cracked and split. The Middle Fork respected fine leather no more than it did a man's body.

Had his brother-in-law found gold? He had passed up new boots in Sacramento City. Some miners wore shabby foot gear because wear had shaped the boots to their feet. Others couldn't wait to rid themselves of their broken footgear. Still others wanted to avoid looking prosperous. Adam could not estimate Mal's success in the diggins.

Finally, their hunger eased, they pushed away from the table. Adam got up and poured more coffee. "How'd it go, Mal?"

"Once I got the hang of it, great. I'm going home with near two thousand. Sold your cradle too for a tidy sum. I was going to give that to you."

"Did you get six hundred for it?"

"And then some."

"Give it to the Squire for the money I owe him."

Alarm spread across Mal's face. "What happened?"

"I was robbed on the way out."

"Here?"

"Between the South Fork and Mormon Bar."

"No! All that work for nothing." Mal's eyes narrowed, and his forehead furrowed. "Adam, I'll bet I know who robbed you!"

Adam reached out and gripped Mal's arm. "Can you put a name to the man?"

"Do you remember Johann Leinenweber? The Dutchman working the cradle next to us? He agreed to work as my partner, but when he heard you pulled out, he lit out in a hurry. Stole my pistol, too."

"The robber stuck a gun behind my ear, said Adam, "but when he got my poke he let me go. Just vanished in the night."

"Leinenweber may not be your man then. I'd guess he would have shot you, left you for dead."

"Why do you say that, Mal?"

"His other pards on the bar told me. He deserted from Stevenson's regiment, the worst army troop anywhere. Most of them came out of the gutters of New York. They were stationed in San Francisco when gold was discovered."

"That explains it then."

"Explains what, Adam?"

"When I went over to see Danny Fisher, the Dutchman disappeared. I never got a good look at him. He probably watched me all the time. But I'm sure he's the one. He couldn't shoot that night on the trail. Miners were camped only a short distance away. They would have caught him and hanged him. Have you heard where he went?"

"Nary a word. When miners leave the diggins, they go to Sacramento City or San Francisco, don't they? I didn't see him in Sacramento, but then I wasn't looking for him. Come with me, Adam! We'll look for him in San Francisco."

Adam shook his head. "Can't. I gave my word I'd stay here until the owner of the ferry gets back."

"Semple's the name, isn't it? I heard men talk about him in the diggins. A big 'un, they said. Where's he gone to?"

"Monterey. He's helping write a constitution for the state of California."

"But California isn't a state, is it? Is it even a territory, the way Oregon is?"

"They want a written constitution to help Congress make it one. I expected him back before this."

"I'm headed home, but if I can't catch a boat right away I'll help you find Leinenweber." Mal yawned, a great gaping yawn that revealed his fatigue. Adam recalled his own condition when he left the diggins.

"We can't do any more tonight."

When Mal left the next morning, Adam said, "Say hello to Miss Mary Jane for me, Mal. Tell her I'll call on her."

Mal's mouth fell open. "Say, are you sweet on her?"

The sudden rush of blood to Adam's face told more than words. Mal shook his head. "I should have told you. She's my step-mother now. Married the Squire last November."

Adam felt as though Mal had punched him in the stomach. "But – your mother?"

"She took sick with the fever again. Our water wasn't very

good at Lafayette. She died soon after you left. You remember, she took sick on the crossing."

But Adam wasn't thinking of Mrs. Wilson. He recalled Mary Jane's many glances toward Squire Wilson's wagon. Had Mary Jane coveted Amanda Wilson's place in the family even then? Did she have an understanding with the Squire? Was that why, when he talked about Oregon, she folded her hands in her lap and looked away, a smile on her lips? If that was what she wanted, she had it now.

Adam busied himself bending the sails to the mast and boom of the ferry. Mal would not see the sick bitterness on his face. Not if he could help it.

But Mal sensed the impact of his words. He boarded the ferry and studied the opposite shore, not even watching Adam weigh out each man's fare on his scales.

As Mal left the ferry, he shook hands with Adam and seemed in a hurry to get away. A pall had fallen over their parting. Adam tried to keep the pain out of his expression.

"Tell everybody hello for me," he said. Or was it goodbye? Why should he go back to Oregon now?

Then, like everyone else who flowed through Adam's life, Mal Wilson was gone.

Before Mal told him about Johann Leinenweber, Adam had found himself increasingly restive. Now he had a name to put to his assailant, if not a face. Now he wanted to see the angular figure of Robert Semple at the Martinez landing.

Changes in the weather added further to the tension. The wind seldom blew as it did during the summer's heat. On some days he shut down although the sun still hung in the sky. The breeze could move an empty ferry across the strait, but ten passengers loaded the boat down. Deep into the water it settled, responding to the current. Adam had to point ever higher into the wind, and it slowed them down. Each day became a test of both skill and patience, each crossing a trial of his pledge to Robert Semple.

He had earned good money. But the promise of profit no longer drove him. Now he thought only of the thousands in gold he had lost. During long nights he wished fervently that Semple would return home.

One afternoon, as he approached Martinez, a wagon drawn by a team of horses waited on the shore. Adam had seen many Conestoga wagons – prairie schooners – on the trail to Oregon. He had driven one himself. But he never saw a rig like this one. It had a square, boxlike canvas top. Canvas sides were rolled half-way up and tied in place. Adam hoped the owner didn't expect him to take it across. No way could he load it aboard the ferry.

Adam docked the craft and tied up. As he was about to load passengers waiting in line, a man approached him. "Mr. Stuart?"

"Yes?" Adam stared, sure he had seen the man somewhere before.

"My name is Semple. I am Robert Semple's brother."

Adam shook his hand and looked about for his employer. "Where is he? I expected him long ago."

Semple led him to the wagon. Propped up by pillows, covered by blankets although the day was hot, Robert Semple turned sunken, anguished eyes on him.

"My God, sir! What happened?"

"I've come to a bad pass, Adam. My old fever turned on me. If the army in Monterey hadn't loaned me this ambulance, I'd still be there. Can ye take me aboard, lad?"

"Of course, sir. Can you walk?"

"I will, if I can lean on ye."

Adam and Robert Semple's brother half walked, half carried the invalid to the dock. "Give way there," said Adam to the men waiting. "We must put this man aboard."

A man swaggered up and said, "Let him wait his turn, same as the rest of us." The man threw open his coat, revealing a frightening array of guns and knives.

At once his companion grasped him by the arm. "Back off, Paddy. You see plain enough the man is sick."

The defiant one bristled and postured before allowing his mates to pull him back in line. Adam led Robert Semple forward and helped him into the ferry and placed him on blankets and pillows from the ambulance. Robert Semple looked at the several passengers he had displaced and said, "Sorry, gentlemen."

At the Benicia dock they struggled to lift him out of the boat. "Take me to the canvas house," he instructed his brother, "and bring a wagon down in the morning. I'll rest better at my house in town. Adam, would ye cross to get the men I stranded there?"

On that trip, which nearly failed because the wind died, many questions burned in Adam's mind. What had happened to his employer? How long had he been ill? Would he release Adam from his pledge?

That night Adam prepared beef stew and cut chunks of bread into bite-sized pieces. He had to feed Semple, who tried to sit at the table but could not. With tortured eyes Semple watched from his bed.

After supper Semple regarded him with bloodshot eyes. "While I was gone, lad, did ye have an easy time of it?"

"Good and bad," said Adam. "The winds died down, making it hard to cross on some days. I'm itching to be on my way. I learned who robbed me of my gold. I want to look for him in San Francisco."

"Who was it, lad?"

"An army deserter from San Francisco. He worked the same gravel bar I did."

"Ye worked beside him and never knew him?"

"Seems strange now," said Adam. "I never saw him close up, and I never spoke to him. That should have made me suspicious, but I didn't think about it."

Semple shook his head. "These scum. I heard about them in Monterey. One more reason we need a government. Well, lad, I won't keep ye. I can't run the ferry, but there's a man or two who can."

"Why did you hire me then?"

"They can run the ferry. I didn't say they wanted to. What will ye do in San Francisco?"

"I don't know," Adam confessed. "I haven't thought about it."

Semple closed his eyes. Adam thought he had fallen asleep. He waited and then turned the lamp low and tiptoed toward the door. "One thing ye might do," said the gaunt man. "Take the rowboat."

Adam stared at him. "You'd part with it, sir? It's a fine boat. I'd gladly buy it from you."

A tired smile crossed Semple's craggy face. "I reckon ye would, lad, but ye stuck by me. There's men who wouldn't have done that. I'll make ye a present of her."

"You're sure?"

"I am, lad."

"Then I'll accept with thanks, sir!"

"Now, how d'ye propose to recover your gold?"

"Go to the law, I suppose, after I find my man."

Semple frowned. "If there be a constable or sheriff in San Francisco, lad, don't trust him. Most folks pack a gun and a knife. Don't go about the streets alone. Ye'll have gold with ye. How d'ye propose to protect it?"

"Why, uh —" With a sinking feeling in his stomach, Adam saw he had no plan at all. "Are there any banks?"

"None I'd trust, but do what ye think best. One thing more. It costs dear to spend even a week there. How'll ye keep from going flat broke again?"

Adam reddened. "I hadn't thought about it, sir."

"Way I heard it, there's traffic between ships and shore. They're building wharves, but not fast enough to handle the custom. Ye might ferry men back and forth. It'll give ye room to move about and keep your eyes and ears open."

"Thank you for the suggestion, sir. I'll do that."

Robert Semple's eyes closed. Adam spread two blankets over the man's long frame and moved to blow the lamp out.

"The villain I warned ye about. The gambler who was pursuing the Wilmotts. I forget his name."

"Charles Dupre, sir," said Adam. "He's come and gone. I didn't tell him about the Wilmotts."

"Good lad. There's a likely-looking lass. Maybe ye can look after her. I'd hate to see her come to a bad end."

With that Robert Semple turned his face away from the light. Adam doused the lamp and went out to his bed.

CHAPTER 11

By the time he sailed out of Carquines Strait, Adam knew he had gained a fine little sailboat. Unlike the ferry, which slammed through the waves with its human cargo, this boat danced on the water. For an hour he enjoyed sailing for its own sake. He owed a debt of gratitude to Robert Semple. Perhaps keeping the ferry running paid some of that debt. He hoped so. Would he ever see his gaunt benefactor again? Semple did not seem sturdy enough to endure the grind of running the ferry. And certainly he would not see Semple in San Francisco.

From the strait he emerged into San Pablo Bay. Here he encountered patchy fog. To the south and west, a gray pall blotted out all landmarks. Unable to see the Golden Gate, fearing he would capsize in its great waves, he clung to the eastern shore. He recalled his awe when the *Western Star* swept into San Francisco Bay a year ago.

Rounding a low point, he steered south. Now waves struck him broadside, slopping over the side. This must be Pinole Point, which Semple had described. He had expected to enter San Francisco Bay here, but another larger point lay farther to the south. When he rounded it, he ran into dense fog, and the tang of salt grew stronger. He had to be nearing the Golden Gate and San Francisco.

Peering into the fog, he made out the eastern shore of the bay. When the waves subsided he thought he must have sailed past the Golden Gate. He brought the boat up into the wind. It was scary leaving the security the shoreline afforded, but he had to cross the bay.

Almost at once he saw land through a break in the fog. Surely he had not crossed already. He had come to an island. He did not recall seeing one near Yerba Buena Cove when he and Captain Howlett slogged through the mud over a year ago. As he sailed past the island, a forest loomed out of the fog. At once he brought the boat up into the wind. Sails flapping, the tremor running through the hull, he wondered where he was. He did not remember any forests near San Francisco.

He decided quickly. He would retreat to the island, if that was what he found, and wait until the fog lifted. He should have taken time to learn how to read the compass Robert Semple had given him. In his haste to reach San Francisco he put himself at risk.

Running in to the island's southern shore, he dropped the sail and rowed ashore and pulled the boat out of the water. Pitching a small piece of canvas for a tent, he built a fire and hugged its warmth. Roasting a chunk of beef Semple's brother had given him, he eyed the fog that obscured the city. Semple had said fog and cold winds subsided in the fall, but apparently it didn't always hold true.

As he chewed his roasted meat, he pondered what to do. Over a thousand dollars in gold lay in his bedroll. He must find a secure place for it. And he needed a place to stay. Then he could search for Johann Leinenweber. Could he find Mal Wilson, who would know the man? He would find out tomorrow. Replenishing his fire from driftwood on the beach, he watched daylight fade before he turned in.

Habit brought Adam out of sleep while the moon still rode the sky above wispy fog. The air was warm, and a golden haze obscured the hills. A faint odor of smoke drifted on a breeze blowing from the north. Only once before had he known such conditions. The forest was burning somewhere in the north.

By daylight he had coffee to go with bacon and bread. As he ate, the sun rose and spread golden light across the bay. Still chewing his bacon sandwich, Adam walked down to the water and looked to the west. And stopped chewing.

The forest still lay in the haze. But the forest he had seen yesterday was not of trees. Masts rose as if disembodied from ships hidden by the smoke. Masts! Hundreds of them! Robert Semple had mentioned ships anchored in the harbor, but this?

Excited now, he stowed his gear aboard and shoved off. The light wind made sailing easy. The welter of masts suggested a solid line of ships blocking access to San Francisco. Soon he found himself sailing among them. The hills of the peninsula, dim outlines ahead, still seemed distant, but the haze distorted his view. They were probably much closer than he estimated.

As he sailed among the ships, their hulls blocked his view of San Francisco. Most of them seemed completely deserted. On some decks a solitary man, often showing a weapon in full view, watched him sail by. There must be several hundred ships in the harbor. How could that be? Yet he had transported hundreds of men across the Strait of Carquines, sailors among them. If this fleet of ships lay anchored off the town, what wonders lay in the village beneath the sand hills? Or had all the men aboard these ships rushed off to the diggins?

Among the ships the breeze became fitful wafts of warm air. Finding it difficult to steer, he dropped the sail, raised the boom, lashed it to the mast and began rowing.

Many of the vessels were derelicts, their decks deserted, sails hanging partly unfurled, flapping idly in the breeze. They would spend the rest of their days rotting in the harbor.

Adam rowed past one ship that seemed familiar. He passed completely under the stern before her name registered in his mind. The *Western Star!* Often he had wondered. Had she remained after she brought him to San Francisco? What happened to Captain Howlett, her New England skipper? Adam rowed around the schooner. She seemed deserted. But some of her ports hung open and smoke rose from her galley chimney. He rowed in close under her stern.

"Ahoy the ship!" he called.

There was no reply. Adam waited.

"Ahoy the *Western Star*! Anybody aboard?"

No answer. Adam grasped the stern anchor chain. There must be someone aboard. The vessel did not look abandoned.

"Who are you?" came a gruff voice. "Show yourself!"

Adam pushed away from the chain. A bearded man — was it Captain Howlett — peered over the railing. One hand shaded his eyes against the sun's reflection on the water. The other held a pistol. "Whoever you are," the shipboard figure growled, "you'll not take *this* ship!"

"It's me, Captain Howlett. Adam Stuart! I sailed with you from Portland more than a year ago."

The figure on deck leaned forward, peering at him. "By the great horn spoon, it is you, Adam! This cursed land swallowed you up. When I saw you last, you wore butternut. Now you wear miner's garb, but you come in a ship's boat. Which are you, miner or sailor?"

"Neither, sir, although I've been both. May I come aboard?"

"Stand by. I'll drop a ladder". The captain vanished and reappeared to lower a rope ladder over the side. Adam made fast to it and climbed up its wooden steps. Captain Howlett had stepped back from the railing. He stood now, pistol cocked as Adam came over the side. Puzzled, Adam froze. "Don't you recognize me, sir?"

"My eyes are going bad on me, lad. I thought you might be

lulling me to sleep so you could take my ship. You've filled out some."

"No thanks to the mines," said Adam. "I was skinny as a fence rail when I came out. But Mr. Semple fed me when I worked for him at the Benicia ferry."

"I've heard of him," said the captain. "A giant of a man, I hear, and important as well."

"Kind and generous too," said Adam. "He was elected chairman of the convention that just met at Monterey to write a constitution for California. He's in a bad way now, sir. He fell sick with malaria and came home in an ambulance. But why do you greet someone with a cocked pistol?"

Captain Howlett shoved gold-rimmed glasses up on his nose. "Ah, lad, a scurvy rat took one of my ships."

"Do you own more than this one?" asked Adam.

"No, Adam. I act as agent for a dozen vessels lying at anchor here. But come below and have a drink with me. I'm forgetting my manners."

Adam followed Captain Howlett down the familiar companionway to his cabin. Howlett had always run a neat ship. Even though the vessel no longer sailed the ocean, the captain kept her shipshape. Adam glanced around. Nothing was out of place. The captain's bed was made without a wrinkle. Only the table showed use. A coffee mug, a bottle of rum and various papers surrounded a ledger. An open bottle of ink and a pen lay on the table. The captain capped the ink bottle.

He indicated a chair at the table and went to the galley for coffee. He was about to pour a dollop of rum when Adam put his hand over his cup.

"Never acquired a taste for the stuff, eh? Unless I'm wrong you're the only miner who hasn't. Just as well. I acquired the habit from my years before the mast. I was a sight younger than you are now" He poured a generous dollop into his coffee and settled with a sigh into his chair. "Now, what happened to you this past year?"

He listened as Adam described events in his life, ending with, "Do you know a man named Johann Leinenweber sir? I believe he came here after robbing me."

The captain shook his head. "I spend most days aboard this vessel or some other in the harbor. I keep track of ships for their owners. I don't go ashore into that pestilent city unless I must."

"What's the trouble, sir? You met me at the rail with a gun."

"A scoundrel turned a ship under my care into a gambling hell. The *Minerva* was a fine trading vessel until she dropped her hook in this harbor. Now the blackguard who took her wants this one as well. We're almost on the beach here, but you'd not know it. You can't see land today, of course, for the smoke."

"I thought ships couldn't come in close to shore."

Captain Howlett added another dollop of rum to his coffee. Again he offered the bottle to Adam, who shook his head.

"Still not having any? Good lad. Ships can't come to shore, so the shore is coming out to the ships."

Adam drained the last of his coffee, and the captain refilled his cup. "Remember the sand hills that surrounded town? Where the accursed dust and sand blew over everything?"

"Who could forget? While here I always had sand in my eyes."

"They're cutting the hills down and filling in the cove, but first they built some docks. Now the cove will shoal in and make the docks useless. Maybe folks on shore will use their heads, but I doubt it. Well, now, Adam, we've traded our woes. What are your plans? Going home to Oregon?"

"Maybe, but not right away. First I need a place to stay."

"Quarters on shore cost dear if you can find them. Beds rent for so many hours at a time. When the man who slept in it gets up, the bed is rented to the next man. You're welcome aboard here. You may have your old cabin. And you can go ashore when the notion strikes you."

"Thank you, sir. I'll do that. And I must find a bank where my gold will be safe. I lost one fortune. I'll not lose another."

"Ah, Adam, there's the rub. There's no bank I'd trust. We may have one someday."

"How do people obtain loans when they need money?"

"Gamblers lend the money here. Most gold flows through their hands anyway. If you keep quiet about it, your gold will be as safe here as anywhere."

Adam nodded. "I'll do that, sir. I'd like to go ashore now. Would you join me?"

The captain heaved his shoulders with a sigh. "There's enough mischief on the beach without adding an old man's foolishness. I'll hang two lanterns, one above the other. If you return after dark, you can find the right ship."

Adam stepped out on deck, and stopped to stare. A wind off the ocean had blown the smoke away, revealing San Francisco scarcely two hundred yards away. Once a few miserable buildings clustered around Portsmouth Square. Now the city sprawled along Yerba Buena Cove clear to Rincon Point. Houses, some of wood but mostly of canvas, climbed up the hills surrounding the cove. Adam had seen thousands of men stream to the diggins. How could so many people still be here?

He descended to his boat and soon was weaving among lighters loaded with freight and small boats like his ferrying passengers. They clustered about a dock on which wooden buildings stood. On the pier a man said as he tied up, "Dollar to tie up, dollar to cross the dock."

Adam paid him and said, "I'm going into the ferry business. May I use this dock?"

The man grinned. "Bring passengers at a dollar a head, you can tie up and cross free."

"It will be a pleasure doing business with you, sir."

As he stepped on shore, a man confronted him. "Baggage to carry, guv'nor? Two dollars to the Square."

Smiling, shaking his head, Adam stepped around him and surveyed the scene. Workmen with shovels and wheelbarrows loaded material from a sand hill and wheeled it toward a lagoon at the north end of the cove, where two men faced each other.

A red-faced man blocked the way of a wheelbarrow. "You'll not dump that sand, sir! I aim to build a dock here." He rested a hand on a pistol stuck in his waistband.

The other spat perilously close to his shoes. "You own the lots out there?"

"Well, no."

"Then in three days you'll be trespassing on my land. You won't have a waterfront. What good will your dock be?"

Wanting to avoid trouble, Adam hurried past. He paused on the beach. Small boats brought passengers to shore, landing at the high-water mark. As boatmen set luggage on the beach, porters hoisted trunks onto their shoulders and set off toward Portsmouth Square, their owners struggling behind, valises in hand. At the edge of the water two men stood beside a pile of boxes. One, his foot resting on a box, his elbow on his knee, pointed to the boxes and said something. The other nodded and handed over a leather pouch.

The buyer's gang, idling while the dickering went on, carried the boxes from the beach up into town. A man trotted up to the seller, looked around and spoke in a low tone.

"What ship?" barked the merchant, looking about to see if anyone heard. He glared at Adam.

The man pointed toward the hill north of town and spoke again.

"Well, don't just stand there. Get me a boat and round up four or five lighters. Not a word to anyone." Again he looked sharply at Adam and hurried away.

Adam stared at the hilltop. Some kind of contraption rose from its summit. It had arms that moved as he watched.

Movement on the waters of the cove arrested his attention. Men in small boats towed an aged ship in toward the beach. All around her barrels lashed to the hull lifted her high above her water line. Fascinated, Adam moved closer to read her name on the stern. *Niantic*. A hole had been cut in her side for a door. No sooner did the sailors secure her than men erected a plank walkway out to her. Adam turned to a man beside him watching also. "Why are they beaching the ship?"

The fellow said, "To make her into a storeship." He flung an arm out toward the bay. "Some of those ships out there are used as storehouses. There aren't many places to store goods on shore. The *Niantic* was a whaler. They used barrels from her holds to raise her."

Over the noise and confusion on the waterfront came the racket of hammers pounding. The city was growing before his eyes. He turned toward Portsmouth Square when bells rang and gongs startled him. Everyone dropped what he was doing; the hammers fell silent. People scurried here and there. Adam stopped a man outside a building where men streamed up the stairs to the second floor. On the ground floor a place sold produce.

"Say, mister," said Adam, "Why all the bells?"

The man looked him over and grinned. "Just came from the mines, did you? You fellers never ate much, did you? It's time to eat. Don't go upstairs. Grub's all right, but the food at Kong

Sung is better. All you can eat for a dollar. Look for long yellow three-cornered flags down near the water."

"I saw them but didn't know what they meant."

The man waved a hand. "Eat while they're serving it up. You won't get another chance until sundown."

At the yellow silk flags a solemn Chinese took his dollar and dished up a bowl of delicious-smelling food. He did not know what it was and didn't care. He hadn't known he was so hungry. He devoured the contents of his bowl and went back for more. He would remember this place.

On the street again, he looked around. A trail led to the top of the hill north of town. Up there he could gain a view of the city reserved only for birds. He climbed past houses of wood and canvas.

On the treeless summit a cold wind blew in from the ocean. Toward the sea massive bluffs blocked a fog bank except at one point. Ragged patches of mist broke into streams drifting across the bay. This must be the Golden Gate.

At first Adam thought he stood alone on the hill. But he saw the man who had talked to the merchant on the waterfront. The fellow trained a telescope on the Golden Gate. These men had strange ways of doing business. He had to learn how things worked here.

As he watched, the man set down his glass and ran to the tower with the long arms. Tugging on ropes, he moved the arms to a different position. Adam thought it must be some kind of signal. He turned back to the Golden Gate. A ship emerged from the fog under full sail, sailing past a rocky island in the bay. Then it came to him. The man kept watch on the entrance to the bay. When a ship appeared, he moved the arms on the tower to signal its arrival. Thus some men knew before others of a ship's arrival. They could bid first on the cargoes aboard.

His eyes drifted east, over Yerba Buena Cove and the ships beyond. A vessel had joined the others, her sails half furled. She was probably the ship the man had run down the hill to report. What had she brought that filled the businessman with feverish anxiety? No matter. He was having none of it.

Looking over the city, he saw it grow into every low area among the sand hills, reaching up the hill he stood on and the hill next to it. He recalled the pounding of hammers he heard earlier. Demand for housing drove the city's business. With the wet season coming, he saw what men paid for whatever housing they could find.

Seeing anchored ships, he thought again of the old whaling ship brought to shore. If a worn-out ship could store goods, why couldn't a vessel house people? Suddenly he wanted to talk to Captain Howlett.

Descending the hill, he strolled over to Portsmouth Square. The streets and the square did not seem as crowded as before. Then he saw why. Men lined up outside the post office, waiting. The ship's arrival drew who hoped to receive a letter from home. He recalled yearning for letters from Oregon. What a damn fool he had been. She married Squire Wilson. With that biter memory he turned away from the post office.

Moving on, he caught sight of a placard on a tripod outside the Parker House, the most substantial place on the Square. He read it aloud.

"Professor Langford Wilmott, late of Kenyon College in Ohio, reading Shakespeare. Miss Francine Wilmott singing the latest Popular Ballads. Nightly 7:30 p.m. in the Dining Room."

His breath caught and his heart beat faster. The Wilmotts were in the city after all. Would Francie remember him? No doubt a hundred men vied for her attention by now. Would she even glance his way?

A sobering thought troubled him. Surely Charles Dupre was here also. Adam never forgot the gambler's threat. Had Dupre learned how the Wilmotts crossed the Strait of Carquines?

He glanced at the sky. There was some daylight left. What could he do to pass the time until the dinner hour? And then another wait for the Wilmotts' performance? He had no love of drink. He would pour all of the terrible stuff onto the ground, if he could, that passed for whiskey. And the gaming tables offered no allure. On either side of the Parker House were gambling hells. He hated the thought of Francie exposing herself to the stares and comments of loafers outside the Eldorado gambling tent.

Charles Dupre was another matter. He had threatened Adam. Would he even know Adam if they met again? Adam had not seen him on the street. Did Dupre even appear during the day? Most gamblers were night people.

He decided against staying ashore tonight. He had much to think about. The placard said the Wilmotts appeared nightly. Tomorrow would be soon enough to see Francie.

On his way to Long Wharf, a familiar voice arrested him. "Gents, try your luck in San Francisco's newest gaming parlor! Come aboard Four-Eyed Johnny's *Minerva!* Win your fortune. Faro, Keno, Monte, Four-Eyed Johnny's got 'em all!"

Adam drifted along with others toward the voice calling on the beach. Sure enough it was Terence Small, his thin, piping voice rising even higher as the crowd gathered. He pointed to the water's edge, where boats were drawn up beneath blazing lanterns.

"Won't cost you a cent to ride out to Four-Eyed Johnny Webb's fine establishment. First come, first served."

Adam took a roundabout path back to Long Wharf. From the dock he tried to pick the *Western Star* out in the growing dusk.

The man collecting tolls sidled up to him and grinned. "Spent the day lining up custom, did yuh?"

Adam nodded. "Tomorrow I'm in business."

Offshore, he rowed toward the blazing lanterns where Terry Small was loading boats bound for the gambling ship. The *Minerva.* Wasn't that the vessel Captain Howlett lost to a lawless scoundrel? He would have to check. He turned his boat and rowed toward the captain's vessel.

As he pulled away from shore, Adam witnessed a scene he would never forget. Canvas houses and tents marching up the hills glowed orange from lamps and lanterns inside. They created a spectacular light show in the night.

He looked for the two lanterns Captain Howlett promised to set. There they were, inside most of the vessels in the bay. Reaching the ship, he doused the lanterns. Standing at the railing, he looked back toward the city. The houses blended into one giant bubble of color. Marveling at the scene, he went below. Captain Howlett's cabin door was closed.

A whale oil lamp burned in the mate's cabin, where the captain had put his bedroll. Soon he lay, head cradled in his arms, listening for the sounds of the city. Through it all came a bumping as ships anchored close together rubbed against one another. Creakings sounded throughout the *Western Star.* A ship never slept. Apparently neither did San Francisco.

CHAPTER 12

When Adam awoke, he felt himself moving. He looked about. When he heard the grinding and rubbing of the ships, together with the aroma of coffee, he remembered where he was. He dressed and joined Captain Howlett, who stood over the coffee pot in the galley.

"Well, Adam," said the captain, "what did you think of San Francisco?"

"It's a wondrous place, not the sleepy village I saw last year."

"It's the devil's own creation, turning the civilized world on end. Well, we'll have our breakfast. There's not much on hand. I'm getting low on money, I'm afraid."

"Sir, I'll provide food as long as I'm on board. Make a list of what you want."

They breakfasted on bacon, hard ship's biscuits and coffee. There was even a pot of wild strawberry jam the captain said came from the Willamette Valley in Oregon. Over coffee Adam asked, "Captain, have any ships sailed recently for Portland?"

"One sailed last week and one two days ago."

"My brother-in-law came out from the mines. Likely he took passage home. Another question. Do you have any paint aboard? I need a sign advertising my boat for hire."

"In the paint locker. It should still be good."

"Later I'm going ashore. What kind of food do you want?"

"Whatever you see and can afford, and I'm beholden to you."

"Before I paint my sign, sir, how would you like to earn some money?"

The captain glanced sharply at him. "Is it legal?"

"You be the judge of that, sir. Yesterday I saw workmen move an old whaling ship into place on what they called a water lot."

The captain stroked his chin. "The *Niantic*. That's part of the foolishness. Most of the cove has been sold into lots. Maybe the pious gentlemen on shore can walk on water. Most of us can't. Do you want us to get mixed up in something like that?"

"Yes, sir. Why not move a ship or two under your care? Do you have any ships too old to return to sea? Preferably large vessels?"

"Do you mean to stay here in San Francisco, lad?"

"There is nothing for me in Oregon."

The captain looked about his cabin. "You have a choice, Adam, whether to leave or stay. I don't. I can't hire a crew. What do you propose?"

"People are seeking places to live. I saw the *Niantic* brought in to store goods. Why not store people overnight in ships? Make them into hotels. Put them on water lots. Ferry people from ship to shore, or build a dock out to them."

Captain Howlett frowned, absently pouring coffee and a dollop of rum. "It might work. Some of us live aboard ships now."

"Would it be legal?"

The captain scratched his chin. "I don't see why not. I'm not a sea lawyer, but I know this. A vessel abandoned may be claimed as salvage and put to use. It's the law of the sea. The rogue who grabbed my *Minerva* said she was abandoned and claimed salvage rights. But I'm the ship's legal agent, and I say she wasn't abandoned."

"Can't you sue for your rights?"

Howlett snorted. "If we even have a court of law it is probably corrupt. We have an alcalde appointed by the military commander. He's a mayor and justice of the peace rolled into one. But might makes right in San Francisco, and this scum has his toughs aboard my ship."

"How did it happen?"

"He just moved aboard one day. When I went out to inspect the *Minerva*, they were cutting a hole in her side for a door. By the great horn spoon! A door in a ship's side! When I objected, the scoundrel laughed in my face."

"It seems half the ships here were abandoned. Why he picked the one he did. . . ."

"She was more ship-shape than most. Now and then I hire a couple of sailors to see if anything is amiss and to set it right."

"I see. Now, sir, if you'd show me the paint locker, I have a sign to prepare."

Adam spent the next hour making a neat sign, black on canvas, advertising his boat for hire. He had to earn money, and quickly, simply to stay even.

The captain declined to go ashore with him, calling the city an abomination. Adam shrugged. Events had passed the captain by. A virtual hermit, sight of the feverish growth on shore soured him.

Adam's sign stretched between poles fastened to the gunwales of his boat. He rowed to the Long Wharf, where a man hailed him.

"Hey, there! Your boat for hire?" The man waved from the dock, a canvas bag at his feet.

"Yes, sir!" Adam guided his boat to the foot of a ladder.

"My ship sails in two hours. Can you take out to her?"

"Yes, *sir!*"

Seated in the stern, his passenger glared at the city he was departing. "God has put His curse on this place," he said. "I can't wait to return home."

Adam, propelling the boat from the dock, said nothing.

"Can you imagine?" the man continued. "We're passing over a lot I own. What possessed the authorities to sell city lots in the bay? Even more, what made me to buy one?"

"You own a water lot? Are you going to abandon it?"

"I don't have time to sell it. I just learned this morning the ship was sailing for New York."

Adam stopped rowing. "I'll take it off your hands for two hundred in gold."

"Coin or dust?"

"Your pleasure, sir."

"Sold. Make it coin."

"I'll have to row to my ship to get it," said Adam. "It'll take only ten minutes more."

Captain Howlett came on deck as Adam scrambled aboard the *Western Star.* "Back already? You didn't spend much time ashore."

Adam grinned. "I haven't stepped on shore, but I just became part of San Francisco's madness. I bought a water lot from the gent in my boat. Decide which ship you want to move." He vanished below, counted out two hundred in gold eagles and scurried topside.

Later he went ashore to purchase food, which he dumped in two sacks in the galley.

"The madness must agree with you," said the captain.

"It does, sir," grinned Adam. "I'm going ashore later. I may want to borrow or buy some casks to float the ship in. Will you live aboard the hotel and manage it?"

The captain looked about. "I'd hate to abandon my lady."

"Tow her over and tie them together. Let's go look for a ship."

For the first time since Adam stepped aboard the brig, the captain smiled. He had stumped the deck with a heavy tread, his lower lip thrust out whenever Adam mentioned San Francisco. Now he descended the ladder lightly and stepped into the boat. "By the great horn spoon," he rumbled, "it feels good to be out and about again."

They rowed among the ships, Captain Howlett pointing the way. As they rowed past one trim vessel, he scowled. "Here's the lady they took over, the *Minerva*. If I had a few bully-boys, I'd throw Four-Eyed Johnny overboard and hold his head under water."

"Four-Eyed Johnny, did you say?"

The captain stared at him in surprise. "Do you know him?"

"Only by name. A man I knew scouts for gamblers for him. I heard him touting Four-Eyed Johnny's place. So this is the vessel. Where's the ship you want to move?"

"Nearly out to Yerba Buena Island," said Captain Howlett. "That's probably why nobody has his eye on her."

They came to a vessel anchored away from other ships. There it did not rub against other hulks. Her masts, spars and rigging seemed intact, unlike many ships abandoned in the bay. Captain Howlett had taken seriously his stewardship of the vessels he represented.

"Row around her and we'll take a look," said Howlett. "Her owner, also her master, and I were shipmates aboard a whaler when we were lads. He died about four months ago. I'd like to see his widow in Essex make a profit from her. Maybe she will yet by renting her as a hotel. If there is any profit."

"After we look," said Adam, "we'll go back to the *Western Star*. When I locate the water lot, we'll scare up a crew to move her. Hotels on shore divide their rooms with canvas, lumber being scarce and costly. We could do the same. Then we won't need to cut her up in case the widow wants to send her back to sea."

"Ah, lad, it's good to hear you say that. My heart broke when I saw them gut the Minerva. But if she sits in the mud," said Captain Howlett somberly, "she'll never go to sea again."

"I'll locate the lot. Then I'm going ashore tonight to see friends."

Nearing Long Wharf, Adam noticed the ease with which a young dark-skinned man handled his boat. He rowed alongside, struggling to keep up, and said, "You want work? Earn gold?"

His passenger snarled, "He's under hire. After he takes me out to my ship, hire him all you want, but until then lay off!"

Ignoring the fellow, Adam called, "I'll wait here."

The other boatman grinned and nodded. With powerful strokes he swept his boat away from shore. In less than ten minutes he returned. "You got job for me, Cap'n?"

"Where did you come from? You handle your boat well. "

"I am *Kanaka*. Sandwich Islands. You savvy Honolulu?"

Adam nodded, although he had never heard of the place. "I need a crew to tow a ship in to the beach."

"Sure, Cap'n. How many boys you want? Five, ten, twenty?"

"Nine besides yourself. Twenty dollars gold per man for one day. An extra five for you if you bring ten men here tomorrow."

The boatman nodded and smiled. "Can do."

"And ten dollars gold if you will help me mark a water lot now."

The man nodded and flashed white teeth again. "Work hard, you bet, Cap'n."

Adam purchased a hundred-foot length of rope and found a couple of willow poles someone had discarded. He tied the rope to the *Kanaka's* boat and directed him out from shore. When he reached the proper place, Adam told him to push the poles into the mud. Thus he located not only the lot but learned how much water covered it. That done, he shoved off the beach with his boat and rowed across the cove to Long Wharf. The toll collector was there again, this time less than cordial.

"Where's the business you was bringin' across the dock?" he demanded. "Two dollars to tie up, one dollar to cross."

Adam grinned and paid, saying ruefully, "I've been busy. Maybe I'll get started soon."

As evening shadows settled over the bay, the bells and gongs sounded again. Once more Adam ate supper at the Kong Sung Restaurant. Then, waiting for the Wilmotts' performance, he edged into the hot and crowded Eldorado gambling tent that reeked of cigar smoke, sweat and raw whiskey.

For a few minutes he watched gamblers, eyes hot with the fever of the game, throw their money away. Recalling how hard, how painful had been his own quest for gold, he could scarcely believe his eyes and ears. Wildly they threw down their pokes and called for the dice.

One man lurched back from a table. "Well, I'm a son of a bitch! Busted again!" In his haste to leave, he pushed Adam into the coolness of the street. "Sorry, friend, I just had to get some air."

"Too bad you're broke," said Adam. "What now?"

"I'll tell you what my father would have me do. Sail home to Baltimore and ship out to the Chinchas. Islands off Peru where they dig bird guano. That's bird shit if you don't know.

He sells it as fertilizer to tobacco farmers whose lands give out. But I'll be damned if I'll sail on his stinking ships. Look, friend, I own a lot in the cove out there. I gave five hundred for it. Would you buy it?"

Adam scratched his head. "All I've got is two hundred."

"Sold! That'll give me a stake."

The gambler signed over the deed and took his ten double eagles. To Adam's amazement he turned on his heel and forced his way back into the Eldorado. While Adam watched, shaking his head, the gambler rolled the dice until he was busted again.

He rushed out of the gambling hell and grabbed Adam's arm. "Got any more gold for a stake? I know I can bust that dice game."

Adam backed off. "Sorry," he said. When the gambler wanted a stake, Adam thought he meant to return to the mines. He had no idea the fellow would blow it on the dice.

The man's face fell. "Well, I'll head back to the Yuba. I'll scratch for gold before I'll haul bird shit halfway around the world."

He lurched through the door and vanished in the crowd pressing by.

Adam's eye following him fell on a line gathering outside the Parker House. So this was how the Wilmotts fared. Not to be denied admission, he elbowed his way into the street and stepped into the line. He paid a giant who stood at the door allowing one man at a time past. He found room at a table near the back. In no time the hall filled behind him until men stood against the wall.

A stage had been set off by footlights: metal canisters each containing a candle. A piano and a door in the back wall, no doubt leading to the kitchen, graced the stage.

Accustomed to the clean air over the water, Adam found

his senses reeling from the sweat, tobacco smoke and sharp tang of raw whiskey being consumed all about him. For a time his stomach struggled to maintain its equilibrium. However, when he thought he would bolt outside to better air, a man emerged from the stage door to light the candles. Adam willed his control to return.

The stage flowed with golden candlelight. There came three sharp raps on the wall behind the stage. The clamor in the house fell silent, and the crowd leaned forward.

The door opened, and a figure stepped into the light. Adam recognized Professor Wilmott at once by his flowing black cape and wide-brimmed black hat. Yet it was not the same. A giant white feather graced his hat. Wilmott's face remained in shadow a moment as he struck a pose, arm lifted to shade his face.

He swept his hat off his head. His face loomed orange with a blush from the candles. His hair had been altered. Before, it was black streaked with gray, but now it was blonde. In the candlelight his eyes glittered. He looked curiously younger yet world-weary.

Wilmott presented his profile to the audience and looked toward heaven. When he spoke, his voice rang with a fervor that transported Adam into a world charged with emotion he had never known before.

"To be or not to be!" Wilmott intoned, "that is the question: whether 'tis nobler in the mind to suffer the slings and arrows of outrageous fortune, or to take arms against a sea of troubles, and by opposing end them."

For the next half hour Adam lost himself in the professor's portrayal of Prince Hamlet. When the monologue ended, he marveled that Wilmott could learn the words and express the feelings of someone else, no, to become someone else for a few minutes. He had never seen or heard anything like it. He could scarcely reconcile this commanding stage presence with the tired, defeated little figure huddled in the bow of his rowboat. As Wilmott's program came to an end, the audience which had strained forward to hear and to feel, now drew back.

For a moment there was silence in the hall. Then somebody began to applaud. It seemed as though a dam holding emotions back burst suddenly, for the audience applauded, stomped and cheered. Langford Wilmott again swept his hat from his head, bowed, hailed the audience with an upraised fist and retreated through the door.

At once talking and shouting broke out among the audience. One man shouted, with a sentiment Adam wished he had said, "By George, boys, don't the perfesser take you outta yerself for a while?"

A man shouldered his way to the door, saying, "He does that right enough, but excuse me, lads, I gotta pee."

For Adam the evening had just begun. He had come to gaze once more on Francie Wilmott. He would not budge until her performance ended.

A sudden hush fell over the hall. The door had opened and a tall, skinny man wearing a red calico shirt with sleeve garters and a bowler hat came onto the stage. He sat at the piano, faced it for a moment, adjusted the garters to free the cuffs from his wrists, drew a deep breath and launched into an energetic rendition of "Oh Susanna."

The audience stamped and whistled and clapped their hands and otherwise showed their appreciation. Energized, the player banged even harder on the piano as he swept through the song again.

But the piano faded and the clamor subsided. Francine Wilmott had slipped on stage and stood, looking small and fragile, her hands clasped before her. Her dark eyes gleamed in the candlelight.

The piano player looked at her, nodded, and went through "Oh Susanna" one more time. Francie caught the beat and sang the words in a clear soprano. The audience joined in keeping time, swaying, snapping fingers or tapping feet, but not a man's voice was raised. No one wanted to miss a note of her young voice.

From the lively opening she moved to the pensive, with Thomas Moore's "'Tis the Last Rose of Summer" and "Believe Me If All Those Endearing Young Charms." She moved on to the tragic as she sang "Barbara Allen." Her finale, "Home Sweet Home," she poured out with every vibrant note of her young voice. Not a sound came from the audience, although men unashamedly wiped tears from their eyes.

As her last notes fell across the audience, her eyes met Adam's. Her eyebrows raised in surprise, and her face broke out into a rosy smile. She nodded to the piano player, who struck up "Home Sweet Home" once more. She sang openly to Adam, so openly that heads turned his way. Eyes filled with wonder and envy searched his face, so that a warm crimson flood crept up his throat. But his heart was pounding. Nothing could have made him happier.

Abruptly Francie looked away, alarm in her eyes. Puzzled, Adam followed her gaze. A chill settled into his gut. He faced the stare of Charles Dupre, who stood along the wall. Adam had wondered whether Dupre would even remember him. But there was no doubt. The gambler bent on him an expression of pure malice. Adam didn't want to lock into a test of wills, so he looked away.

When he glanced back at Dupre, the man was gone. But a commotion behind him turned his head. Dupre stood not six feet away, fury distorting his handsome face.

"You lied to me!" gritted the gambler. "You denied that you had seen the Wilmotts at Benicia."

Adam replied, with a calmness he did not feel, "I said they did not cross on the ferry."

"I know. . . ."

"Quiet, man!" hissed a miner. "The lady is singing."

Dupre ran a cold eye over the men around him. He found equally cold anger directed at him. He glared once more at Adam. "Another time," he promised, and was gone.

Francie finished her song and started forward in a shower of coins, pokes containing gold dust and what Adam recognized as a fifty-dollar gold slug. Smiling, she stepped across the footlights. Puzzled but delighted as she came among them , men made way for her.

Professor Wilmott emerged from backstage with two assistants, who scooped up the gold strewn on the stage and dumped it into a basket Wilmott held. The professor frowned as he saw Francie among the audience.

Adam got to his feet as she came to him, her hands outstretched. He took them in his, thrilling to her warmth.

"For weeks I've watched for you." There was a sudden outburst of applause. She blushed to the roots of her hair.

"I wanted to come sooner, but I promised. . . ."

"I understand," she said. "Loyalty is rare in this dog-eat-dog place. But you're here. Did Charles Dupre threaten you at Benicia?"

"Not in so many words." He didn't want to alarm her.

"Francine!" His collection task completed, Professor Wilmott stood on the stage. "We must vacate the kitchen."

She nodded and turned to Adam. "Wait here. We won't be long."

Adam sat at the table as the dining room emptied. Finally the beefy giant who had taken admission at the door confronted him. "Everybody out," he ordered. "That includes you."

Almost as if Francie heard him from the kitchen, she stuck her head out the door and said, "I asked him to stay, Frank," and vanished.

"You're a mighty lucky fella," said the guard. "Ain't but one other fella has waited for her. A slick type. Gambler."

"Did Francie leave with him?"

"Not on your life. One look at him and she clung to her pa. She didn't want nothing to do with the gent and would I please see him to the door. When he refused, I hustled him out the door, one hand on his coat collar and the other on the seat of his pants. He screeched at me. Told me to keep my hands off his person. Said those very words."

Adam felt relief. For weeks he had wondered. The professor wanted desperately to keep Dupre away. But how did Francie feel?

"Dupre carries a small gun in his sleeve," Adam warned.

Grinning, Frank shook a pistol down from his own sleeve. "Don't you think I know it?"

Professor Wilmott emerged from the kitchen and approached Adam directly. Stiffly he asked, "Just what is your interest in my daughter?"

"Why," said Adam, "she's a delightful young lady, and I'm just happy to see her again. You remember me, don't you, sir? Adam Stuart. The crossing at Benicia?"

The professor peered into his face. "Of course. Stupid of me not to notice." He sagged and offered a limp hand. "Charles Dupre worries me. We must stay in a canvas house, which makes us feel insecure. We, Frank and I, can't watch her every minute."

Francie emerged from the kitchen with a small satchel. Adam took it from her hand. "Are we ready?" she asked. "I'm starved. I didn't have supper tonight. Shall we go to Delmonico's, Papa?"

Wilmott shook his head. "I'm tired tonight. You go ahead. You'll see her home, young man? Immediately after dinner?"

"Yes, sir."

Fog blurred the streets as they made their way to the restaurant. When the waiter presented a card with the day's menu, Adam managed to stifle a gasp. The prices! He could eat half a dozen meals at the Kong Sung for what one cost here."

"Shall we order a big supper?" she asked. "To celebrate your arrival?"

He smiled ruefully. "I don't think I could manage it."

She reached across the table and put her hand over his. "I don't mean for you to buy my supper. We earn a good deal of money."

"It's not that." He recalled her forward manner during the crossing. There was nothing shy about this girl. Yet he liked her style. "I ate a full supper shortly before your performance. I'll have pie and coffee, but you go ahead."

While they waited, Adam told her what he was doing in San Francisco. "I even bought a lot from a man just before your show," he finished. He thought it best to omit the circumstances of the deal.

"You're already caught up in commerce? It's crazy, isn't it, all these frantic happenings every day?" A smile of pure delight lighted up her face. "It's the most exciting place in the world. I love it!"

Adam wasn't so sure he felt the same. She loved being here, doing what she was doing. Why shouldn't she? Francie Wilmott was the darling of all the lonely men like himself. It would turn any girl's head.

When their food arrived, for a time they were absorbed in that. Francie wasn't a bashful eater. She didn't pick daintily at her food as he remembered Mary Jane Carr doing, even at the campfire. Why did Mary Jane come into his mind? Yet Adam knew why. He compared them and Mary Jane Carr came out a pale second.

Adam was under no illusions. Francie Wilmott had shown delight at seeing him again. Did it go deeper than that? Whatever, he would delight in any attention she gave him.

The waiter brought them more coffee. Adam relaxed, but Francie grew tense. She frowned. "Adam, I worry about Charles Dupre. He means you harm."

He wanted to say the obvious: that it was because he, not Dupre, was sitting here with her. But it would sound egotistical. Instead, he told her about Dupre's behavior at the Benicia ferry. "It's his gambler's nature," he suggested. "He was bested by a greenhorn, and he didn't like it."

"Be careful. He has a terrible temper. He challenged a man to a duel at Bidwell's Bar. He would have killed him had the man stayed to fight. I didn't know it when I met him. I was so foolish there. I'd never met anyone like him. I thought him terribly romantic and attractive. Now I know better."

"Are you afraid of him?"

"Papa and I both are. We don't like living in a canvas house." Her eyes widened. "You aren't going to face Dupre, are you?"

Adam smiled. "Hardly. I don't carry a gun."

"Most people here do. People came from all over the world. They don't understand and trust each other. So many bad things happen, especially at night."

"I'll be too busy to worry about Dupre. I'm going to move a ship onto my water lot. And I'm going to squire you around town every chance I get."

A smile lighted her face. "You aren't very bashful, are you?"

"Francie," he said, "I'm a simple Indiana farm boy. But the excitement here is catching. I promise you, I'll be the perfect gentleman when I'm with you."

"Oh, don't go that far," she laughed as she rose. "We must go. Papa will be anxious. He doesn't know you like I do."

Out on California Street the fog had thickened. Flares burning outside gambling tents cast flickering light through the murk. Adam's eyes moved constantly, searching shadows for danger even as he enjoyed the pressure of Francie's hand clinging to his arm. Glancing back, he saw a massive shadow keeping pace with them.

"Quick!" he whispered, pulling her against the wall of a store. "We're being followed."

Francie looked back. "It's only Frank. Papa has him follow me everywhere. It's only a little way to my house, if you call a tent a house."

They came to a canvas house which glowed from a light within. At the door Francie turned and faced him. He wanted to kiss her, but the hulk standing there daunted him. She must have sensed his indecision, for she reached on tiptoe and brushed his cheek with her lips.

"I'm glad you've come," she said softly. "I was afraid you wouldn't." Giving him no chance to reply, she said, in a louder voice, "Frank, go with Adam wherever he goes."

"That'll be Long Wharf. Good night, Francie."

He set off into the night, the giant by his side. Except for one thing his day had gone better than he expected. He would have to deal with Charles Dupre. But even that prospect paled before the glow Francie Wilmott brought into his life.

CHAPTER 13

Through patches of fog Adam pulled on his oars, leading the boats towing the *Trader* from its anchorage. The boats were manned by brown-skinned *Kanakas* led by Hoku, the Sandwich Islander from the Island of Owyhee.

So far their tow had gone well. They took the ship under tow while fog lay over the harbor. Under the captain's critical eye, they raised the anchors using the ship's capstan. Two men held the vessel against the tide until the anchors cleared water. Captain Howlett lashed the ship's wheel and stood at the fiddle-head where he could see out. At the first sign of trouble he could knock out the pins holding the anchors in suspension.

But nothing went wrong. The boats pulled the tow toward shore, where tides would be weaker. Around Brown's Point and then North Point the *Trader* moved easily on the ebb. Adam glanced often over his shoulder at the Golden Gate looming ever closer.

When it seemed Captain Howlett must drop anchor, the flood tide began to pour into the bay. They felt its surge even though the captain said the ebb still ran seaward farther from shore.

They turned the ship and started back toward North Point. They wanted to reach the cove at high water. Then they could ease her into place. Would the *Trader* draw more water than they had over the lot? Whale oil barrels would float the ship higher in the water.

The tow was going well. Adam cast loose and lay into the

oars. He wanted to check again where the ship would finally rest. The markers were in place last evening, but he wanted to make sure of them.

He reached his water lot. Satisfied the poles still marked the lot, he started back to the ship. but a man on shore hailed him. "Hello the boat! I want to talk to you!"

Adam turned back and approached the beach.

"Are you moving that ship out there onto the lot you staked?"

Adam frowned. "We are. Any problem with that?"

"No, no! Want to buy the lot next to it? The next one out?"

"Is it for sale?"

"Here's the thing. The man who sold me the lot said the cove would be filled in by now. But you can see it isn't. I can't wait. I need a stake to go back to the mines. It cost me five hundred. I'll sell for half that."

"Two hundred fifty?"

Adam couldn't believe his good fortune. He doubted the *Trader* would ease onto the shallower lot. This solved a huge problem. Besides, they could move the *Western Star* also, if Captain Howlett were willing. But caution made Adam say, "I heard these lots were selling for seven thousand."

The man snorted. "If I'll take somebody's worthless promise to pay, I can sell for that. I need hard money now."

One cloud lay on the horizon. All morning the captain had seemed distant, almost angry. Would he back out? More than once he had made acid comments about tom-fool events happening on the beach. Division of Yerba Buena Cove into water lots seemed uppermost in his mind.

"Well," said the man, "do you want to buy or not?"

"Can you wait while I get your gold?"

"Sure thing."

The *Trader* rounded Clark's Point and stood in toward the cove. If Adam hurried, he could obtain the lot. He laid his back into the oars, and soon returned with the gold. He still marveled at good luck, but it worried him too. Now he had three properties but no money coming in. He couldn't keep buying; his gold was shrinking rapidly.

"Hope you can wait," said the man as he signed over the deed. "I couldn't."

"Hope so too."

As Adam turned his boat to return to the ship, he saw Terry Small standing on the beach, hands on hips, watching. What was all this to Terry, he wanted to know? But he let it pass.

Quickly he rowed to the ship just off Clark's dock. He ran in under her bow. "Captain! Captain Howlett!"

The gray-haired captain peered over the side. "So there you be. Where'd you run off to? I couldn't tell the *Kanaka* lads where the ship is supposed to go!"

"Ship won't fit onto the lot I staked out. Water's too shallow."

The captain stared at him and then Yerba Buena Cove head ahead. He rolled his eyes heavenward and shoved his cap back to scratch his head. "Then kindly tell me what in tarnation we will do with her!"

Adam laughed. "We'll put her on the next lot out. I just bought it from a gent. The water's deeper."

"By the great horn spoon, Adam, if you aren't a wonder! How does all this good fortune fall your way?"

Adam wanted to suggest moving the brig as well but thought it best to wait. The captain needed to accept the *Trader's* ending her days on the mudflats of San Francisco Bay.

Adam did not rejoin the tow. Instead he watched Hoku direct his crew in turning the ship and nudging it into place. Captain Howlett let the anchors go with a finality Adam felt also.

With satisfaction Adam noted one thing. He insisted the vessel's bow point north, as if she could slip her moorings and sail out to sea. Maybe the captain would accept the move better.

Adam tied his boat to the ship's ladder and climbed aboard. Hoku grinned, but Captain Howlett's brows squinched down over his eyes, as if he personally felt the ship's humiliation.

"How my boys do?" asked Hoku. "Maybe you got more work?"

The captain paid the *Kanakas*. Pointing up at the rigging, he asked Hoku, "Can you take down masts and spars?"

The others were going over the side, but Hoku called them back. He raced across the deck and sprang into the shrouds. Nimbly he scampered up to the first yard and back down. "All same climb coconut tree. You want masts down?"

Adam didn't risk a glance at Captain Howlett. This could be the final blow. He pointed across the cove to the *Niantic*, where a walkway already extended out to her. "The ship will stay here like that one. We must take down all masts and rigging."

Hoku spoke to his fellow islanders. They nodded and laughed, all talking at once. Hoku listened and turned to Adam. "Can do, Cap'n. Three *Kanakas* sail on ship for years. They know how. We help."

Adam hesitated, wondering whether he should commit his remaining gold to the task.

"Go ahead, lad, while we have the chance."

Surprised, Adam turned to the captain. Gone was the pained look. Captain Howlett had accepted the move. "I'm not sure I have enough — resources, sir."

"It's time I paid for something."

"But I thought. . . ."

"What I wanted you to think." To the islanders he said, "In two days we'll take the rigging down."

Happy with the promise of more work, the men from Owyhee tumbled over the side into their boats.

Captain Howlett smiled. "You thought me a pauper with no food aboard my ship? Adam, I protected my savings by acting poor. Can't be too careful. You were a fine lad a year ago but time changes people. But I'm pleased to have you as a partner."

"Well, sir, you're ahead of me. I want to suggest one more move."

"Go ahead, Adam, but I've already decided."

"Decided what, sir?"

"To move the *Western Star* next door, if you have no plans for the lot. A proper landlord I must live close by. You didn't think I had it in me to change We're done with the sea, the ships and I. We need too much overhauling."

Adam gazed at the captain, his eyes wide in wonder. "You're full of surprises, sir."

"I learned from you, Adam."

"From me?"

"You didn't hesitate when opportunity fell your way, did you? You bought these lots under water. I thought you were foolish, but it's working out. If you want something bad enough, go after it."

The captain was talking about business opportunity, but Adam's mind ran along a different channel. The vision of a lovely dark-haired girl rose before his eyes. He wanted Francie Wilmott. "I'll remember that, sir."

They returned to the *Western Star,* where Adam scrubbed the quarters he would offer Francie and her father. He hoped they would accept. But like him they were from the heartland, unused to salt water. Probably they knew nothing about the ships in the harbor.

Before sundown he went ashore, moored his boat at Long Wharf and paid the now-sour attendant. Adam didn't feel bad about it. When he first arrived, he had intended to ferry passengers. But other ventures required his energy.

Adam ate again at the Chinese restaurant. As he ate, he studied the throngs passing by on the street. Every day the city's population swelled. Two more ships arrived, and the *Senator* brought people down from Sacramento City. With a walkway out to the *Trader* they could rent every room. And they could convert the sails into canvas roofs on deck for even more space. One problem remained how to provide heat. A galley below deck gave out little warmth. They would cut up the masts and spars for fuel.

As he ate dinner darkness fell. Flaring torches outside gambling hells threw flickering light into streets churned into mud by the endless tide of people. Adam could only contrast the peace on the water with this madness on shore.

He waited for the Wilmotts' show. The big man, Frank, threw the dining room door open and collected admission. Near the front of the line, Adam paid and found a place near the footlights.

A man came onto the stage to light the candles. Shortly, yells, whistles and stomps greeted the professor as he stepped on stage.

Adam enjoyed the professor's portrayal of Lear, the mad king. For half an hour he was transported to the wild moors of England, involved in Lear's dilemma. Caught up in the words and posturings of the professor, the audience hung on every speech. Shouts of approval ushered the professor off the stage.

Again the door in the back wall opened and the piano

player pushed his upright piano out. The audience fell silent. The accompanist ran through a few finger exercises and then waited, hands folded.

When Francie stepped onto the stage, smiling and blowing kisses, the audience stood and shouted and stomped. If anything, the noise greeting her was louder than before. Adam's heart flip-flopped at sight of her in a bright blue gown. She bowed her head, her hands clasped together, and looked at the piano player.

Once more he swung into "O Susanna," her opening number. The audience clapped and swayed in time to the music. Francie's lusty songs gave way to romantic ballads, and the crowd fell silent. If they had heard them before, they gave no sign. They thought of other times, other places. Adam saw Francie as a musician playing the audience as she would a vast musical instrument.

Midway through her performance her eyes met his, and a smile came into her voice. But she glanced to her left, and a tiny frown gathered between her brows. As surely as if she had stopped to say it, she warned him. Charles Dupre was in the audience.

Francie sang the same songs and the audience reacted in the same way. Again tears flowed unashamed. Adam marveled that the audience seemed not to tire of her. Adam recognized faces in the crowd, but they lost no enthusiasm.

When she closed she came to the footlights. In a low voice she said, "He's here, Adam."

He shrugged. "I can't help it, I guess." But he fingered the pistol Robert Semple gave him in Benicia. He knew Dupre carried a gun up his sleeve. He also knew men killed in San Francisco streets and gambling hells, often with little fear of reprisal.

"Did you see Papa's performance?" she asked.

"It was great! He moved me out of myself into another world. Francie, would you and your father have supper with me? I have an offer that may interest you."

"We'd be pleased," she said. "We were going to eat anyway. Wait here."

When they both returned, Professor Wilmott smiled and extended his hand. "Francie says you enjoyed my portrayal of Lear."

"You were great, sir. You should have become an actor."

"If we remain here, it will come to that. Actors aren't always held in the highest esteem. But we'll see no college here for a long time, if ever. Men here pursue low interests; they are driven by greed and pleasure."

They set off with the giant bodyguard in tow. Adam felt awkward thinking of Frank as a servant. Yet the giant accepted his place. The professor chose Delmonico's, insisting that Adam be his guest. When they were seated inside. Frank stood outside watching the street. The security he offered must cost the Wilmotts dearly, but they seemed to think it vital.

They dined on lobster salad followed by salmon and oysters. Francie enjoyed the latter, but he disliked them. Francie and her father also shared a bottle of wine, which he declined. Again Adam noted that while she displayed excellent table manners, far better than his, she was a hearty diner.

Professor Wilmott finally pushed his chair back. "Francie says you have a proposal for us. I trust it doesn't require the outlay of money." He eyed Adam sternly but his lips curved into a smile as he added, "Of which I have next to none."

"No more than daily expenses now, sir."

He told them of the *Trader* settled in the cove, and of their plans to move the *Western Star* alongside. Francie leaned forward, elbows on the table despite her father's frown. It brought her face near Adam's. He almost forgot what he had to say.

"Your plan shows remarkable wisdom," said the professor. "This was Captain Howlett's scheme, I trust."

Adam hesitated. "At first it was mine, sir, but it became ours together."

"I see. But what has this to do with us?"

With barely a glance at Francie, Adam said, "You live in a canvas house. Most of them have no floors, I hear. In the rainy season they will be cheerless. Captain Howlett offers his cabin for the rent you now pay. It provides security, sir, and far more room. And a tight roof over your heads."

Francie sat up, laughed and clapped her hands. "I always wanted to take a sea voyage, Papa. Now we can without having to go to sea!"

"You approve, Francie?"

"Oh, yes, Papa. It would be exciting."

"I see one advantage," Wilmott said. "Every day I must rehearse my lines. With the infernal pounding of hammers I scarcely hear myself sometimes. Perhaps the ship would give me time to reflect. But how would we reach shore and return to our quarters each night?"

"I'll take you, sir. Soon we'll move the vessel to shore. We will build a dock. And men are filling in the cove."

"Won't you lose your anchorage then?" asked the professor.

"No, sir. I own two water lots where the ship is located."

The professor's eyes widened. "You just arrived here and already you own property? Real estate? Remarkable!"

"What do you say, sir? Will you accept his offer?"

Wilmott smiled. "Gladly. I dreaded huddling under dripping canvas all winter. When can we move?"

"Tomorrow? One o'clock at Long Wharf?"

"Excellent!" said Wilmott.

All the while Adam was painfully aware of Francie, whose eyes never left his face. But he kept his gaze on the professor. He didn't want Wilmott to put him in the same class as Charles Dupre.

Francie put a hand on Adam's arm. "Do you live there too?"

"Why — uh, yes. The captain will occupy my quarters. I will move to the forecastle. The captain calls it fo'c'sle, where the crew lived when the ship was at sea."

"Then I'll see you every day."

Adam darted a glance at her father. His heart sank. Professor Wilmott stared at Francie as if he were seeing her for the first time. But the professor said nothing.

"Maybe," said Adam. "I'll go ashore most of each day."

"But you'll take us to the Parker House, won't you?"

"If you want me to. If I can't, Hoku will take you."

"I'd rather you did."

Adam felt an acute need to get away. He rose. "Thank you, sir, for the excellent dinner. We'll have a boat for you at Long Wharf at one o'clock." He offered his hand to the professor and to Francie in turn. "I enjoyed your performances. Good night."

As he walked past Frank, he glanced up at the man. Frank's face, while friendly enough, was empty of emotion. Quickly he walked to Long Wharf, looking right and left and over his shoulder. Charles Dupre might be anywhere. Likely he was working at his trade. Still, if Francie thought it urgent to warn him, he would stay alert.

Adam's heart sang. When he shook hands with her, she looked into his eyes as she squeezed his hand. He recalled Howlett's advice to follow his dreams. He vowed he would, but slowly. Professor Wilmott seemed even more fearful for his daughter. Adam didn't want to become feared and hated as well.

Early the next morning Adam rowed Captain Howlett to the *Trader* at low tide. The ship looked forlorn, much of her bottom showing. But the captain seemed not to notice. He was about to step onto the ladder when a face appeared over the rail and a pistol pointed at him.

"Back off, bucko, or I'll discharge this weapon in yer face."

Captain Howlett leaned back to look up. "You! What are you doing aboard my ship?"

"Well, Cap'n, it's this way. We seen her driftin' in the harbor. When we caught up, she run aground here. Her crew musta deserted her. So we claimed her according to the law of the high seas."

"You and your gambler boss are liars!" roared the captain. "You watched us move this ship and waited until we left."

The man touched a knuckle to his forehead. "Beggin' yer pardon, sir, ye sees it yer way an' we sees it our'n. Fact is, I'm standin' on her deck an' yer boardin'. If ye'll step off the ladder, I won't be obliged to shoot ye an' report yer illegal boarding to the guv'ment."

Captain Howlett stepped into Adam's boat. As he backed away, Adam caught sight of the dirty-looking man with a half-moon scar across his cheek. Two others, equally villainous-looking, stood beside him.

"You know them, Captain?"

"They turned the *Minerva* into a gambling hell."

"Four-Eyed Johnny Webb, as I remember."

"They're the ones. They knew I was helpless," growled Howlett, "and they think I am again. Take me back to the *Star*."

As they returned to the *Western Star*, the captain fumed. "This damned lawless place. No admiralty courts, no place to go for help."

Aboard the ship the captain stamped below and loaded a pair of matched pistols. "They bluffed me once, Adam. They'll not do it again. Take me back to the *Trader*."

Adam looked from the guns to the captain's face. It was twisted with rage. "Do you think it wise, sir? To go back and shoot it out? They have cover but we'll be in open water."

The captain stared at Adam. He peered at the gun in each hand. "Would you have me give up without a fight?"

"I have an idea, sir. They think they have us outnumbered. But with the *Kanakas* we have ten men to their three. If there were more, we'd have seen them jeering. I'll get Hoku and his mates to board on the back side while we hold their attention. The islanders can throw them overboard."

The captain shrugged. "They're hard men, but it's worth a try."

Adam rowed to Long Wharf to find Hoku. En route to the dock, however, he had an unsettling thought. Tomorrow he would bring the Wilmotts aboard the *Western Star*. Should trouble spread, Francie and her father could find themselves in harm's way.

He left the boat at Long Wharf and hurried to stop them. He couldn't remember where they lived. However, he spotted the giant Frank on Montgomery Street. Frank led him to the restaurant where they were having breakfast.

"Good morning," said Wilmott. "I suppose you ate hours ago."

"Yes, sir, but I'll have coffee."

Francie gave him a warm smile. It was almost the first time he had seen her by day. She looked even lovelier.

"Did you come for us early?" asked Wilmott.

"No, sir. I came to say we should wait, sir."

Wilmott looked at him sharply. "Something is wrong, isn't it?"

"Pirates boarded the *Trader*, the ship we moved into the cove. They're a rough bunch. War may spill over onto Captain Howlett's ship. I'd suggest you wait a day."

Francie's eyes met his. She looked scared. "Will you be all right?" she asked.

"I expect so. But I want you safe."

Professor Wilmott's voice was bitter. "Is anybody safe in San Francisco? Drunken gangs wearing brass knuckles roam about beating and robbing people. Sometimes we're afraid to go out in broad daylight."

Adam suspected the gang called the Hounds was connected to Four-Eyed Johnny's enterprises. But he didn't say anything. He didn't want to worry the Wilmotts any more. He said, "If you'll excuse me, I have business at the wharf."

Adam waited at Long Wharf until Hoku brought a passenger in from the bay. "Hoku," he said after the man paid and left, "we have trouble. Maybe you and your friend can help."

"What you want us to do?"

"Do you know Four-Eyed Johnny's gambling hell?"

Hoku's face clouded, and he made a sharp cut in the air with his hand. "Scum. They throw us overboard once."

"Would you like to throw *them* overboard?"

"After we break the face. When?"

Quickly Adam outlined his plan. Hoku smiled grimly. "We like that."

The next morning a wind blew from the south, creating a rumbling in the bay as ships bumped together. The wind promised a storm, but they set out. The intruders must be evicted now. The captain sat in the stern dressed in his blue uniform, his hat crammed down against the wind. On the seat beside him were his pistols, out of sight but handy. In his hand he grasped a brass speaking trumpet.

Hampered by the wind, Adam guided the boat to a point off the ship's ladder. With some difficulty he held their position as wind, wave and tide conspired to sweep them away.

There was no sign of the marauders on deck. Captain Howlett lifted the trumpet to his lips and spoke the ship. "You men aboard the *Trader*! You have taken this ship illegally. Vacate at once!"

People on shore stopped to stare. But the men aboard the ship did not notice, for they were cavorting about the deck laughing. The spokesman yelled, "Oho! 'Tis the old man of the sea what come yesterday. And all dressed up. Come, Captain! Step aboard and we'll send ye down to Davy Jones' locker!"

"Move in a little closer, Adam," muttered the captain. "A crowd is gathering on the beach. I want them to see this gross act of piracy." In a louder voice he called, "I will repeat. Leave the ship you have taken illegally!"

Again shouts and laughter greeted his demand.

"Let me have the horn, Captain," said "Adam. "I have something to say." The captain handed him the instrument.

"Hear me!" called Adam. "That ship is on my water lot legally, but you are not. You are trespassing! Leave the ship at once!"

The laughter subsided. The rough voice demanded, "Who the bloody hell are you?"

"Who I am does not matter! Leave the ship at once!"

A guffaw greeted Adam's demand.

"It is plain enough they will not budge," said the captain.

"We'll move in closer to make them think we're going to board. We'll keep them occupied on this side."

He grasped the oars and pulled closer as Captain Howlett spoke. "I legally command the *Trader*! If you prevent me from coming aboard, under law you are pirates, and you will hang!"

Again wild laughter greeted his words. The marauders suddenly yelled as brown arms encircled their throats. At once Adam pulled for the ship's ladder. They neared the *Trader* as a wild yell was followed by a splash. He turned to see a second and third man go over the side. Half a dozen grinning *Kanakas* leaned over the rail.

Two of the men swam for their skiff tied at the bottom of the ladder, but the third thrashed about in the waves. "Lor' save me!" he bawled. "I can't swim!" The other two paid no attention, pulling away from the ship.

Adam pulled alongside the struggling man, who grasped the side of the boat but yelled suddenly in pain.

"No, you don't!" gritted the captain. He had produced an oak belaying pin and rapped the man's fingers. "Throw him the painter, Adam. Tow him to shallow water."

With the man clinging to the rope, Adam backed in toward the beach. Some of the shore crowd surged forward, shouting, but made no move to attack. He kept his eyes on them. The soaked fellow found footing in the mud, floundered ashore and vanished into the crowd.

Said the captain, "Look alive when you go ashore. They'll lay for you."

CHAPTER 14

For two days Adam prowled the city, seeking the best lumber and nails he could find. He located them between Clay and Sacramento near Portsmouth Square. Prices made him decide to convert the *Trader's* sails into roofing for the deck house, and to wall off rooms. He walked among fragrant pine boards, picking out ones he wanted, and arranged for them, plus a keg of nails, to be delivered to the beach.

The weather, mostly clear and balmy since he arrived, with breezes out of the interior, began to change. They had few good days left to enclose the ship. When he made his purchases, he rowed out to the *Trader*, where Captain Howlett supervised the crew in lowering the topmasts. Several islanders were cutting spars into firewood.

"Adam said, "We'll have lumber and nails on the beach in an hour. If we don't bring them out, they'll disappear."

"Aye, lad. We've only the foretopmast left to take down."

The *Trader*, built for trade in far places, had ten gun ports on each side. They opened several and loaded lumber and other materials through them.

Constantly he searched the waters for a lurking boat or crew. "Any sign of them, Captain?"

Captain Howlett looked up from paying his crew for the day's work. "No, but we haven't seen the last of the scum."

His tasks done, Adam went ashore, where he ate before going to the Parker House. He found himself in a long line waiting for the Wilmotts' evening performance. He barely gained entrance and had to stand at the back.

The bodyguard, Frank, effectively blocked the dining room door, barely allowing one man at a time to squeeze through. Often he pushed impatient men back, looking carefully at each man who paid. In the third row of standees, Adam stood on tiptoes to see the stage. Finally the professor stepped out and struck a pose. The noise subsided, and Adam expected another memorable evening.

But it was a subdued Professor Wilmott who spoke. Gone was Prince Hamlet's fire. As the professor spoke, so did the young prince. A melancholy actor breathed melancholy into the character. Willmott delivered Hamlet's soliloquy in almost a whisper. The audience had to strain forward to hear. At the end of his show the professor bowed, but a confused audience remained quiet. They had expected the professor to overplay the part, for Hamlet to come off as a hale fellow. But tonight revealed a troubled prince, for something troubled Wilmott himself.

Something had happened. A nameless dread grew in Adam. Would Francie give her lively performance? Or had something happened to her? Had Charles Dupre harmed her in some way? The playbill posted out front said nothing about a solo performance by the professor.

He breathed more easily when the piano player rolled his instrument onto the stage. But when Francie appeared, he knew something had happened indeed. Usually she turned from one side of the audience to the other, smiling, her slender arms and graceful fingers throwing kisses. Instead she looked around, anxiously, he thought, and seemed disappointed when their glances failed to meet.

During her final number she saw him, and her eyes lighted. Her show lacked the usual sparkle, but her audience didn't seem to notice. They whistled and stomped after each number and sniffled as she sang her finale.

She stepped across the footlights. He reached out, clasping her hands. She turned frightened eyes up to him.

"Adam, I know you don't want us yet, but please, may we come?"

"What happened?"

"Last night someone tried to break in. Our house has wooden walls and door and a canvas roof. Papa ordered the intruder to go away. When he persisted, Papa fired a shot through the wall. He didn't mean to hit anyone, only to scare the man off. but someone yelled and cursed. Now we don't know who to watch for."

"I don't think it was Dupre," said Adam. "Unless he was very drunk, he wouldn't make a frontal attack. He would sneak up on you. Where was Frank when this happened?"

"After we are safely inside, if there is such a thing, we let him go to the gambling places. He comes back at noon the next day."

"Someone probably thought you were singing to him alone," said Adam, "and he learned where you live. But I'll take you now. We'll move the *Western Star* soon, so you can enjoy your sea voyage for a half mile. The ships will lie side by side just off the beach."

The professor emerged from the kitchen and hurried across to them. He pumped Adam's hand. "Will you take us out? I will forever rue the day Charles Dupre entered our lives."

"It's my fault, Papa," said Francie. "I let him turn my head. He thinks I'll fall into his arms."

"Let's hope you won't have another devil to deal with," said Adam. "The fellow Captain Howlett fears is ruthless. Do you want to go to the ship tonight?"

The professor hesitated.

"Tomorrow would be better, when it's daylight. Keep Frank

on duty tonight and then give him tomorrow off. I'll be at Long Wharf at daybreak. You will breakfast with the captain."

Pistol in hand, Adam moved swiftly down to his boat.

The next morning he was waiting at Long Wharf when they arrived. A fresh breeze blew out of the south, bumping ships together. Rowing in the cove's calm waters made him careless. Only after he caught several waves on the backstroke did he lift his oars.

Francie's face was in high color. Her coat with its hood framed her curls, and the breeze touched her cheeks with pink.

Her father hunched beneath the cape and broad-brimmed hat he had worn on the Carquines crossing. No doubt he still worried about the intruder in the night. Whenever Adam turned to get his bearings among the ships and lighters, the professor wore a gloomy, gray face.

Captain Howlett stood at the ladder to assist them, introducing himself as they stepped aboard. "We'll have coffee with breakfast in your quarters," he said. "Would you fancy a touch of brandy, Professor? No? Well, 'tis a wee bit early in the day, but you won't mind if I do."

After breakfast the professor yawned. "I slept very poorly last night, I confess. I want to take a nap. How about you, Francie?"

"Later, perhaps, Papa. Right now I'm much too excited. I want to go up and see everything."

Adam joined her, but he offered to row the captain over to the *Trader* where the carpenters were working.

The captain waved him away. "Take your ease today, lad. You've been going hard since you came. I can still handle a ship's boat."

From the bow Francie and Adam watched the captain row toward Telegraph Hill, named after the awkward signal with long arms on its summit. The *Western Star,* with anchors out forward and aft, rose and fell as the waves grew. Adam was glad Captain Howlett had kept the ship clear of others. The bumping ships created almost a cannonade around them.

"Well, Francie, how do you like your sea voyage so far?"

Francie was beginning to look windblown, but she breathed deeply and said, "It's peaceful here even if the boats keep bumping."

"Maybe I can step the mast in the small boat and take you for a sail around the bay," said Adam.

"I would like that."

"Not today, though. It's too rough. Looks like a storm brewing. It might get nasty later."

"I don't care," she said, "I like the change from people under foot. They all run and shout going about their business."

"I thought you liked crowds and excitement."

"I do," she said, "but it gets tiresome. And performing every night wears Papa out. He needs to relax and gather his thoughts. We should not have come to California."

As she spoke, Adam's eyes swept over the bay. A large skiff with two men aboard rowed past. One pointed at the *Western Star.* Adam's eyes narrowed, and his gaze followed the boat around the ship. But he said nothing. He didn't want to alarm Francie.

"This seems such a small boat to cross the ocean," she said, looking back at the cant of the deck and up at the rigging.

"She never has crossed an ocean. At least I don't think so. She sailed along the coast. This ship brought me from Oregon." He turned to keep the skiff, now on the lee side of the *Western Star,* in sight.

"Do you plan to stay here, Adam? In California?"

"I haven't decided yet. I won't go back to Indiana. The fever took my ma and pa there. I might go back up to Oregon."

"Did you come for the gold?"

He shook his head. "I came about the time gold was discovered. I planned to buy cattle and drive them north to the Willamette Valley. I would probably have lost them to the Rogue River Indians."

The boat completed a full circle of the ship but kept fifty yards distant. It drifted by the ship's ladder on the starboard side. Normally the ship's hull would protect the landing stage from the wind. But the south wind made approach to the ship risky. In the evening he would take the Wilmotts in to shore. It would not be easy.

"Adam," said Francie, "why did that boat circle around us?"

Knowing she would sense anything less than a straight answer, he said, "I think they mean us harm, probably after dark."

"We're here alone. Are we in danger?"

"Not until after dark."

At dusk Captain Howlett and his crew returned from the *Trader.* As the men of Owyhee helped the professor and Francie down into the boat, Adam told the captain he expected trouble tonight.

"Likely you're right. Our Sandwich Island lads will sleep in the fo'c'sle tonight. I'll fix a little surprise for Webb's rascals."

That night Captain Howlett took Adam on deck.

"See what I've done with the rope ladder. If the scum board us, cut the cords that tie down the ladder. It'll tumble over the side, but it's got a line on it. We can retrieve it later. I've also put shuttered lanterns in a circle facing the ladder. If they board, we'll shine lights in their eyes."

Hoku stood the first watch. For a while Adam remained on deck. Clouds scurried across the half moon, plunging the bay into darkness. A brief but heavy shower drummed down and the moon reappeared. Adam shook his head. It would be hard to see Webb's blackguards tonight. Finally he went below and lay, feeling the restless movement of the ship.

Had he done right to bring Francie and her father aboard? On shore they felt threatened. But that trouble faded compared to the havoc Four-Eyed Johnny Webb could wreak.

Adam was nodding off when he heard bump, bump, bump. Something was striking the ship's side. He sprang out of his bunk and shook the islanders awake.

"We're being boarded. Wait until the first man comes over the side. Then shine the lanterns in their eyes." They nodded and followed him up the ladder.

Hoku carried a short, massive club. Adam drew his knife.

"Club the first man aboard. I'll cut the ladder loose."

A man's face appeared over the railing and peered around. Apparently satisfied, he stepped over the railing. The *Kanakas* opened the lanterns in his face. Hoku and Adam rushed forward. A knife glittered in the intruder's hand. Hoku struck his arm with the club. The knife fell and skittered across the deck. Hoku lowered his head and butted the marauder, driving him back to the railing.

Adam slashed the restraining cords on the ladder, then helped hustle the fellow over the railing as the ladder clattered down the ship's side. Hoarse yells of rage and pain erupted from below, and flame blossomed in the night. A man fell, screaming. One of the invaders had shot his own mate.

With a scuttling of oars the boat pulled away, but it didn't go far. Cries broke out from the darkness. Apparently the boat was overloaded. When it swamped, men thrashed the water into white luminescence. Then all was quiet.

Appalled, afraid he would retch, Adam leaned over the railing. He hadn't wanted it to come to this. "It's bad business," he whispered to Hoku, "bad business. Men drowned out there." Hoku, at the railing beside him, gripped his shoulder.

"My cap'n say me once man live by sword die by sword. You don't worry no more."

Shaking off the queasy feeling, pulling on the line to retrieve the rope ladder, Adam hauled it aboard.

"What's going on here?"

Emerging from the companionway carrying a lantern, nightshirt fluttering in the wind, Captain Howlett peered at them. He gripped a pistol in his other hand.

"They tried to board us, sir. Half a dozen, I'd guess. Their boat sank. I think they're all lost."

"Go below, lad. We'll not look for them. First thing in the morning I'll go see the devil who sent them."

"I'll stay on deck," said Adam. "I need fresh air."

Captain Howlett peered into his face. "Are you hurt?"

"No, no, it's my stomach."

"Great Jehosephat! You aren't seasick, are you? I know we're bouncing around in these waves, but. . . ."

"Nothing like that, sir. Good night."

The captain shone his light into Adam's face and peered again for a moment. "All right, Adam, good night." He vanished below.

Adam gripped the rail and leaned into the wind. He took in great gulps of air until his stomach settled down. He searched for the vanished boat and looked for other boats but saw none. Crossing to the other side, he studied the bay once more. Feeling better, he started forward toward the fo'c'sle.

He caught a movement on deck. As his hand went to his knife, he whirled, and stopped. "Francie! What are you doing here?"

She stepped out of the shadows. Despite the shawl over her head and shoulders, her dark hair stirred in the breeze. "The rain and noise of the boats bumping kept me awake. I came up for some air."

"You saw the fight?"

"It was awful, but Adam, you were magnificent!"

"You shouldn't have come up on deck."

"I know. You warned me there'd be trouble. But I couldn't sleep, with the boat moving and all. These boats live a life of their own, don't they, as if they're talking to one another."

"If you listen, you can hear them from shore."

"Adam, who were those men?"

How much should he tell her? He didn't want to frighten her, but she needed to know the risks.

"Francie, the gambler who took one of Captain Howlett's ships sent them. His men boarded the *Trader* after we towed it in to shore, but we threw them overboard. We expected trouble tonight."

"They died out there in the water, didn't they? I heard them. Doesn't he care?"

He took her by the shoulders. "Francie, deep down, does anybody here really care about anyone else? We're all strangers. Our paths cross, then we never see each other again. We don't form warm feelings for others."

She shivered. "When we left the mines, Papa said we'd find safety here. That was why he asked Mr. Semple to take us across the strait in the night. But we found no safety, even aboard this boat. If it weren't for you. . . ." Her eyes glowed in the moonlight.

"I did what I had to. Without Hoku and his boys they would have run over us."

Adam released her and looked about the ship again. Although the moon still shone, black sky to the south meant rain again. Francie walked up to the bow and gazed at the city. Lanterns and flares lighted the waterfront, and tent houses rose behind the town, glowing like orange butterflies.

"This place is so exciting," she said. "It hums day and night. It's not at all like Gambier, in Ohio. where we lived. Gambier was a tiny place. Not even St. Louis with its steamboats and Argonauts is as vibrant as San Francisco."

"Did you see gold seekers there?"

"Hundreds. You know what 'argonaut' means?"

He nodded, thankful for Robert Semple's instruction at Benicia.

"I wish Papa liked it better here."

"Tell me, Francie, do *you* like it here?"

"Oh, yes, even when it frightens me." She turned and looked up at him. Her eyes sparkled in the moonlight and her lips parted. The animation faded from her eyes. She stared intently at him.

Adam did the only thing he could do. His arms encircled her and pulled her to him and he kissed her. They broke and gazed at each other. Her lips parted again, and she stood on tiptoe. They kissed again and again, each time more fiercely. He felt her clinging to him, trembling, and he didn't know what to do.

A blast of cold wind and a sheet of rain slanted out of the darkness and pummeled them. They broke and ran for the hatch. Leaving her at the aft companionway, he dashed to the fo'c'sle, where he toweled himself with a spare shirt. Shedding his wet clothes, he climbed into his bunk.

He lay pondering what had happened. What could he do now? One thing was sure. No longer could he be simply a friend. He twisted this way and that, worrying about their embrace on deck. Who started it? He kissed her first, but did she invite him?

He knew so little about how things went between a man and a woman. Except for a few shy schoolyard pecks on the cheek, he had no experience. Lord knew, Miss Mary Jane Carr rode across the continent with him, but she never once invited his attention.

What did Francie intend? Did she succumb to the excitement of the moment, and to his nearness in the moonlight? Or did she mean more? He ground a fist into the palm of his other hand. He wished he knew.

In the morning he awoke cranky and out of sorts. He supposed he should have been ecstatic. Of all the men she could have, Francie had chosen him. He couldn't understand why.

Captain Howlett glanced at him from time to time as he fried bacon and eggs in the tiny galley. Adam sat at the pull-down table nursing a mug of coffee.

"Sure you weren't hurt last night?"

Startled out of his thoughts, Adam shook his head. "I'm trying to clear my head."

"It's simple, lad. Webb wants everything. We stand in his way."

As they ate, the captain said, "First thing, row me over to the *Minerva*. I'll tell that pirate to back off. And as soon as we can, we'll move onto the other lot. There's money to be made from the *Trader*. We need to get about making it."

The wind blew out of the south, kicking up steep waves on the bay. The entire fleet of anchored vessels was moving. Hulls bumped and rubbed each other, setting up a complaint they had to hear on shore.

Adam wore a flat-brimmed sailor's hat made of linen, which a seaman had coated with tar. To keep it on his head, he tied its red ribbon beneath his chin. Having outfitted himself completely from the ship's slop chest, he looked like a blue-water sailor. By now he handled the boat's oars as if he had been born to them.

Adam rowed among the ships, avoiding the derelicts. As they neared the gambling ship, a face appeared over the railing. When they approached the landing stage, the fellow carelessly displayed a pistol.

"So it's you again, old man. Shove off."

"I want to talk to Webb."

The man aimed the pistol at him. "This gun says he's busy."

"Would you shoot me? In front of all the people aboard, and on all the vessels around us? They'd hang you from the yardarm." The captain pointed to the ship's rigging.

The sentry turned and called to someone behind him. Another man appeared at the railing. "You again!"

Glancing up, Adam caught the impression of a hairy black bear at the railing. But this bear had gold wire-rim glasses perched on the end of his small nose.

"Call off your rascals," demanded Howlett. "Taking this ship was piracy. You have no business aboard my other ships."

"What are you talking about?"

"You know, all right. Last night your scoundrels tried to board us. Would you have them murder an old man in his sleep?"

The gambler turned to see whether others had heard.

Captain Howlett went on. "You found I wasn't alone, didn't you? Did your bully boys return last night? Last we saw of them they were floundering in a swamped skiff."

"Shut up!"

"And I'll remind you, Webb. You've no legal right aboard this ship. You and your scum are pirates. You deserve to hang. I intend to see that you do!"

The man leaned over the railing, revealing full black beard and hair. The sun glittered on the lenses of his glasses. Then he said, in a voice low and venomous, "Old man, next time I'll kill you!"

Adam's hands rested on the oars, which lay on the water. But he didn't see oars or rowboat or ship's hull. He pictured a tattered figure limping along a dusty trail, pack hunching his shoulders forward, his feet struggling to keep up with his bent torso. Trail dust, wood smoke and the rank scent of cattle clogged his nostrils. Through the darkness a guttural voice, harsh and rasping, rattled in his ears. He heard it on the trail from the Middle Fork of the American River. He heard it again from the deck of the *Minerva*, unmistakably the same. The growl beneath the hiss had carried a threat against his life on the trail. Now the man threatened the captain.

Although fear gripped him, sudden rage thrust it aside. But he kept his head down. The hat brim shielded his face from Webb's view. Adam knew who and where the man was who robbed him. For now he wanted the advantage of anonymity.

He forced his hands to row, and the boat backed away from the ship. The captain stood and shook his fist, then sat down and looked into Adam's face.

"My God, Adam, what happened? Have you seen a ghost?"

"Yes, sir. A ghost who has haunted me for half a year. But I didn't know until now who and where he was."

"Are you out of your head, lad? Talk sense."

"Was that Four-Eyed Johnny Webb who just threatened you?"

"The same."

"His name is not Johnny Webb. It's Johann Leinenweber. And he isn't four-eyed either. He sees perfectly well without glasses."

"The hell you say!" The captain was not a swearing man. Even saying 'hell' offended his sense of decency. "How do you know this?"

"He's the one who robbed me in the diggins, Captain."

"The *hell* you say!"

Adam rowed furiously, venting his rage. "He was in the army when news of the gold swept over California. Stationed here in San Francisco in a troop from New York. My neighbors on the gravel bar told me a little about him. They didn't know he deserted from the army. And he didn't wear glasses then."

"If you knew who robbed you, why didn't you look for him before?"

"In the diggins he avoided me, so I never saw him close up. He was going to side my brother-in-law when I left, but he pulled out right away. He must have known I had gold."

"But how do you know it's the same man?"

"By his voice. Low and hissing, like a snake, when he threatened you. He used that same tone when he put a pistol to my ear. It was dark then, and I was sick. I'd just taken laudanum for pain in my legs. But I'll never forget his voice. What do you know about him?"

"Well," said the captain, "he came from Monterey about six months ago. I thought it strange. For a man newly arrived, he seemed to know every bully boy and rascal in the city. Likely he was in Colonel Stevenson's New York Regiment. Slackers, most of them. Now they run in drunken gangs, raising Cain. Call themselves the Hounds."

"They're the ones who grabbed the *Minerva*?"

"Laughed in my face when I ordered them off."

"Couldn't you do anything?"

Captain Howlett gusted out a breath. "Damn, lad, your bringing this up makes me angry all over again."

"I'm sorry, sir."

"I went to the military commander. He said it was a civil matter, that I could see the *alcalde*.

"What is an al — what you just said?"

"*Alcalde*. Under Mexican law he's a mayor and justice of the peace. He couldn't settle the dispute. It didn't take place in the city of San Francisco. I went back to the army, but the senior officers moved to Benicia. Your Robert Semple and his partners offered them property if they'd relocate there."

"What can we do now?"

"Only way I know, lad, is to raise a bigger army than Webb's. Trouble is, his old pals hang around."

"Maybe we can get him off by himself."

"Not likely. He eats and sleeps on shore, I don't know where. Always has his bully boys with him."

"Now that I know who he is, I'm going to get my gold back."

The captain looked at him soberly. "Go mighty careful, Adam. The hellions have accounted for half the murders in the city. They'd think nothing of slitting your gizzard and dumping you in the bay."

"Maybe so, sir, but I've got to try."

CHAPTER 15

"This rain is intolerable," grumbled Professor Wilmott as they prepared to go ashore. "Last night when I stepped into a bog, the mud came up over my boot tops."

Adam said, "Sir, would you like India rubber boots?"

The professor shook his head. "I priced them in a store. The pirates wanted a hundred fifty dollars for a pair."

"We have four pairs in the slop chest. If they fit, you are welcome to them."

Wilmott turned to Francie. "What do you think?"

"Anything to keep my legs and feet dry," she said. "Of course, I have to pin up my skirt. It dragged in the dust before. Now it's in the mud."

They both knew she broke an unwritten law. In polite company a female never spoke of her legs. Raised hemlines suggested exposure of her limbs to male eyes.

"We'll try them," said the professor.

Adam waited at the boat while they tried the boots on. When they appeared at the railing, the professor hesitated. No doubt he thought it chancy, descending the ladder in clumsy boots. But Francie came over the side easily, grasping Adam's hand as she stepped into the boat. Seeing his beet red face, she knew he caught a glimpse of pale thigh. A tiny smile curved her lips, leaving Adam wondering. Was she embarrassed also or was she teasing him?

The professor tossed down a canvas bag, which Adam caught and stowed beneath a thwart. He descended gingerly and settled into the boat. They set off through murk from which mist was falling.

"The dust was tedious," grumbled Wilmott. "But the rain and mud are frightful. I hear the rainy season still lies ahead. It worries me. A ship may bring cholera as it did in New York and New Orleans."

"Captain Howlett and I worry about dysentery," said Adam. "The water is poor here at best. Rain water runs into the wells and fouls them. I urge you to drink only the water on board. We catch rainwater with a sail."

They landed at Long Wharf. Francie drew stares from men lounging about the dock. The boots covered her legs, but onlookers ran tongues over their lips at the prospect of hidden delights. They looked at Francie the way they looked at Peruvian and Chilean women in the gambling hells. Was Francie inviting attention she didn't want? Adam took her elbow and hurried her toward shore.

Adam looked back to see Frank following them. No doubt he watched for them, but Adam did not see him when they landed. On shore Terence Small was soliciting customers for Four-Eyed Johnny Webb's gaming ship and supervising the loading of longboats and whaleboats with gamblers.

Adam eyed the one-time miner with new suspicion. Had Terence helped Leinenweber rob him? Adam didn't see how, but the thought unsettled him.

After he escorted the Wilmotts to the Parker House, Adam strolled along Portsmouth Square. There he gazed through the doors of Dennison's Exchange and the Eldorado, gambling hells on the square. The usual crowds jammed the places, many no doubt to escape the rain. Beneath a flaming torch at the Eldorado, Adam watched a man set up a table and lay out a variety of pistols. At once men crowded around. Waiting until they satisfied their curiosity or left with purchases, Adam approached the table. There he admired the clean lines of one small weapon. He reached out and touched its cold metal.

Seeing his interest, the man offered, "She's a beauty, ain't she? Arrived today by ship. You've heard of Sam Colt, of course."

Adam hadn't, but he nodded.

"Colt made this little beauty, the Baby Dragoon. You can slip the three-inch barrel into your pocket easy."

The revolver repelled him, but his need outweighed his aversion. "How much?"

"Hundred dollars apiece, brand new."

"I'll take two." He counted out money for the pistols and two boxes of bullets. Pushing them into his pockets, he moved on.

Frank motioned him inside, where he waited for the show. When Francie appeared, the audience greeted her as they did French and Chilean women in the gambling hells. Did she sense the audience's changed awareness and attitudes, or was she involved too deeply in her art to notice?

There were still damp eyes in the audience after her final number, but Adam heard not a single sniffle. Did this change portend a waning of her wild popularity, or was a new emotion emerging? The footlights established a firm line between her and her audience. No man dared step across that line, but their thoughts penetrated her space. Would words and ultimately more follow?

The assistant came to blow out the candles and to retrieve money and gold from the floor. But the professor did not come out. Francie started toward the kitchen when a commotion at the door stopped her. Frank was jostling somebody. "Show's over, mister. You can't go in."

"But I wish to see the lady," came a voice. "She will like the offer I have to make."

"On your way," said Frank, still blocking the door.

"Out of my way, you fool!"

The voice, low and guttural, shook Adam. Johan Leinenweber, alias Four-Eyed Johnny Webb, had come to call on her.

Francie had returned to the stage. "It's all right, Frank. I'll hear the gentleman."

Adam wanted to leap in front of her, to shout "No!" But he stood dumbly to one side. Leinenweber advanced and stepped across the footlights. The hair rose on the back of Adam's neck, and he cursed himself for a fool. He hadn't loaded either pistol.

"I'm pleased to meet you, Miss Wilmott," said Webb. "Word of your charm has spread throughout the city. A friend from Yuba City extolled your charms and talent."

Francie took a step back. "Thank you," she murmured. "Why did you wish to see me?"

"To offer you a position," he said. "I will pay well."

"What is your offer?"

"Name the figure you now earn nightly," he said. "I will pay five times that."

Francie's eyes opened wide. She glanced at the kitchen door as if hoping her father would emerge. She turned back to Webb.

"That's very generous. I'll discuss it with Papa. We're doing quite well. I don't know whether he will accept, but he will listen."

"Miss Wilmott, I am making you the offer, not your papa."

She frowned. "But we work together. I'm sure you know that."

He smiled. "You can earn much more on your own."

216

"What would he do?"

"Work is available everywhere. He could drive an ox team, or carry bags for travelers. I hear they're hiring men to fill the bogs and holes in the streets."

Her frown deepened. "Thank you, Mr. Webb. We will think it over."

"May I escort you home? The streets are not safe at this hour."

"Oh, no," she said. "I live with Adam here. . . ." She blushed furiously, realizing what she said. Four-Eyed Johnny stiffened. Slowly he faced Adam. His eyes narrowed.

"As you wish. I'll return tomorrow for your answer." He nodded stiffly and turned on his heel.

Francie turned, red-faced, to Adam. "I was foolish." She shook herself and turned back to the kitchen door. When she stepped inside, she screamed.

Adam dashed quickly to look over her shoulder. Professor Wilmott lay on the floor, face up, anguish clouding his eyes, his hand pressing his chest.

"What happened, Papa?"

"Indigestion," he groaned.

"Frank!" called Adam. "We need help!"

Together they lifted him onto a chair. The professor tugged at the cravat at his throat, as if he could not get enough air.

As she loosened the tie, Francie said, "Frank, go for Dr. Smith. You know, Peter Smith, over on Clay and Powell. Papa went to see him several weeks ago. Hurry!"

While Frank was gone, Francie mopped perspiration from her father's face. Tears streamed down her cheeks.

When the doctor arrived, he examined the professor and asked him several questions. Finally he turned to Francie.

"It's his heart. I don't believe he'll become worse, but he

may not get better. He needs rest, but don't take him to City Hospital. If he goes into that pest house, he won't come out alive."

"Sir," said Adam, "Professor Wilmott has an apartment on our ship in the harbor. We can take him there."

"No. It's blustery outside, and the bay will be rough. I'll see Mr. Brown here at the hotel. Perhaps he can provide a room tonight."

The doctor left and returned moments later with the hotel manager. John Brown assured Francie they would care for him until morning. "Away from the gambling rooms," he said, "where he can rest. I'm sorry I can't find room for you too."

The waves in the cove were the largest Adam had yet seen. Francie sat in the stern, her hands gripping the gunwales on either side, her body rigidly upright, dark pools of fear in her eyes. They said nothing as he pulled against wind and waves. On board the *Western Star* she hurried below to her cabin.

In the morning Adam got Hoku to bring a large boat. Helping Professor Wilmott down to Long Wharf, placing him in the stern, they piled blankets about him. Hoku and another Sandwich Islander manned the oars.

On board the ship Captain Howlett had rigged a sling on the mainmast boom, which he swung out and lashed in place. The *Kanakas* lifted Wilmott into the sling and tied him in securely. Hoisting him up, they swung the boom in over the deck.

Despite the tortured look in his eyes, the professor said, "Thank you, kind friends. Where is Francie?"

"She's below, asleep. She needed the rest," said the captain. "I'll get her. Would you like coffee or tea?"

"Coffee, please," said Wilmott.

By the time they got him into his bed Francie was up and

dressed. She kissed him on the forehead and asked, "How are you, Papa?"

He managed a weak smile. "I did it this time, girl. I don't know what we'll do for money."

"Don't worry, Papa. I'll carry on. Mr. Brown offered the dining room without charge. If Adam will escort me. . . ."

"Of course," said Adam.

"But," said her father, "they're getting ready to open the Trader Hotel. The captain will need him there."

"We'll do just fine!" called Captain Howlett from the galley, where he was brewing coffee.

That afternoon they went ashore early. Francie had a new sign made for her solo performance, and they ate dinner at the Chinese restaurant. Francie expressed delight at the cleanness of the place and the taste of the food. "Papa turned up his nose when this place was recommended to him. He considers the Celestials unclean. Don't tell him you brought me here."

The mud was so deep in Portsmouth Square that Francie looked across to the Parker House, distress in her eyes. The hotel and the gambling hells on either side blazed with light. Lanterns and flares reflected off water standing in the square.

Adam scooped her up, settled her in his arms and waded through the mud. Francie snuggled into his shoulder. When he reached the other side, he didn't want to let her go without a kiss. But already the line was forming for her performance. The men, seeing her arrive thus, grinned and cheered. Their good-humored attention daunted Adam so he set her down.

Frank was at the door. "I missed you at the wharf. I went down, but you weren't there."

"We came in early," she said. "I needed a new sign."

"The professor," said Frank. "How is he?"

"Weak and tired. He'll stay aboard the ship for now. It's quieter there, and the air is much better."

She and Adam entered the dining room. She vanished into the kitchen; he took a place along a wall. There he could see virtually everyone who entered. As time neared for the show, the hall was filling up fast when a commotion sounded at the door.

"My man, my money is as good as anyone else's!" shouted a voice. "I demand you admit me to the performance."

"No, sir," said Frank. "Miss Francie doesn't want to see you."

"What's the holdup?" demanded another voice.

"Throw him out!" shouted another.

Frank started to do just that. Charles Dupre sprang back, his face chalk white, his eyes glittering. *"Keep your hands off me, fellow!"*

But Frank gave him a shove. The crowd of miners behind Dupre parted. He skidded back on his heels, sitting abruptly on the ground. Amidst jeers and catcalls he sprang up and disappeared in the crowd.

Adam worked his way over to Frank. "Don't say anything to Miss Wilmott. She has enough to worry about. And Frank, watch out for him." Frank nodded and continued to admit customers, and Adam returned to his vantage point.

The audience filled the hall and waited. The men were quiet, but they showed a kind of tension that worried Adam. Was it because of Frank's altercation with Dupre, or because Francie was entertaining solo, or for some other reason? Adam didn't know, but he didn't like the new feeling.

The piano was already on stage when the man came out to light the candles. The accompanist stepped out and took his place.

When Francie stepped through the door, the house remained silent. She came nearer the footlights than usual, so that her eyes glistened in the candlelight. She clasped her hands and looked left to right. Her voice was choked. "As the playbill outside advertised, my father is not here tonight. He is ill, and I pray for his speedy recovery. Thank you for coming, knowing the program is shortened."

As if a dam had broken, releasing pent-up energy, the audience broke out in thunderous cheers, handclaps and stomps. Francie curtsied. When she looked up, her eyes glistened and tears rolled down her cheeks. She looked at the piano player and nodded.

When he broke into the familiar "O Susanna" she belted it out to handclapping and stomping that shook the walls. Very quickly she turned to ballads of love and loss. The crowd's boisterous enthusiasm melted into an expectant hush. For her finale she sang through 'Home Sweet Home' twice. Adam did not see a dry eye in the place, and he thumbed away a tear from his own eyes. Afterward he helped scoop up the coins and nuggets on the stage.

They made their way through the rain to Long Wharf. Torches and lanterns lighted their way on the dock, which was lined with gambling hells and shops and even a restaurant or two.

"Mr. Webb didn't come," she said.

"Did you want him to?"

"I don't know. He made a very generous offer, but he seemed unfeeling about Papa."

"You did very well tonight," said Adam. "You took in as much as when you both performed. Do you need to accept his offer?"

She walked in silence a moment before looking up at him. "You don't want me to sing for him, do you?"

"The gambler? No, I don't."

"Why?"

"Webb does anything to win. He doesn't care how he does it. If you sing for him, you will lose the loyalty of your audience."

"You sound as though you know him."

"I know of him," said Adam. "We have never been introduced." Without proof how could he describe Johann Leinenweber, alias Johnny Webb, to her? For that matter, despite his vow to track down the man, he had scarcely seen Webb. He knew as little as ever.

He helped her into the boat, removing a waxed tarpaulin on the stern thwart to give her a dry place to sit. They were pulling away from shore when she spoke again.

"I think I'm going to accept Mr. Webb's offer. If Papa needs a doctor's care, we'll need more money."

"Francie, if money becomes a problem, you needn't pay a cent to Captain Howlett. He'll put you up for nothing. If he doesn't, your lodging can come out of my share of the Trader Hotel profits."

Faint light from the receding waterfront lighted her grim face. "Adam, we do not accept charity. We will pay our way."

They rode the rest of the way in silence. Francie gave him a chilly good-night and went below at once. Adam stood on deck, where water dripped from the rigging. A rift had opened between them. He wanted to tell her about Leinenweber, why she should avoid the man. But he didn't want anyone besides Captain Howlett to know who Johnny Webb really was. Shaking his head, he went below to his bunk.

For the next week rain pummeled the city and pounded the *Western Star.* Professor Wilmott lay in bed, his person and his expression turning ever more sour. For minutes on end Francie watched his face with grieving eyes. But the professor lay staring at the overhead, where rain pounded on the deck.

Grudgingly he allowed Adam to help him to the dinner table. Only after Captain Howlett plied him with soups and stews rich in potatoes, onions and turnips did his sunken cheeks fill out and some strength return. But his disposition remained sour.

"What will become of us, girl?" he said. "I've neither the strength nor the will to perform."

She went to him and kissed him on the forehead. "Don't worry, Papa, we earned more last night than ever."

"I don't want my daughter to support me. And face those men alone."

"Rest and read your books. When you're stronger you can do Shakespeare again, maybe some other plays."

Wilmott passed a hand over his eyes. "I enjoy reading, but the light here is not good. And the rain intrudes so that I cannot think."

Adam said, "We'll fix a place on deck for you, sir. A waxed tarpaulin over the main boom with a chair beneath. There you can take the fresh air and look around when you tire of reading."

"I would like that," said the professor, "but I need help getting up and back."

"I can help, Papa. And there's usually someone else aboard."

When Adam and his *Kanakas* rigged the canopy, they also fashioned a crude chair which Adam filled with cushions he brought out from the city. When Wilmott emerged on deck wearing his hat and cape, he flinched from the bright sunlight. He tilted the hat to shield his eyes. When he arranged his cushions and blankets about himself, he tilted his hat more rakishly and smiled.

Glad to see Wilmott's spirits lift, Adam said, "You're a

regular pirate king waiting for your subjects to lay booty at your feet, sir."

"Speaking of pirates," said Captain Howlett later, "have you seen any of that infernal crew?"

"No, sir. Except for Terence Small on the beach touting the *Minerva*, you'd think they vanished from the earth."

"Not that I miss them, you understand. That pipsqueak screeches like a dad-burned seagull. Well, Adam, the Trader Hotel is ready. Suppose we ought to open this afternoon?"

They rowed to the grounded ship. Adam inspected the walkway they built out from shore, and he inspected the cove. Soon the sand would reach the *Trader*. As he stepped off the walk, he looked into the eyes of Terence Small.

"Well, Adam, so you came to the city."

Neither of them offered to shake hands. Adam looked at the flotilla of small boats approaching the beach.

"You moved your landing here?"

"The other place became too muddy. There's room for everybody, ain't there?"

Adam turned away. The *Kanakas* had brought a sign advertising the hotel. They set it up and immediately people started walking out to the vessel, most taking rooms.

"We'll fill every space, Adam," said the captain. "It's so wet in the diggins folks come here for the winter. It's even harder now to find a place. But Adam, we must move the *Western Star*. I can't manage the hotel properly from a distance. I must be on the premises."

Seeing the captain would be busy, even having to stay overnight, Adam returned to the *Western Star*. As he rowed out an ominous black fog bank rolled southward from San Pablo Bay. It was a tule fog flowing out of the cold, wet interior. He wished they had moved the ship. Finding their way after Francie's performance would be hard. He decided to hang three lanterns tonight.

From his vantage point beside the wall, Adam watched Francie's performance. He saw neither Charles Dupre nor Johnny Webb. When they stepped out of the Parker House after the show, the fog was thicker than Adam had ever seen it. They heard noisy crowds at Dennison's Exchange and the Eldorado. But the lanterns were mere pinpoints of light, and flares cast lurid patterns in the murk.

Adam escorted Francie to the Trader Hotel, where he expected to pick up the captain. But Howlett had already left, probably with one of the *Kanakas*.

They made their way toward Long Wharf with Frank a few steps behind. After a few minutes Francie said, "Do you suppose Mr. Webb will come by again?"

"Do you want him to?"

"I don't know," she said. "He made such a generous offer."

Adam didn't say anything. He didn't want to drive another wedge between himself and Francie. But the longer Leinenweber stayed away, the better he liked it. Francie said once she was unprepared to cope with Charles Dupre. But the gambler was merely a vain man who thought himself irresistible to women.

Not so with Leinenweber. He knew what he wanted and would pursue it ruthlessly. He saw Francie as a draw attracting even more crowds to the *Minerva*. Whether he also wanted Francie for himself, who could say? If he didn't now, in time he would.

Darkness pressed in on them after they left Terence Small's station. Clearly confused or frightened or perhaps both, Francie clung to his arm. She relaxed when they approached a lighted area Adam knew was Long Wharf.

Here flares and torches cast lurid moving patterns in

the fog. They stepped onto the pier when a muffled "whuff" sounded behind them. They turned to see Frank pitch forward onto his face.

"Frank!" cried Francie as they rushed to him. But she backed away, a hand over her mouth, her eyes wide. A knife protruded from the giant's back.

Adam drew a pistol and peered into the flickering light. Muffled figures hurried past. One man stumbled over the figure on the planks and sprawled over him.

"Drunken lout!" He raised his fist to strike. But he saw the knife. On hands and knees he scuttled crablike away from the body.

"Oh, Adam! What will we do?"

"Nothing, I'm afraid. He hasn't moved." He stopped people hurrying past. "Did you see anyone back there running away?"

"Sure didn't," said a man, edging past. "You can't see six feet."

"Now, then, what's this?"

A uniformed policeman appeared, standing beside them. Adam stared open-mouthed. He never even heard of a policeman in San Francisco.

"Officer," said Francie, "my bodyguard was following us to the wharf when somebody stabbed him."

"Well, now, d'ye know who done the deed?"

"No, sir," said Adam. "The assailant came from behind."

"Where was ye goin', might I ask?"

"We live aboard a vessel in the harbor. I am co-owner of the Trader Hotel, the ship brought in from the bay."

The officer studied Francie. "Ye're the lass sings at the Parker House."

"Yes. Is he dead, officer?"

The policeman bent over Frank's body on the dock. "He's dead, all right."

"We don't know where to take him." said Adam.

"Leave him to me," said the policeman.

"You'll see he gets a decent burial?"

"I will do that."

After you rifle the body for anything you can turn into a profit, thought Adam. "We'd better get out to the ship, Francie."

As they pulled away from the wharf, the fog glowered above the lights of San Francisco until they faded, leaving them tossing in a black void. Adam rowed, keeping the wind on his left cheek, hoping to reach the *Western Star.* Francie huddled in the stern, sobbing quietly.

Abruptly the ship's lanterns appeared in the murk, and they bumped the landing stage at the foot of the ladder. Captain Howlett appeared with a lantern. He breathed a sigh of relief. "Ah, lad, I feared you'd go on by. This is the worst fog yet."

Below, in the warmth of the cabin, as Francie removed her coat, everyone caught sight of her tear-streaked face. The professor turned to Adam accusingly. "What happened to my daughter?"

"Frank was murdered tonight," said Adam.

"No! Did you see the assailant?"

"No, sir, but I think I know who did it. Frank threw Charles Dupre out bodily the other night. Dupre was furious."

"What now? Frank controlled the crowd at the door."

"I'll do that," said Adam. "Who else can we trust?"

"But you need someone to watch your back," said Captain Howlett. "We'll have Hoku follow you ashore. He's already on a steady payroll."

As Adam crossed the deck to the fo'c'sle, he knew the game had changed. Was it Dupre who stabbed Frank or one of Leinenweber's henchmen? He didn't know. It didn't bode well for Francie.

CHAPTER 16

After Adam made Professor Wilmott comfortable beneath his canopy, he gazed out on the cove and the larger bay beyond. Gusts of wind churned the waters of the cove. Beyond, white-caps marched endlessly out of the south.

"Are winters here always so wet and miserable?" demanded Wilmott.

"Farther north they are." said Adam. "Captain Howlett said last winter here was dry and mild. Sand and dust blew over the city all winter."

"Which is the greater curse, the dust or the mud? I don't know."

Captain Howlett, dressed in oilskins, emerged from below. A sou'wester was clamped down on his gray head. "Bless me, Adam, I want to move this vessel, but the weather defeats us day after day."

"I fear," said the professor, "for Francine on the water in the pitch black."

"There's some risk," conceded the captain, "but I'd fear dangers in dark streets and fog more. Adam, I must stay aboard the *Trader.* We have too much business there."

"How is your enterprise faring, Captain?" asked Wilmott.

"We net eight hundred dollars every day of the week. I doubt the ship ever made so much at sea. Maybe a few thousand after a year's voyage. Her owner will be pleased to have income from her again. When I find time, I'll write to her."

"Where does her share come from?" said Adam.

"She and I split my share, Adam. You earn four hundred a day; we each get half that."

"Is that fair to you, sir?"

"Why not? Captain McRae's widow would receive nothing otherwise. Without your water lots, it would not have happened. Will you row me to the hotel, Adam?"

By the time he bucked the headwind back to the *Western Star* Francie was on deck, standing beside her father, running her fingers through his graying hair.

"How about breakfast, Francie?" asked Adam. "Captain Howlett has gone, but I'll fix it."

"No, thank you," she said distantly, "I'll prepare my own."

Professor Wilmott looked sharply from one to the other. He opened his mouth as if to speak, closed it again, and then said, "May I have coffee please, Adam?"

When he returned with the coffee pot, both father and daughter looked grim. A bright red spot burned in each of Francie's cheeks.

"I brought extra cups in case you'd like some."

"No, thank you," she said.

Professor Wilmott's brow raised. Clearly his daughter's coolness puzzled him. Adam knew what was wrong, but what could he say? Francie's business was her own. If he told her about Four-Eyed Johnny Webb, she would simply think him jealous.

"I'm going ashore this morning," he said. "Would you like to come along, Francie?"

She wrinkled her nose. "And wade in the mud? No, thank you."

"You have a purpose in going ashore?" asked Wilmott.

"To buy some lots in the city," he said. "A new area is growing out on Market Street, where the sand hills block the way.

The sand will be moved to help fill in the cove. I can quickly double my money."

The professor's eyes looked troubled. "Do you think it wise to speculate here?"

"Sir, one day's profit from the Trader Hotel paid for the water lots. There is money to be made in land."

"But do you know enough to carry it off?"

Adam grinned. "I know only one thing, sir. Buy low, sell high."

Wilmott shrugged. "I cannot argue with you there."

Ashore, Adam walked south to Market Street, which angled out toward the Mission Dolores. Despite the sand hills he saw room for vast growth. He bought several lots for a total of fifteen hundred dollars. The hotel brought in gold, but he had no safe place to keep it. He could loan it out to start-up businesses, but how could he tell honest men from scoundrels? He was wiser to put his money into land.

Buying land presented one problem. Everywhere squatters built houses on land they didn't own. It was a growing problem in San Francisco, but so far they hadn't come this far out. If they built on his land, he would enlist the aid of his *Kanaka* friends to eject them.

The next morning a light rain fell. During the day, the blustery wind eased and the skies cleared rapidly. Before he returned to the *Western Star* to take Francie in for her show, he stopped at the hotel. Already tenants had beaten a muddy track to the flimsy catwalk. Every day Captain Howlett paid his workers to bring in fresh sand to fill holes before they became bogs.

The captain presided over the desk in the lobby. He was weighing gold for a week's lodging for several miners.

"Yes, siree, mister," said a miner, "we'll spread the word. Ain't many places here will give full value for our gold."

The captain smiled before turning to Adam. "What mischief have you done today?"

"Bought some more lots out on Market Street."

The captain's bluff expression dissolved into worry. "Adam, is it wise?"

"Sir, I had gold stolen from me once. I haven't figured out yet how to get it back. If I buy land, nobody can steal it. I can always sell it."

"But at these prices, Adam! This madness can't last. When all the gold is dug, the miners will leave. Even our hotel lives on borrowed time. San Francisco will become the sleepy village of Yerba Buena again, and your lots will yield only sand and chaparral."

"When will this happen, sir? Tomorrow? Next week?"

The captain's mouth fell open.

"More ships are coming," said Adam. "The flood of miners hasn't turned into an ebb, or even a trickle. And speaking of ships, that's what I came to talk about."

"You want to move the *Western Star*?"

"Yes, sir, before it's too late. The water lot is shoaling."

"It's bound to," said the captain. "But I'm a step ahead of you, lad. I told Hoku and his crew we'll move her tomorrow."

The next morning a light fog lay over the harbor when the crew assembled. It was a simple matter to raise the ship's anchors, and soon she was making her last voyage. It would be tricky. The cove teemed with lighters moving goods ashore and small boats taking passengers back and forth.

Adam rowed beside the Sandwich Islanders as the *Western Star* moved north toward her water lot. All went well until Captain Howlett howled, "Adam! Come aboard at once!"

Adam quickly rowed alongside and tied his boat to the rope

ladder. Leaping up onto the deck, he joined the captain at the rail. "What's wrong, sir?"

Howlett had his spyglass raised to his eye. "There's another ship moving into the cove. By all that's holy, it's the *Minerva!* She's headed where we are. We've got to let go the anchor and see what's up."

Adam cast a hurried glance toward shore. Their vessel lay directly off Long Wharf. "We can't anchor here, sir. We'll interfere with traffic from the wharf."

"We have no choice. I'm knocking the pawls out of the windlass."

The anchor chain rattled out the hawse as the anchor dropped into the bay. The *Kanakas* stopped rowing and stared at each other.

"Stand by, Hoku" called Adam. "We've got trouble."

"Take me to the *Minerva*," said Howlett. "Webb is up to no good."

Shortly they came alongside the ship under tow from three longboats. Adam didn't recognize the crews moving the ship, but they looked like sailors rather than ruffians. Captain Howlett lifted his speaking trumpet to his lips.

"Ahoy, the *Minerva!*"

A face appeared over the railing. It was no one Adam had seen before.

"Where are you taking her?" demanded Howlett.

"Isn't it plain enough?" retorted the man. "To her place in the cove."

"Onto a water lot? Are you legal?"

"How the hell should I know? I'm just moving her."

Muttering under his breath, the captain stood up in the stern of Adam's boat. "Where can I find her owner? Is he aboard?"

"He's gone ashore."

"Sir, you are moving the ship unlawfully. Her owner lives in Essex, Massachusetts. I am the legal agent for her. The man you are working for has stolen the vessel."

There was the slightest of pauses.

"We were hired to move her. That we will do. If you get in our way, we'll run you down."

Shaking with rage, Captain Howlett sat down with a thump and clenched his fists. "They're taking her to our dock, Adam."

Helplessly they watched the crew maneuver the *Minerva* directly across from the Trader Hotel. With a thump the ship's bowsprit struck the stub of the *Trader's* mizzen mast. Men boiled out of the hotel onto the narrow dock, some of them hopping about on one foot, still trying to get their pants on. The crew backed the gambling ship and turned her inward. Her sprit narrowly missed the house on the *Trader's* deck.

"The scum!" gritted the captain. "The filthy scum! They intend to use the dock we built. It won't handle traffic to both ships. You see what Four-Eyed Johnny intends. He'll try to force us out. He knows the hotel is a moneymaker, so he wants her too. Let's go back. We've got to snake the *Star* in while the tide is still high.

They returned to the ship to find a boat at her ladder. A man on deck was haranguing Professor Wilmott, who struggled to rise from his chair.

Furiously Captain Howlett climbed the ladder, Adam at his heels. "What do you mean, sir, boarding my ship without permission?"

The man in the blue suit with brass buttons common to sea captains whirled about. "And what do *you* mean, sir, blocking commerce on the wharf? The lighter crews are ramming each other trying to avoid you."

"We were moving our ship, sir, when that gambling hell stopped us." The captain flung an arm toward the *Minerva*.

"You didn't obtain approval to move this vessel. Are you going to put her on a water lot?"

"We are, sir. Onto a lot belonging to this gentleman. May I ask, did you give Four-Eyed Johnny Webb permission?"

"That," the other said coldly, "is between him and me."

"I thought as much. Adam, bring the lads aboard. With your permission, sir, we'll finish the job."

The man glared, turned on his heel and went over the side.

Professor Wilmott looked gray and shaken. "Are you all right, sir?" asked Adam.

"I am now. I didn't know what he was shouting about. Who was he?"

"Our esteemed captain of the port sees what he wants to see," muttered Howlett. "And what he chooses not to see."

They resumed their tow, bucking a headwind that sprang up, blowing offshore from the hills beyond San Francisco. Adam was obliged to hook onto the *Kanakas'* boats and pull hard. Finally they brought the *Western Star* around the other two ships and alongside the *Trader.* Men leaned over the bow of the *Minerva*, swigged whiskey and offered advice, further enraging Captain Howlett. Adam's crew pushed and shoved the *Western Star* onto the lot beside the hotel and let go both anchors.

Professor Wilmott watched from his chair. With all the pushing and shoving and bumping of hulls, Francie had come up on deck. She stared at the *Minerva* looming above them and at the city she had rejoined.

The men on the gambling ship's railing eyed her openly. One man finally said, "She's a trim craft, lads, no doubt at all."

The leer along with his words left no doubt which craft he meant.

Ignoring the loafers, Adam and the Sandwich Islanders spent the rest of the day building a landing beside the *Western Star.* Finally they nailed an inclined walkway from the deck to the landing.

That evening Adam and Francie, dressed in oilskins and hip boots, stepped off the Trader's walkway toward the Parker House. Ahead, Terence Small's shrill voice began its nightly harangue. A man with a leather valise asked Small if the dock led to the Trader Hotel.

"No, sir," said "Terence, "it goes to Four-Eyed Johnny's Sporting House."

"And to the Trader Hotel!" shouted Adam. "Step on down, sir. The hotel is on your left."

As he passed Terence Small, Francie on his arm, he said, "If you steer another man away from the hotel, Terry, I'll throw you in the bay."

Small's eyes glittered beneath the whale-oil flares.

Francie played to a full house, as usual. As Adam stood at the dining room door, he saw Charles Dupre in the Parker House lobby. The man kept his distance, glaring at Adam.

After the show Adam said, "Would you like dinner at Delmonico's, Francie?"

Francie's eyes had darted around the hall both during and after her performance. Now she said, shortly, "I'm not hungry."

Her reply angered him. But his anger was not directed at her. Rather, he hated Johann Leinenweber, alias Four-Eyed Johnny. That the man, even though he kept his distance, could influence Francie's thoughts and feelings so deeply was an abomination. Too, he was frustrated by his failure to regain his gold from Webb.

"Well, then," he said, "let's head back to the ship."

They stepped out under the porch that fronted Parker House. Rain drummed down again, streaming off the porch roof. Adam paused. Using the lamps and guttering flares, he looked for a path with solid footing. Washington Street, running along the north side of Portsmouth Square, was a hopeless bog. The path seemed drier on Clay. He directed Francie in that direction. They took a dozen steps when a vast puddle loomed before them.

"To the right," said Adam.

As they sidestepped the puddle, two sharp reports rapped behind them, and something struck Adam. His shoulder and left arm suddenly went numb. He turned to see Charles Dupre. Then Dupre's eyes opened wide, and the gun slipped from his grasp. The gambler pitched forward into the mud.

A great cry rose in the square. "There's the killer!" somebody shouted. "Stop him!" Others took up the cry. Adam stared at the crowd, confused. Obviously the killer lay in the mud. Then he remembered. Hoku was following them on shore. Dupre had not known about Hoku, Nor did the crowd realize that Dupre had wounded Adam.

The numbness dissolved into searing pain, wrenching a gasp from him. Now he grasped what had happened. Dupre had shot him.

"Hurry, Francie! To the ship!" He felt something wet running down his back and knew it was his own blood. When they reached the dock everything swam before his eyes. He toppled to the sand at Terence Small's feet.

Francie screamed and leaned over him.

"Get the captain!" urged Adam. "Quickly!"

When she fled to the ships, Terence Small leaned over him. "Throw me in the bay, will you?" Small kicked him in the ribs.

The captain appeared with several men. "What's wrong, lad? I couldn't get sense out of the girl."

"I've been shot. I don't think she knows." It hurt to talk, even to breathe. But he called to Small, who edged away. "I'll live to throw you into the bay. Count on it."

"Forget about him," said Captain Howlett. "Who shot you?"

"Gambler named Dupre. Don't think I told you about him. Where's Hoku?"

"Nobody's seen him. Let's get you aboard, lad."

When they lifted him to carry him, he fainted.

When next he heard voices, they didn't seem connected to bodies. A face, vaguely familiar, swam before his eyes. "Where did he get all this mud?"

The professor was there also, looking shaken. "Francie?"

"He fell at the dock, Papa. Where the man stands and shouts about the gambling ship."

The man tending Adam grunted. "Not as bad as those pestholes around the square. I've seen people throw everything from garbage to sacks of dried beans in them."

"How is he, Doctor Smith?" asked Captain Howlett.

"He'll do fine if we can keep the fever out."

Adam found, when he tried to speak, that it hurt even to say a few words. "Find Hoku. A mob chased him across the square. He did something to Dupre."

"We'll find him," said the captain.

Francie was there in the room. He heard her voice. But she avoided his bedside. Who would escort her to the Parker House now? He wanted to ask, but he drifted off into a black void.

He struggled toward the light as if from a deep hole. His shoulder throbbed, and cold sweat covered him even beneath the heavy blankets. Yet he felt something warm, and realized someone was holding his hand. He opened his eyes to find Francie by his bed.

"What — where have I been?"

"You've been very, very ill."

He felt tired, drained. "How long have I been here?"

"Five days."

"Five days!"

"We worried about you. You had a high fever. But last night Doctor Smith said it broke and you should recover."

"Were you here all that time?"

"Most of it." In the light of the whale oil lamp she flushed.

He was alarmed now. "Did I say anything I shouldn't have?"

Her face colored. "You said lots of things. I'm sorry I treated you so badly. But you must understand. Papa means the world to me. When he fell ill, I almost couldn't face each day."

"You have done just fine," he insisted.

"What if he never gets well? And then you were almost taken from me — from us. But I must get Papa. He wants to see you."

In a few minutes Professor Wilmott, leaning on a cane, entered the cabin. He sat down heavily and passed a hand over his eyes. "It's almost Christmas, but I find it hard to summon the spirit of the season. So much has happened."

Adam waited. This wasn't what the professor had come to say. He was simply venting his doubts and fears.

"What a thin thread our lives hang by! Adam, promise me. If anything happens to me, do not abandon my daughter, I beg of you."

"Sir, I love Francie."

The professor's face worked with some strong emotion he

never gave words to. "At times she seems to reject you. Bear with her. So many new feelings have come into her life. If she goes off on a tangent, if she behaves strangely, she won't stray far. In this cruel place I pray she won't hurt herself in the meantime."

"I'll stand by her, sir, if she will let me."

"Good." A weight seemed to lift from Wilmott's shoulders. "Another thing." He drew from his pocket a baby dragoon pistol, which he placed on Adam's bed.

"You're returning the gun I gave you?" said Adam.

"This is your weapon. It was choked with mud, I suppose from your fell. I cleaned it and reloaded it. You may need it."

"Charles Dupre?"

"No, Adam, he's gone. Hoku did for him."

"Then it *was* Hoku I saw running after Dupre went down. Is he here? I want to thank him."

"He's hiding until the furor subsides. Feelings are running high. If certain men could find him, they would hang him.. People don't know the gambler shot you because you didn't fall right away."

Adam frowned. "Why would I need the gun then, if Dupre is dead?"

Wilmott waved his arm around. "These pirates have moved in on us. They're becoming bolder. They bait us, wanting us to provoke them so they can move against us. I am not a violent man, and I have never carried a gun, but I advise you to. And don't walk the streets alone. I see the evil in these men. I wish Francie did."

"If I even mention it, she flares up."

Professor Wilmott shook his head slowly. "I know, Adam. She does the same to me. I'll leave now and let you rest."

Adam lay back, exhausted. He would need all his strength. Four-Eyed Johnny would move against them, and soon.

CHAPTER 17

Eager to escape the confines of the cabin, leaning on a cane, Adam made his way onto the deck. Rain drummed down and water dripped everywhere, running out the scuppers, splashing into the cove. He sought shelter under Wilmott's tarpaulin. From there he gazed at the *Minerva* looming so near. Daylight barely arrived, but gamblers called out their bets noisily. Likely they had not given up the night before. Adam shook his head. Working hard for everything he gained, he never understood the seduction of the wager.

Already hammers pounded over the hum of a city pulsing with life. He marveled at the energy of San Franciscans. They drove themselves to get in two hours of work before breakfast. Did their drive stem from ambition, or were they shaking off lethargy born of a poor night's rest? The city offered few creature comforts.

Hearing footsteps on the gangway, Adam drew his pistol. Captain Howlett came up from the Trader, black satchel in one hand, pistol in the other. The night Adam was carried in wounded, the captain put him in his cabin and moved next door. Seeing Adam under the tarpaulin, Howlett came to stand beside him. Together they surveyed the watery world before them.

"Should you get up yet, lad?"

"If I don't I'll go crazy," muttered Adam. "Will the rain ever stop?"

Howlett's breath gusted out in a sigh. "Doesn't seem like it. But this weather is good for our business. In the last week, hundreds, maybe thousands, of miners came down from Sacramento City. Rivers there threaten the city. If the rain continues, they say, the place will go under water."

"How does that help us?"

"Don't you see, Adam? Newcomers must find a place out of the weather. I crowd men into every nook and cranny every night and still they come begging for any dry place to lie down. Water flows through most of the tents and houses on shore. At least one man dies every night in town. Night before last a drunk went to sleep on a lumber pile. It seems he drank himself into a stupor. The owner of the lumber pile couldn't wake him up. Misery has spread her wings everywhere."

Adam said, "I hate to profit by someone else's hard luck."

"It's not your doing. A man needs dry sleeping space. I want to caution you, Adam. Sickness is growing rapidly. Thought of dysentery scares me. Miss Wilmott jammed into that hall every night worries me too, but she seems to thrive on it."

"I have scarcely seen her these days. How is she?"

"She's doing fine," said Howlett. "That girl impresses me. Her father is ill and becoming worse, I think, but she carries on for both of them. The miners can't get enough of her singing. Just her being here makes life bearable for many a lonely man."

"Men are turned away every night," said Adam. "She could throw rocks for all they care."

"Do you blame them, lad?"

"No, sir! She's a delight. But I worry about her going to the Parker House."

"I go with her, and one of the lads covers our backs. So far we've had no trouble at the hotel while I'm gone. I'll go below now, lad, and get breakfast."

With a grunt Howlett lifted the satchel and started toward the companionway. He returned to the canvas. "Adam, do you know how much you earned while you were sick?"

"Whatever it is, sir, I didn't earn it."

"Never say that, Adam. You showed the way. The man who lives by his wits profits even when he's flat on his back. You had a vision, Adam. You saw how to turn a useless ship into a profit. I sat here complaining for a year. I could have made a fortune, but I didn't see it. Besides, the Trader sits on your lot. But I didn't tell you your profit, did I? Three thousand, six hundred. How many city lots can you buy with that?"

After the captain went below, Adam settled again into the chair. Over three thousand dollars! A numbing dread, a fear of losing it, gripped him. Ruthless men schemed even now to grab their hotel and its profits. The *Minerva* reminded him those men were only steps away. They could overpower him and make off with the gold. Without a safe place to keep it he must buy land. It was not easy to run with land.

Should he venture out? He sat down because his legs gave out. He recalled Captain Howlett's warning. Sickness and disease took people every day. What if, through his infirmity, he fell into one of the deep mires on Washington Street? Some of them exuded filth even though rain water carried some of it into the bay.

The smell of coffee brewing wafted across the deck. Realizing he was famished, he started below when he heard a splash near the stern and a voice rasping, "Yer next, nigger."

Adam hurried to the taffrail and looked over. Three grinning bully boys had cornered a Sandwich Islander. The lad crouched, facing them, but he could not fight them all. One of the tormentors, swinging a rope with a knot in it, advanced on him. Adam drew his pistol and cocked it. "Stand where you are!"

"What the hell. . . ." The fellow turned. Sight of the pistol aimed at him not fifteen feet away turned him a sickly gray.

"Get off the walk," ordered Adam. "Toward shore. Move!"

In their haste the three almost fell over each other. Grinning his thanks the Sandwich Island lad pulled a companion out of the water. They scurried into the hotel, where the captain lodged them in the fo'c'sle. Satisfied the scum would not return, Adam went below, where Captain Howlett poured coffee. Adam leaned against a bulkhead and watched bacon sizzle in a fry pan. This was his favorite place in the city, for the stove dispelled the dampness and the cold.

"Are you having more trouble with Webb's bullies, Captain?"

"Every day, one thing or another."

"One of our boys went into the water. Whether he jumped in or they threw him, I don't know. Three toughs were closing on another. I drove them off at gunpoint."

Howlett shook his head sadly. "They've got a bigger and meaner army than we have."

Professor Wilmott emerged from his quarters and joined them. Captain Howlett poured coffee and cracked two more eggs into the frying pan.

"We heard a fuss outside our window," the professor reported. "It's getting so Francine can't get her sleep."

"Adam here settled it. But something bad is going to happen. We can't turn to anybody for help."

"I fear for Francie's safety," sighed the professor. "She wants to sing at a gaming house somewhere."

"Four-Eyed Johnny offered her a place aboard the *Minerva*," said Adam, "for much more than she earns now."

"So you know about it."

"I was there when Four-Eyed Johnny made the offer. I've tried to keep her away from him, but she seems bound to go."

The professor stared into his coffee cup. "Francine has always been headstrong. Her mother could usually dissuade her from foolishness. My bringing her to this wild city has only fanned her willfulness."

Adam couldn't agree more. Yet had they not come, he would never have met her.

They ate breakfast, each wrapped in his own thoughts. Adam wondered whether he could appeal to the *alcalde*, as San Franciscans called their mayor, to remove the gambling ship. He saw now why the constitution convention met in Monterey last summer. Without it no real government could form. Wanton, lawless behavior threatened everyone's safety. He guessed conditions in the diggins were no better.

The melee on deck worked a change in Adam. He had seen himself as an invalid. Now, however, he wanted to return to shore. Curious about his three lots on Market Street, eager to invest in more, he obtained from a reluctant Howlett four thousand in gold.

Wrapping it about his waist, he set out, his cane steadying himself and probing suspicious surfaces in the streets. At once he realized the gravity of his weakness. The weight of the gold already taxed his strength. Should he fall. . . .

Even though the rain beat down, pounding hammers mingled with the other sounds: ships bumped each other in the bay; businessmen shouted orders overseeing deliveries of goods from storeships; bells and gongs announced breakfast.

Moving deliberately, seeking sure footing, Adam headed toward Market Street south of Portsmouth Square. Here the ground was less trampled. However, quagmires would spread this way as well. The need for government to repair the streets became apparent.

When he reached his lots, he stared at the change. Most

of the sand hill was gone, probably into Yerba Buena Cove. Another sight disturbed him. Piles of lumber lay on his lots. Had somebody squatted on them? He approached the lumber.

"Not your lumber, mate!" growled a voice behind him.

Adam turned to the burly speaker, obviously a sailor come ashore. "I agree, sir. The lumber is not mine. But the land it sits on is."

"We're in luck then!" called another voice. A man emerged from the scrub chaparral. "I have been looking for the owner. I wish to build here. Are your lots for sale?"

"At the right price," said Adam.

"Would three thousand in gold meet your requirement, sir?"

"Sounds fair." Adam reached into his pea jacket pocket. "I have the deeds. If you have the gold, they're yours."

"Excellent. Tovey, go for the builders. Have the draymen deliver the rest of the lumber. It is a pleasure doing business with you, sir."

A few slips of paper lighter, his coat three thousand in gold heavier, a tired but satisfied Adam Stuart eyed another area, also covered by a sand hill. A man was driving stakes, marking out lots. It was the fellow who sold him the lots earlier.

"Mr. Jocelyn!" called Adam, limping up to him.

The man turned around. "I remember you. Mr. Stuart, isn't it?" He extended a hand. "I saw you talking with the fellow who brought the lumber up from the wharf. Did you sell?"

"He made a generous offer, said Adam. "I accepted on the spot."

"May I ask what you sold for?"

"Three thousand for the three of them."

Jocelyn wagged his head. "Mr. Stuart, you got the worst of

that deal, I'm afraid. Yesterday I sold six lots for two thousand apiece. You probably didn't know land values have risen."

Adam smiled ruefully and shook his head. "I've been flat on my back for a week." He remembered his earlier boast. *Buy low, sell high.* It didn't happen, even though he received double what he paid.

"Try to keep in better touch. Can I interest you in land today?"

Adam looked over the tract Jocelyn was marking out. If the sand were removed, it would be level enough. He pointed to the hill. "Will you level these lots too?"

Jocelyn nodded. "We're building a tramway from the cove. We'll haul this sand to the cove also."

"What would six lots cost?"

"Thousand apiece to you, if you're buying that many."

"Twice what you asked only a week ago."

Jocelyn shrugged. "City's growing. Mark my words. In no time this will be the center of the city, not that swamp beside the cove."

"Very well," said Adam. "I'll taken seven lots." He paid out the gold and received his deeds.

"You won't go wrong," said the seller. "Just don't sell too hurriedly."

Relieved of his burden, Adam took a leisurely walk back to the cove. Dusk settled in when he returned to Portsmouth Square. Knowing the captain had left with Francie by now, he ate supper at the Kong Sung.

It was dark when he returned to the *Western Star.* Terence Small stood beneath his flares as usual, haranguing passersby about the attractions aboard the *Minerva.* The hustler smirked as Adam hobbled by, leaning upon his cane. Remembering the kick in the ribs, Adam fixed him with a hard look.

Aboard the ship he returned his gear to the fo'c'sle. The exertion left him shaking and sweating, but he had troubled Captain Howlett long enough. For a while he sat on his bunk. After the strenuous day every muscle and joint ached. Putting on his pea jacket and black woolen watch cap, he clambered up onto the deck.

The skies cleared, allowing the moon to shed ghostly light over the ship and its neighbors. He leaned against the bow railing and listened. The city roared as if it must fulfill its destiny before the night was out. Only the pounding of the hammers had ceased.

When he first returned to San Francisco, it seemed an alien place. He never understood its frantic pace. Now he owned land and thus part of the city's destiny. The clusters of light, mostly gambling hells, and the dotted orange glows on the hills surrounding the city's heart beckoned to him.

Even more so did the Parker House. Francie was still there singing her heart out. He wanted to go ashore. But his good sense told him to rest.

He sat on the forward hatch and closed his eyes, but his mind responded to noises about him. Terence Small still shouted in his squeaking voice. Adam wondered whether the tout ever slept. Probably deep in the night he crawled into a warren long enough to rest his weary feet and voice.

Adam thought of Four-Eyed Johnny Webb. He had not seen the gambler since Webb's visit to Francie at the Parker House. Webb frustrated him. He was no closer to regaining his gold than he had been at the Benicia Ferry. If anything he seemed farther from his goal. Now he knew who and where the robber was but could not touch him. No way could he board the *Minerva*. If he did, he was a dead man.

Voices from the catwalk brought Adam alert once more.

He heard Francie's animated laughter. She was always excited after her performance, feeding on the miners' enthusiasm as she sang to them. Captain Howlett rumbled in response.

He wanted to get up and meet them and go below and talk to Francie. Yet he couldn't bring himself to leave the hatch. He watched them step aboard, cross the deck and disappear below.

His lack of initiative distressed him. When he entered the same room with Francie, she found a reason to leave. He wondered what he had done to annoy her. He suspected the fault lay elsewhere. She was going through a hard time. Professor Wilmott was declining rapidly. He walked like a feeble old man, taking halting steps, steadying himself on his cane.

Adam stood to go below when a figure emerged from below. In the moonlight Francie stepped back to the stern and faced the *Minerva*, which was alive with sound. For a long time she stood there. He knew why. She wanted the income Webb offered her. Could he blame her? She wanted no more than he did. Didn't they all strive for a better life?

With Francie's yearning came peril. She would place her safety, even her life, into Webb's hands. How could she not know the danger? She misjudged when she welcomed Charles Dupre's attentions. For all her confidence there remained a great deal of the little girl in her, dreaming of a future offering promise and peril in equal amounts. In Gambier, Ohio, Francie Wilmott would have grown into a confident, capable young woman. What were her prospects here? Adam wished he knew.

He became aware of another figure, a man lurking at the gangway. Silently the man moved toward Francie, whose eyes yearned toward the gambling ship. The fellow was going to attack her! Adam wanted to shout, to warn her, but he didn't want the fellow to grab her as a shield and force her from the ship. Slowly he stood up, drew his pistol and moved aft. It was a long shot, and he didn't feel confident of his aim. Amidships he stopped and raised his pistol.

The deck lighted up with a flash, and a sharp report racketed across the deck and the water. Francie whirled as the man took two steps toward her before crashing to the deck. She recoiled, her back against the taffrail.

"What the hell. . . ." came a voice from over the side. "The shot came from up there."

Said another voice, "I ain't goin' to see what happened."

Yes, Adam agreed, *what the hell indeed?* He had not gotten a shot away.

The intruder thrashed about. His heels drummed on the deck for a few seconds. Then he lay still.

Slowly Adam approached. The sharp odor of burned gunpowder wafted across the deck. Now he saw, under the tarpaulin, a figure struggling to rise from the pillowed chair. Professor Wilmott got unsteadily to his feet before pitching forward. The pistol slipped from his hand and clattered on the deck.

"Papa!" screamed Francie. She edged around the body and flew to her father. Kneeling on the wet deck, she lifted his head and cradled him in her lap. Adam peered into the shadows. He didn't know what happened to Wilmott, but he wasn't going to be surprised by another intruder. Seeing no one else, he knelt beside Francie.

"Papa," she cried, her voice low, broken. "speak to me, Papa." There was no answer. She shrank back when Adam put a hand on her shoulder.

"It's me. Adam. I saw it happen, but I was too far away. I didn't see your father here." He put his hand to Wilmott's neck. "I feel a pulse. Stay here. I'll go below and get the captain." He opened the hatch and called down the companionway.

"That you, Adam? I heard a shot. Soon as I find my confounded britches I'll come topside. What happened?"

"The professor shot a man and then collapsed."

"What's he doing up there at this hour?"

Adam shared his sentiment. What was any of them doing on deck? If Francie had not come up and stood at the stern, would the fellow have come aboard? Did he see her from the dock below? Or had he been aboard the entire time? If the professor had not been here, the intruder might not have died. But what might have happened to Francie?

Under the canvas Adam turned the professor over and laid him out on the chair cushions. Francie was crying softly.

"The captain will be here. Then we'll get Doctor Smith."

Captain Howlett joined them with a lantern. He examined the professor and then shone his light on the body of the intruder. "I've seen this one before."

"We've got to get him below," said Adam. "It's cold and wet here. I'll take his feet. I can't carry his head and shoulders."

Together they moved the unconscious man to his berth. Adam leaned against the bulkhead, gasping for breath, sweat popping out on his forehead. He was weak as a kitten.

The captain said, "Stay here, Adam. I'll get the doctor." But he nodded his head toward the companionway. Adam followed him topside. Again they looked at the body on the deck. "Was he wounded?" said the captain.

"I think he's dead."

"I'll send a couple of boys to remove the scum."

It seemed an eternity before Doctor Smith arrived. Adam lighted lamps and made a fire in the galley stove. He put coffee on to boil and then sat beside Francie. The golden light of the lamps revealed Langford Wilmott's wasted features, creating a caricature of the once vital man, as tragic as the figures he created on his little stage.

Francie sat nearby, her head bowed, her body wracked by

spasms of silent weeping. Adam reached out and touched her shoulder. Fiercely she thrust him away and drew back, her tear-stained face twisted with anger. "Were you spying on me too?"

Adam rolled his eyes and lifted his arms only to let them fall to his sides. Her words galled him, yet he knew grief prompted her stinging words.

Footsteps on deck announced the captain's return with the doctor. The lean man with dark mustache and sideburns cast a sharp eye at Francie as he shed his coat. When he examined Professor Wilmott, he shook his head. The right side of Wilmott's face was slack, the corner of his mouth sagging. Doctor Smith lifted it to a semblance of its normal position, but when he took his hand away, it caved in as before. It gave the professor an evil-looking lopsided leer.

"Apoplexy," said the doctor. "Probably a second attack. I can do nothing for him. I can't even tell if he's suffering pain."

"Is there a hospital in the city?" asked the captain.

"There is," said the doctor grimly, "but I wouldn't put a mongrel dog in that pesthole. No one there gets decent care. If you can pay, I know a woman who can come during the day. For care at night. . . ." He shook his head.

"We understand," said Howlett. "Please send her."

Doctor Smith turned to Adam. "You're recovered from your gunshot wound."

"I tire easily," said Adam, "but I'm all right."

After the doctor had gone, Adam and Captain Howlett retreated to the galley for coffee. When Adam offered Francie a cup, she seemed not to hear him.

"We have grief on our hands now, Adam."

"I know, sir. I'm sorry I brought this upon you. I didn't know it would turn out this way."

"Of course you didn't. Don't blame yourself."

It was late when Adam went forward to the fo'c'sle. It was even later before he felt drowsy. Brooding over the wedge driven between himself and Francie, he knew his objection to her singing for Johnny Webb lay at the bottom of it. He sighed.

CHAPTER 18

"We're in a bind, Adam," growled Captain Howlett, "Whether the fellow after Francie was sent or came on his own makes no difference. The scum from the *Minerva* have hounded our Owyhee lads. Now they menace our hotel guests. They chased some away. We haven't lost paying customers yet, but if the rascals keep it up, we will."

"What can we do?" asked Adam.

"Nothing. They understand only one thing: my shotgun at the ready. I must stay at the hotel during the evening. So who's going to escort the girl to the Parker House?"

"I'll do it," said Adam.

From a coffee pot on the galley stove the captain refilled their cups and added a dollop of rum to his. "How'll you do that, lad? Can you fend off some admirer who's bound he'll take liberties? You need to regain your strength first, Adam."

He spent most of the night in pain, but he'd not let it show. From his pocket he drew his pistol and set it on the table. "This will make up for a lot." Even as he said it, however, brandishing the weapon dismayed him. Two months ago he would have refused. But this was San Francisco. In the mines now, he reflected, he might do the same.

He finished his coffee. "I'm going ashore today. I'll return in time to take Francie. Unless you want me to back you."

The captain shook his head. "I'd not chance your butting heads with the bully boys. You could be hurt or worse. No, Adam, follow your own interests. I have half a dozen lads with me."

When Adam went topside, fog swirled about the vessel, shutting off view of the beach. Even shouts of commerce and the incessant hammering seemed muted. Today was Christmas Eve, but no letup in business showed. The weather was unlike anything he knew during the Yuletide season. Would tomorrow bring a day of peace and rest? Would men and the few women ponder the meaning of the season and their own destinies? He doubted it.

Snugging his coat collar about his neck, he set off toward Market Street. There he had found his calling. Would he find his future there as well? In the entire city, only along the mission trail did the land open up enough for the business district to grow. Logically the city would expand in that direction. Some maintained the city had reached its limit, that it would decline. But he didn't agree. Each ship arriving with throngs of passengers bolstered his belief.

As he crossed California Street and neared Market, using his cane past the muddiest spots, incessant pounding reached his ears. Dimly he saw men moving about, their shouts and grunts coming through the fog. He came upon them before he realized what they were doing. One gang of men was laying timbers in a level sandy bed. Another crew grunted as they lifted iron rails and laid them in parallel tracks. He approached the boss, who faced him, hands on hips.

The burly supervisor growled, "Don't ask what we're about, like all the other gawkers before ye."

Adam pointed inland. "I know what you're doing. You're laying tracks for trams to move sand to the cove."

The boss grinned. "Ye're a regular marvel, ye are."

"I own half a dozen lots out there."

The boss nodded. "I see. We got a steam paddy to dig the hills down. They're just waitin' for us to lay the tracks."

Adam followed the grade until he came to his lots. A steam shovel waited nearby. Hugh Jocelyn was talking to several men and pointing farther inland. He saw Adam and beckoned him over.

"Glad you came, Adam. These gentlemen want to purchase land, but I don't have any lots surveyed. I said you'd sell them for fifteen thousand."

Fifteen thousand! And the Trader still earned four hundred a day. He felt inundated by gold.

"Yes, gentlemen," he said, hiding his elation, "that would be satisfactory. Fifteen thousand in gold."

One man, apparently the spokesman, stepped forward. "Come to the Parker House tomorrow," he said. "Ask for Hillman. That's me." He stuck out his hand and introduced Adam to the others. "Wait a minute. Tomorrow's Christmas. How about the day after?"

Adam shook hands on the agreement, and the group walked down the grade toward Portsmouth Square. In the fog it provided the only sure path and direction.

"You named a good price for me," Adam said to Jocelyn. "More than I would have dared ask."

"Stuart, seize every opportunity. Business men will pay for what they want. Cultivate them, invest in some of their enterprises. Wharves must be built, water brought in. Some of our water comes from Saucelito, across the Golden Gate. They're talking about street railways, and manufacturing gas for heat and lighting. There's money to be made in those schemes. Look into them. Did you come to see about more land?"

"Do you have more lots for sale?"

Jocelyn shook his head. "All sold. That's why I made the offer on your behalf." He pointed beyond the sand hill. We are laying out another plat. If you wish, we can climb the hill and take a look." Jocelyn glanced down at Adam's cane. "If you want to try it."

"I'm mending," said Adam, eyeing the sand, "but I'll take your word for it. You've done well by me. Will the lots cost more?"

Jocelyn held out his hands, palms up. "You see how it is. They cost more to develop. The steam paddy, the tracks and cars. . . ."

Adam nodded agreement. "I trust you, sir. Pick out and save for me the number of lots fifteen thousand will buy. No, make that eighteen thousand. I'll be back after Christmas."

Jocelyn rubbed his hands briskly. "Be glad to, Stuart. Obviously you have other income. May I ask what it is?"

Adam saw no point in evasion. "You've seen the Trader Hotel, the ship converted into living quarters? I am a partner in that venture."

Jocelyn smiled. "And I suggested you consider some business schemes. I pegged you as a miner recovering from an injury."

Daylight was fading. He needed to return to the *Western Star,* but dinner bells and gongs were sounding when he reached the beach. He stopped to eat at the Kong Sung. He would need to give Francie's show his full attention.

She was pacing the deck when he returned. "I thought I'd have to go alone."

Aware of the cross tone in her voice, he shrugged.

She did not take his arm. Resigned to her displeasure, he hoped she would work her bitter mood out. As they crossed the square, he noted the usual envy in the eyes of men they met. But he took no comfort in it.

At the door Adam faced the usual clamoring crowd. He recognized faces now, but he saw changed attitude in the audience. When he first came, the men seemed wistful. They responded to Francie's little-girl air. They saw in her the sisters and daughters they left behind.

Now, however, their manner was bold. They didn't come to see a little girl. They came to see a woman. Adam wondered what the professor would think now – if he could think at all. Surely he would seek a different profession or move on. But Professor Wilmott was on his death bed. Perceptions and decisions were beyond him now.

Francie stepped on stage and came to the footlights. Her noisy reception reached new heights. She waited, rosy-cheeked, smiling, lowering her eyes until the audience subsided. "Gentlemen," she said, "This is Christmas Eve. I shall add a few songs for the occasion."

The miners stomped and roared their approval. Only when the pianist struck up "O Susanna" did they subside, and only after he had gone through the song twice. Quickly Francis sang her lively numbers, her air bright and gay. When she came to the sentimental songs her mood changed, and with her the mood of the audience. She reached out, her slender arms hovering, beseeching them to understand. A hush fell over the audience. Even the coarsest among them sensed her suffering, her yearning for a happier time.

Adam felt tears welling in his eyes. Partly they stemmed from his adoration of the girl who lamented happiness lost. But part of his sorrow sprang from his own sense of loss. As Francie grew into a lovely, desirable woman, she became more distant. She no longer turned to him for support. He recalled his first night here. When she saw him in the audience, her face lighted in simple joy, and she poured out her songs as if to him alone. Now she didn't even look his way.

But Francie Wilmott was not finished yet. Before she sang her signature finale, "Home Sweet Home," she paused.

"I shall sing a new Christmas hymn recently arrived from Germany."

At once her soprano voice lifted into clear notes:

"Stille Nacht, heilige Nacht,
Alles schlaft, einsam wacht,
Nur das traute, hoch; heilige paar. . . ."

Adam had no idea she knew the song. He had never heard it before, even when she sang the words to "Silent Night, Holy Night" in English. She went on to "Hark the Herald Angels Sing" and finished with "Home Sweet Home," singing the song three times as if she couldn't bear to part with it.

There was not a dry eye in the audience. Usually when the crowd filed out, looking to an evening of dice or monte, there was much good-natured laughing and shouting and shoving. Tonight the subdued crowd dispersed to face their loneliness and their wish to be home with families and loved ones.

Soon everyone was gone and Francie, assisted by two helpers, scooped up coins and nuggets showered on the stage. His left side still too sore to bend over. Adam could only watch. Suddenly his attention centered on one of the men, and he watched closely. The man's eyes darted often to Francie. When she wasn't looking, he slipped something into a coat pocket.

"Hold it!" shouted Adam, darting from the doorway. "You, there! You put something in your pocket. Out with it, man! Turn your pocket inside out and let it fall to the floor."

A snarl formed on the fellow's lips. But Adam drew the pistol from his pocket. The snarl crumpled into a whimper and the follow complied. Half a dozen coins and nuggets fell to the floor. Adam scooped up two gold eagles. He glared at the fellow, who hung his head and scurried to the door.

Adam turned to Francie. Hands on hips, her face twisted, she ground out, "I suppose you think I can't manage my own affairs."

He lifted his arms, palms upward. "Francie, the man was stealing from you."

"Oh, now you're the expert on money affairs, aren't you? You know how to do everything."

He clenched his fists and stifled the impulse to tell her of the fifteen-thousand-dollar deal. "I was only trying to help."

"Well, I don't need your help."

He faced her directly. "Shall I leave now? Then you can walk the streets alone with the money."

Her eye fell on the other assistant, who stared dumbly at them, his mouth agape. "Well, Mr. Morse, don't just stand there! Help me."

Even though pain stabbed through his side and shoulder, Adam retrieved coins and nuggets, dropping them on the bandanna she spread on the floor.

Silently they walked to the *Western Star*, Francie beside him, carrying the bandanna tied into a pouch. She gripped it fiercely, as if daring him to offer to carry it.

There was no wind, and the flares and lamps cast a baleful, quivering orange light on the underside of the gloom overhead. For several weeks Adam had not walked the streets at night. He had forgotten the excitement of the crowd and the dangers lurking in the shadows. He kept a hand on the pistol in his pocket.

Without incident they reached the waterfront, where Terence Small held forth as usual beneath flaring torches. With barely a glance at him, Adam pointed Francie toward the catwalk. He pulled out his pistol and held it low beside him. The last few feet he considered the most dangerous of the entire route. Often he and the captain debated whether to place a lantern at the hotel doorway. Always, however, Howlett declined, fearing men from the *Minerva* would smash it and start a fire.

Once on deck, he waited until Francie disappeared below. He turned to the fo'c'sle.

For a long time he lay awake, wondering how he could turn her anger aside. He twisted the situation this way and that and could come up with only one answer. He stood between her and the *Minerva*. There she could earn much more, if they could believe Four-Eyed Johnny Webb. Finally he could worry no longer, and he fell into a fitful sleep.

What awakened him he didn't know. Because there were no ports in the fo'c'sle he left the hatch cracked open to let in fresh air and light. His mind choked with sleep, he saw a narrow strip of overcast through the hatch. It flickered wildly from orange to red and back to orange.

His mind snapped awake, and he heard bells and gongs and men shouting, "Fire!" The sounds seemed to come from the gambling ship, but no gongs had ever sounded there before. The din must be coming from shore.

When he sat up in his bunk, he saw a single sail dangling from the *Minerva*'s rigging. The flickering pattern created in the canvas a living, evil quality as the reds and oranges danced upon it and gave the spars a deep burnished color.

Grabbing his clothes and boots, he dashed up the ladder, pushed the hatch open and stepped onto the deck. The clamor came from shore. Dancing on one foot and then the other getting into his pants, he crossed to the railing and stared.

Above shadowy buildings soared a great gout of flame. He couldn't pinpoint the fire's location, but it was no more than three or four blocks from shore. He ran aft, dropped below and pounded on Captain Howlett's door. From inside came a muffled, "What do you want?"

"There's a fire in town, sir, a bad one!"

Moments later they stood together on deck. "Should we awaken the hotel guests?" asked Adam. "There's no wind right now, but should it come up, we'll be in the fire's path. They would have no escape."

"I'll go," said the captain.

"I'm going ashore," said Adam. "Maybe I can help."

"Adam, you're still mending from your wound."

"At least I can warn you if it comes this way."

He started toward the gangway when a voice called behind him. "I'm going with you!"

Francie, fully dressed, had come topside and was staring at the flames.

"Shouldn't you stay with your father? In case he realizes what's happening?"

"He doesn't know anything anymore," she said bitterly. "If the fires comes this way, what will he do?"

"I'll put him in the boat," said Adam, "and take him out in the bay. But we must know what's happening first."

They went ashore. Men streamed from the *Minerva*, crowding the walkway. Adam took Francie's arm and hurried her ashore. By the light of the flames they saw their way clearly. A crowd stood between the fire and the cove, watching. "Why don't you do something?" Adam asked a bystander. "That shopkeeper is begging for help moving his goods."

"It's not my town burning," the fellow retorted. "They give no even breaks in their gambling hells."

"Help!" cried the shopkeeper, standing before his store holding out half a dozen pails. No one responded. "I'll pay a dollar a bucket for water."

Half a dozen men ran to grab buckets and headed for the cove, returning with pails sloshing water. They threw them against blankets the storekeeper had tacked upon the walls facing the fire. "More water!" he shrilled "Keep it coming!"

Adam and Francie moved toward Portsmouth Square. People ran toward the iron house Francie had pointed out to him. They carried boxes, sacks and valises and placed them inside. Then three people stepped inside and closed the door. Cast iron houses would not burn, said the men who sold them on the waterfront. What better place to store their valuables?

Steadily the fire spread. Wooden and canvas walls of houses and stores shriveled and blackened. They burst into flame, shooting yet more fire into the sky. The burning structures closed in on the iron house, now outlined against the flames. As they watched, the house glowed an ominously dark red. It began to smoke, and the walls and roof turned a cherry red color.

Suddenly the door burst open, pieces of iron falling this way and that. A black figure staggered out, fell to the ground, got to his feet and fell, not moving.

Adam started forward to him, but Francie clutched his arm. "Where are you going?"

"He needs help," said Adam.

"No, Adam. He's beyond help." She turned and buried her face in his coat. "It's terrible, isn't it?"

The iron walls twisted and writhed as if in mortal agony, bending down to the treasures within. They burst into flames and burned furiously.

Said Adam, "A man tried to sell me one of those contraptions. He assured me the iron house would withstand anything — fire, flood, storm. It's just a glowing heap of rubbish now."

The milling throng hovered just beyond the fire. They watched building after building succumb, lighting the sky. One man ran back and forth as his canvas gambling hell began to smoke.

"Won't anyone help me?" he implored the bystanders.

"Why should we?" shouted a man in the crowd. "You've got our gold. It's your problem."

"Where and how did the fire start?" Adam asked a bystander.

"Dennison's Exchange, the way I heard. Don't know how."

Francie grabbed Adam's arm and pointed. "The Parker House!" she gasped.

"Mostly gone," said the stranger. He peered closely at Francie. "You're the girl who sings. You sang your last song there, missy."

"Let's go closer," she said. "I want to see."

Across Portsmouth Square the flames subsided as the last walls of the Parker House fell in, sending showers of sparks into the sky. New columns of fire leaped up elsewhere.

"What if it spreads to the ships?" asked Francie.

"I'll take you and your father off. Captain Howlett oversees other ships in the harbor. We'll have a place to stay."

"What about all the gold? Profit from the hotel? Won't you have to save it too?"

Wasn't she aware of his dealings in city lots? "I don't have much. I've been buying city lots over on Market Street."

"But the city is dying. Your lots will be worthless."

"Maybe." When the fire first started, Adam knew the Parker House lay in its path. He thought of the man Hillman who promised him fifteen thousand for the lots on Market. Did Hillman escape the flames, and would he still want the land? Or would he depart the crippled city? That became Adam's biggest worry now.

Silently they watched Parker House crumble into a charred heap. Other buildings, unable to withstand the heat, burst into flame and collapsed also. But the fire was diminishing. As long as no wind came up, as it often did at night, little more of the city would burn.

Sadly they made their way toward the *Western Star.* "Now what shall I do?" Francie wailed. "I have no place to sing."

As if in answer to her question, Four-Eyed Johnny Webb, flanked by burly toughs, approached from the *Minerva.* He bowed. "I'm very sorry, Miss Wilmott, to see your performing hall destroyed. My offer to you stands."

She gazed uncertainly from him to Adam. "Why – thank you. I'll think it over."

"Would you like to see the place where you would sing?"

"No, not tonight – yes! I'd like to very much."

Webb offered her his arm. "The *Minerva* offers less space than the Parker House did, but you'll find the audience spirited. And your pay doesn't depend upon numbers. May I call you Francine?"

As she took his arm, she said, "My friends call me Francie."

"Francie it is. I'll see her home, sir," Webb said to Adam. As they walked away, the gambler glanced over his shoulder, a grin of pure malice on his face. Adam felt as though Webb had kicked him in the stomach. Francie was slipping away, and he was powerless to stop her. He suddenly understood Charles Dupre's torment.

CHAPTER 19

Adam emerged from the fo'c'sle before dawn. He dressed and climbed to the deck, ghostly in the fog. He looked and listened for movement. The uproar continued aboard the gambling ship. A breeze carried smoke and the odor of charred wood over the cove, reminders of dreams vanished with the flames of last night. He slipped up to the fiddlehead and looked toward shore. From this vantage point he saw dimly a dark gap in the city's lights.

He crossed the deck and dropped below deck. Already Captain Howlett had coffee on the stove and was slicing bacon.

With barely a nod at the captain, Adam poured coffee and slouched at the table. He stared into the cup, his mind numb with events of the last twelve hours. Finally the captain turned, hands on hips, feet apart as if he were maintaining balance on a heaving deck.

"Out with it, Adam. What is it? Did you lose something in the fire?"

He gusted out a sigh. "Francie went aboard the *Minerva* with Johnny Webb last night."

The captain scowled. "The devil you say! Why did she do a fool thing like that?"

"Webb offered her more money to sing there. You know the Parker House burned down. Webb saw us there. She went with him to look the *Minerva* over."

"Did she come back for the night, or is she still there?"

"I don't know."

Howlett shook the skillet on the stove to keep the bacon from scorching. "After all the trouble that scum has brought on us, hasn't the girl any sense at all?"

Adam looked at the skillet smoking on the stove. "The bacon is burning. I'm not sure she realizes Webb is the cause."

The captain stirred furiously with a fork. "We don't need any more smoke, do we, after last night. I'd better pay mind to my cooking. That girl vexes me. Now that he's paralyzed, she doesn't give her father the time of day."

Adam said, "Her world came crashing down. Now this fire, taking out the Parker House. But it hurts to see her go to Webb."

"She needs spanking, if you ask me. Maybe it would jar some sense into her." With one hand Howlett cracked eggs into the bacon grease in the skillet.

"She says she needs more money. She's been angry because I opposed her going to Webb. He's the one I fault. Maybe he hopes to increase his business. Maybe he's doing it to devil us."

"Maybe he wants her for himself," ground out the captain. "Somebody ought to shoot him." He dished up the bacon and eggs and they sat down to breakfast.

"Nobody can get near him with the toughs at the *Minerva's* gangway."

"I know. See 'em every time I go to the Trader."

"In town he's surrounded by a gang. I don't know where he sleeps at night, or when he leaves the ship."

"He'll make a mistake," said the captain. "He's riding high now, but he'll bring himself down. What are you doing today?"

"I won't sit around and feel sorry for myself. Soon as it's light I want to see how much of the city burned, and find a man who stayed at the Parker House. I want to offer him a bunk in the fo'c'sle."

"Any particular reason?"

"I hope to sell him some lots on Market Street."

"I've wondered, Adam. How is that business going?"

"If he still wants to buy, I'll gain fifteen thousand."

The captain set his cup down with a clatter. "So much? I had no idea. If the fire doesn't kill the town, buy me some lots."

Adam went ashore. Already he heard voices shouting near the square and the pounding of hammers. Men swarmed everywhere. Some poked in the ashes. Others tossed charred wood and metal into wheelbarrows. Still other raked debris off their property into the streets. There was a great gaping hole in the city north and east of the square.

Leaning on his cane, Adam looked about at the ruins. He recalled his first sight of San Francisco. Sand and dust enveloped adobes and frame houses. He thought of the city now: noisy, dustier than ever, growing before his eyes. Then with the rains it became a bog. Now it was a fire-scarred blight on the cove.

He stared at the blackened ruins. Stores and houses stood at the fringes of the fire, their walls scorched, soggy blankets still hanging. It seemed the fire burned the heart out of the town. Its most pretentious hotel and the two major gambling hells lay in ruins. Yet through it all — growth from village to city and now this ruin — one thing remained: the land.

Andrew Jocelyn had invited him to invest in the city's business. Many of those enterprises were destroyed or damaged. He would invest only in land. If San Francisco faltered — even slipped back to the sleepy village he had seen — he would move on. Travelers spoke highly of Pueblo San Jose, near the head of the bay, and of Monterey down the coast. But for now he would stay and watch and wait.

Using his cane for support on Washington Street, he listened to excited talk of rebuilding. Elated, he hurried back to the Trader. There several toughs were taunting Captain Howlett from the catwalk. The captain puffing calmly on his pipe, advanced, his shotgun at the ready, driving the gang back to the *Minerva*.

When the catwalk was clear, Adam hurried to the hotel. The captain, sitting behind the desk, looked up. "You saw them?" he asked.

"I saw," said Adam. "We're headed toward trouble. But I came to get your gold to invest."

"You must have good news."

"They say they'll rebuild bigger and better. The Exchange is to be finished in fifteen days or the builder pays a penalty. The Parker House will go up in brick instead of wood."

"Maybe the fire just slowed things down," said the captain. "Well, let's go get my gold."

Laden with the captain's three thousand plus two thousand of his own, Adam set out to find Andrew Jocelyn. Already the rail line extended halfway to the sand hills. Even though it was Christmas day, the tracklaying gang was pushing the rails through. It began to rain once more. Even out to Market Street the sour odor of the fire's ashes pursued him.

Jocelyn was nowhere to be seen. Eyeing the sand hill, Adam noticed the path someone had dug into the hill. His cane didn't help much in the sand, but he climbed up, gasping for breath. The loose footing, even though the rains packed the sand down, taxed his strength. Lying flat on his back his weakened him more than he thought. Legs trembling, he descended to level ground. Jocelyn was sighting through a surveying transit while a man drove stakes in the chapparal. Jocelyn waved as he approached.

"You survived the fire, I see. Was your hotel destroyed?"

"Thanks to the calm night we were safe. If the wind had been blowing . . . . Have you seen Mr. Hillman today?"

Jocelyn nodded. "He was here first thing this morning looking for you. I said he could find you at the Trader."

"He was burned out of the Parker House. I came to offer him temporary quarters."

"He'll like that. He didn't know where he would sleep tonight."

"I'll hunt him up. Before I go, what can five thousand buy? In addition to the other lots."

Jocelyn smiled. "You're certainly a good customer. Lots here are fifteen hundred apiece, but I'll let you have four lots for five thousand."

"Done!" said Adam. "I thank you."

He paid, received the deeds and left. Once over the sand hill he had to rest again. He studied the giant digging machine waiting for the rail line and tram cars. What did Jocelyn call it? A steam paddy, that was it. He supposed it was named for the Irishmen who tackled tough jobs. It had, on a long arm, another arm worked by pulleys and cables. The machine would scoop up this and the other sand hills. He would bet Andrew Jocelyn also owned water lots near the foot of Market Street.

Rested, Adam returned to the Trader, where he found Captain Howlett behind the desk. He held up the four deeds, saying they held them jointly. Adam did not say he held the property in his name, and the captain didn't ask. Not that it mattered. The captain would realize sixty per cent of the profit when Adam sold them.

"What do you suppose they'll bring in?" asked the captain.

"If we hold them a few days and let the price go up, you stand to double your money."

"Six thousand!" breathed the captain. "With profits from the hotel, I could go home and live out my days."

"Is that what you want, sir? If so, I'll buy your share of the hotel for six thousand."

"No, by gum! Before you came I wanted to go. Now I want to see how things turn out, Adam. You're the son I never had. And — it hurts me to say it — I want to see where this infernal city is headed. By the way, the man you were looking for came here. Meet him for dinner at the Delmonico. Tonight at seven."

"The Delmonico? But it burned down, didn't it?"

The captain shrugged. "He said to meet him there. Hill-man, wasn't that his name?

Adam nodded. Maybe his land deal would go through after all.

He boarded the *Western Star,* where he dropped below to look in on Professor Wilmott. The sick man's eyes were closed. Adam drew a chair beside his bed, ignoring the odor of sickness that pervaded the cabin.

He found himself nodding off. The long walk out Market Street with the gold had taxed his strength. If Hillman paid him fifteen thousand in gold, no way could he carry it out to pay Andre Jocelyn. After napping a few minutes, he opened his eyes to find the professor staring at the ceiling.

Adam touched the hand which lay at the side of the bed. To his surprise the professor gripped his hand fiercely as if to cling to his strength. Wilmott turned his head and tried to smile. But the side of his face had caved in, so it came out a leer instead.

"You're getting stronger, sir."

The professor's jaw worked, and his lips twisted to form words that never came. He succeeded only in giving voice to a series of grunts. Adam puzzled over what he was trying to say.

"We had a big fire in town last night. Did you know that?"

Wilmott's eyes dilated and his mouth worked, but no sound came.

Curtains swished behind Adam, and Francie emerged from her space. She was dressed for the street in her familiar long coat and hood.

"If you're going out," said Adam, "I'll escort you."

"Not necessary," she said. She kissed her father on the forehead and left.

The professor strained to follow her with his eyes. A frown gathered on his forehead, a questioning without words. But Adam understood. He pressed Wilmott's shoulder and headed for the companionway. By the time he reached the deck she was gone. He drew a watch from a pocket. It was still too early to meet Hillman. But he strolled to town and watched the cleanup and rebuilding which continued by lantern and torch light. He hoped to see Francie. She shouldn't have set out on her own after dark.

At ten minutes to seven he entered the Delmonico. Already Hillman sat with three others at a table, all clad in fashionable suits. He looked down at his own sailor's garb drawn from the ship's slop chest. To associate with these gentlemen he needed new clothes. On the other hand, he didn't want to look overly prosperous. Now he walked the streets with little fear of being robbed.

Hillman waved him over, moving valises onto the floor to make room. Hillman introduced him to his partners.

"Steward!" called Hillman. In a lower tone he said, "You don't know whether a doctor, lawyer or sailor will come to your table. So you don't call for a waiter." *Or college professor.* A man came, took their orders and vanished toward the kitchen.

Adam didn't think the porterhouse steak was as tasty as the food at Kong Sung. It certainly cost more. Silently they ate. They would talk later.

After dinner the four partners lighted cigars. A man named

Sehorn offered Adam one, but he shook his head. Hillman questioned him about his experiences in California. They seemed intrigued by his accounts of placer mining.

"You might try the mines," said Adam. "Satisfy your curiosity at first hand."

Hillman smiled ruefully. "I'm not cut out for it, I'm afraid. But you found more success than some."

"I came early to the American River, sir. We couldn't stroll about picking up nuggets, as some claim, but gold was plentiful. Easy to wash out of the gravel." He saw no gain by telling of his growing infirmity and the robbery.

When conversation lagged, Adam looked around the restaurant. And froze. At a table in a corner sat Francie having dinner with Johnny Webb. Unable to bear the sight, he turned back to Hillman and pointed to their luggage on the floor.

"You were burned out of the Parker House. Do you have quarters for tonight?"

Hillman stifled a yawn. "As a matter of fact, we don't. I suppose we'll spend the night in a gambling tent that escaped the fire. Any place out of the weather."

"If you can stand close quarters aboard ship, I can help, sir. If we have sufficient food, we'll provide breakfast. The sleeping quarters won't cost you a cent."

Hillman smiled. "I'm delighted, Mr. Stuart. If I could find places for these other gentlemen. . . ."

"I meant all of you," said Adam.

The partners smiled broadly at one another. Hillman leaned forward. "This calls for a drink. Bourbon from Kentucky, Mr. Stuart, or perhaps a fine brandy?"

"Thank you, but I don't care for spirits."

Hillman frowned. "Did I offend you, sir?"

"No, sir, I just don't like the taste."

The partners glanced at each other. Hillman said, "You are a remarkable man, Mr. Stuart. Perhaps the only tee-totaler in the entire city. You'll go far."

"Thank you," said Adam. He wished Francie could hear that. He glanced her way to find her staring at him. Under the lamplight her face was white. Apparently Webb noticed her pallor, for he turned to stare at Adam.

"Mr. Stuart?" Hillman looked at him, eyebrows raised.

"Oh! I'm sorry. I just saw someone I know."

"The lovely young lady, perhaps, or her companion?"

"Yes, sir. Miss Francie Wilmott."

Recognition lighted Sehorn's eyes. "The singer. Of course. I knew I had seen her before. A beautiful girl. You are lucky to know her."

I'd be luckier if I were sitting with her now.

Hillman said, "May we conclude our business on your ship? I don't fancy prying eyes."

"Fine," said Adam.

Before they could rise Francie and Webb left their table. On their way out they had to pass by. She nodded and hurried past. Webb fixed him with a cold stare.

"A bad fellow," muttered Sehorn, looking after him. "We were gaming aboard his vessel the other night. I don't know what started it, but he ordered a man beaten and thrown into the bay."

"I know him from the mines," said "Adam. "Francie's consorting with him worries me, but I'm not her guardian."

"A pity," said Sehorn. "She'll come to no good."

Outside, they looked about. Mr. Hillman held a handkerchief to his nose. "This burnt odor distresses me," he explained. "I would find it dismal to locate here."

Suddenly Adam felt uneasy. Had he set the price too low

again? But Jocelyn had set the figure. If anyone knew a fair price, he did.

"This way, gentlemen," he said.

Their route to the ship took them past the Kong Sung restaurant, dark and silent now. Adam was pleased to find it still standing. "If you wish to sample Chinese cooking," he said, "I recommend this place. Of course, you'll find little elbow room between diners."

Hillman said distantly, "Perhaps we will try it sometime."

They passed Terence Small, who paused to sneer at Adam. One day, Adam promised himself, Terence would get that saltwater bath.

When they boarded the *Western Star* Sehorn stopped. "We've been here. There's Webb's *Minerva*." He pointed to the ship's rigging, much of it ready to crash down, lighted by torches and flares.

"We don't have the best of neighbors," said "Adam, "but you'll be secure. If you'll wait, I'll go below and light a lamp."

Below decks they set down their luggage, eased around each other and looked around. "It's snug, as you say," said Hillman.

"Only the Chinese crowd more people into a space than ship captains do," said Sehorn.

"But it's warm and dry," said Hillman. "We thank you."

One of the men felt the straw-filled pallet on a bunk and sighed. "Except for sitting down to eat," he said, "I've been on my feet since the fire."

"Maybe you'd rather rest. We can finish our business in the morning."

"No," said Hillman. "We'll conclude it now."

All four men unwrapped money belts from around their waists. They laid them in a pile on Adam's bunk. "You have no idea," said Hillman, sighing, "what a burden gold can be on your person."

Adam smiled. When he left the American River, he carried as much gold as any two of these men. He knew, all right, what a burden it could be.

"We'll wait," said Hillman, "if you want to count it."

"Not necessary," said Adam. "You are honorable men." He would count it later. If they tried to cheat him the land would still be there.

He produced the deeds and signed them over. Their transaction completed, he said, "I'll tell Captain Howlett you came. He manages our hotel, the ship berthed next to us."

On deck Adam waited to let his eyes adjust to the dark. It did not pay to stumble about in darkness, even aboard the ship. From the *Minerva* the clamor seemed louder than ever. It grated on him. Then he heard a new sound. Francie's clear soprano rose above the din. He clenched his fists.

"She's done it," he muttered.

He moved quickly to the Trader's doorway. There he paused to listen. He sensed a new note in Francie's voice. It had become more strident. At the Parker House she was the central attraction. She set the tone and the audience responded. Aboard the gambling she vied with the clamor at the gaming tables. It wouldn't surprise him if she could scarcely hear the piano accompaniment.

Men came to the *Minerva* to gamble. If they heard a pretty girl sing, so much the better. She had become a gambling hell entertainer, like the Chilean women who sang and encouraged men to drink in the lesser gambling tents. When would she realize that? When she did, would she stay? Johnny Webb would not willingly let her go.

When he entered the hotel lobby, Captain Howlett sat at his desk, his head cocked to one side. "Is that Francie I hear?"

"She's gone over to him."

The captain shook his head.

"Sir, I brought four gentlemen to stay the night. I need blankets. Can we give them breakfast in the morning?"

The answer was yes in both instances.

Returning to the fo'c'sle, he saw his guests had closed the hatch. Already the air was heavy. The lamp burned low. All four men had stripped down to long underwear and were already asleep beneath their coats. Gently Adam removed the coats and hung them on wooden pegs. He covered each man with a blanket.

Feeling not the least bit sleepy, he returned to the deck, drawing his pea coat tightly about himself. He looked and listened carefully. Nothing. He moved under the tarpaulin and settled into the professor's chair.

Sitting in the shadows, he saw movement on the gangway. Quickly his hand went to the pistol. But his fingers relaxed. Francie stepped on board, paused, started forward toward the fo'c'sle and stopped.

"Francie."

She gasped and whirled. "Oh! Oh, it's you, Adam."

"Francie, don't walk alone in the dark. Have Webb provide you with an escort."

"It's only a few steps."

"Death or worse lurks in these shadows. Demand an escort, a reliable one. I'd come to get you, but I'd never leave."

"Aren't you exaggerating?"

"Not a bit."

"You hate Mr. Webb, don't you?"

"No, I don't — yes, I do! I hate what he does to people."

"Tell me about him."

He paused, staring at her face so pale in the poor light. "Would it change your mind? Would you even believe me?"

"I suppose not."

"Then why say anything?"

She sighed. "I'm tired. Good night, Adam." She was gone.

In his bunk he lay awake for a long time. Of all the days of his life this had become the best and the worst. He had gained more wealth than he ever expected to see. That wealth he could turn into even greater profit. If only he had the eight thousand Four-Eyed Johnny Webb had stolen from him. Yet Webb had taken something he valued more than gold. Like the gold, he despaired of getting it back.

CHAPTER 20

Adam plunged into buying and selling land. No longer did he need a cane. But he took care to save his strength. Cold rains continued to plague the city. It turned streets into nearly-impassible swamps. He could not afford illness again.

He bought two suits and a hat and an India rubber raincoat. But it made him sweat inside while it repelled the rain. Between rain showers he frequented Portsmouth Square, where merchants gathered to buy and sell. There he listened closely. When a man asked about land, he introduced himself and negotiated a sale. Seldom did he come away empty, for he offered a tract for five hundred dollars less than the next man and still made a handsome profit.

No longer did he seek out Andrew Jocelyn. He reserved half a dozen lots at a time, which he sold sight unseen for twice what he paid.

When rain swept over the city he retreated indoors to the Delmonico bar. Here he met wealthy investors and listened to their talk. Now and then he bought a share: the Mission Dolores toll plank road and a scheme to bring more fresh water from Saucelito across the Golden Gate. But most of his profits he poured back into land.

During one meeting with a buyer over lunch, Adam looked up to find Francie staring at him from a nearby table. When their eyes met she quickly looked away. Johnny Webb glared at him. He nodded, bound he would be civil although murder lay in his heart.

Adam rarely saw her, but every night he stood on deck, listening to her sing above the roar aboard the gambling ship.

Although he rarely took profits, he amassed ten thousand in gold. More and more he worried about fire in the wooden ships.

"Captain," he said at breakfast one morning, "we should do more to protect our vessels. Ever since the big fire, smaller ones have popped up in the city. According to talk, some were set deliberately."

"Aye," grumbled the captain, "if they didn't want our ships, the scum across the way would burn us out. What are you thinking, lad?"

"There was not a single fire company in the city. People had few ways to fight the fire," said "Adam. "Some hung wet blankets on their houses and threw water on them to keep them wet. I want blankets and buckets. We could bring water butts from other vessels. Set them up on deck and let the rain keep them filled."

"Good thinking, lad. I'll take Hoku and his boys to get the butts. Hoku is coming out of hiding."

"Want me to take the hotel desk while you do that?"

Captain Howlett shook his need. "No need. I've got Kahele trained now. He meets people well and has a fine eye for detail." Howlett grinned. "Besides, you can't afford a day on the water. You haven't figured out yet how to turn it into gold."

"I agree," said Adam. Lowering his voice, he added, "Counting the value of lots I hold, I'm up to thirty-four thousand."

The captains mouth fell open. He recovered enough to say, "You've truly got the Midas touch, Adam."

"Midas? Is he one of the gamblers here?"

Howlett laughed. "After you make your fortune, Adam, you need to educate yourself."

The next morning Captain Howlett set off with his *Kanakas*. Adam dressed for business ashore. But he weighed the risk posed by their both leaving the ship. Kahele learned quickly, but he was little more than a boy, no match for the brutes around the *Minerva's* gangway.

He took a pot of coffee up on deck and settled beneath the tarpaulin. At once Kahele's alarmed voice rose. "Please, sirs, not to go into hotel."

Adam leaped up, drew his pistol and ran down the gangway. Kahele stood, arms outstretched, in the hotel doorway facing three bruisers.

"Aw, mate," said one with a broken-toothed grin, "we just wants to visit our shipmate what's staying in your hotel." They advanced upon Kahele, who dropped into a crouch and doubled his fists.

"Stop!" yelled Adam.

The men turned and stared. "It's you again. Mind yer own business."

"This *is* my business. I am half owner of the Trader." He aimed the pistol at them. "Get out or I'll shoot."

The men muttered among themselves and backed away, vanishing up the gangway into the gambling ship.

Adam watched to see if they would return. Finally he turned away when Francie emerged from the *Minerva*. She stopped, eyed the pistol in his hand. They stared at each other. White-faced, she descended the gangway. As she brushed past him, she said, in a tight voice, "Must a proper gentlemen dress up in a suit before shooting?" She swept up the gangway to the *Western Star*.

Blood pounding in his ears, Adam stared at the pistol in his hand. Heat rising in his throat, he tugged at his black silk cravat. He jammed the pistol into his coat pocket and started ashore when he saw movement above him. On the gambling ship

Four-Eyed Johnny Webb, his eyeglasses reflecting light from the water, grinned and disappeared.

Glowering, Adam returned to the professor's chair beneath the tarpaulin, for rain had begun again. He poured coffee into his cup, but it had gone cold. He emptied it over the side.

He wondered why the toughs hassled Kahele. So far as he knew, it was the first bald attempt to breach the hotel's security. Were the roughnecks seeking sport at the expense of the defenseless lad? Or were they acting under Webb's orders? Did it mean the gambler was stepping up the pressure? If so, he could have simply set fire to the hotel. Failure to do so meant only one thing. Four-Eyed Johnny meant to goad the captain into violence. Then he would come down hard: drive them out if he could, kill them if he must. He wanted the hotel and its profits.

Several times during the day Adam climbed the ratlines of the ship's remaining rigging, searching for Captain Howlett and his crew. Familiar traffic flowed across the cove, but fog and rain obscured most of the ships. In the last month the anchorage had become even more crowded. Still, he saw a fair expanse of water but no Captain Howlett.

Between searches of the harbor he sat under the tarpaulin pondering Francie's behavior. Had she stayed aboard the *Minerva* last night? Or had she gone over early this morning? Knowing the routines of her days, he concluded the former seemed more likely.

Again he pondered why she turned against him. As always, he came up with the same answer. Merely his presence reminded her of the more pleasant life she had led earlier.

Fog descended over most of the bay, obscuring the ships at anchor. Late in the afternoon the captain emerged from the fog with his crew. Two boats, side by side with spars lashed together across them supported two large water casks. A third boat towed them in.

They planned to bring the boats alongside the *Western Star* and use the mizzen boom to hoist the casks aboard. But dumping of sand into the cove had shoaled the water. Too, the tide was running out. Using a speaking tube, Adam directed the captain to the open water alongside the *Minerva*. This put them across the catwalk from the ship's gangway. They maneuvered the boats and secured them alongside the walk.

The captain scowled. "I hoped to return before the ebb tide so we could use the boom. Now we'll have to carry them aboard."

Adam sized up their cargo. "Can four men carry a barrel?"

The captain shook his head. "I don't know. They're made of oak and they're waterlogged. What are you thinking?"

"Lash two oars together to form a platform. With a man on each corner tote the butt up the gangway."

"Sounds good," said the captain. "We'll try it."

First they set blocks under oars laid out on the catwalk. Hoku cut rope and lashed the oars together three feet apart. They eased a butt onto the oars. Sudden lurches of the overburdened boats forced all hands to hang on until they steadied.

Men gathered on the catwalk, some bound for the gambling ship, others leaving. A gentlemen rapped a gold-headed cane on the catwalk. "You, sir, are blocking a public thoroughfare."

Adam straightened up from tugging at the butt. "You, sir, are mistaken. This is a private dock constructed for guests of the Trader Hotel. You are trespassing."

"Why – ah –" the florid man spluttered, pointing to the *Minerva*. "That vessel is. . . ."

"Trespassing. Squatting on a water lot the gambler does not own."

"Harumph!" The gentleman stomped up the gangway into

the gambling ship. He returned moments later with Johnny Webb. Webb took one look at the gathering knot of men on either side of the water butt.

"What do you mean, blocking the way and saying we're squatters?"

Retorted Adam, "I know the man's name on the deed registered with the port captain. You, Mister Leinenweber, are not that man."

Johnny Webb blanched and drew back. "You are mistaken."

"I think not."

"My name is Webb."

"Webb, Leinenweber," said Adam, "yours is not the name on the deed. You are here illegally."

Johnny Webb's eyes bulged in a face turning red. "Produce the owner if you are so sure."

"I have never met him," said Adam, "but I know his name. Now if you and the gentleman will show patience, we'll clear the catwalk." Adam turned to the others waiting. "We are sorry to inconvenience you."

"Oh, that's all right, lad," said a bystander. "We'll look elsewhere for our pleasure."

At sight of gamblers turning away toward shore, Johnny Webb turned livid. He fixed Adam with a look of pure hate, spun on his heel and stamped back aboard the *Minerva*.

"All right, boys," said Adam, "ease her onto the oars. That's the way."

During Adam's exchange with Webb, Captain Howlett had vanished. Now he stood beside Adam. "You know this means war." He brandished his double-barreled shotgun, the muzzle pointed downward. "You showed Webb up for a liar and cheat. He'll never stand for it."

"I suppose not," said Adam. "I don't want Francie caught in the middle, but we didn't start it." He told of the attempted invasion of the hotel.

"You haven't gone ashore all day?" asked the captain.

"We have an investment to protect here."

Howlett frowned. "Maybe we should close the hotel. You earn more in a day ashore than in a week here. I'd hate to see you come to harm."

Adam laughed. "A day won't make a difference. The hotel income backs up my dealings. But should we risk our lives? It's something to think about."

The Sandwich Islanders moved the first water butt onto the deck. Now they caught their breaths after their exertion. Adam looked up at the mizzen boom overhead. "We can move the next one just a few feet and hoist it aboard."

He took down the professor's tarpaulin. The crew tied a sling around the second water butt and heaved on the halyard that lifted the boom. Its gooseneck screeched against the mast as the boom raised. The water butt appeared over the stern and swung in to the stern counter. "This is where we'll need the water," Adam observed.

It was nearly dark when they moved both butts into place. Adam stretched the tarpaulin over the boom. He wanted a dry place from which to observe the deck. The rain, which had held off most of the day, began once more. Adam placed buckets where they would catch water dripping from the rigging. He wanted the water butts full at all times.

Satisfied, he went below and stoked the galley range. Soon the professor's soup was simmering on the back of the range. Adam sliced bacon and arranged it in a cast iron skillet. In minutes eggs sizzled in the bacon grease. He completed his meal with bread and coffee.

He looked in upon Professor Wilmott. By the light of a whale oil lamp the professor's features appeared sunken and wasted. Adam knew the futility of his life, yet he did what he could. He recalled Wilmott's need to escape Charles Dupre and his forceful stagings of Prince Hamlet and King Lear. He looked sadly upon the wreckage of the man.

Wilmott stirred, and Adam found the professor's eyes on him. He smiled and said, "Wanted to see if you were awake. I'll bring your supper."

In the galley he filled a bowl with soup and cut off a chunk of bread. These, with a glass of water, he took to Wilmott's bedside. With the spoon he forced the professor's mouth open and fed him small chunks of bread dipped in the soup. Now and then liquid dribbled down the professor's chin. Patiently Adam wiped it away with a handkerchief.

The curtains that separated Francie's quarters from her father's parted and she stepped into view. Adam gasped. She was wearing a new red gown cut low and in such a way that it pushed her breasts up. Her shoulders and most of her bosom were thus exposed. Her hair was swept up from her neck and secured by whalebone combs. A large ruby suspended on a gold chain glittered in the cleft between her breasts.

She approached her father, color rising in her face. Shocked, Adam retreated to the companionway. Francie bent over and kissed her father on the forehead. "I must go to work now," she said. "I've learned some new songs."

Her father's eyes dilated and his mouth opened, making sounds but no words. His brows drew together in a frown that expressed his dismay. Francie cradled his face in her hand, turned and started past Adam.

Shocked out of his numbness knowing she would expose herself thus aboard the gambling hell, he muttered, "You said my suit made me a proper gentleman. Does your gown make you a proper lady?"

She stopped, the color blanching from her face. "You dare. . . ." She slapped him with a blow that drove him back. He put a hand to his face and watched her climb the companionway. Then he saw the raised hemline. He caught more than a glimpse of calf and thigh.

He wanted to grasp her ankle, to stop her until she came to her senses. Yet he did nothing. He had no claim on her. She was gone.

He turned to the professor. After trying to feed him, he gave up. Wilmott stared, first at Adam and then toward the companionway. Adam sensed that the professor was willing him to go after her. He continued, uttering squeaks and grunts until Adam slipped into his India rubber coat and went up on deck.

Everything gleamed in the light shining from the gambling ship, the town and the low-hanging clouds. Adam went aft to the counter, where the water butts loomed in the pale light. As he leaned over the railing a great roar came from the gambling ship. No doubt Francie had appeared in her new costume. Obviously her audience approved of the new Francie Wilmott. But what would it cost her? Did she realize what she was becoming? Adam held his fevered face in his hands. *Ah, girl, you don't know what you have done to your father. Or to me.*

When the wind chilled him he trudged forward and dropped down the fo'c'sle ladder. Shedding his damp clothes, he climbed into his berth. But he could not sleep. Over and over he saw Francie as she had left. Could he ever bring her to her senses? Could he ever show her the real Johnny Webb? He could force a showdown, but he would endanger Captain Howlett and the men from Owyhee. Most of all he didn't want Francie caught in the middle.

His eyelids grew heavy when he heard a muffled scream. Instantly he leaped up, danced on one leg and the other while he pulled on his trousers. Cursing Johnny Webb for failing to escort Francie, he grabbed his coat and pistol. On deck he looked wildly about. Again the scream. But it came from below decks. He clattered aft and down the ladder as Captain Howlett emerged from his cabin.

They stared at each other. From the main cabin came the cry of a woman with a broken heart. They looked in upon Francie on her knees before her father's bed. The professor lay, mouth open, eyes staring, a clawlike hand reaching out.

"I came and – and found him - like this."

Adam started forward but with an arm Captain Howlett barred his way, shaking his head. Adam stepped back. Seeing the pistol in his hand, he shoved it into a pocket.

Captain Howlett drew Francie away from the bed. "Come, child, your father is suffering no longer."

She buried her head in his chest, broken sobs wracking her slender body. "It's my fault. I let him see me like this. I'm so ashamed!"

"What's done is done." With his eyes the captain motioned Adam topside. As Adam moved up the companionway, the captain spoke gently. "I'll make arrangements in the morning."

On deck Adam clenched his fists. If he could catch Johnny Webb, he'd beat the man down into the mud from which he had crawled. For a moment he considered boarding the *Minerva* and shooting him down. His shoulders sagged. Even if he succeeded, what good would it do? He wouldn't leave the gambling ship alive.

All night Adam tossed and turned and rose tired the next morning. Wanting to go ashore, he donned his rain gear and set off. He could return in time for the burial this afternoon.

Rebuilding after the fire proceeded at a furious rate. Already the void left by the flames had vanished, with buildings framed like white skeletons in the uncertain light. This section of the city would be brand new, yet except for a few brick buildings brick, all was rebuilt of wood. It would burn again. Since the fire he had heard rumors of arson. They renewed his resolve to avoid chancy investment. It also raised his concerns about the Trader Hotel and the *Western Star* and the gold he accumulated faster than he could invest it.

"Mister Stuart!"

Adam turned to see Hillman and Sehorn approaching with a man they introduced as William Ward. "Mr. Ward has just arrived," said Hillman. "He wants lots on Market Street near ours. We believe San Francisco will grow in that direction. We drove out to see Mr. Jocelyn. He says you hold a dozen lots where the sand hill used to be.

Adam concealed his astonishment. The sand barriers were gone already?

Adam addressed Mr. Ward. "I'll show you what I have but not today. I must attend a funeral. How about tomorrow about one?" He could look up Andrew Jocelyn and determine which lots were his.

Ward agreed.

Adam returned to the *Western Star.* Captain Howlett was dressed in his finest blue uniform and cap. He shook his head over coffee.

"That girl aggravates me, she surely does. We will follow the body, but she rode off in a carriage with that devil Webb."

Adam shrugged. "We'll have to live with it."

The captain got to his feet. "After I give Kahele instructions, we'll take the coffin to North Beach. A cart should be here any time."

Patches of blue sky appeared as they set out. They walked behind the cart. The *Kanakas* who had borne the pine box to shore followed. They passed Telegraph Hill. As they moved out toward the beach, the sun broke through. Finally they passed Russian Hill. The bluffs beyond the Golden Gate shone chocolate brown in the sunlight.

They had to wait for Francie and Johnny Webb. Captain Howlett gazed out on San Francisco Bay. Here the water was clear of the ships that cluttered the harbor. The captain's eyes followed a ship inbound, all sails set. No doubt he was reliving happier days at sea.

Although the occasion was stern, Adam felt cheerful. The salt breeze blew in through the Golden Fate. He filled his lungs with the crisp air. Until now he had not realized how malodorous the city had become. Waste and trash filled the holes in the streets, and the fill being dumped into the cove included garbage of every description.

Adam decided to buy a lot on the hill above the city, far enough above Little Chile to catch the ocean air. He thought it high time to remove himself from the *Western Star* and especially the *Minerva*. From the hill he could watch gulls soar on the wind and pelicans crash into the bay in pursuit of a meal.

Waiting at the burying ground, they looked back toward the city. But the carriage did not come from there. Instead, it traveled at a leisurely pace along the shore from the Golden Gate. As they waited, the carriage approached. Adam saw Johnny Webb handling the reins with one hand, his other arm about Francie. The horses moved at a slow walk, as if they were out for a Sunday afternoon turn down a country lane.

"The devil is taking his time," muttered the captain. "He's telling us time is not important, or the reason for coming. Will the girl have sense enough to realize it?"

Finally Webb stopped the horse a distance away and helped Francie down. As they neared the grave, Francie on his arm, Webb nodded almost pleasantly. She gazed at the pine box and then at the white clouds above.

The men of Owyhee placed the coffin over the grave, supported by two plants the grave diggers provided. Ropes were slipped under the coffin as well. The diggers stood off a few feet, their hats in their hands.

"Ladies and gentlemen," said Captain Howlett, "I could not find a man of the Lord on short notice. I will say a few words and then urge anyone to offer a thought. If that meets your approval, Miss."

With a start Francie pulled her gaze away from the sky. White-faced, she barely nodded.

Aware the captain had buried men at sea, Adam expected a nautical point of view. Captain Howlett would say words he had spoken many times before. But the captain took a different tack.

"Lord," he said, "Thy will works in mysterious ways, and we accept Thy wisdom and mercy even though we may not understand. Each of us is dealt a hand in this life, given a number of cards. One by one we play out those cards according to our own wisdom, which does not match Thine own."

Adam glanced at Francie, who seemed not to hear. Johnny Webb, however, studied the captain's face.

"The game is not done until the last card is played. Only then do we know whether we have won or lost. Langford Wilmott has played out his last card, Lord. We consign him into Thy care, knowing he played the game well. Amen."

The captain waited for others to speak. When no one did, he motioned the Sandwich Islanders to lift the casket by the ropes until the grave diggers removed the boards. They lowered the remains of Professor Wilmott into the grave. Howlett threw a handful of dirt into the grave. Adam followed suit, but neither Francie nor Johnny Webb stepped forward. Instead, Webb steered Francie toward the carriage and they drove off toward town.

The captain eyed a black cloud sweeping in through the Golden Gate, threatening to obscure the sun. "We'd best shove off, lad. We'll get wet as it is." He paid the grave diggers. One of them knuckled his eyebrow as Adam had seen other former sailors do when dealing with the captain.

The rain caught them approaching Little Chile under the brow of Telegraph Hill. At once the streets became treacherous quagmires. Howlett, obviously ill at ease on shore, picked his way carefully. They were drenched by the time they reached the *Western Star.*

"Coffee will shake the chill," said the captain. "I'll look in on Kahele at the Trader. You go ahead."

Adam stoked the galley range, poured coffee and sat down to await the captain. Francie was nowhere in sight. But the captain did not come. Only when Adam resolved to look for him did he hear the familiar footsteps on deck and the captain's grunt as he descended the stairway.

"Kahele is nowhere to be found," growled the captain. "I searched the hotel and even looked for him on shore. Now what?" He held hands out to the heat of the stove as Adam poured his coffee.

"All the *Kanaka* boys are looking for him. If anybody can find him, they will."

Francie descended the companionway. "I need help moving my things," she said.

Adam got up and followed her to the master cabin, which she had occupied with her father. Francie pointed to a valise.

Surprised at its heavy weight, nevertheless he thought it tragic that in her young life she had acquired so little. Yet wasn't it true of almost everyone here?

He followed Francie onto deck and down to the catwalk. There Johnny Webb met them. Webb picked up her grip and led Francie away. Adam stood, a hollow feeling in his stomach. The girl had broken the final link between them.

CHAPTER 21

Adam stepped off the gangway on his way to meet Hillman and Sehorn. He almost reached shore when excited voices shrilled behind him. Two *Kanakas* knelt on the catwalk and hauled something out of the water beneath the Trader's stern. Adam dashed back to peer into what was left of Kahele's face. He stiffened. The captain's hotel clerk had been a gentle lad, too gentle for this place, intelligent, quick to learn, loyal. Webb's crew had sensed this and trampled him. Kahele didn't deserve to die like this.

"Ho, lads!" A scarred face with lopsided grin leaned over the bow of the *Minerva*. "Ye caught yerselfs a big 'un this time. Hold fast now. Don't let him get away!"

Attracted by the noise outside his door, Captain Howlett emerged from the hotel. Seeing the bloated remains of his former clerk, the captain turned white. He glared up at the *Minerva*, where a wild laugh floated across the vessel. The grinning face vanished. No doubt the man had gone to report the finding to Johnny Webb. What would he hatch next?

In a low voice Adam gritted, "I'll bring that butcher down if I do nothing else in my life."

Captain Howlett put a hand on his arm. "Careful, lad. They're itching for trouble."

Adam relaxed his clenched fists. "You're right, of course. But it angers me that Webb got his start on gold he took from me. And it hurts even more to see him get away with it."

"There's another rub, Adam. Francie's turned against you. Don't drive her further way. There's still hope."

"She's making her bed. She can damn well lie in it."

"You can't mean that, lad. It's Johnny Webb's bed she'll lie in. You don't want that. Wait and watch, Adam. Your chance will come."

Adam said nothing. He returned to the *Western Star*, where he changed into seaman's garb. He dropped a rope ladder over the side to Hoku's boat, tethered to the ship. Hoku was using Adam's boat to ferry passengers between Long Wharf and the anchorage. Pushing away from the ship, he pulled on the oars, moving well out into the bay and approached the *Minerva's* stern from Long Wharf. Easing under the stern, he searched for an open port, any way to gain the captain's cabin. But all the ports were secured; he could not access the hulk.

"Hey, you! What're ye doin' down there?"

Adam didn't answer, and he kept his head down.

"I see ye under there. Shove off before I put a bullet in ye!"

With powerful strokes of the oars he shot away from the ship. Now and then he glanced up. His challenger remained at the taffrail, waving a long-barreled pistol. Adam rowed to Long Wharf. There he mingled with craft plying the cove. Then he made a long circle outside pistol range and came in close under Telegraph Hill. When he reached the *Western Star*, he climbed up the rope ladder to the deck.

Captain Howlett was waiting for him. "Your friends – Sehorn and Hillman – came by with a man I've never seen. They're going out Market Street. The new fellow wanted two lots. He said you'd meet them there at one o'clock."

"I'll meet them there. And I'll eat on shore tonight."

"Good. I'll stick close to the hotel. Kahele's body showing up stirred Webb's bully boys, like seagulls when the cook throws galley slops over the side. I don't want them in the hotel."

"What about Kahele?"

"I sent his body out to North Beach. His friends will bury him."

"If I'd known, I'd have gone too."

"They understand. Hoku is in a rage, Adam. No good will come of this. Now be off to meet your friends."

Adam changed back into his suit and set out for Market Street. Except for the tramway track, the entire street had become a bog. The softly falling rain didn't help. He caught a ride on an empty car whose contents had gone into the cove.

The first sand hill was leveled, and men were laying track beyond to the second hill. Adam walked on until he found Andrew Jocelyn surveying. Jocelyn called his assistant in and invited Adam to share their sandwiches. The assistant took his sandwich and went back to watch the steam paddy attack the hill.

Adam pointed to the transit and the stakes they had driven thus far. He gazed out in the direction of Mission Dolores. "You seem to have unlimited land to divide."

Jocelyn waved his sandwich in the air. "I buy as I go. In a little town called Benicia I could have bought huge tracts for less."

Adam sat bolt upright. "Did you go to Benicia? Did you meet Robert Semple there?"

Again Jocelyn waved his sandwich. "I know Semple. A remarkable man."

"How is he, sir? I helped him run the ferry. When I left, he was down, ill with the fever."

Jocelyn stared at him. "He was weak, but he appeared to be mending. He and his partners have set San Francisco back. They got army headquarters to move there, and they're after customs too. But Semple's let down about his town's future. His partners favor Sacramento City. Semple talked about a young man who wanted to found a new city in Oregon. That wasn't you, was it?"

Adam grinned. "I must have sounded pretty foolish."

"Not at all! He praised you for having ambition and vision, a sense of the future. That's important here, Adam. Would you join me in this land venture?"

Adam had been about to bite his sandwich. He set it down. "Are you serious?"

"I need someone to sell the land. When I talk to a buyer, it slows me down. You wouldn't found a city but you'd help one grow. Think about it. Let me know what you decide."

"I don't need to think about it. I'd be honored to join you. I can contribute thirty-five thousand to the enterprise."

"That much? You'll earn much more. Three times more in the next year."

A hundred thousand!

Jocelyn went on. "You must have saved every dollar."

"Yes and no," said Adam. "I saved most of my money. But on the American River I lost eight thousand in gold to a robber." He gazed toward the bay. "I know who robbed me. And I know where to find him. I'd shake the gold out of him, but he surrounds himself with the scum of the waterfront. Do you know Four-Eyed Johnny Webb?"

Jocelyn frowned. "Who doesn't know him? Watch out for him."

"I'm careful. First he stole the ship. Then he beached it at the dock we built for our hotel."

Jocelyn emitted a low whistle. "Does Webb know who you are?"

"No doubt. He smirks and grins at me as if he knows he put one over on me. I confronted him the other day and called him by his real name."

"He knows who you are and you're still alive?"

Adam produced a Colt revolver from each pocket. "I don't go anywhere without these."

"I see. Now we'd better lay out our plans, Adam. I do one thing very well. I survey land. But I don't have time, nor the desire, really, to look for buyers."

"I can do that," said Adam.

Jocelyn cocked a critical eye at him. "How would you go about it?"

"First I'd hang around the Delmonico bar."

Jocelyn's eyebrows raised.

"Not to drink," said Adam. "I hate the stuff. Men you meet there have money. And I'd put a sign on Long Wharf. Most newcomers pass over that dock. I'd watch for new ship arrivals and men returning from the mines with gold, but they're hard to spot. Some of them disguise themselves as busted miners. And of course I'd spend time here also."

Jocelyn eyed him keenly. "Obviously you have thought this out."

Adam grinned. "I listen to men on the street and in the saloons. Many of them are looking for land to build on."

"By George, Adam, Robert Semple said you had a head on your shoulders. You're a modern-day Midas."

That was the second time someone called him by that name.

They concluded their agreement and shook hands. Adam promised to return in two days' time with buyers.

"Speaking of prospects," Jocelyn said, "your friend Hillman has another man in tow. The fellow wants two lots. They're over by the steam paddy. Sell any lots you have left. Then we can start over."

Adam found them admiring the steam shovel attacking the

shrinking sand hill. Hillman introduced the stranger as William Lynch. Quickly Adam struck a deal with him.

"My deeds are aboard the ship I live on," said Adam.

"Then let's go there," said Lynch. "I want to start construction at once on a large hotel."

To rent rooms to gamblers at fancy prices. But it was none of his concern.

They caught the tram hauling sand to Yerba Buena Cove. Shadows of night stalked the city when they reached the waterfront. The clamor of bells and gongs greeted them.

"How about dinner to celebrate our deal?" said Mr. Lynch. "I'm partial to the food the Chinamen put out. I believed they call their eatery Kong Sung."

"An excellent choice!" said Adam. Hillman and Sehorn exchanged dubious glances.

In the cramped and clamorous tent they talked little. Hillman's eyebrows shot up at the first taste of his food. Sehorn returned for a second bowl of chow mein.

By the time they boarded the ship, darkness had fallen. Adam invited them into the captain's cabin for coffee. "I'll be back with the papers," he said.

Hillman and Sehorn looked about appreciatively. "More spacious than the quarters we enjoyed before."

"This cabin was occupied then," said Adam.

"Oh," said Hillman, "don't get me wrong. We felt lucky indeed to find any roof over our heads."

Adam and William Lynch were signing the deeds when a dreaded call sounded.

"Fire!"

Other voices took up the cry. "Fire! Fire! Fire!" But no gongs or bells sounded.

"Gentlemen!" cried Adam. "Go up on deck. Quickly, until

we learn what's burning." He slipped the poke Lynch had given him into a coat pocket.

On deck Adam turned a puzzled eye toward town. Torches and flares cast fitful, wavering light at the underbelly of clouds hovering over the city. But no flames leaped up from the dark buildings.

"Fire!"

He wheeled about. The shout came from the *Minerva*. There men stumbled over each other, racing down the gangway toward shore.

Adam ran to the ship's taffrail. Still he saw no fire, but smoke poured from the gambling ship's stern and drifted across the water. The cove's choppy waters reflected a baleful red glare.

"Adam!" bellowed Captain Howlett. "Come quickly!"

He sprinted down to the catwalk, where Howlett held off an angry mob with his shotgun. Adam drew both pistols and cocked them. "Right here, Captain!"

The men turned. At sight of his guns they shrank into a tight group, each man trying to get behind the other.

"Take the *Kanakas* in hand," said the captain. "Show them how to fight the fire. If I leave, these rum lads will torch the hotel."

The Owyhee men edged past the mob and followed Adam aboard the *Western Star*. Half of them he assigned pails of water. "If burning embers fall onto the deck or the hotel roof, throw water on them. The rest of you stand by with soaked blankets to smother fires."

Adam, guns in hand, stood ready to shoot the first intruder at the gangway.

They stood, watching, waiting. The *Minerva's* stern blossomed into flames shooting out the ports and leaping skyward.

From the taffrail Adam could not see the larger ship's deck. He heard no sounds of men scrambling to fight the fire. Men still fled the burning vessel, stopping only when they reached the safely of shore.

By now a crowd had gathered. Above their excited clamor Adam heard his name shouted as the villain who fired the ship. A pistol in each hand, he stood ready to shoot. Shouts and curses continued, but no surge came.

A ringing voice sounded above the crowd's roar. Johnny Webb appeared on the catwalk, Francie on his arm. At the same time Captain Howlett appeared, his shotgun ready. The catwalk now cleared of men. Only Webb and Francie advanced. Webb stared up at Adam. One of the toughs growled from shore. "He done it, Johnny! His boat pulled away just before the fire started."

"Hoku," murmured Adam. Hoku had used his boat all day.

"You!" gritted Webb. He stared at the *Minerva*. The ship seemed a giant roman candle now, spewing flames out and up. "My gold is aboard!" shouted Webb. But none of his henchmen moved from safety. Webb shook off Francie's arm and darted up the ship's gangway, deserted now.

"Stop, you damned fool!" roared Howlett. "No gold is worth your life!" But Webb disappeared into the ship.

Staring at the place where Webb had vanished, Adam was startled by Francie's voice so near on the catwalk below.

"How could you do this?"

He looked into her blazing eyes. Her accusation flooded him with despair. Hard on that thought came another equally crushing. Did Johnny Webb mean so much to her? She turned to stare with anguished eyes at the *Minerva's* gangway. His eyes followed hers. Would she too dash into the burning ship?

He set his pistols on the deck along with his poke of gold and sprinted down to the catwalk. There he brushed past Francie and started up the burning ship's gangway.

"Adam! No!"

He continued on, pausing at the top of the gangway. The decks had been cleared and canvas spread over all in a makeshift roof. Brilliant whale oil lamps revealed empty tables and roulette wheels. Drinks lay untouched as if awaiting the players' return. In one corner stood a battered upright piano. But he saw no Johnny Webb.

Knowing a companionway led to the captain's cabin, where the fire burned furiously, he started aft. Heat increased, pulsing from the fire still contained below decks. At the top of the stairway he recoiled from heat and gases rising from smoking paint and varnish.

Webb lay huddled at the foot of the stairs. The closed door of the cabin was smoking. Did he dare go down? At any moment the passageway would explode in flames. Even as his senses screamed at him to run, Francie's piercing accusation forced him forward.

Shielding his face with an arm, holding his breath, he dropped down until he stumbled over Webb. He grabbed the man's coat and dragged him up the steps. Surely his lungs would burst, but he dared not breathe. He would inhale the gases and he too would die. *Got to get out fast!*

Smoke curled up from the companionway. Backing up the steps, he reached the deck and dragged Webb away from the ladder. As he strained to reach safety, elation flooded his mind. Four-Eyed Johnny Webb, only minutes before a menacing figure, was reduced to a pitiful lump whose clothing began to smolder.

Vaguely he saw figures appear at the gangway and rush toward him. Hands grasped him and pulled him toward safety.

"Get the other one too," Adam rasped.

"To hell with him!"

"Get him! She wants him."

As they reached the catwalk with Johnny Webb in tow, a sheet of flame erupted from the companionway. It rolled across the deck beneath the canopy, igniting it until all seethed with fire. It reached into the rigging. Sails, dried by the superheated air, burst into flame, which spread to the rigging. Burning tar rained down.

But they reached cool air outside the ship, and Adam drew ragged breaths into his tortured lungs. In minutes the *Kanakas* hustled him aboard the *Western Star.*

"Get some whale oil!" barked Howlett. "Smear it over his hands and face, wherever skin shows. I'm going below for laudanum."

Adam tried vainly to recoil from pain searing his hands and face.

Men brought Webb, unconscious, and laid him on the ship's deck beside Adam. Everything whirled before Adam's eyes, but he didn't pass out. He struggled upright and propped himself against a mast. Hoku smeared his hands and face with oil. The *Kanaka's* hands were incredibly tender, and the pain eased somewhat as oil cut off air to his burns. Captain Howlett hurried forward, uncapped a bottle and ordered, "Drink this." The liquid was bitter and the taste familiar. He gulped some down. He leaned against the mast, staring about, trying to make sense of what happened. The pain evened out into a muted nightmare.

The fire ate its way forward until the entire vessel was engulfed. Flames climbed tarred ratlines. Soon bits of tar fell onto the Trader's roof and the *Western Star's* deck. Adam could only watch Captain Howlett direct his crew. They smothered spot fires with water-soaked blankets and hurled buckets of water onto those they could not reach. As flames consumed the *Minerva*, the captain left two men to douse fires on the ship while they set about saving the hotel.

"Come with me, lads. Bring buckets. We'll douse the *Minerva's* bow and our own ships to cool them down."

Apparently believing themselves safe, Adam's friends remained on board. Flames crept closer, but an offshore breeze carried smoke and heat out into the bay.

Sehorn asked, "Should we move the injured men ashore? Just in case?"

Adam roused himself. "Hear that lawless crew howling on the beach?" he croaked. "They'll tear me apart."

"Wouldn't it serve you right?" demanded Francie, her voice dripping with scorn. "Look at what you've done."

Adam hadn't realized she was still there. But then, where could she go? At least she had sense enough to stay.

A shout rose from the gangway. Half a dozen men appeared and advanced toward Adam and Johnny Webb. "We'll just collect this pair an' take 'em to the hospital," said their leader. Adam recognized him as Webb's man Hoku had thrown overboard from the Trader weeks before.

"We think not." Lynch, Hillman and Sehorn emerged from the shadows, cocked pistols in their hands. "Take Webb. If you touch Mr. Stuart, you are dead men."

Lynch was a man accustomed to command, perhaps in the recent war against Mexico. Even Adam, who had never seen the military, recognized authority in his voice. So, too, did the gang, but still they edged forward.

A flash and roar lit up the deck. Captain Howlett had fired his shotgun into the air. "Take Webb and go. Else I'll cut you in half."

Johnny Webb groaned hideously when his men picked him up and bore him away.

William Lynch stepped forward. "Miss," he said, "did you accuse Mr. Stuart of setting the ship on fire?"

"Well, didn't he?"

"He couldn't have. This afternoon we met Mr. Stuart out on Market Street where we went to buy land. We came here to complete the sale. On the way we stopped for dinner."

"I didn't see you at the Delmonico."

"Of course not. We ate at the Chinese emporium on the waterfront. Mr. Stuart was with us the entire time. He couldn't have started the fire."

Francie's face drained of all color. Her hand went to her mouth. "But Mr. Webb's men saw Adam's boat at the *Minerva*."

"They may be quite right, Miss, but Mr. Stuart was not on that boat. He was on shore with us."

Francie stared at him before bursting into tears. She flew to Captain Howlett, whose arms enfolded her. "I don't know what to think!" she wailed.

The captain held her at arm's length. "You've had a hard time, lass. But you must face facts. Four-Eyed Johnny caught you at a bad time. He offered you money and I don't know what else. But his name isn't Johnny Webb."

She stared at him. "Then what is it?"

"On the American River Adam knew him as Johann Leinenweber. When gold was found, he deserted Colonel Stevenson's army regiment stationed at the Presidio here in San Francisco. The New York Volunteers.

"Are you sure?"

"As sure as we are of anything."

"Why didn't Adam tell me?"

"Would you have listened?"

She hung her head.

"Francie, Johann Leinenweber robbed Adam of his eight thousand in gold."

Her eyes flew open. She spoke as if Adam were not there. "He didn't say anything."

"He didn't want you to think jealousy prompted him. He hoped you would see for yourself. Your father knew, and he was afraid for you."

Francie looked at Adam, who stared at the burning ship.

Lynch, Hillman and Sehorn stirred. "We'll be going, Mr. Stuart. If we need more land, or know someone who does, we'll look you up."

Adam watched them go. He was aware of only one thing: the need to sleep. He mumbled as much to the captain, who shook his head. "Nobody goes below until the fire is down."

Howlett left to help wet down the hulls. Adam, from his place at the main mast, watched fire leap about in the *Minerva's* rigging. First the mizzen mast fell, then the main. They collapsed over the side. Must he wait until the foremast came down?

Off a ways Francie stood, her hands over her face, crying softly. Now and then she looked at him, and her shoulders shook anew.

Steadily the fire ate through the *Minerva*. Aft, flames licked down to the waterline. Rain began to fall, first as a mist. Soon drops of water drummed on the deck. They dampened the fire until it seemed to retreat into itself.

Adam mused that all was over. But with startling suddenness the burning ship's bow sprit, which had loomed overhead, crashed down. Its white-painted tip thudded onto the deck and quivered just beyond him. Excited voices yelled on the catwalk and faces appeared at the gangway. Captain Howlett's startled face peered at him.

"Are you all right, lad?"

Fighting through a growing torpor, he nodded. The captain picked his way thorough chains and ropes to look into his face. "Never gave a thought to the sprit coming down. Should have moved you. Now we can go below. Can you stand up and walk?"

Careful to avoid brushing his hands, the captain helped him up. Equally carefully he walked Adam through the debris. At the ladder he turned to Francie. "Come below and rest."

"I don't think so. I wouldn't be welcome here."

"Nonsense!"

"Besides, all my things burned up."

"I'll lend you a night dress. Tomorrow we'll buy new things. Come along, child."

Below, in the relative warmth of the cabin, Adam tried to flex his hands. But the burns had drawn the skin taut. His hands with their splayed fingers resembled a bird's claw.

Francie had followed them down. She removed her heavy coat. The scarlet dress Adam had reviled revealed her shoulders and the cleft between her breasts. In an odd detached way he studied her until blood rose fully into her throat and face. She turned away.

The captain helped him stretch out in the bunk formerly used by Professor Wilmott. "Adam, I sent for Doctor Smith. I don't know when he'll get here."

Adam nodded. With a sigh he rested his hands on his chest and allowed sleep to engulf him.

CHAPTER 22

Dimly aware of food and coffee smells, Adam ate when the captain forced soup down him. After each feeding he lay back, exhausted, and drifted into sleep. Sometimes he heard Captain Howlett and Francie talk in low tones, but he couldn't make out what they said. Nor did he care. He awoke fully one morning when Doctor Smith came to see him.

"Feeling much pain?" the doctor asked.

"Some."

"We'll take you off the laudanum. Don't want you addicted to the stuff. Don't try to do anything yet." He pointed upward, where constant thumpings told of activity on deck. "Let your island boys cut up the masts and spars and stack the firewood."

"How long have I been here?"

"Four days. I worried about infection. But everything looks good. You should know the man you rescued — what was his name — oh, yes, Johnny Webb. He died this morning. Damn fools took him to City Hospital. Anywhere but there. His burns mortified right away. By the time I saw him it was too late. Probably too late anyway."

Had Francie heard the doctor through the blanket curtain? If so, how did she take it? Had she fallen in love with the gambler? Or had Lynch and the captain opened her eyes? He didn't know, and he was too tired to care. He had his own future to think of.

After the doctor left, the captain brought him another visitor. Andrew Jocelyn entered carrying a stack of deeds, each describing a lot he laid out on Market Street.

"Don't mean to rush you, Adam. I heard the doctor say to keep still for awhile. But I want you to see what we've done. Also, I bought a tract where the hills rise north of Market Street. Folks say the air is healthier there. Can't say I disagree. Do you want me to reserve a corner lot for you?"

Adam nodded. "Can't do anything for a while."

After Jocelyn left Adam tried to sleep, but without opium he remained wide awake. He caught himself listening. It puzzled him until he realized he was listening to silence. Gone was the clamor of the *Minerva*. Shouts and curses, jovial calls and greetings, the excitement of winning big, all these had become part of their lives, however unwillingly. On deck he heard the ever-present hum of commerce and gambling on shore. In the captain's cabin he heard nothing.

The sharp odor of charred wood was pervasive. He seemed to taste it in his food, in coffee the captain brought him. It would take a long time to fade.

He heard the thumps topside as the Sandwich Islanders stacked firewood on the deck. In the evenings he heard voices in the galley. Once Francie cried, "Oh, thank you, Hoku! I thought it was lost."

Finally Adam felt strong enough to go topside. He breathed deeply of the fresh air and reveled in the sunshine. Activity quickened his blood. All around them pile drivers hammered pilings into the cove's bottom. Spidery docks reached out even as men with carts and wheelbarrows dumped sand into the water. The struggle between those who would fill Yerba Buena Cove and those who would build docks flourished. More ships crowded the anchorage. As he watched, two more vessels rounded Telegraph Hill and dropped anchor.

Each night Captain Howlett could fill the hotel three times over, so great was the demand for housing. In town the chorus of hammers swelled as new dwellings went up before Adam's eyes. At night, when he went topside, he marveled at how much farther up the hills the tent city, glowing orange, had spread.

One morning Adam leaned over the taffrail. Below him the *Minerva* lay, a blackened hulk burned to the waterline. The men of Owyhee attacked a mast until one end lay across the hulk and the other trailed in the water. He marveled at their progress. Evidence of their work lay stacked around the tarpaulin which sheltered the professor's chair.

What could they do with the hulk's bottom? Nothing, he guessed, except wait for fill to cover her ugly remains. She would become part of the city pressing out toward deep water.

"She's a sorry sight, Adam, a sorry sight." The captain had moved up to the rail beside him.

"True, sir, but the air is cleaner and quieter where she lies."

"Hoku did us all a favor, there's no doubt of that."

"Did Hoku set the fire? Webb's henchmen saw my boat near the *Minerva*'s stern. Hoku was using it that day."

Captain Howlett glanced around. "Not so loud, Adam. People are angry about the fire. They fear arson more than anything in this shack and tent city. If they catch someone who set a fire, they'll make short work of him."

Adam turned and gazed across the city. "Do they believe the Christmas Eve fire was set?"

"Nobody knows how it started. It began in Dennison's Exchange, that's all anyone knows."

Adam spoke in a low voice. "Strange how hard Hoku works to clean things up. Especially after burning the ship."

The captain wagged his head. "Not at all, Adam, if you know the lad. In the Kau region of Owyhee he became a warrior, with a warrior's tendency to fierce deeds. He didn't like it, so he shipped out on a Yankee trader much like the *Minerva*."

"I could never have set the fire," said Adam. "Not that I didn't want to. But tell me, sir. While I was down on my back I heard you and Francie talk. How is she taking all this?"

"Hard, Adam. She's had a bad time of it."

"I can see that. Losing her father, then the Parker House and finally the gambling ship. I must say she deserved Webb after treating her father as she did."

There came a gasp behind them, and a cry. Francie rose from the chair beneath the tarpaulin, a book in her hand. She fled to the companionway and vanished below.

"I'd better go ashore," said Adam. "The sight of me sickens her."

"Now, lad, don't be hasty. She needs time. Working with me at the hotel desk has done wonders."

Finally Adam moved from the captain's cabin back to the fo'c'sle. There he could come and go as he wished. Wearing light and loose sailor's garb, he went ashore in the morning darkness, before Francie arose. There he ate breakfast and returned to his usual haunts.

Most buildings destroyed in the Christmas Eve fire had been built bigger and more grand. They exuded the aroma of pitch oozing from newly-sawn lumber. New canvas tents and frame houses gleamed beneath the sun that shone more often now. Adam admired the new structures. But they would soon turn gray from soot and mildew. And, he reminded himself, they burned once. They would burn again.

The Parker House, its bricks bright and new, went up more slowly. Would Francie return there to sing? He hoped not. After her exposure aboard the *Minerva* she would attract the worst element in the city. Men who applauded her at the Parker House and those who ogled her aboard the *Minerva* were likely the same, but now they saw her differently. Professor Wilmott had shielded his daughter in an aura of decorum. Johnny Webb exploited her youth and sex.

Perhaps she would never expose herself to audiences again. Demand became greater than ever for space. Many hotel rooms were leased for gambling. Maybe Francie would never again command the space she needed. Fervently he hoped so.

Rarely did he see her. While he was in bed he had awakened to find her peering around the blanket curtain. He studied her through half-closed eyes. If anything, she had become more lovely. Gone were her girlish cheeks and open innocent gaze. Although her face was composed, he saw suffering in her eyes. Did she mourn Johnny Webb's passing, or did other emotions grip her? Before opening his eyes fully, he sighed deeply. When he showed signs of awakening, she vanished.

Now he saw her more often, with a book in her hand. He recognized one as her father's copy of Shakespeare. Another was an account of a voyage to California written by a young seaman whose name he had forgotten. Captain Howlett had suggested he read *Two Years Before the Mast*. It told about commerce in animal hides before gold was discovered. A different kind of commerce occupied Adam's mind now. He would read later.

One morning when he returned to the Delmonico still dressed in sailor's loose-fitting tunic, a deep-voiced bartender accosted him. "This is a gentleman's bar," said the mustachioed man. "You'll find sailors' bars nearer the waterfront." The bartender peered more carefully at him. "Oh, excuse me, Mr. Stuart. I didn't recognize you. Still selling land on Market Street?"

Men's eyes turned. One man asked, "Do you have land for sale?"

Soon buyers ringed him. Some outbid others to buy property sight unseen. Sharp-eyed men among them offered large sums, giving a promise to pay instead of gold. When they opened their gambling hells, Adam thought, they might pay. Then again they might string him along with further promises.

So he smiled and said, "Gold in my hand will get you deeds, sirs. If I took a note, my partner would roast me over a slow fire." Jocelyn said nothing about how he should conduct business, but Adam's refusal made a good selling point. He quickly sold the lots, sometimes for more than the shady gamblers promised. There was no doubt about it. Times were heady.

Each day his store of gold increased. And with it grew his fear of fire. Often he saw Johnny Webb's followers standing on the beach eyeing the Trader Hotel. If they could, they would burn her to the waterline. He could lose his wealth and Andrew Jocelyn's as well. But he still didn't see a bank he would trust.

One evening, as he returned from town after dinner, he paused at the catwalk. A giant moon was rising above the hills across the bay. A cold wind raised waves which shattered the moonlight on the water into a million golden crystals. The golden bay outlined black hulls and spars of ships anchored near and far. Quiet and darkness had come to this section of the waterfront. Gone were the pine-knot flares that burned all night and the shrill wheedling cries of Terence Small. Gone was the clamor of the gambling hell Johnny Webb had thrust upon them. Sometimes he regretted he had not thrown Terence Small bodily into the bay. However, the man was no longer important.

But Adam remained wary. The darkness masked dangers lurking everywhere. When he reached the *Western Star*'s deck he stopped. In a habit born of fear he searched out every nook, every corner of the ship. Webb's men could waylay him even here. William Lynch and his associates made a point of telling whoever would listen that Adam Stuart could not have torched the *Minerva*. Even so, he heard grumbling and threats and armed himself when he went ashore.

About to cross the deck to the fo'c'sle, he saw movement beneath the tarpaulin. His hand went to a pistol but stopped. Francie stepped out, wrapped in her heavy coat.

"Adam."

He relaxed. "You shouldn't be out here alone."

She turned flashing eyes on him. "Will you stop telling me what I should and should not do?"

"I'm sorry. What do you want?"

"To talk to you." She crossed the moonlit deck. "You spend so much time away, I think you're avoiding me."

He shrugged. "There's money to be made on shore."

"And you make lots of it?"

"Since the big fire I've cleared nearly forty thousand."

"So much? But I don't want to talk about that. What about us?"

"Us? What about us?"

She looked up in his face. In the moonlight he saw her shiver. She must have waited here a long time.

"I've hurt you, haven't I?" She put her hand on his arm. "Very deeply."

"Francie, you're cold. You should go below."

"Won't you talk to me? I've waited hours to see you."

"Then let's get out of the wind." He drew her to the shelter of the tarpaulin, rendered nearly windproof by stacks of fire-wood. The smell of pitch was strong and sweet.

"You've hated me these past weeks, haven't you?"

"Francie, I never hated you. I hated what you did, but I have no claim on you. You're free to do what pleases you."

She gripped his arm. "Please understand, Adam. Papa's illness frightened me. I tried not to let it show. But if he died, what would I do alone in a place like this?"

He shrugged. "You were never alone."

"But I felt I was. When I first came to California, I enjoyed singing. You have no idea, Adam, how sweet was the applause. But it was more than that. It was assurance to me. I could make my own way. When Papa fell ill, I needed that assurance. When the Parker House burned down, I became more frightened than ever. Johnny — Mr. Webb — assured me of a place with a future."

He faced her squarely, trying to keep calm. "A future? Francie, he would have ruined you. He dirtied everything he touched. That red gown was just the beginning. Tell me straight out, did you sleep with him?"

Her eyes became large and luminous in the moonlight. "Would it make a difference if I did?"

"I don't know. I don't let myself think about it."

"Well, I didn't. He pressed me, but I said I needed time." She was silent a moment. Adam thought she shivered, whether from cold or emotion he couldn't say.

"Francie, why did you turn from me — from us? The captain and me."

She looked away, stared at ships outlined against the moonlight. "I don't know. I became angry with Papa for leaving me. And I was ashamed of the way I treated him. I should never have let him see me in that dress. Right now I'm ashamed you cared for him more than I did."

"I hardly knew him."

"But I didn't know him at all. Or you."

Adam took her icy hands in his. "Francie, I love you. I have loved you since that night of the Benicia crossing. I lost you then, but I vowed I'd find you again. When I did I wanted to protect you from men like Dupre, from this place."

She sighed. "But don't you see, I didn't want protection. I wanted to be swept off my feet."

"I couldn't do that. I grew up a simple farm boy, and that's the way I'll always be."

They stood, gazing at the city lights, listening to the hum of a city in headlong pursuit of pleasure. What was a simple farm boy doing here? Yet most San Franciscans were young men like himself, with one great difference. Unlike him, gold lured them here. They came seeking wealth and excitement. Most of them found cold, misery, whiskey tents and gambling hells, even death.

"I hated you for that, I suppose," she said. "No, hate is too strong a word. I was disappointed in you. That was foolish of me, wasn't it? Now I know you're a rock to cling to in a world gone mad."

Bitterly Adam laughed. "Rocks don't move much. Mostly they gather moss."

"I needed a rock to steady me, but I didn't see it. I have thought much lately about wants and needs."

"You may think you need me now, Francie, but someday you won't. Then what?"

She sighed. "I wish I could say, but I don't know." Again they fell silent. Finally she stirred and sighed again. "We're so different, you and I."

He took a deep breath. "Francie, will you marry me?"

She became very still. Again the city's sounds, awakening from the winter's pall, pulsed with life. Out in the harbor, ships bumped one another, setting up a low rumbling rhythm.

She said, in a small voice, "After all I've done to you?" Tears welled up in her eyes. He had hoped she would say yes without hesitation. But she didn't give him the answer he wanted. Did she find him dull? Or did she have doubts about herself? Or even worse, did the ghosts of Charles Dupre and Johnny Webb linger in her mind?

"Don't answer now," he said. "Think it over."

"There is nothing to think about. I'll marry you, if you'll have me."

He pulled her to him. For a long time they clung to each other. He felt the warmth of her even through their heavy coats, saw the warmth in her eyes. All along he had sought human warmth. Closeness with someone. He had yearned for it across the plains, in the new Territory of Oregon. Beneath his cold, lonely tarpaulin on the American River he had wanted something gold couldn't buy. And especially after he met Francie Wilmott at Benicia.

They broke apart, held each other at arm's length. Wonder filled him, wonder that this lovely girl consented to marry him. In the moonlight he saw softness in her eyes he had never seen before. For a while, at least, she was his.

"We'd better go below."

They found Captain Howlett having a cup of coffee. He had pushed his dinner plate away. Beef stew simmered on the range and a loaf of bread stood on the table with a bowl of butter.

"Couldn't wait any longer," he said, "so I ate. Dig in."

"Later," said Adam. "We have something to tell you." They told him of their decision.

As they spoke, the captain's broad whiskered face set in a fierce scowl. It almost unnerved Adam. Did the captain disapprove so strongly?

But Captain Howlett suddenly beamed. "So you've both finally come to your senses. Now hear me out. It's been a grand adventure, but I'm done with it. I'm going back to a snug harbor called Fairhaven, out of New Bedford. I'll make it my home port for the rest of my days."

"But, sir, you'll stand up with us before you go?"

"Wouldn't miss it, lad. Now let's decide what to do with the hotel. Francie, will you manage it? I'd give it to you outright, but I have an obligation to the owner of the *Trader*."

"I'm not sure I can manage," she said.

"Certainly you can. You know what to do. I've already spoken to the Owyhee lads. They'll stand by you. All except Hoku. He sailed for home on the morning tide. Which reminds me."

The captain went to a locker and pulled out three leather pokes. The smallest one he held out to Francie. "Hoku left this for you."

She stared at it. "Why? He already returned my gold from the *Minerva*."

"He held out a share in your father's name. Take it, child, and remember his kindness."

Francie burst into tears. "I wish Papa could be here."

"And these are yours, Adam. The gold Leinenweber stole from you."

Adam's mouth fell open. He looked from the leather bags to the captain.

"Hoku recovered the gold from the hulk of the *Minerva*. Wasn't the easiest diving he ever did. He divided most of the gold among his mates. Took a good share himself, of course. And he took a share home to Kahele's family."

Adam brushed his brow with a shaking hand. "I'm not sure I understand. Captain, we thank you for all you've done, but I don't want to live aboard the *Western Star*. The sand will soon engulf us, and everybody throws garbage into the fill. I intend to build a house on the hill above Market Street. It's cleaner there, and the air is better there, and. . . ."

"And the grand folks are settling there. The men you do business with. I understand. But wait six months. Divide the proceeds of the hotel between you. Build up a stake. You don't need it, Adam, but Francie does. Do you follow me?"

Adam nodded.

"If you sell the Trader, send half the proceeds to me. I will share with a lady in Massachusetts. Now I propose to drink a toast to the bride."

The captain drew from a locker a bottle and a glass, which he poured full.

Before he could lift the drink in toast, Adam said, "I believe the bride would lift a small glass with you, sir. So would I, if you can spare just a drop."